Photograph of Senator Robert F. Kennedy and
President Lyndon B. Johnson. White House,
Oval Office.: 06/22/1966

ARC Identifier 192488 / Local Identifier
A2676-17a

Front Cover Photograph
Signing Cuba Quarantine Proclamation.
President Kennedy. White House, Oval Office.:
10/23/1962
ARC Identifier 194218

Disclaimer

Autopsy in the Oval Office is a novel based on
established historical facts. All the characters are
fictitious except historical personalities. Any
statement concerning a historical person's action,
which is made to develop the plot of the novel, is
fictitious. All historical claims made about a
historical character have been double sourced
and every effort has been made to describe
accurately the historical record about them.

Autopsy in the Oval Office

A Novel

Kenneth Braunstein, MD

ISBN-13:
978-1475277784

ISBN-10:
1475277784

Prologue

September 1963, in the expansive parlor of a red brick Federal mansion on St. Louis Street midway between Bourbon and Dauphine Streets in the French Quarter of New Orleans:

A sizable crowd pulled themselves away from the birthday celebration to gather loosely about him. Cutting a formidable figure, he stood in front of his large altar to Erzulie and motioned for all of them to come closer so that he could initiate them into her cult without having to raise his voice very much. Dressed up in a white top hat, a black tailcoat, and a vest with pink and white sequins, he waved his outstretched hands, signaling them to stop chitchatting. His only concessions to the heat were not bringing a bow tie and intentionally leaving his white ruffled shirt unbuttoned above midchest. In place of the bow tie were four strands of Mardi Gras beads, each strand a different color, and a long, thick black silk cord with a shrunken head attached above a human foot bone.

His entire face and neck were pale white from ghost makeup. Blackface greasepaint, painstakingly applied and highlighted with black pencil liner, encompassed his eyes, created a Van Dyke-style beard, acted as rouge on his cheeks, and dotted the tip of his nose. A full moon was out, and he was indoors. Still he wore dark glasses. Conforming to the Haitian tradition for preparing the dead for interment, small cotton balls plugged each nostril. Fixed over his own teeth, close-fitting, hand-molded artistic, finely detailed fake ones clenched down onto a Churchill cigar he had just put into his mouth. With that, the revival of Baron Samedi, the skull-like spirit of death and custodian of the pathway to and from our world and the next, was complete.

A waiter brought him a tall tulip shaped wine glass. The bony fingers of his white-gloved right hand cradled it as the waiter poured rum from a decanter. His black-gloved left hand clasped an imposing walking stick with two perpendicular metal tridents forming the tip, from which a large python slithered in a spiral up its shaft. He had sculpted it out of a lower branch of a monumental live oak that he professed broke off the old tree in Mississippi the instant the innocent black man hanging from it grew limp and took his last gasp. Serving as its knob, a large human skull with a very visible fracture sat securely glued to four enormous carved fangs. He swore, when asked, that the skull belonged to the Klansman who had done the lynching and whom the falling limb had struck down. "The Voodoo were appeased," was his succinct take on that day.

He loudly thumped the point of his staff on the floor to gain their full attention and silence and subsequently began his spiel. All the while training that skull towards the table behind him, he faced them and spoke formally and elegantly but with a heavy Cuban accent. "Honored guests, Erzulie Fréda Dahomey is the Loa or female spirit of passion, comeliness, dancing, opulence, flowers, and all sorts of ornaments for the body, both rare and precious. More important to those who follow her, she can rejuvenate a weary soul or bestow great financial success in both regular commerce and gaming. Her powers may inspire intense romantic ardor including the renewal of a love affair gone bad, even one from long ago. Above all else, she is beloved for her ability to reverse any wanga without limit, no matter how wicked or vile. So wondrous is she that her

6

essence alone by just embracing you is an antidote for every poison and nullifies any and all evil magic and potions."

Hired as the evening's entertainment, he brought Erzulie's altar especially to festivities that, like this one, were celebrated in the French Quarter. Since gay men were considered to be under her particular patronage, Erzulie had a great many loyal disciples in that part of the city. Over a rectangular dining room table he had draped a bright, laced pink cloth, which flowed down to the floor and on which were partially layered solid colored silk kerchiefs in her favorite colors: primarily pink and white intermingled with a smattering of navy blue and yellow/gold. For a backdrop to the altar, a large white satin bed sheet, only fastened at three spots along the top of its stand, dangled precariously from above. In its center a sword pierced a prominent embroidered pink valentine heart bounded by tarot cards with images of the Empress. Adding to the spectacle was a gold-colored canopy fashioned from some glossy piece goods that floated from the peak of the frame without visible support.

The focal point of the altar was a rococo style coin silver chalice that almost overflowed with water. On each side of it stood matching Martelé silver candlesticks, one holding a pink candle and the other a white candle. Looming over the goblet from behind and leaning to one side of a sterling silver ice bucket with a pierced grapevine border was an uncorked magnum of pink champagne. Four strands of Mardi Gras beads, pink, white, blue, and gold, swathed its long neck. Over the tabletop he had randomly strewn at least a dozen strands of both fake pearls and Mardi Gras beads in every imaginable color as well as three golden rings, a single large gold chain, several silver chains and daggers, and many heart shaped gems and medallions. Opened bottles of drugstore perfumes fancied by Erzulie graced the four corners of the altar. Sixteen little glass bowls seemed to be everywhere. Four each brimmed with Florida Water, pink or white roses, or basil floating in sacred rainwater, collected from the urns in the nearby cemeteries during the midnight walking tours that he regularly conducted.

Amid all of this clutter, adding random bits of color to the tablecloth, were mini-bottles of various liqueurs, above all Crème de Cacao another of her preferences. To satisfy her sweet tooth he had set out crystal cake stands holding Doberge cakes with pink strawberry frosting fresh from Gambino's Bakery. Next to the perfume bottles, small Old Sheffield Plate trays were teeming with aluminum foil take-out baking cups. The chef at the Potpourri restaurant in D. H. Holmes on Canal Street that afternoon had ladled into them cinnamon-laced white Creole rice custard.

In front of him, an austere pure white linen tea cloth dropped to the floor and spread over a plain wooden table that functioned as a less formal and much smaller altar. Following paying homage to Erzulie, he had carefully and ceremonially arranged on it the symbols of the four elements. Two saucers represented the Earth. To his left the smaller one kept salt. To his right the other, a larger saucer, had an abundance of a special blend of graveyard dirt, dug up from nine separate cemeteries and the grave of a child between the break of day and before sunset at a time no vampire would be awake and about. Incense in a burner in the middle of the table smoldered on behalf of Air. Stationed in the right rear corner, two lit white altar candles, thick enough that they called for no holder and tall enough to tower above everything else, signified Fire. After consecrating all of his ritual objects and both altars prior to the arrival of the guests, he had laid a deck of fortune telling cards next to the lit candles in case anyone wanted him to read their destiny. Finally, on the right side of the incense burner, a humble stone compote held holy Water sanctified that very day at the Cathedral-Basilica of Saint Louis King of France down on Pere Antoine Alley.

On the left flank of the table, stacks of empty coin-purse-size, vibrantly colored cloth bags and a few made of leather obscured the sides of shoeboxes crammed with odds and ends. Their contents included diverse things such as, blossoms, feathers, colored stones, essential oils, herbs, small bones, horsehair weavings, bird's nests, and an assortment of talismans. Each amulet was chosen for its unique occult and astrological symbolism and powers. By now the guests nestled closely in an arc in front of the table eagerly waiting their turn to be handed a gris-gris bag custom-made on the spot. Before entrusting a gris-gris bag to its new owner, he would dress it with anointing oil and then activate its magic by blowing upon the bag.

He paused shortly to allow the guests to appreciate the details in the altars before continuing. "Ladies and Gentlemen, please permit me to elucidate the significance of gris-gris bags. You may know them as a mojo or mojo bag. We prepare them to attract and influence the voodoo spirits that surround us all. During the old days to insure their safety, every law enforcement officer in New Orleans carried a gris-gris bag crafted initially by the Voodoo Queen, Marie Laveau, who popularized them in the mid-nineteenth century. Sealed in her bags were bits of bone, colored stones, salt, red pepper, and her own exclusive goofer dust. She concocted her goofer dust starting with batches of the most excellent available graveyard dirt procured from recently dug graves. Once having personally inspected them and handpicking which selections to use, she next mixed the chosen few with anvil dust, pulverized snakeskin obtained only from the exceptionally venomous serpents living principally in the bayous of Louisiana, and a combination of dried pigeon droppings and sulfur ground together to a fine powder in an extraordinary mortar and pestle. Early in her career, the people of New Orleans presented it to her in gratitude for her valiant efforts in a yellow fever epidemic. Her followers had the mortar and pestle chiseled out of a log of the highest quality petrified palm wood ever discovered even to this day in Flatwoods.

"For doing good she would add soil from the last resting place of an innocent toddler who had died from the fever. Conversely, an order for a gris-gris bag to produce maleficence or malice required her to search for soil from a freshly dug burial site of a criminal, usually a murderer still warm after his hanging. Most desirable was one who had not yet had the benefit of a priest performing a proper death ritual ceremony to release his soul to God and whose unrepentant spirit would still be trapped there for at least nine days. The number of objects ordained to be in the gris-gris bag is always an odd number: three, five, seven, nine, eleven, or thirteen." For emphasis he raised and then brandished his finger in front of his face. "Never an even number and no less than three or greater than thirteen."

A man in front asked, "Did anyone else besides the police routinely carry them way back yonder?"

He nodded emphatically. "Oh yes. People would

pay thousands of dollars for Marie Laveau in dragon's blood ink to pen onto parchment a vévé, a supernatural icon. Each one is unique for an individual Loa and compels them to return to the earth. She would then stitch the paper into a gris-gris bag made of the finest textiles or leather.

"Frequently, a gambler would have her stir dove's blood and pine-tree sap together to blend an ink with which to inscribe on a piece of chamois the amount of money he desired to walk off with from the games of chance he was about to play. Then as the ends of the red flannel being wrapped around the chamois touched each other but before they were hemmed, she interspaced a shark's tooth between the fabrics. This was all seamed together with cat's hair, which she insisted be from one whose fur was unadulterated black. The gambler would then insert the gris-gris bag into his left shoe before scurrying off to wager his bets. More often, the high rollers would have the red flannel made into a bag in which a magnet or lodestone was deposited along with the appropriate amount of anvil dust to feed them. This would most definitely secure their success at the conclusion of their risking their weekly wages."

The woman furthest away from him bellowed out, "I'm about to be divorced by my good-for-nothing husband so that he can marry some young slut from Baton Rouge. Were they ever used to promote bad luck?"

"Absolutely, and, as I said a moment ago, there were those for harm and mischief. Red pepper or gunpowder in a gris-gris bag thrown at one's enemies or their doors meant that they had been admonished and were no longer in the good graces of the Voodoo. In antebellum times before the great misery, owners who were cruel to their slaves might find under their pillow a gris-gris bag, containing gunpowder, salt, black pepper with saffron, and la pièce de résistance, freshly crushed dried dog excrement pounded by the femur bone of a buzzard in one of the water buckets belonging to the master's house until it resembled manure for the cotton fields. Now, Marie Laveau, it is claimed, assembled a gris-gris bag that would most assuredly make the intended victims die if slipped into their handbags or under their pillows."

"What the hell did she put in it? As soon as I'm finished taking that son of a bitch to the cleaners, I think I'll have need for one of them." She laughed. "Make that two of them!"

His smile quickly turned to a solemn expression. "My dear and much wronged Madame, it may be very problematic to fill your most righteous request nowadays and acquire for you the justice you seek and deserve. For you see, the bag itself was sewn from the burial shroud of one who had departed this world exactly nine days prior. It was much easier for her to come across such a winding-sheet then than it is for us at the present time. Furthermore, she packed it with a multitude of articles with the strongest supernatural powers and of varying degrees of rarity: a rooster's heart, a dried one-eyed toad, an owl's liver, a bat's wings, a dried lizard, an absolutely black cat's eyes, and, most difficult of all to procure in this day and time, the little finger of a full blooded Negro, who had recently committed suicide. Perhaps we can accommodate you with something that is not so troublesome to obtain."

The host, who had just arrived late for his own party in honor of his wife's turning forty, approached the houngan asogwe and patted him on his back. Good-naturedly, he asked, "I know you rank among the highest members of the voodoo clergy, but do you ever intend to start making my guests their gris-gris bags or do you only plan to talk about them?"

His playfulness returned and he spun around to look up at the host before grinning. "I was presently about to do precisely that, sir. First, I need to conclude telling them the type of bags they can select." After putting his glass of rum on the altar behind him and parking his walking stick against its border, his hands were free to line up along the edge of the altar in front of him ten bags, every one a distinct color. His right hand circled above the shoeboxes to accent them. "Depending upon what your intended purposes are for the gris-gris bag, I will select from these boxes the appropriate stones and ingredients that Erzulie, herself, directs me to choose both to improve your lot in life and to protect you."

He laid a finger on each bag as he described them one by one. "Here you have a black bag for fending off harm and negativity and attaining healing through silent rumination and reflection. Rest it under your pillow at twilight. Now, the blue one is for triumph and great joy and attracts all things that are good, love and health above all. Men, plant it firmly in your right pocket. You women leave it in your purse or left pocket. You politicians will want this next one in purple. For gaining power of all types, particularly forcing others to bend to your will, the purple bag works best. Through it you may achieve peace, protection, and abundance. During an exorcism, you must dangle one from around your neck on a long necklace to press firmly against your heart and shield it from Satan, Beelzebub, Ashtoreth, or Azazel, themselves, or from one of the remaining lesser princes of darkness or any of the fallen angels who reside in hell. Otherwise, bear it as you would the blue bag.

"To answer difficult questions or such things in court," he continued, "you lawyers, particularly those of you from the FBI, will need to tuck a brown bag under your pillow. Wrap that green bag in some folding money and always keep it close to you. That will facilitate your realizing harmony in your life through wealth and godsend. At work you will need to suspend this orange gris-gris bag over your desk to encourage your creative talents in the arts."

He stopped and laughed before proceeding. "I see your eyes all keep being drawn to the pink bag and the red bag and for very good reasons. Both go between the mattress and box spring of your bed. Pink makes for fervor and fruitfulness in your bed. On the other hand, the red one only at the moment of your completely anointing it with the appropriate love oils and herbs and your puffing on it will then bestow upon you power, adoration, and much lovemaking, including seduction.

"Now I caution all of you to be careful with this red bag. Anything in red, if misused, may cause a benign spirit to become malevolent and curse you with bad health or worse, death!

"For you Secret Service agents there are both the white and yellow bags. You'll hang the white one in your home since it generates good karma and will protect against all kinds of wickedness and misbehavior, and can revoke jinxes. On the contrary, carry the yellow one in your pocket to increase your mental agility and beget good fortune, especially riches, and to heal both the body and soul."

14

The host's wife came over and whispered into her husband's ear, "It's time for you to join the rest of your guests. By the way, they have staked out the bar set up in the living room and have spilled out across the foyer into our dining room. While patiently waiting for you to tell them all about your meeting today at the White House and the reelection, they've been thoroughly enjoying themselves by depleting your stocks of Highland Park and Rémy Martin and smoking what little you have left of the Cuban cigars Jack secretly told you to buy before the embargo. If you don't get in there now, I'm going to have to send someone out to the liquor store!"

Mention of the White House caused the host to remember something he needed to ask the voodoo priest and, consequently, to tap him again on the shoulder "Did you happen to bring that special voodoo doll you suggested you could make?"

"Yes, sir." he said earnestly. "It's right here under my table with the rest of them. The concern that I alluded to over how difficult it would be to render the likeness to your satisfaction turned out to be justified. It took a long time for me to make it, but I think you will be pleased with it. In all modesty, I must say it looks just like the Vice President." He bent down under the table and pushed aside the tablecloth to hunt for the carton next to the cage housing his huge boa constrictor. He found the doll, stood up, and handed it to the host along with several red pins.

The host gave the voodoo doll the once-over, quickly lifted it above his head so that everyone could see it, and hollered, "Damn, if it isn't the spitting image of Lyndon!" He then shook hands with the houngan and said, "You're the best! Bobby will be thrilled when I give

15

it to him next month. I'll be back in DC then visiting his brother."

While grabbing for his deck of cards, he volunteered, "Would you like me to do a written reading of Mr. Kennedy's future? You could include it with the doll."

"Oh no, I don't think that will be necessary."

Chapter 1

Death and divorce, the two Ds, are both my friends and business partners from whom I eke out a living. Of course, overwhelming debt and corporate downsizing are similarly invaluable to me but are much less reliable allies. Without these four human perils, I would never legally be able to rip-off relics of the past previously treasured by their owners and still be thanked by those very same people for being so generous in their hour of need. Although the Tenth Commandment strictly forbids us from coveting anything that is our neighbor's, that is precisely what we do. Ironically, death is considered a good career move in this regard. The value of one's estate frequently increases dramatically upon one's passing, particularly when that someone is assassinated while occupying the Oval Office. However, when it comes to being collectables, Presidential memorabilia are not all equal. Interest in either John F. Kennedy or Abraham Lincoln far exceeds that in William McKinley, Jr.

Materialism has become the driving force behind the world's economy. Whereas in the prior century inventors or innovators garnered the great riches, currently it is the salesman or better the pitchman for some overpriced commodity who is included on the Forbes list of the wealthiest persons. And do not think that those real estate billionaires are not doing the same thing. They just call it deal making. The Dalai Lama likes to say that ignorance leads to misery. In my case, it makes me a profit. The lack of knowledge about what other people are really willing to spend, or, as we say, give for an item is key to my take-home pay.

Twelve times a year we all meet near the airport for "the show." There are thousands of scavengers out there just like me, and, in the dark of the morning of the Thursday before the second Saturday of each month, we begin to cluster together in the parking lot of an old Home Depot whose floor has been divided with black painted right angles into hundreds of numbered square cubicles. Overhead, hanging from the ceiling, are signs with a dark blue capital letter and a bright red number that indicate the section that each booth will eventually occupy. Meanwhile, outside we are lining up our trucks and vans in a sinuous procession, allowing first the senior dealers to enter the side doors from which they claim their assigned more desirable locations: silverwares in front and furniture in the back. Jewelry is scattered about the building to prevent a shoplifter from grabbing a handful of diamonds or gold and darting out of the exit before there is time to alert security.

Thieves are our nemesis. Ironically, we are actually in the same business. They just prefer not to buy their merchandise and then sell it to intermediaries who eventually try to become our sources. I spend my free time scouring the pawnshops and second hand stores of the city searching for the items I have reported stolen to the police. That and learning how to tell fakes made in China and South America can become our second occupation. However, even more vital is protecting ourselves from the highway robbers that follow us home from "the show." This is self-preservation. Except for the jewelry, they are generally only interested in the money we carry rather than our goods. After all, mine is predominately a cash and carry trade.

"The show" is the great melting pot for people with disposable income and an appreciation of objects made

18

by artisans who signed their work with the pride of knowing that it was the very best that they could do. The quality of their masterpieces remains evident even today. I can never predict who may make an appearance there. Movie stars, politicians, CEOs of Fortune 500 companies, and rock stars haggle along with the doctors, lawyers, accountants, and schoolteachers. Although having deep pockets helps, it is frequently irrelevant in getting the buy of "the show." Expertise in stuff that most people do not even care exists usually trumps legal tender. Because anything and anyone may be at "the show," each weekend it is held has the potential to be magical.

Today I let my middle-aged, slightly overweight and balding, gray haired self sleep in late. It is preview day for the auction. The intrigue that I will witness over the next two days makes the monthly goings-on at "the show" seem bush league. Auctioneers are the wholesalers to my industry and are therefore one of its vital links. They are also prone to hyperbole and balderdash. Everything they sell is the best, the very best with that "WOW factor." Our mutual tendency to overstate is one reason why antiques dealers feel a special kinship to them. On the top of the front covers of the catalogues for this auction house is its owner's motto: "Buy something at an auction and it may change your life forever." Although this has never before happened to me, I, the eternal optimist, certainly expect it will this time and have planned accordingly. For weeks I have scrutinized the catalogue for this auction on line and reprinted it into my own spiral bound book. Each lot in which I am interested is copied on an individual sheet of paper and the recent prices paid for it or similar items on Internet sites or at other auctions are written in the margins. I feel I am better prepared for this one than the last one where some international dealers, who I only recognized as friends of the auctioneer, kept bidding me up and then dropping out at the last minute. I am determined not to overpay tomorrow. After contacting a few of my out of town customers to ascertain their interest in particular items, I will be ready to leave for the preview.

While still lying in bed under the covers, I reach over to my nightstand and turn on the lamp before grabbing my preview book. As I leaf through its pages with my left hand to find Lot 250, I call a usually reliable silver collector with the index finger of my right hand touching the number to his private line on my cell phone's speed dial directory. "Hey, Leonard, you keep reminding me you're after a knock out Tiffany vase and, remember, you made me promise to give you the right of first refusal on the next one I got. It just so happens that I may be offered one this week by my Delta pilot customer from Milwaukee if he doesn't back out of the deal. Are you still interested?"

He is coy. "Ernie, I'm always interested; however, it all depends. I don't have to tell you that the market hasn't been the best, but for the right piece I might be able to swing it."

I go for the jugular. "How about a Columbian Exposition piece?"

His excitement is evident from his quick response. "Awesome, you definitely have piqued my attention. Which one is it?"

Reading from the catalogue's description, I pretend to be conversant about a vase, with which I am unfamiliar and that in reality I have never seen first hand. I really outdo myself. "The 'Wild-Rose Vase,' designed by John

T. Curran for Tiffany. Only the 'Magnolia Vase' at the Metropolitan Museum is better. As you recall, they only made twelve sterling and enameled vases for that World's Fair. If I am successful, it will be one of the finest examples of Tiffany I've ever handled."

He clamors, "It's on the market!" I am at a loss. All sorts of concerns cross my mind. Is he pleasantly surprised or horribly disappointed for some reason? In each antiques field there are the cursed items. Rumors about their provenance or their "being right" kill any potential sale. Even famous masterpieces in museums may be suspect. Fearing saying anything that will squelch the deal, I hold my breath. Finally, he breaks the silence. "Well, how much is it going to set me back? Even if only half of its mystique is true, it won't come cheap." That is exactly what I wanted to hear. Yes, he is hooked. I tightly clench my right fist before jerking it downwards.

This is where dealing becomes more art than crass salesmanship. "I can't tell you yet. As I said, I'm still waiting for that old customer of mine to finally commit. His wife is eaten up with cancer and he needs to raise some money fast to help pay for her round-the-clock nursing care at their home. I just wanted to inform you that it may be available and to see, if I succeed in getting it, whether you would want me to drop by for you to just admire it."

Never one to be subtle if he truly is after something, he lays his cards plainly on the table. "I appreciate that. If you are able to obtain it, which by the way may not be as easy as you think it will be, call my secretary, and I'll fly you up here in my jet so that you can show it to me." It is at an auction. How much trouble can this be?

A few more quick transactions like Leonard's and I will have a very good month. It has always surprised me how the exceptional curio sells itself, no matter how bad the economy. Hell, in February 2010 in the middle of the worst recession since the Great Depression, a copy of the original comic book, which featured Batman, sold for over a million dollars; whereas a little over 19 years before that, another one had gone for a mere $55,000. That same week a copy of the first Superman comic as well went for a million dollars, $683,000 more than a lesser grade Action Comics No. 1 sold for a year prior. That record lasted barely a month when in late March 2010 another copy of it went for $1,500,000 on an Internet comic book auction website. A million and a half dollars for a comic book, what will they pay for some real art: how about $104.3 million with fees, again in February 2010, for the bronze, "Walking Man I," by Alberto Giacometti? That was over three times more than his "Standing Woman II" brought 2 years earlier, which had set the record price for one of his works. And they are not even antiques. He made "Walking Man I" in 1960. Sotheby's sold it, Lot 8, in ten minutes for Dresdner Bank in Germany, which acquired it in 1980: easy money in hard times. These stories are what keep me in the business. Too bad I am not an auctioneer. Sotheby's made just shy of $12 million off of Lot 8. I find it amusing that for the little time they invested in promoting "Walking Man I," they made more money when annualized than the bank did from owning it for 30 years. As I said, these stories are what motivate me. Every time I hear them it rekindles my belief that some day I will stumble on that one thing, which will be my grand slam in the world of antiques.

Beginning my pre-preview rituals, I finally get out of bed and move to my closet where I sort out my most worn shirts and pants. I always have difficulty deciding what to wear for these occasions. Is it better to appear worse at its preview or at the auction itself? For the preview, my local rival likes to jog from his condominium to the auction house in his sweatsuit. He claims people leave him alone when he does that. He hates the **canards** that are told there. I, on the other hand, like them. A lot must be worth a bundle if people are willing to lie about it. I especially enjoy it when someone loudly challenges the authenticity of a clear signature or trademark when it is patently correct or report to anyone who will listen repairs that have never been attempted. I make a point to bid more aggressively for those items even if I am not interested in them. God forbid that the son of a bitch should get a misbegotten bargain. Of course, it is prudent to observe the real authorities when they take a special interest in something. Either they really want it or they do not feel it is quite right. Regardless of their motive, they keep it to themselves. For today's action I admire how really grungy I will look as I lay out my clothes on the foot of the bed.

Next, I sit beside my tattered jeans and link up with my bank via my cell phone. My letter of credit is due at the auction house upon the opening of the preview today in order for me to register and get my number. I like having a low number. It is one of my superstitions. Besides, I am an obsessive-compulsive, who would not sleep the night before an auction without already having my number. Sure enough it has been sent. Finally, I inspect my cell phone. Is it fully charged and does the Internet connection work? Somehow the auctioneer never has available that very reference which I really need to verify a crucial detail. I would be an idiot to bring my own material with me since reading from it while standing in front of a particular lot would be a red flag to the bulls in the room to gouge me tomorrow at the real event when that very lot opens for bidding. Accordingly, my book for this auction stays at home today while my phone is good to go.

Oh, by the way, coming to earlier preview events is also folly. Why give the auction house advance warning about on what I plan to bid? Those security cameras are not there just to prevent heists. I can only imagine who will be standing in the very back of the room or on the other end of the phone call bidding against me?

It also helps to be friends with the auctioneer, but not too friendly. They can give me an edge by telling me who my competition will be for the day and how big a player they are. As I said before, who were those international dealers at the last auction? What did they want so badly later on in that auction to have had me shoot my wad so early that evening? Naturally, I may pay a price for that insider information. If I make a misstep by underestimating my competition's credit limit or actually believing the auctioneer's baloney given to me in strict confidence, I may end up going home with an expensive mistake. As we say about a dealer's own estate sale, it has either the very best, what they would not sell, or the very worst, what they could not sell. Then again, the sign hanging over the entrance to "the show" says, "One man's garbage is another man's treasure."

Just before I am about to leave, I do my last rite. Emails are both a blessing and a curse, but regardless, they have to be answered in a timely fashion or else risk incurring the wrath of customers and forever lose their business. For days my inbox has been full of clients asking me what to pay for lots at this auction. I lie back on the head of the bed with my Mac Book on my lap. I have to overcome my temptation to reply, "If you are stupid enough to ask a person who may be bidding against you, what to pay for a lot, you will never win the item." Let me be clear. My advice has never caused one of my "friends" to overpay for anything at an auction nor by some quirk of fate to outbid me. I sincerely forewarn them about auction fever and the ridiculous prices that people have paid at them in the past. After giving them a reasonable range to consider, I counsel that if they really want the piece, they should have me, a professional, bid for them and pay me a commission. In reality, both of us would end up ahead of the game. Many in fact have done just that for this auction, and I hastily print out the information about their lots for my book. Meanwhile, I open the top drawer of the nightstand and take out the auction catalogue that I will use at the preview and circle those lot numbers in it.

Chapter 2

No two auctions are the same nor are their previews. Today's preview promises to be something special. When I walk into the large exhibition room, it does not fail. Along the walls, which are covered with undistinguished wallpaper in neutral colors that some decorator undoubtedly charged a small fortune to select, are the display tables. Black tablecloths totally conceal their tops and legs as well as the storage boxes underneath them. They abut each other so tightly that the lots, which have been neatly arranged consecutively by their numbers, appear to form one continuous row that outlines the entire perimeter of the room. Bright halogen light towers are placed periodically behind the display tables to show off each item at its best. Because the auction had been so well publicized, the crowd is abnormally large. Furthermore, the quality of the offerings has drawn more than the usual number of out-of-town dealers and collectors. While I really like a good sale with a high degree of rarity, I prefer them to be kept quiet, an unthinkable happening. John, the auctioneer for this one, reportedly went to New York to hype it personally to the dealers there.

Draped with the same black tablecloth used to create the illusion of elegance for the display tables, which actually are just cheap folding tables, the registration table stands prominently in the middle of the exhibition room so that everyone notices it upon entering the preview. There sits an impeccably dressed clerk, who immediately recognizes me, and smiles accordingly. I personally have never asked John why he does it, but it is an established fact that at each of his events he uses the same young, buxom, blond Southern belle, Jenny, to check us in. I suspect that, since she is also the one who checks us out, it is a psychological trick of his to encourage us to outbid each other in order to gain her attention and favor.

Jenny matter-of-factly hands me the one page form to fill out to register for the auction. While hunting for me on her iMac, she states with her soft, sultry Southern accent, as slowly as blackstrap molasses dribbles from its jar into the gingerbread dough, "Dr. Kopp, if your information has changed, please write it down for me so that I can update our computer. From your profile it's really clear that the bank has been most generous with your line of credit this week. We must have something one of your customers truly wants."

I smile. "Jenny, I keep telling you to stop with the Dr. Kopp bit. I only went to medical school to please my parents. Just call me Ernie. By the way there are no changes. As for my line of credit, remember what Teddy Roosevelt said, 'Speak softly and carry a big stick.' Seeing all these people who you all have persuaded to come down for this auction, I may need to get a baseball bat for tomorrow."

Careful not to come across as a flirt while still being just playful enough to lead me on, she flutters her long eyelashes, green from her mascara. "Well, you have always carried a big stick in my mind, but tomorrow you will need that bat. The Tiffany vase in Lot 250 has brought in the big guns from New York and Europe. They all want to set their eyes upon it before they bid on it. It's strange that we haven't had a single phone bid or absentee bid for it. Usually for something that significant we would have had a ton of them already. Instead, they

27

all came down here. I guess they all hope to be that someone who hits the winning home run of the last game of the World Series and leaves the field with the trophy ball."

While these guys may enjoy going to a Yankees game and may even envision themselves as Babe Ruth, they would very much prefer visiting the shark tanks at the New York Aquarium at feeding time since there is never enough blood shed over home plate for their tastes. I wonder out loud, "That or are they circling their prey?"

Always a quick wit, she asks as she hands me my paddle, "Are you going to be one of the sharks or their prey? Here's your bidding paddle, you're number 125."

This cannot be right. "125! How can this be? You just opened."

"You should've seen the line to get in here when we first arrived. Besides, most of the major league hitters from out of town preregistered earlier this week. You would plotz if I showed you their lines of credit. But there is no need for you to worry. After all, you are the man." She winks again, beaming a coquettish smile towards me.

After nodding back at Jenny but before leaving her table, I ask myself, *Is this what Leonard meant when he said this might not be as easy as I thought it would be?*

I make it a habit to start a preview at Lot 1 and proceed from there in the order that the lots will be offered at the auction. That way I do not miss a sleeper that did not photograph well in the catalogue or about which the auctioneer had not been given the skinny.

Besides, it keeps everyone from recognizing what I really want. Only suckers go first to the lots they plan to bid on. Why not just place signs over them that say, "Go ahead, bid me up. Paddle X doesn't care. It's going home with me no matter what the price." That and spending too much time at a particular lot is bait for those barracudas, stealthily eyeing me all the while pretending to be concentrating on the preview. Fortunately for me, I have my customer's lots to examine. They are good cover for mine.

The first several items at most auctions are either dogs or damaged merchandise. The auctioneers are not dumb. They are wise to the slowpokes, who no matter what will not arrive on time, and do not want to have a tardy well-heeled bidder miss an extraordinary rarity. However, some experienced auctioneers will place a couple of their best lots near the beginning. I once asked one why he did that. He patted me on my back and said, "It didn't take me long when I first got started to realize that I was losing my shirt on the first twenty five lots since everyone was waiting to bid until they saw if they had won Lot 26. I haven't lost any money since I've moved what would've been Lot 26 to Lot 5. Once, I made my best lot be Lot 1. You would've thought I had violated some auction superstition when I did that by the number of people who came up to me during the preview and asked me if I was crazy." He then smiled. "I made a ton of money on Lot 1. Everyone who wanted it made damn sure they came ahead of the opening and had a sufficient bankroll. Didn't do so bad on the other early lots either that day."

When I reach Lot 10, I open the catalogue to read its description, "Extremely rare! 16½" AMERICAN BRILLIANT PERIOD CUT GLASS HANDLED

DECANTER --'WEDDING RING' PATTERN (aka Crystal City) By J. Hoare--Triple Notched Handle, Hobstar Base--Fine Piece!" I have a love-hate relationship with cut glass. While I love the way it sparkles, it is a royal pain in the ass to vet. My customer wants me to bid big on this item if it is right and has a soft-top number for it, which means he has given me some latitude, if I need it, to bid above that amount. As I said, being certain about the piece is a pain. Fortunately, this auctioneer has a black light box in the corner for me to use to tell if it fluoresces green. Green means it is probably old and good, pink is probably new and bad. I have to wait in line for my turn since the porcelain dealers, busily examining for repairs done on the Chinese wares, are bathed in the purple radiance from the Wood's lamp.

During this hiatus, I survey all around to see what lots appear to be hot. There is one in particular that seems to be drawing quite a crowd about it, Lot 250, that Tiffany vase. Leonard's prophecy seems to be coming to fruition.

Finally, I get my chance. Boy, does it glow lime green. One would have to be color blind not to see it. Next I go over it for chips, cracks, flaws in the glass, interior stains, and notable restorations. Finally, I examine the handle to inspect for a heat check. Those cut glass collectors go nuts over heat checks. Just because the junction of the handle and the body of the glass has a crack that was caused by a faulty annealing process at the factory over a hundred years ago, they will discount what they will pay for an item. I am about to put the decanter back on the table when I remember to test the stopper. Yep, its plug fits snuggly in the neck. I must agree with the catalogue that it is a fine piece and rare, too.

Nevertheless, I hope I get outbid. Worse than anything is having to pack cut glass. It does not forgive careless wrapping as silver does. Shipping it is another pain. However, once it is washed and properly displayed with good lighting, this decanter will compete favorably with anything Tiffany made. Hell, Tiffany may have even sold it originally in the 1890s.

After giving the next twenty-three lots respectable but short once-overs, I finally arrive at some of the Tiffany offerings. Although pleased by the lack of competition to inspect them, due to the extraordinary attendance today I am at a loss to explain my good fortune. Lot 34, the catalogue says, "TIFFANY CURTAIN BORDER HANGER designed by Clara Driscoll for Louis Comfort Tiffany (known to dealers as LCT). Spectacular Arts & Craft ceiling hanging lamp in a geometric motif whose top is made of dichroic glass, which turns from a subtle nicely mottled light yellow color in natural sunlight to a wonderful rich orange when illuminated by incandescent light. Along the shade's bottom, mottled green and brown rippled glass create a curtain border. Signed 'Tiffany Studios New York.' SIZE: 24-1/2 in. diameter." If cut glass is a pain in the ass, Tiffany lamps are hemorrhoids. I never feel comfortable telling a customer that one of them is bona fide. If I can find out who the seller of the lamp is, I will generally be confortable that it is right. In this case I do not have to worry about that. This auction house has a letter of authenticity next to it from the leading authority on Tiffany and will take it back if another true expert subsequently finds fault with it. The glass appears genuine with only the occasional expected hairline fracture that comes with its age and has no replaced pieces. The metal and its patina seem to be original without repairs, but more crucial, all the exposed copper foil adhere nicely to each piece of glass and are completely coated by lead solder at each foil joint and in the outer edges. I lift the shade off the table and turn it upside down to read the impressed metal signature tag; sure enough, it says Tiffany Studios New York. After thumping it and hearing it rattle, a telltale sign that the shade is old since the beeswax used to hold the glass pieces in place has dried out, I acknowledge that it is OK by nodding. But what are those New York dealers going to give for it? My customer has rightly made a firm top bid for me. He may not get it, but he will not have overpaid for it either, should he win. If he is lucky, I will pay the auction house to ship it since it will need the special insurance that they already own on it and they have the hatbox shaped shipping crate that came with it. Buying antiques is easy. Being confident that things are as advertised and arrive home safely is hard.

As I approach Lot 250, I see where all the Tiffany dealers and collectors have been hiding out. The crowd that I had spied earlier has grown even larger. That is commonly held to be a good sign by auctioneers. However, the closer I am to it, the more the intensity of the dealer's grumbling convinces me that someone must be committing the highly unorthodox sin of openly challenging the vase in public. That turns out to be exactly the case.

John is surrounded by naked hostility. Normally, at one of his auctions he is unflappable. No one dares to challenge him. His size alone intimidates his customers. He used to play college basketball and has subsequently gained a lot of weight. He is not obese, just large. One of his hands will completely engulf most decanters. Because he still has all of his hair, which is turning gray, he cuts a dashing figure with his sideburns and retro western shirts adorned by apache or string neckties. He usually defuses conflicts with his small town Missouri humor and charm. Presently, he is visibly upset with his face flushed and sweat beading upon his forehead. "I may have to remove it from the auction. I've been told that an identical vase is housed at the Museo Nacional de Bellas Artes in Havana. I've called Tiffany & Company to learn what their files show about a second Wild-Rose Vase. Until I have proof that mine is not a fake, I am reserving my right to pull it tomorrow. For those of you who came here specifically for it, I apologize."

Someone cries out, "You wouldn't be pulling it because you've had an offer you couldn't refuse? I've heard you won't reveal the name of its seller and that there has been unusual interest in it from a foreign country. Can't stand the heat, John?"

John becomes indignant. "No! Whoever you are, if you knew me, you would have never said that. That is not how I run my auction house! Some of my customers don't want their names disclosed; that shouldn't come as a surprise to any of you. As to who is interested in this lot, all I can tell you is that I expect to make a nice commission off of it tomorrow. Why would I deny myself that by pulling it and then selling it to someone without giving you the benefit of outbidding him and paying the buyer's premium? Goes against everything I stand for: true capitalism and my making money even if you don't."

The crowd slowly disbands allowing me to take in the vase from a distance. It so far is good. I have personally held the Magnolia Vase at the Met when they auctioned off curator's tours as part of their annual fund raising a few years back. Of course, I had to wear white gloves. Unlike the others here, I have a photographic memory and recall exactly how it was hallmarked. The silver curator showed me an additional very small mark that was incused under a much larger mark, a capital 'T' over a globe, placed by Tiffany on each of those twelve enameled vases to indicate that they had been shown at the Columbian Exposition. Since it is negligible and had been left on a curve, that other mark does not photograph well and shows up as a smudge on all the Met's images of it. He told me it identifies the artist responsible for the enamel work for each of them. Evidently, Tiffany was so concerned that the enamel on one of his exhibition pieces might get damaged at the World's Fair of 1893 that he had gone to this extreme measure to insure that any required repair be done by the original artist for that particular vase. Only someone who had seen the real hallmarks on one of those wonders would be clued-up to seek it out since it is not mentioned in any of the literature about them.

Once the crowd dispersed, John approaches me. He shakes my hand and simultaneously turns me so that our backs are to the few remaining hangers-on. In an undertone he solicits my help, "Ernie, you're the only dealer here who I trust. Study that vase and tell me what you think. I can't believe a communist country has anything of Tiffany's that's worth having."

I previously had not grasped how little he knew about Russia and Cuba before communism. "John, the whole goddamn interior of the Museo de la Revolución in Havana was designed by LCT around 1918 while it was being built as the Presidential Palace. His Magnolia Window was purchased by Baron Stieglitz, a close courtier of Tsar Nicholas II, for his own collection in St Petersburg in 1901. Pre-revolution Russia and Cuba were hot beds for Tiffany and the art nouveau movement."

Already upset from having just dealt with that mob, he becomes even more flustered. "You mean to tell that that bastard Castro was an art collector and I never knew it. Can you imagine how much money I could've made off of him? Those Cubans in Florida collect their homeland's art and I've passed on it every time they've offered it to me."

Curiosity gets the better of me. "Who told you that the vase might be a fake?"

My question really makes John angrier. I can honestly say I have never seen him this agitated before. "You remember those two dealers who kept underbidding you at my last auction? Apparently, they told it to every Tiffany silver collector and dealer in the world. Everyone wants to see it and make up his own mind before bidding on it. If Tiffany doesn't come through, I may have to pull it just to prevent those two from getting it for a song. I don't have the time to send someone to Cuba to get the run down from there. And to think I thought they were my friends. I've never heard of such an underhanded move to undermine the bidding at an auction."

I say to myself, *They didn't get to Leonard. If he had heard about this, he would have flown his secretary to Havana to check it out.* Come to think about it, maybe he has already done so and is aware that it is real. He never goes to an auction or even reads their catalogues since he claims he makes more money working than wasting his time at them. He'd rather have me do all the legwork and collect my finder's fee. I wonder if he just feels they are beneath him or is afraid he'll get ripped off if people recognized him or knew he was bidding.

My protracted silence only heightens his desire to find out what I am thinking. "Well, have you heard anything about the vase?"

"To be perfectly honest, John, before you mentioned it, nothing other than the vase should command a nice price. Nor have any of my customers. They are all excited about it. This is a real shocker. Maybe those two didn't think I ranked high enough to threaten their little ploy. The only problem with what you are suggesting is what would they do with it once they owned it? Who would buy such a tainted piece of Tiffany? They would never get their money back."

My reassuring him has not abated his fury. He persistently waves his finger in my face. "There are people out there who don't care about getting their money back. All they care about is owning the object. They have so much that losing a million dollars doesn't keep them awake at night. Even better, in their wills they frequently leave their possessions along with an endowment to a museum instructing it to create a major collection in their names from the core that they have bequeathed to it. They come here all the time. Two of them will sit on opposite sides of the room and try to outbid each other no matter how outlandish the price gets. They live in a different world than the one we live in. If they want something, they buy it. The rarer it is, the more they want it. If a one of a kind happens to come through here, the sky's the limit on what they will pay for it. And the history buffs are the worst. They would hock their businesses for the dagger that killed Caesar or the pistol that assassinated Lincoln." He laughs. "It's sad but true, but, if you're murdered while you're President, almost anything connected to you, even your worn-out top hat, becomes valuable. And anything even remotely associated with the crime is an instant sought-after collectable. Stuff surrounding JFK's assassination is today's hottest Presidential memorabilia."

"How come? I always thought that Lincoln and Washington were the most popular Presidents."

"It's the only presidential assassination done long distance with a rifle. Nothing is definite about what really happened in Dallas. The conspiracy nuts want that last bit of evidence that clinches the case, and will they ever shell out dearly for it."

Everyone else has finally moved on and we are at last alone. John hands me the Wild-Rose Vase. I turn it around and then peer into its interior. For all that I can tell, it is a true sibling of the Magnolia Vase. Four large rose blossoms, hand tooled out of the silver, are covered with peach colored enameled petals. Trailing beneath each blossom are green and brown enameled leaves and branches along with peach colored rose buds. In the background is densely acid etched foliage consisting of more rose leaves and an overwhelming abundance of ferns. Inside, the original gilding is preserved with the appropriate wear marks, signs of age, along the rim. If this is a fake, I want more of them. John's unease prompts him to interrupt my assessment. "So, what do you think?"

Antiques dealers when holding a true masterpiece can get turned-on by the experience. At this moment I am having such a sensation while discreetly fondling it with my hands. "As luck would have it, I've held the Magnolia Vase. This is just as magnificent although quite a bit smaller. Who these days could fake it? It was acid etched in at least two layers. If I were to use my loupe, I bet you I would make out even a few more layers. The silversmith then lightly repoussed from the inside under the flowers, buds, and some leaves and stems. After he did that he had enamel applied in several layers with several firings into the spaces created by the acid bath. No one makes this champlevé enamel anymore. Hell, only Tiffany did it in the nineteenth century. Besides, it would cost so much to make one currently, nobody could afford to buy it."

My unabashed enthusiasm for it causes him to become very excited and boosts him to smile for the first time today. "So, it's right!"

I am so convinced about its being genuine that I have not yet bothered to confirm it. Consequently, I resist answering him until with one hand I turn it upside down so that I can pore over the hallmarks, particularly the enameler's mark. With my other hand I take my chrome plated jeweler's loupe out of my pocket and its leather case. Carefully scrutinizing the base, I find the enameler's mark is there on the curve below Tiffany's special Columbian Exposition stamp that capital "T" over a globe, which is below "TIFFANY & CO/11182 T3164/STERLING." I smile back at John. "It's right!"

This minute, nothing else matters more to John. He is elated and vigorously shakes my hand. "I knew it! From the bottom of my heart I thank you, Ernie. Although I have Tiffany Tom's receipt from that vase's last sale, which I will give to the winning bidder, I personally needed your Good Housekeeping seal of approval. You see, I refused to pay $1500.00 to that son of a bitch to certify the piece again since he had said it was fine when he had done its last appraisal for estate planning. You won't believe this, but I brought him all the documentation I had on it. Rather than certify that they were not forgeries, that bastard literally tore up his old letter of authenticity and would not issue another one without a new complete inspection. He would've done the same thing to his sale receipt, if I had presented it to him first. Fortunately, I was lucky to have had the presence of mind to have kept it locked up in my attaché case before showing him his letter. Pulling that vase would have cost me a small fortune. As you recall, the bigger Tiffany Daisy Vase from that World's Fair brought $284,800 in 2005."

Thoroughly familiar with how paranoid I am about anyone spying on me during preview, he leaves me alone to finish my surveying it. Once I complete my rounds on all of the lots, I head for The Blue And The Gray, a Civil War themed upscale meat and three restaurant in midtown associated with a small motel, where dealers for "the show" stay. Although not its real name, everyone calls it The Blue And The Gay because most of its patrons are either retired straights or gay antiques dealers and/or interior designers. Its owner, Bill, is one of those history buffs that John had referred to earlier today. The walls of his restaurant display his mini-museum. Visiting it is also one of my pre-auction rituals. The food there is good home cooking, nothing fancy, at a reasonable price. I do not think the menu has significantly changed in the eighty years it has been in business except for the prices. But it has been years since I bothered to open one. Everybody has decided what they want to order before they get there, and the wait staff has ingrained in their memory what everyone is going to order. It is a mere formality to hand them a menu.

Going to The Blue And The Gay is both entertaining and a business expense. One reason that it has survived so long is its customers are also the show there. The matrons are all dolled up with their gray hair being a light shade of blue from over using Mrs. Stewart's Bluing and the gents wear suits, usually cotton poplin, and silk ties. If they are lucky, they come alone and leave with a date for the evening, who after a short walk across the large parking lot accompanies them to the motel. The gays wear whatever they have that is clean: worn-out blue jeans with tee shirts or loud, gaudy cotton print shirts with the buttons open to their navel and expensive designer pants that amazingly match their shirts. Gold jewelry is plentiful and always flaunted: the more ornate and garish, the better. Middle-aged men bring their twenty-something boyfriends and, per their request, are seated at the most conspicuous tables. Despite their cultural differences, everybody gets along there. After preview and before the regulars descend upon the restaurant and leave no empty tables for us, each and every dealer, local or out-of-towner, heads for The Blue And The Gay. That is where the deal making is done.

While all this is entirely illegal, we nevertheless collude to decide who will bid on what and how high. If there is a complete set of dishes or glasses that will need to be broken up, the dealer who will bid for it and later divvy up the place settings to the rest of us needs to be appointed. After all, it is just business and we have to protect ourselves from those putzes who call themselves collectors. They wear out their welcome whenever they refuse to lower their paddles and ruin a deal I have worked on for weeks.

My talk with John has made me late. I must push my way through the crowd in the entrance way and the small official waiting area on its left to view the main dining room. Only one large round oak table remains with a vacant chair. Tablecloths would be entirely out of character for The Blue And The Gay's family atmosphere, rather eight white paper placemats are equally spaced along the edge of the table. Sitting at it are seven dealers who have consumed more than their fair share of the restaurant's liquor by the time I arrive.

Paul, a dealer friend from Nashville, happens to be there and calls me over to the table. He has a matinee idol's smart appearance and works out every day to preserve his slim physique. In keeping with his hometown and his country music star clients, he maintains a mullet, which he holds in place with mousse, and wears rhinestone studded shirts, blue jeans and lizard skin boots. While most of us would feel ridiculous wearing his haircut and attire, he pulls it off. "Come sit with us, Ernie. We all want to hear what you and John were saying to each other with your backs turned towards us. It was very impolite for you two to have done that."

Still standing, I smile the best good old boy smile I can muster. "Heaven forbid, Paul, you wouldn't have wanted us to discuss how ugly and fat you've become in front of you and everyone else. We did the honorable thing. We did our hatchet job on you behind your back."

He laughs. "You're so kind. Under the same circumstance, I would've shown you the same courtesy. What did you think about the Tiffany vase? John rarely gets fooled."

As I sit down, I say, "And I don't think he did this time. It looks right to me. He told me that part of his problem is that he refused to pay $1500.00 to Tiffany Tom to certify the piece again since he had said it was fine when it had last been appraised for estate planning.

The prick ripped apart his original letter of authenticity!"

"How come? I don't need to tell you that that's highly unusual and suspicious!"

"He claims he would need to examine the vase again since he had not seen it in over a decade. After all, as he insists on telling everyone, he is the nation's leading Tiffany expert and has his sterling reputation to protect."

Chapter 3

Auction day always invigorates me like the opening day of the regular baseball season. It is a mystery to me why, but it does. Maybe, because just before either of them begins, anything is possible. It likewise reminds me of a Thanksgiving Day Midnight Madness sale. You never can predict what true bargain you will bring home from one of them. Moreover, auction day compensates for the myriad unsatisfactory treasure hunts that I must endure on a regular basis. I waste a lot of time visiting recently deceased people's homes that are filled with what their children claimed were exquisite antiques, but turn out to be just reproductions. As for going to "estate sales" held by divorcing couples or families moving out of town, they are really nothing more than glorified garage sales. Most of my finds come from managers of true estate sales inviting me to them prior to the public event. I have to laugh every time I pass by one of them early Friday or Saturday morning before the doors open and spot the long line of eager buyers with their price guides in one hand and tape measures in the other. Do they not realize that anything of value has already been picked over by the pros like me?

"The show" is another good source for referrals to virgin works of the decorative arts. Some innocent couple will walk into my booth and lust for almost everything there. Seeing my prices inspires them to ask the infamous question: "My Grandmother gave me something that's just like that punch bowl you have marked for $50,000. But it doesn't go with the rest of our things. You wouldn't be interested in coming over and appraising it, would you?" Dealers will sit in their booth for hours in stark boredom waiting for the magical invitation. More than likely their grandmother's punch bowl is a fine example of Macy's best. However, occasionally the supernatural occurs: it is the real deal. A big decision must be made right then and there. Do you have them bring it to "the show" or do you go to their house and behold it along with what else grandmother left them? Experience helps me decide. A few minutes of discussion about my booth tells me whether they have lived with antiques in their parents' homes or think anything with dirt and tarnish is a 100 years old national prize. I go to the former's home with my checkbook and have the latter schlep their legacy to "the show." Either way, if it is right, I give them a fair dealer's price for it, which in any other business transaction would be called a steal. However, today the treasures come to me.

There is a routine that I have developed over the years for the morning of the auction. I do not eat anything nor do I drink unless I feel that I will pass out from dehydration. An unscheduled visit to the restroom from a cup of Joe can be costly. Today will be a marathon. It takes training to develop the endurance required to sit for 4 to 6 hours in a room without losing my attention or worse nodding off. With over 470 lots to sell, the auctioneer moves fast. His gavel will strike at least once a minute on average. I must be completely aware of my surroundings at all time. Is it my paddle or the one directly behind or next to me that is the highest bid and is going to be recognized as the winner? Which dealer has which number? Getting up to stretch my legs by walking around the room can lead to disaster. The auctioneer may lose me in the crowd and my bid goes overlooked. I will be married to my chair for the duration.

A sociable spouse or partner is a valuable ally in

today's struggle for a successful auction. My wife, Gloria (yes, I am straight) on the other hand follows none of my rules. She has a large breakfast and will need two cups of coffee or more to stay awake during today's contest. Visiting the ladies' room is a must for her. While I, with the aid of my book containing the computer printouts from the catalogue, in solitude and silence hastily go over each lot one more time before we are asked to take our seats, she schmoozes with the collectors and dealers, especially their wives. This is not because she lacks interest in the auction, but rather she is obtaining my last bits of reconnaissance. She learns a ton from this. Women discuss everything in the ladies' room: divorce, infidelity, upcoming marriages, new grandchildren, deaths within the family and foremost recent victories or catastrophes in the stock market. On the floor casual chitchat can be most revealing. Recent hospitalizations are particularly key information.

Her being a thin, attractive, tall brunette with long straight hair that just curls at her shoulders only aids her today. Unlike me, she is all dolled up and has made every effort that her ample breasts are well displayed. I learned from John that men at auctions fawn all over pretty women who do that and will tell them anything. I guess it is our pre-auction hormonal rushes that make us that way, but not all men. Gay dealers and collectors are immune to this tactic, which gives them an unfair advantage.

Gloria and I have only one issue that ever divides us. As proven after the previous auction, she will stew for weeks if I overpay for something. My beautiful and doting bride becomes a Queen Bitch when that happens. She claims it is a sign of lack of discipline and a true professional would never do such a thing. Only when I sell it at a profit does she relent.

All of these ruses and seemingly trivial data are critical for victory. Why? Without them, I will not be able to predict how generous or frugal my friends will be today. Everyone at The Blue And The Gay last evening had deep pockets and a long wish list. Any impending major expense may turn last night's conspicuous serious competitor into just an interested observer of the day's activity. Meanwhile, an inheritance or a killing on Wall Street may leave me going home empty handed.

At 9:50 AM sharp, John approaches the lectern, which is positioned just right of smack center on the small stage of the auction theatre adjoining the exhibition hall. Once there he turns on the LED projector sitting on a black tablecloth covered pedestal to the left of him and establishes that his MacBook on the lectern is hooked up to it and that the photos of each lot will project clearly on the screen behind him. He tests the microphone on the lectern to prove it works and the sound system to find out if it is at the correct volume. Once his equipment check is completed, he starts his introduction. "We will begin in five minutes. If you haven't registered already and received a number and wish to bid for any item up for sale, please do so immediately. Each article will be sold without a reserve and as is, per the general policy of this auction house unless stated otherwise prior to the bidding. There is a 10% buyer's premium placed on each successful bid, as well as the local sales tax unless you have a resale tax license. An item is sold when my hammer strikes. So if you want to win it, make certain I can catch sight of you. And remember, if you bid every time, you'll get it. There will be a ten minute break taken at 1:00 PM. Beverages and refreshments are in the back. Feel free to partake of them throughout the auction. Please take your seats before the first lot is announced. I thank you."

Sounds innocent enough, please take your places. But which one of the hundreds of red velvet chairs lined up in parallel semicircular rows is best? My colleagues and I debated this piece of strategy last evening at The Blue And The Gay as closing time approached and the bartender felt it was sensible to refuse to serve us any further adult libations. I prefer the back row, which allows me to view all who are bidding against me without their having the same advantage. Plus, my neck muscles are not strained by repeatedly turning about to monitor my opponents. Paul made a very cogent argument supporting being in the middle of the pack. The anonymity provided by that location is afforded by no other seating position. John, who had joined us later in the evening after we had finished our business meeting, forcefully asserted that the front row is best. He has never had a bid from someone in the front go ignored. Correspondingly, he insisted, "If you want the damn lot then just keep your paddle raised and don't turn around. Why do you care who's bidding against you? You guys make the two simple rules of this game complicated: he with the most gold rules and the highest bid wins."

Gloria has saved a seat for me in the middle of the back row. She insists on sitting to my left so that she can pull down my paddle whenever I suffer from auction fever. She is right-handed. I am left-handed. Boy, after taking up weight lifting, can she yank my arm down when she gets upset. Upon sitting, I place my book of printouts on my lap. She leans over, cups my ear with her hands, and whispers to me, "Mitch won't be a threat on that Tiffany hanger. His daughter just got accepted to Yale without a scholarship. Despite many an argument over this, Helen won't let him refuse to let her go to their alma mater even in the face of Harvard's offering her a full scholarship. As for that rare cut glass decanter, you can kiss it goodbye. Paul is planning on taking it home. Kelly told me that their new neighbor just moved down from New York after he bought Jack Daniel's from the Brown-Forman Corporation. And guess what, he collects rare decanters! Finally, are you positive that Tiffany vase is authentic? The scuttlebutt in the ladies' room is that John wouldn't have threatened to take it out of the auction unless he had serious misgivings about it. He basically told everyone not to bid on it."

I do not have time to reply. The first lot is about to be presented. Its picture is on the screen and one of John's assistants for the day has placed it on the table between him and the projector. As I tell everybody, the beginning lots are usually either damaged merchandise or dogs. Nevertheless, I cannot resist bidding on them. Usually, I will be the opening bid and then stop. Whatever happens to get no other bid, as long as it is under $25, will ultimately sell for a profit at "the show." One would be amazed at what "parts" can bring; just go to a car auction and see what junkyards pay for salvaged autos. A sterling stopper alone is worth more than the cracked decanter and it together bring at an auction. What fails to be snapped up becomes future wedding presents or birthday gifts. What can I say? Every dog has its day. Occasionally, John will have a surprise mystery box or a lot full of rubbish among the last lots. I also have a particular weakness for them. Early on in my career, I won one of the multiple junk lots. It was a bunch of "candy cane" wine glasses that did not match each other. One of them turned out to be a one of a kind eighteenth century British color twist firing glass. They were used to make toasts back then. I sent it to England for auction. Someone bought it for $20,000 because it had a terraced foot! Ever since then, always hopeful, I keep going back to the well. Goodwill has been quite gracious in accepting the vast majority of these purchases.

Finally, Lot 10 is up. I turn to its page in my book as John begins his spiel. "Lot 10. A 16.5-inch decanter in a slight variation of J. Hoare's Wedding Ring. The lapidary stopper is felt to be original. I don't need to tell you how rare and exquisite this piece of American Brilliant Period cut glass is. The American Cut Glass Association ranks it among the top five patterns. Pearson rates it a 1:1. Who will start the bidding at $5000?"

No paddle is raised. "$4000? $3000? $2000? Come on ladies and gentleman. You won't see another one in this condition anytime soon. You'll regret not getting it. Who'll give me $1000?"

I cannot count fast enough to figure out how many paddles are lifted up. As his three assistants, moving about the room, shout out and point to the bidders, John rapidly increases his tempo as well as the bid amounts, "I have $1000. Do I hear $1100? I have $1100. Do I hear $1200? I have $1200. Do I hear $1300? I have $1300. Do I hear $1400? I have $1400. Do I hear $1500? I have $1500. Do I hear $1750? I have $1750. Do I hear $2000?"

The number of paddles bidding at this point is cut in half. John does not slow his pace. "I have $2000. Do I hear $2250? I have $2250. Do I hear $2500? I have $2500. Do I hear $2750? I have $2750. Do I hear $3000?"

Eventually, it is only a collector in the front row, a telephone bidder, and me. "I have $3000. Do I hear $3500? I have $3500. Do I hear $4000? I have $4000. Do I hear $4500?"

The collector has stopped bidding. I hate telephone bids. I never feel confident if they are legitimate. A friend of the owner of the lot may be jacking up the price. This is a particular concern when there is no reserve placed by the owner. I glimpse down at my printout for Lot 10 to see at what price to drop out. I continue to show my number. "I have $4500. Do I hear $5000? I have $5000. Do I hear $5500? I have $5500. Do I hear $6000? I have $6000. Do I hear $6500? I have $6500. Do I hear $7000? I have $7000. Do I hear $7500? I have $7500. Do I hear $8000? I have $8000. Do I hear $8500?" The telephone bidder hesitates and the room is suddenly silent. John glances at his assistant handling this bidder and repeats himself, "Do I hear $8500? I have $8000. Do I hear $8500?" The clerk nods her head. "I have $8500. Do I hear $9000? I have $9000. Do I hear $9500?" He scours the room but this time stops to stare at his phone bank. "Do I hear $9500? Do I hear $9500?" No one else is bidding. "$9000 going once, going twice, fair warning." John peers at me and then at the sales associate listening on the cell phone and shaking her head, no. Finally, he goes back to me and wallops the sound block on the lectern with his antique walnut judge's mallet. In a softer tone of voice and at a much slower cadence, he says, "$9000. Sold to paddle number 125."

I am surprised that I won and turn to Gloria. "I thought you said that Paul was going to bid on it for his new neighbor."

"That's what Kelly seemed to be implying. Let me go over and talk to her."

She gets up and walks over to the middle of the bidders where Paul and Kelly are seated. Taking the empty chair next to Kelly. Gloria asks under her breath,

"Why didn't Paul bid on the decanter?"

Kelly appears perplexed and replies, "Why should've he?"

"I thought your new neighbor collected them."

"He does, but he already has a matching pair of Wedding Ring variant decanters just like that one except neither one has a handle."

Gloria barely makes it back to her seat before Lot 34 is up. She mumbles, "I'll tell you later."

I browse my sheet pertaining to the Tiffany hanger. Along the margin in red ink is written $50,000, no higher. From the number of clerks calling phone bidders, I can tell that this lamp has attracted significant interest. Although expensive, it is still in the range of most collectors. I search the room to find out where the New York dealers are all sitting. While not together, they are close enough to each other to tell who is bidding and when. Lamps like this one have recently been going for between $40,000 and $50,000. However, the Russians and Chinese have been creating a supply shortage for them because of their insatiable hunger for anything Tiffany. Mitch has a number of them as clients. If he does not bid, then I have a shot at this one.

After he does a microphone adjustment, John announces, "Lot 34, ladies and gentlemen, one of the finest Tiffany hanging lampshades I have had the honor to sell in many a year. Everything about it screams Arts & Crafts. This hanger is featured in Neustadt's *The Lamps of Tiffany*. It comes with a letter of authenticity certified by Tiffany Tom, himself. And as with all

Tiffany lamps, if it is subsequently found not to be right by one of the other experts on our list, we will take it back and return your money. "What will you give? $50,000? 40? 30? 20? 10? Ten thousand dollars for a genuine Tiffany hanging ceiling lamp! It's been decades since one has sold that cheap. You can't own it at this price if you don't bid on it."

One of the New York dealers waves his paddle in front of his face. John smiles broadly. "OK. I have $10,000 from the gentlemen from Manhattan. Thank you, sir. Glad you remembered how to use that paddle. How about 15? I've got 15. How about 20?"

A clerk at the phone table hoists his paddle. John points towards him. "$20,000 on the telephone. Who'll give me 25? $25,000 again from the gentlemen from New York."

I decide it is time to enter the bidding and show my paddle when John asks, "$30,000?"

His assistant is holding a phone to one ear while elevating his paddle again with his other hand and keeping it up as John pleads, "Do I hear 35? I have $35,000." He shifts back to watching me. "Do I hear 40?"

I yank my paddle above my left shoulder. John combs the room for other bidders and finds none. "I have $40,000. Do I hear 45? I have $40,000. Do I hear 45? $40,000, going once, going twice, fair warning." Then he cries out, "I have $45,000 on the phone!"

Not yet out of any further bidding, I raise my paddle. "I have $50,000." Mitch enters the bidding at $55,000. It is Mitch versus the anonymous telephone bidder. While waving at each bidder, John continues his chant increasing the bidding in $5000 intervals. Now 55. 60? Now 60. 65? Now 65. 70? $70,000?"

He eyeballs the telephone bank without receiving any response and then Mitch. He peeks back one more time at his sales associates. "$65,000, going once, going twice, fair warning." As he turns to Mitch, he hits the gavel on the lectern and in a lower register says, "Sold to paddle number 147 for $65,000."

Gloria winces. "I'm going to keep my mouth shut next auction."

I laugh. "It's all part of the game. What did Kelly say?"

"Their neighbor already has a pair of them!"

"I wish we had neighbors like that. Go find out why Mitch bought the lamp."

Gloria again gets up and scans the room for Mitch who is sitting at the edge of the audience on the left side near the front. If Paul is country, Mitch is all Brooks Brothers. It is never difficult to find him. He is the only one in at an auction who will be wearing a gray pinstripe suit with a tricolor striped tie. He cannot help himself. His earlier life in the Ivy League and as a corporate lawyer on Wall Street has permanently made him this way. Worse, his short stature and male pattern baldness has given him a Napoleonic complex, particularly around John. He dresses both for success at the auction and to overwhelm his competition. After finding him, she bends over and asks him softly, "Why did you get the lamp? Helen said you were trying to save for your daughter's

Yale tuition."

"Actually, this will help out. A Chinese customer emailed me towards the end of the bidding to go for it. The dollar tanked in New York today, which makes the hanger a lot cheaper in Yuans. I can't wait to see what the vase goes for. Is Ernie going to try to get it?"

"Of course, he thinks he has an immediate sale for it."

Mitch chuckles. "I hope he knows what he's doing. If he's wrong, it's going to be painful for him."

Gloria smiles when she approaches me. Once seated, she explains in an undertone, "He's as bad as you. His Chinese Tiffany collector emailed him just before the bidding ended to buy it at any price. It seems the dollar is down again today in New York. All of our best antiques are going to foreigners."

I nod. "What goes around comes around. We did it to them after World War II. I guess there is some sort of justice in the antiques world. Did he have anything else to say?"

"Yeah, he said you better be convinced about the vase. He's curious. How much pain can you endure if you're wrong?"

"Hopefully, I'll be the only one who is going to bid on it, assuming John doesn't pull it. If I'm wrong, the Goodwill Store will bail me out with a nice tax deduction."

Between Lot 34 and Lot 250 I make some decent

buys for my customers, who are doing better than I am. While I haven't yet bought anything that great or that pricey for myself, the stuff I did get will sell well at "the show." By this time half of the audience is wandering about the exhibition hall, having lunch, or catching up with their friends' news. However, as everyone realizes that Lot 250 is near, they settle back into their chairs. Silence enshrouds the room. No one stirs. The lull manifests the anticipation we all feel that something major is about to happen.

John pulls an envelope out of his coat pocket. "I have a letter faxed to me this morning from Tiffany & Co. that states they only made one Wild-Rose Vase for the Columbian Exposition. Furthermore, the hallmarks on this vase match the hallmarks their records show were incused on that vase. I will be glad to show this letter to anyone interested in bidding on Lot 250, which is next."

The New York dealers, en masse, approach the lectern to inspect the letter. Once they are satisfied, John restarts the auction. Just as he begins to introduce the next lot, those two international dealers make their flamboyant entrance. I can tell that John is perturbed by their presence. After they had so maliciously maligned the vase by claiming that exact same vase was on display in Havana, he had expected them to try to steal it by telephone bidding. Why are they bidding in public? He scowls at them when they take their seats. "Lot 250, the 'Wild-Rose Vase,' designed by John T. Curran for Tiffany & Co. in 1893 and exhibited at the Columbian Exposition that same year in Chicago. Only the 'Magnolia Vase' at the Metropolitan Museum is a better example of Tiffany sterling silver with enamel work. This is one of twelve silver and enamel vases displayed at that World's Fair by Tiffany. It is 7.5 inches tall and weighs

6.4 troy ounces. I will start the bidding at $100,000."

The entire audience turns to witness what I will do. Realizing that he is starting way low on it, I show my paddle. John says, "Thank you, Ernie. I have $100,000. Do I hear 125?"

His eyes search the room. For what seems to be a minute, but is not, there is no other paddle. Why is he hesitating from banging his gavel on the lectern? I sense he wants everyone in the room to have the time to note and consider that the international dealers are there. Sweat begins to bead above his brow. Not believing my good fortune, I too peer all around me. Then I hear him say again, "Do I hear 125?"

As if on cue, the bidding begins in earnest and so frantic that I do not get a chance to enter it. With excitement being clearly evident in John's voice, he is barely able to bellow out the numbers in time and motions only with his hands in rapid-fire gestures to whoever just bid. "125. 150? Now 150. 175? Now 175. 200? Now 200. 225?"

From the seats where all the bidding is coming, I can tell that it is the New York dealers who are doing it. Then I hear someone with a blatantly Hispanic accent shout out, $225,000. It is one of the international dealers. Stunned, I peek at Gloria who equally shares my amazement. She whispers, "What are they up to? They can't believe that they aren't going to steal it from those New York dealers. Are you going to bid again?"

The New York dealers do nothing. Once more I am the focus of all who are present. John leans forward on the lectern and stares at me, while awaiting my decision. This makes no sense to me. Maybe the international dealers had plotted to have no one, particularly the New York dealers, bid on it with the hope of taking it home cheap, cheap. Perhaps their ploy has failed, and they are being forced to bid against those dealers at a much higher level than they had planned. Whatever the case, the instant I pick up my paddle, a New York dealer lifts his. John goes back and forth between us. The rate of the bidding does not slow down from its previous pace. As quickly as he can, he points to whoever is bidding while turning to see what the other wants to do. "250? Now 250. 275? Now 275. 300? Now 300. 350? Now 350. 400?"

The New York dealer pulls his paddle down. Gloria glares at me. In her head she has just done a hurried calculation. I have at this moment exhausted my business line of credit and entered the verboten: playing with our personal funds. One of the international dealers shouts, "$500,000!"

This is not poker. He has raised the bid on his own. He is not following the rules. For a second time watching me intently, John asks, "I have $500,000 bid. Will anyone give $550,000?"

Without thinking, almost instinctively and before Gloria can pull my arm down, I heave my paddle over my head. John states, "I have $550,000. Do I hear $600,000? Do I hear $600,000?" That moment of serenity before the bidding had started returns. No one breathes, makes any sort of movement, or speaks while his eyes pan the room. "I have $550,000. $550,000 going once, going twice, fair warning." His wooden hammer whacks the sound block on the lectern causing it to bounce to the floor. Despite the relief John is feeling, the intensity in his voice this time does not change when he smiles at me and announces the winner. "Sold to number 125 for $550,000!"

The walls of the room echo the applause from the audience. Paul jumps up and scurries over to me. "Are you nuts!"

Gloria asks the same question. "Yeah, are you crazy!"

Still a bit high from all the excitement, I reply, "Yes, I am!"

Chapter 4

I try to settle down. The auction is not over and there are still lots I have to bid on for my customers. Needing both to stand up to stretch and to get away from Gloria, who is in a stew, which comes as no surprise to me, I walk over to where that international dealer had been sitting. I want to ask him why he bid so aggressively on the vase after telling everyone that there was an identical one in Havana, but he has already left. Even odder, so have the New York dealers. Are they not interested in the remaining Tiffany offerings? Once back in my place, I mutter to her, "Damn, they've done it to me again!"

No longer giving me the silent treatment, she asks antagonistically, "Who's done what to you?"

"This is the second time those international dealers have had me shoot my wad too early in an auction only to drop out. I was going to confront them to find out why they keep doing this to me, but they've already gone. Cowards!"

Paul chuckles. "If I were you, I would want to discover what they really see in that vase. He upped the bid on his own $100,000 to $500,000. With the buyer's premium that's just shy of twice what the Daisy Vase went for."

"Damn straight it is! I was going to find that out too as well as who they were bidding for. If Leonard reneges, I may need to talk to their backer."

Paul is thinking clearer than I am. "He may be contacting you. If he had them bid $500,000, he probably wouldn't think much about going up $50,000."

That observation confuses me. "Why wouldn't he have just told them to bid whatever it takes?"

"If it were a museum, maybe the one in Havana that has the other one for the sake of argument, they would had to have been authorized prior to the auction to bid on it. Whoever controls the purse strings there probably set a limit that they felt was so high that no sane individual would outbid them. Certainly bidding twice what a much larger one of the Columbian Exposition vases went for a few years ago would fit that scenario."

"If that's the case, why would they want it so dearly?"

"*Museums*! They live in a world of their own. It could be that the curator is a true Tiffany collector at heart and wants a pair of the Wild-Rose Vases. Hell, we always say, 'A pair is more valuable than twice what a single would bring.' Or possibly, the other one is damaged beyond repair. After finding out that there's a duplicate, they want to replace it with yours."

Although that makes perfect sense, there is still one issue he has not addressed. "If Tiffany only made one Wild-Rose Vase for the Columbian Exposition and mine is it, where did theirs come from?"

"Tiffany in their fax never said that they didn't make another one later on. Just that there was only one made in 1893. The Spanish were active buyers at that World's Fair. They even bought tons of cut glass from the

Libbey glassworks. In fact, they ordered so much of it that the company named the pattern Isabella after the Queen of Spain, Isabella I, who sent Columbus to America."

"So, the Cubans want the original?"

"Ernie, that's what this may well be all about."

He seems to have all the answers. "Paul, why then have they been bidding me up and then dropping out at the last minute?"

"I haven't the foggiest idea. But it's reasonable to suppose that they either have the same taste as you do, but not as fat a wallet, or wanted to make your wallet a bit thinner before this auction. Again, if they were bidding today for a museum and were smart, they would have tried to make your line of credit be as low as possible."

Gloria interrupts. If looks can kill, I'm a dead man. "Speaking of your line of credit, how do you plan to pay for all of this stuff you've bought so far today? John may be your friend, but he doesn't extend credit."

"It's cool. The instant, I tell Leonard I got it, he will wire our bank with the down payment for the vase as he usually does and pay the rest when he sees it and takes possession. I mean, he was salivating over the phone when I told him about it. He'll assume that I will be showing it to others if he doesn't lay claim to it. It's just too expensive and rare a piece for me not to do so. I bet I could sell it over the phone to almost any of my customers this afternoon if I hadn't already offered it to him."

Paul stares at me in disbelief. "At that price? I don't think so."

"Paul, I've got a waiting list of people who want one of the Columbian Exposition enameled vases. Leonard's been pestering me for years to get him one after the Daisy Vase was purchased by someone who didn't give his dealer-bidder a limit of $275,000 at Christie's. I'm not worried about this one."

Gloria continues just to glare at me after Paul leaves to return to his seat. Finally, she emphatically declares, "You buy anything else except for a surprise mystery lot or something a customer has specifically told you to buy for him and I'll divorce you on the spot. I told you I won't put up with you risking our own money on these overpriced toys for your wealthy customers."

There is probably nothing more frustrating than having no more money in your bank account and sitting at an auction. As we like to say, you've got to keep your powder dry. Nevertheless, one can still have fun. In between bidding for my customers, I begin to raise my paddle for all sorts of things that I never deal in. I drop out when I become only one of three bidders. Hell, it keeps me awake until the end when those surprise mystery boxes and junk lots are offered.

They are unique opportunities. Most of them are items that have not sold repeatedly at other auctions (John's or one of his friends') or have been consigned to John by people who have no interest in owning them any longer and just want to get rid of them. Because they have not been researched in any detail nor cleaned, it is the simplest of deals. They are sold as oil painting signed or unsigned, silver spoon (it's up to the bidders to determine if it's sterling or plate), or art deco bracelet. Of course, no guarantee is made beyond they have not been reported stolen to the police. Best of all, these items are not advertised. One has got to be physically at the auction to view them and to buy them. He even sells guns, swords, and knives in the surprise mystery boxes.

When registering, everyone at the auction is given a background check just in case they end up winning a weapon. Most of us have a Title 3 Federal Firearms License anyway. The rifles ironically are most popular. I can buy one for a sawbuck and unload it on the first day of "the show" for a nice profit to one of the many gun dealers who shop there for the bargains that they have no problem selling in their stores: the decent ones go to hunters while kids wanting something cut-rate to use for target practice end up with the crap. If all else fails, they will strip them down for parts. Frequently, they are worth more that way than if they are kept whole. Of course, lucking out by getting an actual collectible gun or sword from the Civil War is what we all hope for. World War II era rifles have gained somewhat of a following, but usually are wholesaled by the pound. Because they are so liquid, anyone who gets a weapon and does not want to mess with it can have a dealer, like myself, take it off their hands in the checkout line. Mind you, these are not automatic or semiautomatic arms. Criminals have no interest in these weapons since most of them need a thorough professional cleaning before being used.

It has been awhile since I last seriously bid when Mitch ambles over to me. Thankfully, he rids me of the boredom that has been oppressing me. "Buying that vase has kept your number from being mentioned lately."

"Yeah, Gloria was less than thrilled about the

amount I paid for it."

"I wouldn't worry about it."

If Gloria were not next to me, I would say *Well, I am.* However, since she is, I can't. Taken aback by his remark, I pat the seat of the empty chair to my right. "Why do you say that? One of your Chinese customers wants it? Come, sit next to me."

Mitch settles down there. "Nope. But I talked to the dealer who lost out to you after he and the New York dealers had a relatively heated pow-wow in the exhibition hall. Was he ever pissed! He didn't say it, but he definitely acted like you got a bargain. He asked me if you knew the history behind it. I said I doubt it and that all you've said about it is that you think it's right. He shook his head and then stormed out of the exhibition hall."

"Do you know who he is?"

"Not really, I've seen him at a few auctions. He likes to bid on Tiffany but doesn't seem to have a Tiffany size checkbook. He's usually the bridesmaid but not the bride. However, he is discerning. Only major pieces with a remarkable provenance attract his attention. I'm suspicious he's fronting for some Latin American museum that is undercapitalized for what they are trying to acquire."

"Why do you say that?"

"The way he acts. He never goes after bargains. He comes for an item or two and leaves immediately when they've been sold. He doesn't take an interest in

64

what anything else goes for. How many dealers behave that way?"

Before I am able to mention that Paul came to that same conclusion, Gloria cuts in and points at me. "Mitch, how about this one who's going to start doing just that."

"Gloria, give Ernie a break. That vase will put his name on all the major antiques websites. You can't buy that kinda publicity. Every Tiffany collector will be calling you for it. They don't care about the price. The fact that it cost so much is enough to make them want to own it even more. You might luck out and have a bidding war for it."

At last someone has endorsed my purchase. I smile at him. "From your mouth to God's ear. Paul thinks almost the same way you do."

"What's that?"

"That those two international dealers are representing a Cuban museum."

"That definitely would explain why they lose so often."

"Any idea why a Cuban museum would want it so badly?"

Mitch hesitates. "I have to confess, I've never been to Cuba. I am aware that LCT filled the Presidential Palace full of his studios' work. I have no idea how many of the lamps and other objets d'art that he placed there ended up being sent out of Havana by Batista to the US or Portugal during the revolution. Perhaps it was originally at the Palace and they just want it back."

Since life is never that simple, I state the pressing issue. "Then why would those two guys tell everyone that there is already one in Cuba, which Paul has speculated was made after 1893?"

"Do you have independent confirmation that there is one there? That unproven statement effectively kept the number of bidders to a minimum for such an important piece of Tiffany. Strange, that in the end it was you and the New York dealers against him. And I don't understand what they and he were up to after the auction."

"So you agree with John that it was a hoax to keep the bidding low."

"It wouldn't be the first time someone tried to do such a thing. By the way, they never claimed it was a fake nor not right. John can't allege they besmirched his merchandise."

Despite hearing his upbeat analysis of my plight, Gloria remains miffed. Realizing this, I place my hand on her shoulder and say, "See, it's a museum piece."

She snarls back at me. "Yeah, and you just paid more than the one that wants it the most was willing to give for it. Leonard better be in a good mood when you tell him how much that vase is going to set him back. And if he isn't willing, how do you plan to finagle a passport to Cuba? None of your Latvian relatives live there, and, the last time I inquired, selling antiques isn't on the State Department's exemption list for the boycott.

Of course, John could give you the address for the underbidder and you can sell it to him at a loss."

Mitch is about as frustrated with her attitude as I am. "Gloria, Ernie isn't about to lose any money on that vase."

"You guarantee that?"

"Well, I don't deal in his silver, just his lamps. However, the foreign market for Tiffany is driving prices up. Best of all, they pay in cash! Those Russians come in to my shop and will buy $2,000,000 to $3,000,000 worth of lamps and have me deliver them to their private jets at the airport that very day. And the Chinese are almost as bad, but they don't have the private jets yet."

"If they are such fanatics, why don't you think that guy was representing one of them?"

"Gloria, if he were, he wouldn't have stopped bidding. No, with his Hispanic accent and precise instructions when to give up and pull his paddle down, he is dealing with the next tier below the Russians and Chinese. It doesn't have to be the Cubans. It could be the Brazilians. After all, ever since Tiffany opened a store in Sao Paulo, they have shown an increased interest in all things Tiffany. Once their oil and gas explorations start to pay off, they will be real competition for the Russians and Chinese."

His proposal of a non-Cuban backer for that guy makes me ask, "Is his accent Spanish or Portuguese? Up until you asked, I haven't paid that much attention to it."

"I believe it's Spanish. But I'm no expert."

I raise my head to see where John is in the auction. He has moved ahead quite rapidly and the mystery boxes are coming up. "Mitch, do you have any interest in the junk items?"

"Are you crazy? Only you can make a buck off of them. The people who come into my shop don't buy Depression era glass or costume jewelry. And would they have a fit if I had a World War II vintage military rifle or Japanese sword for sale. Those things just aren't politically correct, particularly when you deal with Orientals. Did I mention the special interests? Hell, I had to remove an umbrella stand made out of an elephant's foot despite its having a Tiffany sterling collar. The animal rights groups were threatening to boycott me and picket my store. They didn't care that I had a letter from Tiffany stating that it had been a presentation piece given to Teddy Roosevelt and that the foot had come from a man-killing elephant from P. T. Barnum's circus, which he was obliged to destroy in 1855. Ivory is even worse. By the time I do all of the documentation for the Feds, I've lost interest in the piece. Carved Mammoth tusks, on the other hand, sell well to the Orientals. But shipping them is a pain in the ass. They literally weigh a ton."

"How about those fossils and meteorites that occasionally show up? They don't interest you?"

"No. All they end up being are paperweights on my desk. My customers are only interested in objects of vertu. Fortunately for me, they will pay dearly for them, no matter what the economy is doing."

With the auction coming to an end, I get up to skim over the last items for sale a final time to see if anything is of interest. Mitch joins me. Since they are not listed in the catalogue, I have to measure them and hold them to determine how big and heavy the object hidden inside may be. Very small boxes that are light are probably jewelry, hopefully not reproduction paste. Very large boxes that weigh a lot are probably cast iron relics from some demolition site but potentially could be Tiffany architectural bronze. It's their element of uncertainty that attracts me to the surprise mystery boxes. Plus, I learn a lot from doing research on their contents before giving them away to Goodwill.

Unlike me, Mitch is attracted to the small boxes. He holds them up to his ear to hear if they make any sound that may hint at the identity of what is inside. He makes a game of predicting that. He actually is pretty good at it. If he tells you one contains a sword, rifle, knife, or fragile object, he is usually correct. He will not tell me his secret but I suspect that he does it by the shape of the box, its weight, and the absence of any noise when he shakes them. John really packs breakables well so there is no movement in them. Unfortunately, even Mitch cannot distinguish between an antique large Chinese garden stool and a used toilet being the surprise. No matter how hard I try, I cannot sell a used toilet, unless, of course, a celebrity owned it. The Toilet Museum will buy every one of those I can get and authenticate. As the sign hanging over the entrance to "the show" says, "One man's trash is another man's treasure."

"Mitch, which ones should I bid on?"

"Lots 453 to 458 are probably rings. Lot 460 is a knife, probably a Bowie knife. Lot 467 is a rifle. Lot 471 is a sword, probably Japanese and old and possibly valuable."

I cannot help myself and ask, "What makes you say that about Lot 471?"

"It's the right shape, size, and weight for a Japanese sword, but it is packed so tightly that there was no shifting of its contents when I held it upside down."

"So?"

"If it is a sword, John only does that careful packing when it is an old sword. He doesn't want the pommel or cross-guard to come loose from everyone doing what I do."

We return to the back row and await the bidding. I decide that I will pass on the rings. I have never had any real luck with John's junk jewelry, and, after all, I have already shot my wad.

When Lot 460 starts, John says, "Let's see who learned the Presidents of the United States in grade school. Who'll give me a Grant for this lot?"

No paddle is waved. "How about a Jackson?"

Again, no one bids. "How about a Hamilton?"

Someone in the audience shouts, "He wasn't a President and the box ain't worth a sawbuck."

John laughs, "I stand corrected. How about a Lincoln?"

Nobody stirs. "Will anyone give a Jefferson?"

Finally, I raise my paddle. John points to me. " I

have $2, any one give $3?" After a few seconds, he hits the gavel on the sound block and declares, "Lot 460 goes to paddle number 125 for $2."

Gloria takes out her frustration with me when she gives me a solid poke in my rib. "You couldn't have waited for a Washington?"

Chapter 5

The auction is finished. Along with the other winning bidders, I stand in the relatively straight line leading to the checkout table, which earlier today had been the registration table and which John has moved next to the exit door of the auction theatre. Once there, we carefully compare our lists of the lots we've won and their final price against the auction house's computer's record. There is no second chance to correct an error. We, therefore, move painfully slow. I survey those in front and in back of me. What a change has come over them. Just before getting up to check out, the collectors had been dozing off after being mentally drained from spending hours listening to John prodding them on to increase their bids. Are they ever all keyed up from the adrenaline rush that immediately spikes with the last strike of the hammer at an auction! Each and every one of them is showing off their bargains to whomever they can corner.

The majority of dealers are still wrapping their new inventory items with bubble wrap and paper of all sorts including diapers and carefully placing them in large cardboard boxes. The sincerely obsessive then secure the cartons with plastic tape. Many neatly stack them on the very tables, which just hours ago were displaying their contents. While others stow the boxes next to the chairs in which they had been sitting. Those dealers, who are finished, stand in line, busy calling their customers to notify them of the exciting treasures that they must see this week in their shops or at "the show."

I, however, am still feeling soreness in my left rib

from Gloria's jabbing me there. It reminds me that I have exhausted my line of credit. I will be writing two checks to cover today's bill, which is something I have never had to do before. It is strange how the confidence felt while bidding is so fleeting that just shortly later in the checkout line buyer's remorse sets in. Heaven forbid, I will never let on to Gloria that I may have overbid. Paul and Mitch did admirable jobs of backing me up. I hope to be able to return the favor to them at some other auction. My feeling regret is cut short. Five of the New York dealers come up and congratulate me.

The dean of their group, a somewhat overweight, tall, grey-headed elderly man with a full beard, says, "Good job, Ernie. It's about time those Columbian Exposition vases were given the respect they deserve. We were talking amongst ourselves and want to make you an offer."

I am flabbergasted. These guys are so arrogant that they felt it was beneath them to join the rest of us at The Blue And The Gay last night. Needless to say, they have never bothered to acknowledge my existence before. Maybe my outbidding them has somehow made an impression upon them. "Thank you. What kinda offer are you pitching?"

"Last night, we had decided that $400,000 was a fair valuation for that vase. Evidently, we were wrong. After discussing amongst ourselves what a fair offer should be, we can propose to you $600,000 plus the buyer's premium John will charge you. That's a $50,000 profit for one day's work."

What is he talking about? "Are you all acting as a group or as individuals?"

73

He speaks haltingly as if searching for the right words. On top of that, he commences to stroke his beard with his left hand, which I take as a sign of his unease. "Let's just say that we have a client, who has let it be understood that he will be troubled, to say the least, by our not obtaining it for him. He had sent us all down here to validate its authenticity and bid for him. For this auction, for this vase we were acting as a purchasing group, so to speak."

These guys' reputation stinks. Word is that they will do anything shy of something that will buy them jail time in order to get what they want at the lowest price. Are they actually telling me the truth or had they stopped bidding to keep the final cost down, figuring they could haggle with the winner after the auction? More intriguing is why had they been bidding against each other if they were acting as a cartel? They have caught me completely off-guard. This does not happen often. "Why doesn't your client just contact me and negotiate directly with me? I assure you I will be fair with him. Besides, I've already committed the vase to a good customer of mine."

"Oh, I promise in the end Leonard won't mind if we get it."

How the hell did they find out I have offered it to him? I had just done it yesterday. Besides dealers never reveal their sources or their customers to other dealers who are not their friends and, even then, only begrudgingly. We are all a bit paranoid. So, who are these guys? Or better, who is their client? "And he told you that?"

"Not exactly. Leonard's been bragging to everyone that he's going to be getting the Tiffany Wild-

74

Rose Vase. Watching your performance today, we concluded that you were his agent. If our analysis of your business' probable line of credit turns out to be correct, you should be dipping into your personal savings to pay for the vase. It would be awkward for you and Leonard, to say the least, if he somehow found it necessary to pass on the vase."

Did I just mention that my buyer's remorse had disappeared? Well, I was mistaken. It was just taking a siesta. These guys sound like Marlon Brando in the *Godfather* trying to "make me an offer I can't refuse." Although I find that to be humorous, my discomfort with the situation compels me to ask, "Why should he do that? Are you suggesting that it would be because he lacks the funds? That's ludicrous!"

He laughs. "My friend, people back out of deals all the time for all sorts of reasons. I'm just suggesting that it would be prudent to take our offer in cash today rather than risk a freak collapse of what you think should be a sure-fire deal tomorrow. Hell, you'll be making the same amount of money."

"No problem, if Leonard backs down, I'll give you right of first refusal. I don't want to insult a very good customer and friend by not completing my part of the transaction."

There is a smile, perfected by women, which is not done out of friendship. That is exactly what his face expresses. "I'm sorry. I failed to mention that my offer is limited."

"In what way?"

"If you buy the vase today, it will no longer be valid. Our client is funny about this. He insists that his name be on the auction records as the new owner, not yours."

This proposition reeks. His client's self-esteem is unbelievable. He does not want it documented that someone else outbid him. I have heard about this type before but have never dealt directly with one. He measures people's worth by the size of their testicles. Similarly, bragging rights are more essential to him than the artistic value of the object. "Well, I guess we don't have a deal. Keeping my relationship with Leonard intact is more valuable than massaging your client's oversized ego. Tell him that I will do as I said earlier and grant him right of first refusal if Leonard declines the vase."

The dean of the group and the other four New York dealers walk a few feet away just out of hearing range and huddle together. I am hoping that they will be reasonable and accept my counter offer. A $50,000 profit for that vase will assuredly take the heat off of me. As for Gloria, I will be vindicated. He quickly approaches me again. "We can tender you a $100,000 profit this afternoon. Take it now or we leave pronto."

$700,000 for that vase! I cannot conceive of Leonard spending that much for it. Even he has his limits. I remember my favorite saying, "The lack of knowledge about what people are really willing to spend, or, as we say, give for an item is key to my take-home pay." In this case, it is my ignorance not my prey's that is crucial. What are the Russians or the Chinese willing to give for this vase? Their backer has to be of one of those nationalities. No American collector, of whom I am aware, is going to better that offer any time soon. More

76

critical, why would he want it so badly? I wish I knew who currently owns the Daisy Vase or its recently rediscovered sister, the Bud Vase. And I must not forget about that ugly Mexican inspired piece with all that turquoise that showed up on the Antiques Roadshow. Is a foreigner trying to corner the market on these vases? He has to be. In my mind I am kicking myself as I say, "While that's a most generous offer, I must pass. I cannot screw Leonard."

He pats me on my back and then starts to walk away shaking his head in disbelief. "I hope Leonard realizes his friendship is worth a $100,000 to you."

The dealer behind me taps my shoulder. "What was that all about? Who was that guy?"

"That's Ira Wynn. He was selling Tiffany when you and I were being weaned from our mother's tits. That's the first time he has ever spoken to me."

"Why was he so interested in the Wild-Rose Vase?"

"I can only imagine! Perhaps, because this is the first time I've ever outbid him, he and his partners are really pissed that they were one-upped by me. He was frank about his not wanting it recorded that some upstart had beaten him out of a masterpiece. On the other hand, he could have an eccentric foreign customer who's trying to accumulate all the Columbian Exposition vases that are not in museums, like when that Japanese developer, Takeo Horiuchi, bought up the great Tiffany in the 1990s before the real estate market in Japan went bust."

"Wasn't he the one who was duped by Alastair

Duncan?"

"Yeah, that's him. He bought a 9-foot-tall Tiffany mausoleum window that Anthony Casamassina had pried off a large tomb in a cemetery located where the borough lines of Brooklyn and Queens meet. Despite having been convicted in federal court of selling stolen merchandise, Duncan claims that he had been kept in the dark about the window's having been pinched. Instead, he blames that grave robber and another dealer from the Bronx, who he claims originally contacted him about the window. After having been deceived by them per his story, he paid $30,000 to Casamassina for his 50% interest in the stolen window. Together, he and the Bronx dealer sold it to Mr. Horiuchi for just shy of $220,000 yielding them each an $80,000 profit. That case brought a chill to the prices of Tiffany windows and made provenance a key issue with all things Tiffany."

"Why did you turn down his deal? That's a helluva lot of money for that little vase."

His objection is well-taken and causes me to pause for a minute to collect my reasons for doing such an outwardly foolhardy thing. "In this business you always have to ask yourself why. Just consider Alastair Duncan. I remember all the details of his case so that I can use them to teach my customers to be cautious and always ask why. If he is telling the truth, he should've been savvy enough to have raised the issue with Casamassina about how he had acquired that over 500 pound Tiffany mausoleum window. After all, it suddenly materialized out of the blue; and Duncan wrote the standard text about Tiffany windows. In regard to the vase, I don't understand why they are so eager to own it and pay so much for it. Until I have the answer to those two questions, I really don't want to do business with them. You can never be too careful."

Gloria approaches me and, for the first time since I bought the vase, is smiling. "I heard you sold the Wild-Rose Vase for $700,000. I'm proud of you."

"How did you hear that?"

"News like that travels fast at an auction."

"Well, it's not true."

Suddenly, her face is flushed from anger and her smile has turned to a frown. "What's not true? You weren't offered $700,000 in cash, or more likely you were but turned it down."

"I turned it down, Gloria."

Everyone near us hears her ask, "You did what?"

"I turned it down. I just didn't trust those New York dealers."

"What's not to trust about $700,000 cash?"

"What makes them or more important their customer be so generous? If he's willing to pay $700,000 today, he probably will be willing to pay $800,000 next week. How come he wants it so badly?"

"I'm not a psychologist, Ernie, and neither are you. I could give a rat's ass if his mother's stopping breast feeding him too early or starting toilet training before he was ready caused him to want it, just so long as we leave here with $100,000 in cash in my purse."

"Well, I do. And until I know why, I'm not going to sell it to them."

She sticks her index finger in my face. "Well, you better be damn willing to sell it to Leonard as you promised me. Have you bothered to consider how much interest we will be paying on $600,000?"

I am reticent. "Unfortunately, I have."

From the middle of the theatre, Helen beckons to Gloria who wanders over to find out what she wants. "Mitch, Paul, Kelly, and I are going to go to The Blue And The Gay for supper with the rest of the gang for our usual post auction get together. Are you and Ernie going to join us?"

"Probably later. Ernie wants to put the vase in our safe the minute we leave here."

"That's understandable. It's not the type of thing you would put on the window table in the front bay window with the drapes open."

Gloria nods in agreement. "It will be lucky to see the light of day."

"Well, in that case, I have an idea."

Back at the checkout table I am reading the computer printout when Gloria returns and grabs the receipt from my hands. All she sees is the final total before crying out, "A million dollars! You are crazy. Where are you going to get the money to cover those two checks?"

Jenny, the clerk, glances up from her computer screen. She bats her long eyelashes at me. Her Southern way of talking softens the blow for me. "Having a cash flow problem Ernie? Like it says in the catalogue, John doesn't usually extend credit or hold checks; but, if you need us to hold the one for the vase, I will ask him. I just can't imagine him not understanding your predicament. We all appreciate your bid. No one thought it would ever go for that much!"

To say the least, I am embarrassed by Gloria's outburst and Jenny's helpful proposition. Because I anticipated the cost of my acquisitions prior to the auction, I had arranged for all of my customer's purchases to be covered by them by wire transfers to my bank in the morning. If technology works as advertised, my checks will clear without a hitch. Loudly, but not obnoxiously so, I declare, "That won't be necessary. I have it covered."

Gloria is not through with me. "How many of these lots are ours and how many are your customers?"

"Only the vase and Lot 460, along with a few minor purchases that I'll be able to sell on set up day of "the show," are mine. For the rest I have firm commitments from my customers. Quit worrying about this."

The dealer behind me could not help but overhear everything that was being said. "Ernie, you wouldn't mind sharing your customer list with me?"

"In your dreams! I don't do that. Besides, after

today's auction they probably won't be buying anything for a while. Their wives' divorce lawyers' fees will temper their appetite for antiques."

He laughs. "You get that comment too. My customers all seem to be cowards."

"What do you mean by that?"

"To quote the Bard, 'Cowards die many times before their deaths. The valiant never taste of death but once.' Every time I sell them anything expensive, while they write the check, they foretell their imminent death at the hands of their wives that evening when they go home."

I chuckle. "You have any idea why all the collectors are men with wives who constantly threaten them with divorce or death?"

Gloria butts in. "Because only you men are stupid enough to spend all your money on expensive toys. We women all outlive you and have to figure out how to unload all of those toys at a profit to pay the damn estate taxes. You should know that, Ernie. You spend half your time schmoozing widows out of their inheritances."

Chapter 6

After every auction I have a let down. That adrenaline rush I had in the checkout line is over and lament about what I did not get sets in. Of greater magnitude, the reality of how much I have spent on what I did get glares at me. Unquestionably, a successful dealer is a profitable dealer. Making a profit comes from being able to hype one's stock. It too demands that one does not overpay for it. The Wild-Rose Vase both excites me and scares me. I have never had nor heard of a situation like the one I have just experienced. Despite the bravado I have displayed all afternoon after winning it, I really do not have the faintest idea what it is honestly worth. Worse, since I need to move it ASAP, I do not have the time to find that out.

The rest of the items are basically paid for. First, I will inspect them for any damage or flaws and, after carefully photographing them in case anything happens in transit, I will await my customers' bank transfers and then ship them. What I did not get today was all the new inventory I really need for my booth at "the show," and I will not be able to buy on set up day unless my customers come through on time.

Driving home from an auction in our son's van is always an experience. We use it since he is in residential construction and has his company's logo all over the sides and back of it. No one will suspect that it is hauling valuable antiques. Besides, he prefers his truck and hardly ever needs the van, which he has relegated to picking up and delivering things that would be damaged by inclement weather. I always go below the speed limit.

An accident would be disastrous. Gloria rides shotgun and tries to spot any suspicious car that seems to be trailing us. Her suspecting one means a visit to the nearest police station. Usually along the way, we discuss what to charge for the items we have just acquired. Tonight is different.

Gloria is no longer berating me over what I paid for the vase. She has something else on her mind. "Where do we store it until Leonard buys it?"

I crisply remark, "In the bank safe in the basement, of course."

She sighs before objecting. "I don't want it in the house. That's the first place thieves will expect it to be."

This surprises me. Our insurance company certified our antique bank safe to be essentially burglar proof. If it could be unbolted from the concrete floor, they would find it easier to forklift it out of my house than to attempt to pick the lock, which has a modern digital movement in place of the old tumblers. I am a bit indignant when I ask her, "Where do you recommend I put it?"

It is clear that she has deliberated more about this than I have, which is basically not much. "Helen and I have agreed that Mitch's and her place would be a more discreet location."

Our downtown bank's safe is my usual back up site when something will not fit in my basement. I have never considered using their house. "How come?"

She though has her reasons, which are rational.

"His Tiffany lamps will dwarf the vase. Besides, their house is a fortress. No one wanting to steal his lamps or our vase will be able to invade it. He even has armed guards patrol it when they're not home. He takes no chances. Helen claims it's more protected than their shop."

I yield to her better judgment. "When do we go over there?"

"No time like the present. Take a right at the next stop light. She'll meet us there and then we'll go to The Blue And The Gay."

My customer's booty is almost as valuable as that vase. "Why not unload all the other stuff first?"

Gloria has been reading just too many crime novels. "Because it will be less detectable that the vase has been placed in a secure place, if the van isn't empty."

While her logic is formidable, I still have one concern. "Do you think someone will try to break into the van while we're in the restaurant?"

Genuinely prepared for this trip home, she pulls out a blue and white handicap sign and places it on the windshield's mirror arm. "Not when we're parked right in front of its entrance adjacent to the valet attendant's stand."

She is like a magician tonight. "Where did you get that?"

"Helen lent it to me. It's her mother's. They use it whenever they go on long buying trips."

"We won't get in trouble using it, will we?"

"Hell no! Why would anyone question it?"

I see no reason to pursue this any further and decide to change the subject. "Did you see Jim Cook at the auction?"

"No, why do you ask?"

"He did not bid against me like he usually does. Plus he wasn't at the preview yesterday. You don't think the son of a bitch is sick or better, dead?"

One thing Gloria does not stand for is my wishing ill to my rivals. Something I do at least once a day. During "the show," I must confess, it is an hourly event; particularly, if I watch them sell anything to one of my customers. "Don't say such a thing."

He is actually a very nice man who just happens to deal in the very areas I do and, unfortunately, has a bigger wallet. Nevertheless, I will not forgo casting the evil eye on him: one of my valued pleasures. "Why not? Over the years he has cost me a fortune always upping the final price of things or winning choice pieces after he has made me shoot my wad while keeping his powder dry."

Her face becomes quite stern and her tone of voice is very judgmental. "That still doesn't justify your wishing harm to him. He has never done anything unethical to you. It's just business. I have no doubt he would help you out in a pinch. Besides it lessens you. Whoever has an evil eye will never experience true joy but only anguish and agony when the rest of the world

86

prospers."

I usually can judge when it is time to quit annoying her, and I think I have reached it. "Well, did anyone mention where he was? He never misses one of John's auctions and this would have been one he would have relished."

"As odd as it may sound, nobody mentioned him. Which is really strange when you think about what a presence he has at auctions."

"You mean he stinks from not showering after taking his morning jog."

"No. And you're not much better, dressing as if you were homeless and didn't have a nickel to your name. Which I might add that after today's little adventure, you don't!"

She had to bring up what I had paid for the vase again. I had hoped she had gotten over it. "Well, he does it so that no one will sit near him and spy on his bidding book to read what he has written down as his highest price for what he's bidding on."

Gloria sulks while I silently and attentively seek Mitch and Helen's house. All the homes along their street are hidden from the road by trees while the mailboxes and front yards all appear the same to me. The driveways are really long and curvy on their block as well as being narrow with deep ditches on both sides. Needless to say, it is a pain in the ass to turn around in them to get back out whenever I realize I have made a mistake, which I inevitably do. Gloria though somehow instinctively recognizes which one is their house. She breaks her pouting. "It's the next house on your left."

"How do you always do that?"

She smiles at me. "You're not very observant. Theirs is the only one without a security service sign in the front."

After glancing around, I have to admit, "You know, you're right."

"A long time ago, Helen told me that their company specifically decided not to issue them anymore."

"How come?"

"They claim it's just an advertising gimmick for the service and actually makes you less safe."

"In what way? We have a sign out front."

"It tells the burglars our house has something worth protecting and, therefore, worth stealing. Also, since the pros are not stupid and are acquainted with each company's system, it tells them what devices have been installed in our house. They like that. Takes them less time to disarm the alarm system."

I feel like an idiot. "So, we ought to get rid of the sign."

Gloria likes to rub it in when she has done this to me. "That, or leave cookies and milk out for them on the kitchen table whenever we go out."

The light in the living room tells me that Helen has beaten us here. Gloria jumps out of the van once it comes to a stop, opens the gate to its back, searches around, and asks, "Which one of these damn boxes has the vase?"

"It's not in a box. It's in that wooden crate in the back underneath the other boxes. I figured that I shouldn't make it easy for anyone to steal it from the van. I'll come back and find it."

"Sometimes you're a real putz. They wouldn't have bothered to jimmy the lock to open the gate to steal it. They would've just taken the whole van or worse carjacked it. Anyway, why the crate?"

"John said that's how it came to him."

"Does it look old?"

I nod in agreement. "Yeah, it does. John figures it's the original one Tiffany had made for it."

"What makes him so secure in saying that?"

"Someone branded both Tiffany Studios and their Columbian Exposition mark on it."

Helen opens her front door and calls out to us. "It's about time you came. I was beginning to get worried about you two."

Gloria pulls her head from out of the cargo bay area. "That's Ernie; he's incredibly careful packing his boxes and loading up the van. He's always the last one out of the auction house. Sometimes I believe that John

89

would have him lock up the place if he could."

When I finally find the crate after unloading most of the other boxes onto the driveway, I feel the need to defend myself. "I don't have the advantage of having those custom crates like you do for your lampshades. I have to individually roll everything in paper diapers. Besides filling up the van is an art in itself, those boxes have to be positioned just so. There can't be any movement or shifting of them. I don't want one piece of the glassware to crack coming home."

Helen observes, "Well, Mitch didn't have that much stuff to bring back. He was really pissed. When the New York dealers returned from whatever they were doing after you won the vase, they took out their revenge on him. Every time he bid, one of them would raise a paddle. Mitch finally gave up. Ernie, who bankrolls those guys? They don't seem to worry about how much they are spending."

"Yeah, yeah. They like to pass themselves off as big shots. They were probably bidding for customers who work on Wall Street. When that happens all you can do is prevent them from getting it cheap, which is what they are after when they come down here."

"Hurry up and come on in. If I keep the door opened too long, the security company is going to call us to find out if everything is all right. It's a royal pain in the ass having all of these Tiffany lamps here. You lose all of your privacy to their surveillance devices. They are more familiar with what we're doing than we are."

I laugh. "Why don't you just get rid of them?"

Helen pauses for a blink of an eye. "The lamps or the security company?"

"The security company. Mitch will never sell all of his collection."

"We would but the insurance company insists that we use this particular security service. I feel sympathy for the President having to put up with the Secret Service."

Reloading the van a second time does not take much time. With crate in hand and Gloria locking up the van, I walk into their foyer. Something is different. I peer all about it before asking, "New hanger?"

Next to the room's 20-foot ceiling and walls, Helen gives the impression of being much shorter than she is. A model in her youth, she has kept her figure. With Mitch's well-established Napoleonic complex, she of course has big breasts. She rarely wears a bra, which makes the absence of the expected droop insinuate that they are really too big to be natural. Her long wavy blonde hair and green eyes just add to her trophy wife appearance. However, they have been married since his law school days. "Yeah, it's from a San Francisco mansion. It was sold to Mitch as being from a New York mansion, but after extensive research he decided that it was from a home destroyed by the 1989 earthquake. Do you like it? I only wish we could find some brighter bulbs that we could use in it. Mitch doesn't agree, but I think it makes the room too dark."

"There are some expensive LED bulbs that might work or just put some lamps in here. I mean modern lamps or some sconces with some real wattage. Who wouldn't like it?"

91

Gesturing towards it all the while being openly pleased by how well it displays, she adds, "We even had to reinforce the supports up in the ceiling just to bear its weight."

Gloria lets herself in and watches both of us gaze towards the huge multicolor Tiffany lampshade. "Which garage sale did you get that from?"

"Christie's."

"She would! That girl has more junk to sell than anyone I know. Where did she find the Morgan Library lampshade?"

I correct her. "It's from a house in San Francisco."

Gloria becomes indignant and squints at me. "No, it's from the Morgan Library. After all, I did my master's thesis on Tiffany hangers, and I better be able to distinguish them."

Mitch overhears her as he strolls in and stares at what undeniably to him is the Holy Grail of Tiffany lampshades. "OK, Gloria, why am I wrong and Christie's turns out to have been correct?"

"J. P. Morgan, Jr. saw the Tiffany hanger at the new building of the First United Methodist Church in Los Angeles while visiting there on business almost immediately after it had opened. Although an Episcopalian, he went to church services there one Sunday just to see all of its Tiffany glass in all of its glory in its intended setting. He had seen them in New York while they were being exhibited there before being shipped to Los Angeles and was so taken with them that he had to observe them in the Church, itself. You are right about its having been moved along with the three glass panels, Te Deum Laudamus, to the San Francisco Bay Area, actually to a Methodist Church in Oakland, after their home for sixty years was sold in 1983. Anyway, after seeing the original in its intended setting, Jack Morgan commissioned LCT to build him a bigger version of it. That one's the bigger size. And it's a reproduction."

"How can you be so smug? I had several experts including Tiffany Tom inspect it while it was on preview at Christie's. Everyone agrees it's authentic."

"I said it was a reproduction, not a fake. The President of Cuba had LCT duplicate and install two Morgan Library hangers in the Presidential Palace. They are exact copies, well, as exact a copy as Tiffany ever made. I had the privilege of seeing the original designs for all four shades while I was doing my research for my thesis."

"You mean this came from Cuba."

"Must've. The Morgan hanger was still in its original location last time I was there. That Church hasn't sold its Tiffany. I can't comment about the two in Havana."

The crate is getting heavy. I interrupt Gloria by asking Mitch, "Well, where does this vase that may have come from Cuba go?"

He motions to me. "Follow me. I've got a locked display case that will be perfect for it in the den."

His large den with walnut judge's paneling is full of antiques with a Tiffany lamp either sitting on any available side table or standing in any open space on the floor. I have to concede, "Nobody will even mind the vase in this room."

He smiles. "That's the idea. By the way, a lady came in to my shop two weeks ago. She wants to sell some family papers at auction or through a dealer. I went out to see them but decided that I don't handle that kinda stuff. Are you interested?"

"Only if the papers are historically notable. Most of those types of things that I've been offered are of interest only to the family or a local historical society that doesn't have the funds to pay anything significant for them. They usually want them donated. You see, people just won't pay for other people's dead relatives' papers."

Mitch unlocks the polished brass and glass cabinet door. "I haven't actually seen them, but her father had worked in both JFK's and LBJ's administrations in the White House. She claims he had access to the President whenever he wanted it. So, he must've been influential. She even sang at one of the LBJ inaugural balls."

I help him take out and shift some Tiffany glass pieces to place the vase in a corner of the cabinet where I confirm that it is out of view by nodding. "That sounds interesting. How many documents are we talking about?"

Satisfied with its location and where he repositioned the original items, Mitch closes the door and locks it. "I didn't count them, but they were in a bunch of cardboard boxes stacked in her kitchen."

Documents need to be stored properly or else they deteriorate rapidly. Therefore, I wince from exasperation. "Why the kitchen?"

"Don't ask me! All I can say is she's a little strange. I've got her address here if you want it."

"Sure, what's the most I can lose: an afternoon?"

"More like a day, Ernie. She lives in another state."

Chapter 7

As soon as the auction is completed and they have paid for and packed up their purchases, the out-of-town dealers immediately depart en masse for home. Their long caravan of small trucks and vans meanders through the side streets heading for the nearest interstate entrance from which they will disperse. Those of us who live here gather back at The Blue And The Gay for a post-mortem analysis of the day's activity. Bill always has several smaller tables arranged into one really big U-shaped table that will be ready for us in the back room of the restaurant where, after he closes its pocket doors, we will not disturb his regulars. We are a rowdy bunch, still pumped up from today's action. Decorum is not something we are noted for on these nights. He calls us his dirty dozen times two, since after a good auction there will be at least twenty-four of us.

First order of the evening is determining whether prices were firm or weak. Firm prices mean a good economy and the prospect of good profits. However, weak prices are a mixed bag. We got what we wanted for less than we had expected, but why? What were the others aware of that we were not? Will the customers at "the show" be willing to give what we expect them to pay? Auction prices these days are almost immediately available on the Internet. A poor day for John may mean a bad month for us.

The second order of business is horse-trading. What did you win that I could use and how much do you want for it? We have for the most part a symbiotic lifestyle. Calls to customers after the auction to notify them that they did not get what they wanted frequently result in their being willing to dole out more if the other dealer will cooperate. Sets of crystal, china, and silverware are the most vulnerable to being divided. Collectors no longer strive to have services for 12. They just want a place setting as an example. It seems no one these days has enough display or storage capacity to maintain the unity of what has been lovingly cared for for over a hundred years. What we will carve up in the matter of a few minutes will take decades to piece back together, if anyone would ever care to do so.

When Gloria and I walk into the dining area, the dealers who had arrived ahead of us rise up and give us a standing ovation. Paul, one of the few out-of-town dealers not to have left, cries out, "Hey, let the good times roll." They then all sit back down.

Another person shouts out, "Oh great one, we are not worthy."

I blush. I am not used to this type of attention. "My coronation is a bit premature since I haven't sold it yet. So don't come around trying to unload your overpriced treasures on me."

Boy, is Gloria ever peeved by their adulation. "One of you get bamboozled and you all make him a hero. Great! Who amongst this pack of thieves will be paying our mortgage next month if he gets stuck with that vase?"

Along with two waiters, Bill has been serving champagne to everyone in the room and brings her a glass of it. "Loosen up Gloria. Your husband is famous. His record breaking bid for that vase is already on the cable news programs. They are even broadcasting his picture."

Her anger is not assuaged. "That's not being famous. That's being infamous. The whole world at this instant appreciates that he's its biggest sucker!"

He is not dissuaded and raises his own glass of champagne. "To the world's biggest sucker."

The others remain seated, lift up their glasses, and chant in unison, "We are all suckers and he is our leader."

Gloria sighs out of frustration. "You all have gone looney-tunes."

I feel it is time to calm her down. I straighten up with my glass of champagne held over my head and address my loyal followers. "As the freshly anointed king of the suckers, I would like to agree with my wife. You have to be deranged to be the highest bidder and still think you got a great deal. Therefore, I propose a toast to the greater fool theory, which protects us all from financial ruin." I then take my seat, but Gloria is still too upset to do so and keeps on standing.

Again, they all hoist their glasses and cry out, "To the greater fool theory, may it reign forever."

Paul then rises and offers, "I propose that we all pledge our lives and fortunes in support of our noble leader's valiant quest for that bigger fool and wish him great success in his contest to slay our worst enemies, apathy and a bad stock market, on our field of honor, 'the show.'"

My entire court gets up and echoes him, "'The show,' 'the show,' long live 'the show.'"

Having finally agreed to be seated by Bill, Gloria begins to laugh at the spectacle that she is witnessing, yanks her glass of champagne from the table, and aims it towards the ceiling. "I propose another toast. To the rule of the law that governs all the markets: bulls make money, bears make money, pigs get slaughtered."

We all rejoin with our glasses thrust up high, "To the pigs, to the pigs. Pigs get fat, but hogs get slaughtered."

She is not finished and arises to make one more toast. "Pigs don't know that pigs stink."

One by one, all of the waiters who can leave their stations have entered our room. They realize that they will have a good time. We are all out of our chairs exclaiming as we heave up our glasses of champagne and mugs of beer, "To the stinky pigs. We love them all. We all want to be stinky rich, we all want to be stinky rich."

In one last grand effort to put us all in our proper place, Gloria, still standing, proclaims, "Pigs don't fly."

She fails. The crowd successfully counterattacks. Everyone extends an arm upward and forward with a drink in hand. "Pigs don't fly, but dragons do. We are all dragons. Long live the dragons of the world." We again sit down.

Vanquished, she silently slumps back down into her chair. When I turn to console her, she whispers into my ear, "You all are incorrigible."

The last of the dealers have arrived and are sitting in their respective seats when Mitch announces to the whole table. "Ernie's going to visit Denise Reid."

There is a murmur of surprise among them. I do not understand their reaction. I ask loud enough for everyone to hear me, "What's the big deal?"

Finally, someone answers me. "You mean, she hasn't approached you before?"

"No, why do you ask? Should she have?"

Mitch surveys the assemblage. "Is there anyone here who hasn't been asked to handle her father's papers?"

Each and every one shakes his head, no. I do not understand. "Why have you all passed?"

"Because of the conditions of the will."

"What will?"

"She'll show it to you when you get to her house. Her father stipulated in it that the papers cannot be shown publicly or sold to the public until December 2017."

I am dumbfounded. I have never heard of such a thing. "Does he give a reason?"

"No. Just that this is an absolute requirement."

I see a self-evident concern, "Well, what's in them that he placed such a weird condition on their sale. This wouldn't have to do with some oddball statue of

100

limitations?"

Mitch once more searches the U-shaped table. "Anyone actually examined what's in those boxes she has in her kitchen?"

For a second time, they all shake their heads, no. I move on to the other relevant issue, "Who was he and why would anyone care to buy his papers?"

Mitch cuts in, "I asked her that very question. She was very evasive. As I told you earlier this evening, he seems to have worked in the White House for both JFK and LBJ and had the President's ear whenever he wanted to speak to him."

One of the dealers adds, "I think he worked in several Presidents' administrations, including Eisenhower's. However, when I asked her in what capacity he had served them, she forthrightly said she couldn't say. I can't exactly remember the reason why. On the face of it, what he was doing must've been classified at the time and he either never told her later on before he died or had sworn her to secrecy."

I am getting nowhere. "OK, what's in the boxes? I mean, there is no reason for me to drive to her house for nothing."

Mitch laughs, "You know those surprise mystery boxes that you can't resist bidding on, like your $2 one today. They're sort of like them. When I was there, they were numbered and all taped up like registered mail. I don't think she is even familiar with what exactly they contain."

The other dealer nods in accord with him. "She has an envelope that is also sealed and that she claims her father had in his safety deposit box. In the will the contents of that envelope are stated to be the index of what each of the numbered boxes contains and a short summary of all their material. She hasn't opened it either."

Baffled, I shout out, "Then why the hell should I bother to meet her?"

"Because of the deal!" someone else says.

"What deal? Am I supposed to buy these boxes sight unseen or what?"

Mitch confesses, "I never got that far. She was too creepy for me. Besides, as I told you, I don't usually handle papers. I only went to see them out of curiosity and because of who had recommended me to her."

The first dealer concurs, "After I knelt down to note the condition of the boxes and my knee cracked a bunch of goose eggs and my pants were covered in their yolks and the goose shit on the floor, I left."

Mitch adds, "I left after a goose pecked my ass when I bent over to count the boxes."

Gloria could not resist asking, "What's with all of these geese?"

A third dealer mentions, "She's a bit eccentric."

Mitch and the first dealer both laugh and together declare, "A bit eccentric! How about a whole lot eccentric! In fact, how about the mother of all eccentrics!"

The third dealer concedes their judgment. "She's nuts, Gloria. She lives with geese, lots of geese. They are everywhere in her house. And none of them is Mother Goose. They are all mean and will attack you if you let them get near you."

I am forced to press them. "Then how are you confident what she's telling you is true? If she's crazy, she may be making the entire story up. Those boxes could be filled with old newspapers that she has collected over the years."

The third dealer addresses me. "You're right. We can't be positive that the boxes contain anything of importance."

"Why do you think they do?"

"There is a special tape that the government only uses when it seals key White House documents or papers in those special archival white boxes they use to store them in. Both her boxes and the tape used to seal them are authentic for the White House before the Ford years, when they changed the colors of both the tape and the boxes so that they would fluoresce under a black light with a special code that dates them by year. Each year's unused boxes and tape are destroyed on January 1 of the next year."

"Why did they change them?"

"To be able to guarantee that a box has not been tampered with and the papers altered. Watergate changed the rules."

Still confused, I turn to Mitch. "So, the boxes came from the White House before 1974 or so. Despite that tape, that doesn't mean they are of any consequence. I'll betcha that 99% of the crap that aides to the President write is of no interest to historians. Most of them, in all likelihood, are submissions for policy statements that never make it to the final drafts or are background for speeches for his speechwriters to review before writing them. Those aides' egos make them think everything that they are ever involved in will make a great movie or documentary. They probably routinely use that tape on whatever is going into storage."

He is of the same opinion as I am. "You're right. They may be of no value whatsoever. After all, who would keep the darkest secrets of the Kennedy and Johnson administrations in their kitchen guarded only by attack geese? But what if they do contain just one of them? What would they be worth? How much would a collector pay to have the original source material on a White House exposé?"

Gloria butts in. She knows what type of hook will get me to open my checkbook, and she is in no mood for me to do so until I sell that vase. "So, what's the deal? Ernie's having a cash flow problem this week."

Mitch shrugs his shoulders. "I never got that far."

I go back to the first dealer. "Did you talk turkey with her or only goose?"

He frowns. "I'm afraid only goose."

The third dealer volunteers, "I did."

"Did what? Talk turkey or goose?"

"Turkey. I was about to sign on to the deal but backed out at the last minute."

Gloria stares at him. "That usually means it was too rich for your blood."

"You're right. It was."

"How much is it?"

He pauses before slowly replying. "$3,000,000."

She explodes, "$3,000,000! Is she crazy?"

He nods. "I think we have all agreed to that fact."

I am accustomed to these deals and how they usually are constructed and believe there is more to it than what he has just said. "$3,000,000 up front or in stages?"

The third dealer explains the covenant. "In stages, of course. $1,000,000 to take possession, $1,000,000 to read them, and $1,000,000 in December 2017 upon their sale."

"Why $1,000,000 to read them?"

"It's all in the will. There's a million dollar fee to be the first person to be granted the right to read all of her father's papers. If you don't feel you can sell them, then you may return the boxes back to Ms. Reid but forfeit your $1,000,000 reading fee. You'll get the other million back. She will then be allowed to sell them to someone else. Oh, by the way, you're sworn to secrecy about their contents until after they've been sold."

This is more than a bit bizarre, and it has been a long day. I lean back in my chair and wipe my eyes with both of my hands. Bill has been standing behind me quietly listening to all of this. He is a history buff. I turn around to ask him what he thinks. "Does this deal make sense to you?"

He shakes his head. "Her father must've thought he had a helluva story to tell." He then gestures towards the third dealer, "In the auctions and private placings of historical papers there is usually an appraisal of their worth before the sale. Does she have one or did her father have one done prior to writing his will?"

Once more the third dealer nods. "There is an old appraisal attached to his will."

I ask, "What did it say?"

"It was dated 1984 and said that based upon what the appraisers had read was in the boxes, the papers were worth $3,000,000."

Gloria becomes excited. "That was a lot of money in 1984. If my math is correct, that would be a bit over $6,000,000 today. It had damn well be a helluva story for that kinda money."

"No doubt about it! On top of that, she even claims it's a bargain!"

106

That is a lot of money. Bill asks for a clarification from the third dealer. "You said appraisers. How many were there?"

"Three."

"Can Ernie contact them to see if they still hold to that estimate?"

"Unfortunately, no. I tried to do that. Strangely, they all died shortly after giving the appraisal."

Gloria does not like the sound of that and with both elbows on the table leans forward before asking him. "From natural causes?"

"Yes, per their newspaper obituaries, they all died from natural causes at their homes."

Mitch feels the need to add one additional twist to the story. He comes over and whispers in my ear, "Ernie, your friend Leonard gave her my name to call!"

Chapter 8

It is never a good sign when the appraisal outlives the appraiser. It defies logic; but, when it comes to money, people just do not bank on the opinion of the dearly departed, whoever they may have been. Trust me on this. Families are always coming to me to find out what their deceased parent's possessions are really worth. Did they not tell their children the value of their things when they were alive? The matter at hand for me is far more complicated. How do I figure out what a fair price is for those papers without paying the million dollar reading fee Ms. Reid is demanding? I am about to ask my friends how they would do just that when a waitress comes to our table. "Anyone here have a van marked All Pro Contractors?"

Ever since Gloria had mentioned it, I have suspected that that handicap sign was not going to pass muster and nervously gaze up at the waitress. While trying to act as innocently as I can, I state, "Why yes, I do."

"Well, you better hurry outside and claim it. Because it's about to be towed."

Gloria and I get up immediately and do exactly as she had said. Unfortunately, by the time we arrive we can only see our van on the flat bed portion of a rollback tow truck heading out of the parking lot. We are standing next to the valet parking booth dumbfounded by what we are witnessing. I am really perturbed with her and cry out, "Good going, Gloria, and since when do they tow your car for using someone else's handicap sign?"

All she can say is, "Shit! How did they find out?"

Before we have a chance to have a real argument, the attendant approaches us and asks, "Is that your van?"

At a loss for words, I initially do not speak. Eventually, I say, "It's my son's."

Gloria corrects me, "Well actually, his company's van."

"In that case, the driver told me to hand you this note. He was very apologetic about towing your van but said he had to do it anyway."

She is not in a forgiving mood. "He couldn't have just written us a ticket!"

He gives me a sealed envelope with a return address for the Allied Commercial Credit Company. Needless to say, I am surprised since I've never heard of them. After I tear it open, Gloria and I read from a sheet of paper, "Dear Sir: Your van has been repossessed for failure to pay last month's payment. Sincerely, ACCC." Included are a photo of the van and its license plate, as well as, a copy of the loan agreement."

Call the cops, or call my son? My wrath over losing what is in that van has frozen my brain's ability to choose which one to do first. Gloria, on the other hand, is already dialing our son. In that tone of voice mothers use to warn their children that they are very displeased with them but not yet to the point of yelling at them, she asks, "George, why didn't you pay your last month's payment on your van?"

Since her phone is set to loudspeaker, I can hear him quickly and aggressively defend himself, "Because it's paid in full and has been for over a year. Why do you ask?"

"Because the Allied Commercial Credit Company just repossessed it for failure to pay last month's payment."

To say he is surprised is an understatement. "Who the hell are they?"

Her anger over the situation is peaking and she becomes quite terse with our son. "What do you mean by that? You don't know them?"

He does not back down and is becoming irritated with his mother's accusation. "Hell no! Never have dealt with them before. I used our bank to finance all of my vehicles. Are you convinced they didn't make a mistake in identity?"

"Son, don't you swear at your mother! They have a photo of your van and its license plate along with a copy of your loan agreement included with the repossession note. You have no memory of having done business with them? All of your father's purchases from the auction today are in it."

He does not answer her right away. No longer cross with her but rather upset by what has just become apparent to him, he states, "Yes, I'm positive! I just searched the Internet. The only thing close to the Allied Commercial Credit Company I can find is in Gig Harbor in the State of Washington. That's all the way across the country!"

Gloria glimpses at the envelope again. "Well, this company is in McLean, Virginia."

"You better call the cops. I'm going to the police station and report my stolen van."

Gloria phones the police to do the same before we return to The Blue And The Gay to await them at its bar. When you enter it, you go through a long narrow foyer with double glass doors at both ends. After about 6 p.m. this is where the overflow of customers lingers until their tables are ready. The Blue And The Gay does not usually take reservations, except for us after an auction. Then you face the cashier's booth on which is a glass bowl that is always kept near overflowing with giant lentil mints and a tablespoon embedded in them. To your left is a small, square waiting area with bench seats on all four sides that hold at most twelve customers and the lectern with its microphone where Bill stands to orchestrate the evening's activities and call out the lucky party to be seated next. He resembles W. C. Fields and is always jovial. However, he takes being the maître d' quite seriously, despite never wearing a coat or tie. Even if he has been calling a customer for decades, he requires them to introduce themselves before then writing their names in an appointment book. Only once this formality is completed, will he render his ruling as to when the next available table will be ready for them. As I said, after 6 p.m. until 9 p.m. all hope is abandoned for a quick seating, and one must therefore ferret out a spot to dawdle away their allotted amount of time until being called by Bill for him to hand out the menus, the all important sign that the table is ready. To the right is the bar where most of his customers ultimately decide to go. It is a fairly expansive room with sofas and wing chairs upholstered in hotel type fabrics and solid oak tables stained in a honey

111

oak color. On the far side of the room is a fireplace with gas logs blazing away even in the summer and across from it is the bar proper with about eight stools and a TV screen above both ends of the counter. A large mirror with two rows of thick glass shelves holding all sorts of liquor bottles covers its gantry. On the bar itself are small wooden bowls, which the bartender constantly refreshes with the house recipe Chex Mix.

Usually when Gloria and I come to The Blue And The Gay, only other dealers and our friends recognize us at the bar. Tonight everyone appears to wave to me or stare at me. We are in the dark until Gloria taps my shoulder and calls my attention to the TV to the left side of the bar. There I am on the screen or, more accurately, my picture from Facebook. The sound is turned down so low that we cannot hear it. However, on the lower part of the screen runs the news banner headline stating that I had just set a record price of $600,000 for a Tiffany silver and enameled vase. I do not like being the center of attention, and we decide to go back to our table with the other dealers.

Paul asks us, "Was it your van?"

Gloria replies, "Kinda. It was our son's with all of Ernie's purchases in its cargo bay."

Mitch adds, "Not all of his purchases. We had him drop off the vase at a secure location on the way over here."

"Thank God you did that. How much did the rest of your stuff cost?"

"Paul, is that with or without the $2 surprise

mystery box that Ernie couldn't pass up?" Gloria asks while still taking a dig at me.

"Let's be bold. With it."

"$400,000."

No one says anything. Finally, Paul breaks the silence and asks what is on everyone's mind, "Is it at least insured?"

I am hazy about this and have to confess, "I hope so. But I've never claimed a loss by repossession."

Bill opens the closed pocket doors and walks over to me. "I think the cops you called are here. Where do you want me to take them?"

"Bring them here. I've got nothing to hide and maybe some of the other dealers can be helpful."

When he returns, he has two policemen with him. Neither of them is particularly oversized or overwhelming. If they were not wearing a uniform, I doubt if I would have guessed they were in law enforcement. Actually, they resemble more the actors in *Beverly Hills Cop* than *The Terminator*. But they are very professional and courteous. The older of the two starts the questioning. He shakes both Gloria's and my hands. "Hi, I'm Officer Duncan." He points to his partner who nods to us. "And this is Officer Perkins. What exactly happened?"

Gloria answers him. "An Allied Commercial Credit Company repossessed our son's van even though it was fully paid off and they did not have a lien against it."

"Did they leave any paper work explaining why they did this?"

Handing him the envelope from inside her pocketbook, she complains, "Yeah, they even have a phony loan agreement."

"How have you corroborated it's fraudulent?"

"Because our son told us he has no current loans taken out on it with anyone."

"Could it just be a case of mistaken identity, and they were after some other van?"

She takes back the envelope and after reaching within it for the photo shows it to him. "I only wish."

The younger cop, Officer Perkins, studies it and says, "You wouldn't have the name of the towing company?"

Both of us reply, "No. I never saw the truck up-close."

He then surveys the crowd. "Anybody see the truck's markings?"

There is silence until Bill notes, "The valet attendant should have spoken to them and seen their truck up-close."

"Can you go get him and bring him in here?"

"No problem." He then leaves to retrieve the attendant.

While Bill is gone, the policemen confer among themselves. In a few moments Officer Duncan says to me, "I don't think we have jurisdiction over a repossession. Even if it was a mistake."

Before long, Bill returns with the attendant. Officer Perkins asks, "What did the driver of the tow truck tell you?"

"He said he was here to repossess the van for failure of payment of last month's payment."

"Anything else?"

"No."

"Did he show you any form of identification or paperwork?"

"No."

The cop is frustrated. "Was the tow truck marked in any way?"

"No."

Officer Duncan interrupts. "You mean to say that you allowed a total stranger to tow a van from the parking lot of The Blue And The Gray based solely on his saying he had the right to do so."

The attendant does not like the tone of that question and begins to act jittery. "No."

"What else did he say?"

"He didn't say anything else. He flashed a badge that seemed legit."

Office Perkins has never heard of a tow truck driver having a badge. "What kind of a badge was it?"

"I'm no expert but it resembled some sort of a federal law enforcement badge."

"How could you tell that?"

The attendant smiles. "Because it had United States Government on it."

"Anything else?"

"Yeah, when he lifted his jacket to show me his badge, I saw that he had a gun in a holster. I didn't feel I was in any position to challenge him just then."

The cop agrees. "You did right. Did you see the license plate of the tow truck?"

"Of course, I'm no idiot."

"Do you remember it?"

He smiles again. "Most of it, except the numbers. It said US GOVERNMENT on top and FOR OFFICIAL USE ONLY on the bottom."

Gloria answers her cell phone. "Hello. George what did the police tell you?"

"They said that they have no jurisdiction over an Allied Commercial Credit Corporation repossession."

She places it on speakerphone so that I can hear too. "Was that all that they said?"

"No. They told me to contact the U.S. Attorney's office in the morning, which handles any complaints regarding the Allied Commercial Credit Corporation. They also warned me that there had better not have been any illegal drugs in the van."

"How come?"

"Evidently, the DEA uses them to repossess vans and trucks that are suspected to be owned by gangs and drug dealers. It avoids having to get search warrants."

"Is that legal, George?"

"They don't care. It's a given among them that gangs and drug dealers know better than to go to court to claim their vehicles."

I grab the phone from Gloria's hand. "Did they tell you how I can get my merchandise back?"

"Yeah, but you're not going to like it, Dad."

With that remark I instantaneously guess what they had told him and George is right that I do not like it. "Not at one of those government seized property auctions?"

"Yep, at one of those. The captain wished you good luck at it. He said he has gotten some great bargains at them. He also mentioned it may be online."

One obvious question remains unanswered. "Did they have an explanation of how this happened? After all, we are not drug dealers and aren't members of a gang."

"He mentioned that occasionally this happens as an act of revenge where someone will set up their enemy's vehicle for repossession claiming that it is used to deal drugs."

"I can't imagine that happening to me. I make it my business not to tick anyone off. Have you been naughty and not nice recently, George?"

I can hear him laughing. "I'm in construction. I piss people off all the time for their shoddy work or shoddy materials. But no one does that. Everyone realizes it's part of my job."

Gloria takes the phone back. "Did the captain have an explanation where the loan papers came from?"

"He said they have stacks of them. They just fill in the name of their target and hand them out. So many of these loans have been sold to assignees that most people don't have a notion who actually holds their notes."

"George, none of this sounds kosher. How can they just make up a story and tow away your van?"

"The captain knows it's not legal and says that the DEA knows it's not legal. In fact, they hope the gang members and drug dealers know it's not legal and will challenge them in court. That way they can get firm identification of who they are."

"What do you mean by that?"

"The government wants their legal names, not the

street names they use. That way they can deport them if they're here illegally or get hold of their real rap sheets."

Once more, I grasp the phone to ask my final question. "How did they find out that the van was here?"

"The captain said that the DEA places a GPS tracking device on the vehicles they intend to seize. Usually they're placed in the glove compartment or under the hood."

After hearing what the captain has said, Officer Duncan says, "We'll make a report, but I can't promise you it will do any good. Good evening." Having said that, the two policemen leave.

Chapter 9

Disheartened by all that George had discovered, Gloria and I decide it is time to go home. We have no further interest in wheeling and dealing tonight. I will contact the U. S. Attorney's office in the morning and hopefully straighten out this mess. Mitch and Helen volunteer to drive us home. As we gather up our things, the valet attendant approaches us. "I'm really sorry about your van, but there was nothing I could do."

I nod to him. "I understand that. I just wish I knew who fingered us and for what?"

"Well, there is one thing the police officers didn't ask me but might help you."

My curiosity peaks with his comment. "What's that?"

"There was a passenger in the tow truck who became upset with the amount of time the driver was spending with me. He said, 'Hurry up. We don't have all night to find it. And we've got to repack all of this crap by midnight when they want it back.'"

"He didn't mention what the it is or they are, did he?"

The attendant slowly shakes his head. "No, but he was really anxious to get out of here."

"What did he look like?"

The attendant again shakes his head. "I never saw him. I just heard him yell at the driver."

Gloria is fuming. "What the hell would the DEA want with that Tiffany vase? Do they think it belonged to a drug lord? Or are they claiming that John stole it from one of them?"

Mitch is more analytical. "We haven't established for a fact that it's the DEA behind this. That's that police captain's opinion. The real question is what's happening at midnight?"

Helen has the most experience in this line of thinking since she graduated with a master's in applied intelligence. "Let's be logical. If it really is the DEA who impounded your vase, they must have a deal going down early tomorrow morning and somehow need that vase to complete it."

Things begin to click for me. "Of course, those international dealers must've been representing a drug lord and the New York dealers must've been working for the DEA. But why is the vase of any interest to a drug lord?"

Out of left field, she asks, "What makes you think it's the vase they want?"

What is she talking about? "Unless this was just a routine heist and it sure as hell doesn't smell like it was, what in particular did I have in the van that would be worth going to all of this effort for? My $2 mystery surprise package?"

"Maybe something you bought is evidence for a

drug bust and they need it to obtain a search or arrest warrant?"

Laughing out loud, I declare sarcastically, "Yeah, the cut glass decanter is going to send a Mexican or Columbian drug lord to prison."

Helen yields. "You're right. It has to be the vase. Did John tell you who owned the vase?"

"No. He said if I really needed that information to sell it he could give it to me. But the vase and another lot were consigned to him by one individual with the stipulation that the seller's information not be made public. I freely admit that breaks the rules for dealing in Tiffany, but John has proof that it's not stolen. He gave me a copy of the sales receipt for it the last time it was sold by Tiffany Tom and the most current Interpol-Stolen Works of Art DVD. Of course, the consignee's name was blackened out on the receipt. I really don't need to have the seller's name and would hate to create a problem for John since Leonard and most of my customers only care that it's not hot."

Mitch adds, "You're lucky. I couldn't sell a Tiffany lamp or window to save my life without its provenance."

Gloria is shaking her head violently. "You guys are idiots! If the DEA needed the vase for a warrant they would have confiscated it from John prior to the auction as material evidence of a crime."

Helen also begins to shake her head. "I disagree. They could've done it that way, but the dealers would have recognized that some law enforcement agency had gone after it. Too many of them heard about its sale immediately after John had posted this auction's catalogue on the Internet and would have demanded the reason why it was pulled. Then the antiques blogs would have gone haywire with conspiracy theories about whether John was telling the truth or not. The drug lord would've gotten wind of what the DEA was up to."

I butt in. "She's right. He was getting a lot of heat during the preview just about his threatening to pull the vase. I can only imagine what the uproar would have been like if he had actually gone through with it."

"Precisely, Ernie. The DEA had only two options: Plan A to obtain it at the auction before the drug lord did. And when that failed, they went to plan B."

Her words make me unexpectedly recall Ira Wynn's odd proposal. "If you buy the vase today, it will no longer be valid. Our client is funny about this. He insists that his name be on the auction records as the new owner, not yours." A cold shiver flies down my spine. I start to breathe rapidly and my heart begins to race.

Gloria detects the change in me and asks, "Are you all right? Do you need to sit down? I don't want you fainting again."

I snap back, "I'm physically fine, but not mentally. I just realized that we might indeed be dealing with a drug lord!" Heeding her well-founded caution, I take a seat without delay.

Helen is stunned. "What makes you think that?"

"I just figured out what Ira Wynn was doing when he made me that offer." I explain further, "I thought he was being his usual New York jerky self. Now, I see he was trying to save my life!"

I have gotten to Gloria. She is trembling. "What do you mean by that?"

"Think about it. If the drug lord knew the importance of the vase and he must've because he sent those two dealers to buy it for him, he would go after whoever got it. And that's me. He may have stolen the van just to get the vase!"

The attendant breaks in, "But from a distance that badge for all the world was real. My brother's in the FBI and I've seen his umpteen times."

Helen pats him on the back. "It probably is real. When the drug lords kill agents they take their badges."

Mitch starts to dial a number on his cell phone. I ask him, "Who the hell are you calling?"

He sternly says, "The police. We need those two officers back here."

"How come?"

"Because when the drug lord finds out the vase isn't in the van, who do you think he's going to visit to find out where it is?"

"Me, of course!"

"Yeah, you. And you need police protection. That drug lord won't follow the Supreme Court's rules for interrogating suspects. Last I heard they didn't give out

Miranda rights either."

For a while today I thought I had my grand slam. At present, I am afraid I have the ultimate strike out. "How much trouble do you think I'm in?"

"Listen, you were a forensic pathologist before you became an antiques dealer. You've seen their work. How long did it used to take you to get a final ID on their masterpieces? I don't need to tell you how deep the shit is."

Gloria is almost hysterical. "You mean to say we're going to have to have police protection?"

Mitch nods. "Maybe even protective custody."

She brandishes her fist at my face. "Ah, shit. Ernie, you had to be macho today and buy that damn vase. Let's face it, your check to John is going to bounce since I suspect that drug lord won't let you sell it to Leonard in the morning."

Helen is the only cool head in the group. She asks the attendant, "What did you say the passenger said about midnight?"

He promptly answers, "He said, 'And we've got to repack all of this crap by midnight when they want it back.' That's all."

She ponders what he has just repeated before explaining, "The drug lord must be planning to leave this country a little while after midnight with the vase. But I can't figure out what he wants with the rest of the stuff in the van?"

Mitch promptly turns away from his cell phone to say, "Cover. He needs it for cover."

"What do you mean by that?"

"When customs or whoever stops him at the airport, he wants to pass off as a legitimate antiques dealer. If all he has is that vase, he won't be successful. The airports are probably already on alert for it. He's probably going to head for a smaller private civilian airport since he's got to have figured that the TSA would pick it up even in checked baggage when it passes through security at one of the majors."

Gloria vents. "You mean, we've lost $400,000 worth of stuff tonight. Our insurance agent is going to kill us. We definitely won't be able to get our policy renewed and they'll probably cancel us when they hear about this caper. We're out of business!"

Mitch starts to talk on his cell phone, "911, we need Officers Duncan and Perkins back at The Blue And The Gay."

The Operator asks, "Do you mean The Blue And The Gray Restaurant on King Boulevard?"

"Excuse me. Yes, ma'am."

"What is the nature of your call?"

"A van was stolen from the restaurant's parking lot and we've discovered some material information regarding the theft."

"I'll send them back over, but it may take awhile."

"Thank you."

Gloria's rage just grows. "Why didn't that damn drug lord just have those dealers bid whatever it took to get the damn thing?"

Mitch, who at the beginning of his legal career had been in the U.S. Attorney's Office, observes, "They only deal in ready money. That guy probably only had a half million dollars in cash today. No wonder he got so teed off when Ernie outbid him."

I add, "And the DEA only had authorized $400,000 before the auction. Ira must've called them up and got the $700,000 authorized after they lost."

"Yeah, that's the same way I piece it together."

I feel the acute need to sit down. "Oh my God, what have I gotten myself into? How about my just giving the vase to the DEA tonight?"

Mitch casts his eyes down upon me and places his right hand on my shoulder. "They would be thrilled. But the drug lord would be pissed and would probably kill you just for spite when he finds out that the vase isn't in the van. You can be damn certain that he's going to be watching out for you. Hell, he was probably tailing you ever since you left the auction."

I get another quiver down my back, and my fingers and lips begin to tingle while my feet and hands start to cramp. Without warning, I am paranoid. Who can I trust in the room? All I mull over is *do not give out the vase's true location, do not give out the vase's true location.* Carefully choosing my words while launching into some serious panting, I ask, "You don't believe he found out where we really hid it and would go there?" Am I ever glad to be sitting!

"I doubt it."

"Why do you say that?"

"First, they couldn't see the van from the road there and, therefore, have no idea that it was taken out of the van. Second, if they did suspect it was there, they would've gone there first. The security system at the hideout would have detected a second unauthorized car coming down the driveway following yours or after we left, and the service would have called us immediately if anyone had tried to break in there. As I told you, it's impregnable. Just to be safe, I'm going to have the service keep someone there around the clock."

Gloria is beside herself. "Where are we going to spend the night? I'm afraid to go to my own house. Hell, they may already be there. Ernie call the service and tell them to have the police search our house." I begin to phone them when she adds, "You better alert them to have a SWAT team available. You know, they may even kill our dogs!" She calms down enough to joke, "That would be the only good thing to come from today! You are aware how much I hate those two dogs. After they're gone, no more animals, you hear me!"

After acknowledging her disdain for them by curtly smiling at her, I return to the disaster at hand. I dither about what to tell the service. I do not want to sound hysterical or crazy, but at the same time Gloria is right. They need to be warned of what may happen when they get there. I cannot figure out why I am so winded, but I

128

am. Puffing away, I am only able to say slowly, "Hello, we need someone along with the police to check out our house."

Just from the caller ID from my cell phone, they already identified our home's address and me. "Can you speak up, sir, I can barely hear you. Now, what seems to be the matter, sir?"

I pull myself together and talk louder. "Well, I purchased an antique vase, as you can see from our profile I am an antiques dealer, and that antique, we think, is wanted by a drug lord, who may be breaking into my house as we speak to get it."

"Is it in there?"

"No, it's somewhere else, very well protected."

"Have you notified the police of this problem?"

"Somewhat."

It is explicit from the tone of his voice that the dispatcher did not like that answer. "What do you mean by that?"

I try to cool off. "Well, the drug lord stole my van a few minutes ago in order to get the vase. We reported that to the police. We just realized that since the vase is not in the van, he will most likely try to search for it at our house."

"Do you have any information that the burglars will be armed?"

"Yes, the driver of the tow truck that took our van was carrying a pistol in his holster. We suspect that they will have assault rifles with them."

There is a long pause from the dispatcher. "I've spoken to the supervisor and he thinks we need to call the police and have them send a SWAT team out to your house. This is beyond what we contracted to do for you."

"My wife thought you might want to do that."

"They will request documentation if there are any explosives, dangerous animals, or special weapons in your home."

"Nope, none of that. However, we do have two dogs at home, but the worst they'll do is bark at them."

Gloria interrupts me. "Or lead the thieves to where my jewelry is stashed. Boy, are they ever dumb dogs!"

"OK, sir, we will notify the police. Listen, until we tell you it is safe there, don't go home."

"Thank you."

Officers Duncan and Perkins arrive just as I finish up with my security service. Officer Duncan is smiling when he asks, "What have you discovered since we left here?"

With his law enforcement background, Mitch decides that he is the best suited to explain our conclusions and speaks up before Gloria or I have a chance to do so. "We have deduced that a drug lord has stolen the van in order to abscond with evidence that the

DEA is seeking in order to arrest him."

Both policemen break out into a roaring laugh. We, on the contrary, are confused and upset by their seemingly unprofessional reaction. Gloria in particular is not pleased. "What do you two find to be so funny? Our lives are at stake."

Noticing her palpable irritation at them, Officer Duncan holds her hand in an effort to pacify her. "Ma'am, first thing we did when we got back to the station house was contact the DEA regarding your son's van. They told us that they have had no covert operations the entire day in the metro area and have none planned for tonight."

This is not enough. She is still not satisfied. "What about a drug lord?"

"We also asked them if there was any ongoing investigations that would in any way have involved your son's van, yourselves, or anything you bought at the auction that may be in the van. They said that they were unaware of anything involving you that would be remotely of interest to them or anyone they were investigating."

Confident that he has finally placated her, he then turns to me. "The supervising field agent we spoke to wanted me on behalf of his family to congratulate you on winning the Tiffany vase. One of his relatives owns the Daisy vase, whatever that is, and he appreciates how proud you must be today for owning yours. They also are grateful to you for more than doubling the value of their vase."

I am humiliated but, thankfully, no longer short of breath. Gloria remains angry and pursues the issue. "If it wasn't them, then who the hell took the van?"

Chapter 10

Officer Duncan, who is still holding Gloria's hand, shrugs his shoulders. "I don't have the foggiest idea. We also asked the DEA agent who he thought might have impounded the van. He said he didn't have a clue. What bothered him was that whoever did it used a government vehicle and flashed a government badge."

From his past experience, Mitch does not understand this concern. "Why? We used to do that all the time when I was at Justice."

"He said because he couldn't find any court order to do this when he did a computer search on the van. The Attorney General is strict about the agencies using government vehicles only when there is a court order. Unequivocally, when they use that Allied Commercial Credit Corporation scheme to repossess a vehicle they have to contract with a private towing service."

"OK. But I don't see the difference."

"It's because the ACCC is used when it's a matter of national security or drugs are suspected but not proven and not when a crime per se has been committed."

I, too, am terribly confused. "I don't see their reasoning, either."

After laughing at our ignorance of the nuances of law enforcement, he explains, "It's clear as a bell. They don't want a drug dealer, spy or terrorist to learn that the government is onto them. The Department of Homeland

Security has had more than a few investigations flat out spoiled by a suspect watching his car being carried away by a tow truck with U.S. government tags."

Mitch finally comprehends what Officer Duncan is saying. "I see. That DEA agent was indirectly telling you that the ACCC, among other things, is a front for the National Security Court. When they order a vehicle impounded or searched, the government uses the ACCC to do it."

"He didn't put it in those words, but I think that's the gist of it."

Meanwhile, Gloria is settling down and pulls her hands away from Officer Duncan's. "So, who took the van? A rogue federal agent who doesn't go by the book?"

"I am unable to substantiate that ma'am, and neither is the DEA agent. However, we have issued a stolen vehicle alert on it."

There is still one question no one has asked. "Why?"

Officer Duncan screws his face. "What do you mean, why?"

"Why would a rogue agent want a van full of antiques? None of them was stolen. None of them on the face of it was used in carrying out a felony. None of them has national security importance. All of which means none of them should be on a federal agency's radar."

"Unless this is just a horrible misunderstanding, no

134

one who we can contact tonight has an answer to your question. The DEA agent did mention that, since whoever took your stuff has created the strong suggestion of being a federal employee, you can file a claim with the U.S. Attorney's Office in the morning."

"And how am I supposed to prove that those two are federal agents?"

Officer Perkins perks up and smiles. "I took the restaurant's surveillance videos of its parking lot when we left earlier this evening. Like the attendant said, the tow truck was carrying U.S. Government tags but the numbers were blurry, as if they put some sort of clear reflective tape over them."

Gloria immediately asserts, "So, it was a government truck!"

"Yes, ma'am."

"And they tried to hide its identity!"

"Yes, ma'am."

"Thank God for that! At least we're not bankrupt and out of business."

Always the lawyer, Mitch is still not ready to celebrate our return to financial soundness. "What makes you think that the tow truck wasn't stolen and that was why the tags were covered with tape?"

Officer Perkins continues, "I enquired into that, too, sir. The government hasn't reported any stolen, missing, or unaccounted for tow trucks." With that revelation, I get up.

Upon re-entering the room, Paul joins us. "I see y'all haven't solved the crime of the decade, yet. Well, while y'all were ruling out a drug lord coming to get yah, I called a friend of mine in Nashville. He's one of those conspiracy nuts who think the government is always doing wacky things to its law-abiding citizens. Despite his high BS content, he does seem to closely follow what the government is up to. He raised the issue if Elvis had owned any of those antiques."

I snicker at what is a transparent mini version of one of Paul's notorious larger than life jokes. We are always on our guard on the first of April. Several years ago he somehow had every physician in Nashville awakened and on their way to the hospitals for a midnight air crash. They did not think it was a funny April Fools' joke when they dashed to the ERs only to be greeted by clowns who sprayed them with seltzer water. He made up with them for it with a big donation to the Children's Hospital at Vanderbilt. "Why would he ask that?"

"He claims it might help prove that Elvis is still alive and is being held in protective custody by the government under an alias."

All of us roll our eyes in disbelief. He cannot be serious. I unwittingly continue to be his foil. "Why would the government have done that?"

"Because Nixon in 1970 covertly made him a real 'Federal Agent-at-Large' in the Bureau of Narcotics and Dangerous Drugs since he was already working as an agent for the equivalent state agencies in Tennessee, California, and Colorado. Elvis hated the hippie drug

136

culture. Acting undercover, he was informing on all the drug trafficking in Memphis and the entertainment industry that he encountered. They made him disappear when his name began to show up on some Mafia hit lists."

"How would one of my antiques prove that?"

"My friend said that if Elvis was the consignee for that vase, that would prove he is still alive. I overheard you say that John wouldn't reveal the name of the seller unless under duress."

"Paul, I said he was instructed not to reveal it publicly and only if it was absolutely required for me to make my sale."

"Whatever, Elvis, it turns out, was a secret collector of Tiffany. He didn't let it be spread about since he was concerned that dealers would take advantage of him if they suspected that he was really serious about it. His reputation for poor taste was great cover for him. He took his collection with him when he went into the government's witness protection program. None of it was left at Graceland. He may have been forced to sell the vase to raise some money since he has been cut off from his estate to protect his new identity. Word in Memphis is that he is getting old and sick and is selling off what things he still has to pay for his care and more than modest lifestyle."

Mitch loathes Graceland; nevertheless, he asks, "That's silly. His estate is worth a fortune. Why doesn't he just have the DOJ transfer funds from his estate to him?"

Officer Duncan answers him. "They can't do that."

"Why not? It would be legal."

"A money transfer can be traced. Once the Mafia puts you on their hit list, your name is never removed until you're buried. The Mafia has so many connections, particularly in Vegas that they would find out about it before the IRS did. All they would need to suspect is that Elvis is really still alive and they would try to get him. The U.S. Marshals Service isn't interested in having its first failure be the King."

Curiosity gets the better of Mitch, who refuses to believe any of this. He turns to Paul and asks, "God forbid, but did the King in fact collect Tiffany lamps?"

"Rumor in the antiques world of Memphis is that the gold, green and peacock blue light shade over his 9 foot pool table is really a knockoff of an original one he owned but was afraid to hang. He allegedly feared that Graceland's depression era ceiling timbers wouldn't support it, and one day it would fall and be ruined. He had a local stain glass company make it, two small hangers for his kitchen, and some panels that separated his living room and den as updated substitutes of the originals he had stored in his basement. But the gossip is the real reason he did that was that true Art Nouveau struck him as being too old fashioned for Graceland. We can all agree, can't we, that actual Tiffany wouldn't have meshed with his kitschy design ideas for it?"

Crossing his arms, Mitch manifests his condescension in his slow nods and tone of voice. "You know I would never set foot in Graceland for fear that both my feet would turn gangrenous and have to be

138

amputated. However, I unquestionably agree with you from the pictures I've seen of it. How someone with those decorative notions, if you can call what he did to that place decorative, could have a passion for LCT is beyond me! Placing one of his masterpieces among that Rock & Roll dreck would have been blasphemy. One day I'll show you the bill I received to strengthen the supports for my new authentic Tiffany hanger."

Rather than listen to their recurring argument about Graceland, I try to recollect the events of the day. Even if we had gotten it wrong about the New York dealers and the Hispanic dealers, maybe we still were not too far off from the truth. I speculate out loud, "Let's suppose that Paul's friend is not entirely off his rocker. Could the New York dealers still be working for the government but not the DEA?"

Mitch welcomes the move back from the Graceland digression. "Which government agency do you suspect?"

Before I have a chance to say what I'm thinking, Paul bellows, "The U.S. Marshals Service, of course."

Them! Mitch is unimpressed and scowls at him. "Why them?"

"Because it would fit. They arranged to have Elvis sell the vase at John's auction under their name. That's why John was told not to reveal it. Then they would have the New York dealers buy it for $400,000, which Elvis's estate had already supplied to them. All Ira and his friends would be told is that they are buying a Tiffany enamel and silver vase for the Elvis Presley Trust as an investment. No treasury funds would be used, so no rules would be broken, and no Congressional investigation would be indicated. That's why those dealers had to stop and let Ernie take it. Then the New York dealers had the Trust arrange for the release of an additional $300,000 from its bank account allowing their offer of $700,000."

I enter the fray. "Why did they tell me that my name couldn't be recorded as the buyer?"

Mitch has an aha moment. "That's simple. If they paid you with funds from his estate's trust and you were still recorded as the purchaser, then the Mafia may be paying you a visit. Obviously, the U.S. Marshals Service had the Presley Trust instruct Ira not to buy the vase unless its name was listed as the buyer."

"Why?"

"To prevent the Mafia from seeing the cashier's check Ira would have given you and to keep them from having you find out who the consignee really was from John."

"How would discovering either the bank account that Ira used or that the U.S. Marshals office was the consignee help them?"

"Because they're better at tracing bank accounts than we are. They pay in cash and at greater than civil service rates. In addition, they would trace the seller on the receipt you were given by John and have him 'voluntarily' reveal who he sold it to years ago. Hey, we all keep those records so that, when we have a new customer for it, we can call our old customers to find out if they will sell back to us one of the treasures we sold them years ago. If he didn't have the records, they would go to Tiffany Tom, who keeps everything he has ever done on his computer. Son of a bitch charges $1500 to reprint each of his old reports with an updated date. Finally, how many federal witnesses collected rare Tiffany before they entered the program? Not many I bet."

"So, Ira was trying to protect me from the Mafia."

"Yeah, not intentionally, of course, if you believe Elvis is still alive."

Wagging his finger towards my chest, Paul softly interjects, "Elvis may be in this very restaurant as we speak and we don't even realize it." He raises his voice. "Listen everyone, Elvis is in the house!"

This is going from being fun to being stupid. I feel like I am the quizmaster in Twenty Questions. "OK, who were the Hispanic dealers representing?"

Helen waves her hand. "That's simple. The Mob."

"Why did they stop at $500,000?"

"It's the Mafia. They charge a fortune for their services and pay a pittance for yours. Just ask Mitch. He'll tell you how little those crooked politicians and judges he sent up the river for being on the take actually got. However, $500,000 wasn't being cheap. They really must've wanted it. Besides, they would've been paying in cash, not cashiers check, and probably never imagined that you would pay $600,000 with the buyer's premium for it. That's probably all that they brought. But they could be at your booth at "the show" with two suitcases full of dough."

141

Gloria shouts in my ear, "And you better take it!"

I am beginning to feel uneasy about each of our scenarios ending up with my having to deal with criminals. "Anyway those Hispanic dealers could have legitimate clients?"

Mitch is disappointed that I want a less interesting thesis. "Of course, it's just not as much fun. I told you earlier today that I think they represent that museum in Havana. They, like you, may be innocent bystanders in whatever intrigue the government is up to. However, as I mentioned to you at the auction, the one who lost out to you was curious if you were aware of the vase's past history. Can't we assume that his patron was more than your average Tiffany collector?"

"I came to that conclusion by the way he was bidding. He wanted that vase in a bad way. He seemed to think I was bluffing when he went on his own from $400,000 to $500,000. He was not happy when I did not fold."

"He definitely wasn't happy. The way he acted in the exhibition hall you would've thought his life depended on getting that vase."

Helen interrupts him. "Mitch, maybe it did. Before the Allied Commercial Credit Corporation became a front for the National Security Court, it had other purposes."

"Like what?"

"I guess it is OK to tell y'all this. It's no longer a Top Secret. But back in the Sixties, the ACCC under a different name was the CIA's way of funneling funds for the Bay of Pigs invasion and to the subsequent other anti-Castro groups. It would establish lines of credit at local banks for our operatives to use to topple him."

"Made following the money trail difficult."

"Yeah, it took congressional investigators decades to figure it out."

I do not like the sound of this. "Helen, you're not implying that those dealers were working on a plot to overthrow or worse kill Castro?"

"I claim ignorance about what they are up to, but I don't think the Company is still in that business, Ernie."

The two policemen are ready to leave. After hearing our theories, they have had enough of amateur police work. Officer Duncan comes over to Gloria and me. "Do you two have a ride home? We'll be glad to take you."

"Thanks, but Mitch and Helen have offered to take us home."

"Good. We'll be contacting the auction house in the morning to get their information on the antiques you bought. We should have it on the Interpol Website by the afternoon. All the pawnshops in the state will be notified by noon. If whoever stole your stuff plans to sell it, he better do it pretty fast because by the end of business tomorrow that vase and everything else in your van will be smokin' hot. By the way, there weren't any weapons in your van?"

"I don't think so. However, I did buy a surprise mystery lot that could contain a weapon. I never bothered to open it to see what's in it."

"How come? I would think you would be curious to see what it was."

"Officer Duncan, it only cost me $2.00."

"Oh, in that case I understand. By the way, will you be showing at 'the show' this weekend?"

"I plan to be there unless the drug lord's or the Mafia's bogeymen come after me. I may not have much to put out, but I've already paid this month's booth rent. Why do you ask?"

"Perkins and I will be doing night security there. I thought I'd update you then on where we stand in the investigation."

When they leave, Bill comes by. "This is the most excitement we've had around here since one of those old geezers choked on a piece of steak a year ago. I got to try out the Heimlich maneuver. We had an ambulance and a fire truck come for that call. He was mainly drunk but they took him anyway to the ER on a stretcher with oxygen. It was quite a show."

"I hope we weren't too much of a distraction for your other guests."

"Nah, they kinda enjoyed it. There you were on the TV and the police were here investigating the van's theft. They felt they were right in the middle of all the action."

"Good, I would hate to have caused you a problem."

144

"Ernie, I only have one question for you. Look around here; you see I'm a Civil War buff. Did John Wilkes Booth by chance meet Tiffany?"

I laugh. "Not another conspiracy theory, Bill. No, he was shot about 28 years before that vase was made. It didn't have anything to do with the Lincoln assassination."

Chapter 11

At first, the ride home is surprisingly quiet. Gloria and I are leery as we leave The Blue And The Gay. Will our house be as we had left it? Although our security service had been forewarned about what had happened to our son's van, was then told later to stand-down, and has not called back about anything unusual occurring there, our sense of dread swells as we approach home. My imagination starts to unnerve me.

I feel compelled to vent my growing fears. "What do we do if there's someone in our driveway?"

Helen is calm. Her years in government espionage serve her well tonight. She tries to decompress us with a joke. "I'll jump out of the car and just unbutton my top. There isn't a hitman in this country who can stand up to my two lethal weapons!"

Mitch agrees with her and nods. "The Agency never felt the need to issue her a gun. Really!"

I laugh and finally relax. "What do you do with them? Smother them to death?"

She is in the front seat and turns to face me. "It's a helluva way to die. The undertakers can't wipe the smiles off of their faces for the open casket. And they don't rest in peace because their wives hire private dicks to find out what they were up to when they were killed."

The joke falls flat. Gloria does not laugh and is still uptight and in a fighting mood. "Well, what if they're in the house? Do we call the police and wait and risk their getting away or do we confront them? I do have a black belt in karate."

Helen stares at her. "So do I. But I'm trained not to try to be a hero by confronting them. We'll call the police and do our best to keep them from escaping. I want to discover who the hell is up to this just as much as you do. You let me handle this. You're too much of a Rambo."

When we finally arrive, there is nothing in our driveway and the house is dark. Mitch tries to cheer Gloria up, "Now do you think that you have anything to worry about?"

I am convinced, but she is not so confident. "They could've come and gone."

We all get out of Mitch's car and slowly walk together to the front door. It is locked. Still cautious, we then move onto the back door. It too is locked. Helen cracks another joke. "If someone has invaded your house, they're the most courteous burglars I've ever heard of."

I give Helen the key, and she unlocks the back door and opens it slightly. She listens intently to ascertain if anyone may be scurrying about inside to hide. Our two dogs immediately start to bark. They are beagles and, once they do this, you hear only them. Gloria is now convinced that we are safe. "Just go in Helen. If there was anyone in our house those two hounds would have been raising hell when we got here."

We all agree she is right but, nevertheless, venture cautiously into the kitchen after Helen turns on the lights. It is as we had left it earlier in the morning. Then we

147

proceed onto the living room, dining room, and den. Everything is undisturbed. I concede, "No one has been here. I guess the dogs scared them off."

Mitch discerns one thing out of the ordinary. "Where are they? Usually they charge over and greet us."

"I put them in the basement so that they could use its doggy door to get out if they needed to. I knew we wouldn't be back until late this evening."

This raises a red flag for Mitch. "Isn't that dangerous?"

However, I do not perceive an issue. "What do you mean? It's approved by the Humane Society."

"I'm not worried about them. I'm worried someone could enter your house through it."

While smiling at the absurdity of Mitch's concern, I observe, "They're beagles. That opening wouldn't let a two year old in. Those dogs would worm their way through a tomato can to get to a rabbit that happened to be passing by in the back yard."

Gloria adds, "Besides, the door to the basement is a steel door with a steel frame and a commercial dead bolt lock. Even if they could get in it, they can't get to the rest of the house without a blow torch." As she turns on the lamps in the den, she spots the telephone's voice mail light is blinking. She motions to me to check it out. "Ernie, see what messages we have. The police may have found the van."

"We should be so lucky." I go to the phone, which

sits on the end table by the sofa, and dial our access number. I punch the speakerphone button so that Gloria can hear the messages as well.

"ATT, You have two unheard messages. To listen to your unheard messages, press 1." I do so. "First unheard message: message from unknown caller at 5:10 PM today: 'Do not sell the vase. I repeat, do not sell the vase.' Click. To save this message press 9 to delete it press 7." I, of course, press 9. "Second unheard message; message from unknown caller at 9:20 PM today. To listen to your unheard messages, press 1, to re-save the message press 9." I press 1. "Your car will be ready in the morning. Click. To save this message press 9 to delete it press 7." Again, I press 9.

Since everyone heard the messages, we all instinctively gather closer to the phone. I am speechless. So is Gloria. Mitch begins to laugh. "By God, it didn't take Paul very long to figure out how to play a trick on you two."

We, both, stare at him. I note, "That didn't sound like Paul."

Gloria agrees, "I don't recognize either of the voices."

Helen asks, "Do you have caller ID to trace the calls?"

I nod, yes. "But when I was getting the voice messages, the caller ID said unknown number both times."

Mitch is impressed. "Paul may have outdone

himself this time. How did he so quickly stumble across a phone that blocks caller ID?"

Helen frowns at him. "You putz. All you do is dial 67 before you enter the number you're calling. It probably took him 30 seconds to have his phone company set him up to do this. I wonder who at The Blue And The Gay he got to make the calls, because I don't recognize any of the voices either."

Mitch, however, counters. "He may not have done it there. I didn't hear any background noises on those messages. That place is never quiet enough to have avoided them."

"Unless Paul did it in Bill's office," she correctly insinuates.

"You're right, but I was standing next to him at 5:10 PM. He didn't duck out to Bill's office then."

We listen to both of the messages again. Mitch wants to hear the first message a third time. Afterwards he says, "Damn, if I haven't heard that women's voice before. But I just can't place it."

I face Gloria. "We don't have a car in the shop do we?"

She shakes her head, no. "Not unless you took it there."

"Could that message have been left by mistake?"

Helen is adamant. "No, repair shops routinely leave their numbers so that you will call them back. Do you think we should call the police?"

"What for? So that they can tell us that they can't trace the calls and neither of the calls constitutes a threat. Besides, we've bothered them enough tonight. The best I can hope for is that whoever stole the van understands how to handle fragile antiques, and this won't be a complete loss for me."

Mitch and Helen leave to return to their home. Gloria and I decide just to go to bed. Neither of us is interested in watching TV.

Very early the next morning Dumb and Dumber startle us with their baying and barking at the front door. This is unusual because it is before their routine awakening time. Lying in bed, we face each other and hope that the other will take the initiative to go downstairs and find out what has caught the attention of our dogs. I lose the standoff. I put my slippers on and then grab my robe off the left corner post at the foot of the bed. As I tie its belt around my waist, I yell at the dogs, "What the hell is wrong with you two. The sun isn't even up."

At the top of the stairs, I turn the downstairs lights on. I inadvertently peer out through the transom window over the front door and spot what for all the world is my son's van parked along the curb under the streetlight. I call out to Gloria. "Take a gander out the window and see if that's George's van."

She is still half asleep. "What did you say?"

"Get up and see if that's George's van outside."

151

Once in the foyer, I see that they are perched at the front door with their front legs pawing at it and their tails pointed straight back. They are on a hunt. I struggle with them. They will not budge. Finally, I am able to move them enough to allow me to open the front door. They shoot out of it and probably wake up my next-door neighbors with their howling. Gloria is very excited and shouts out. "Oh my god, if it isn't it."

I waver between hurrying over and delving into it or calling the police and waiting for them. What if it is booby-trapped? All sorts of other possibilities zip through my brain. Very shortly, I regain my composure and just walk up to it. The dogs have scoped it out ahead of me by sniffing all about it. They then leave for more interesting smells up the road before I can grab them. The light from the lamppost is bright enough that I can canvass the inside of the van without any difficulty. Everything has the earmarks of being OK. The driver's side door is unlocked. I open it and rummage around. Nothing has been damaged; even the keys are in the ignition. I push the unlock button and go to the gate in the rear of the van. When I lift it up, all of the boxes from the auction are there, but not as I had packed them. Whoever had taken the van had done a better and neater job of positioning them than even I had. The boxes are also taped differently and more securely than is my practice. They had without question searched all of the boxes and had been extraordinarily attentive to insuring nothing got damaged. Normally, I would just lock up the van and empty it later in the morning. However, a combination of curiosity, nervousness, and my obsessive-compulsiveness makes me go back inside, walk up the stairs, and get the keys to the house out of my pants that are hanging over the back of a chair in my bedroom. There Gloria is in her robe at the door about to go downstairs. She asks, "Is it

152

George's van?"

"Yes, ma'am. And everything turns out to be present. I'm going to go move it into the garage and take the boxes inside so that we can inspect them for damage and see if anything is missing."

She rushes down the stairs and goes outside to confirm that. When I catch up with her, she is greatly relieved. "What did those sons of bitches want with the van?"

"Hell, if I know. But whatever it was, it wasn't in the van."

When I drive the van into the garage, I say to myself, *I better call the cops and have them check for fingerprints. Come to think of it, they probably won't want me to unload the boxes.* Once back in the kitchen, I go to the portable phone sitting on the countertop next to the refrigerator and dial 911.

"9-1-1"

"I need the police to come to my house and dust my son's van for fingerprints."

"May I ask why?"

I immediately realize how odd that must have sounded. "Oh, I'm sorry. My son's van had been stolen last night and then this morning shows up in front of my house. I thought that if there were any fingerprints from the culprits left on the van that might help catch whoever did it."

"Let me get this straight. They stole your van yesterday and then returned it to your house this morning."

"That's right."

"Anything stolen from your van or damaged?"

"No, not that I can tell."

The operator asks a question that makes me rethink this entire situation. "You sure this wasn't some stupid practical joke?"

One person comes to mind, Paul! "No ma'am, but, if it is, you will be arresting me on murder charges later today."

"What was that, sir?"

"You made me think about a friend of mine who is devious enough and capable of doing this. I'll get back to you."

Despite the hour of the day, I call Mitch. "Hello, Mitch. This is Ernie. Do you have any idea where Paul is staying?"

"Ernie, have you looked outside? It's still dark! And why do you care about that?"

"Because I think he took George's van yesterday and not long ago returned it to my house."

"Come again."

"You heard me. Someone just parked the van outside of my house."

"And you think Paul did it?"

I am certain of it. "Mitch, who else would do such a thing?"

"You do have a strong case. However, this is way over the top even for him."

"Again, who else would've done such a crazy prank?"

"Ernie, someone who was after that vase. Have you called the police?"

"9-1-1 is who got me thinking it was Paul."

"Call them again."

Before I have a chance to do that, Gloria races back into the house screaming to me. "You better come help me get those damn dogs before all of our neighbors call animal control and have them picked up. I don't want to go to doggy court again and pay another fine for their barking."

I go down to the basement to get their leads. As we leave to retrieve the beagles from hell, we can hear them chasing something in the next street over. "Gloria, we may not need to call the police. They maybe are already coming to pay us a visit."

"I hate those dogs. I have mentioned that to you before, haven't I? When George wanted a dog, I told you it was OK. One dog I said. I never agreed to two dogs."

"But they're litter mates. You wouldn't want just one. It would get lonely."

If she could have, Gloria would have lynched me on the closest tree with one of those leads. "Lonely, my ass. Ever since we got those damn dogs, we've been the talk of the neighborhood. People, who I didn't even know existed, recognize me and come up to me at the grocery store solely to badger me about how appreciative they are of our dogs serenading them at all hours of the day and night. And how about those lovely anonymous letters we receive with printouts on the latest technology in bark control? Best of all, everyone in the neighborhood has our telephone number on speed dial to notify us that our dogs are bothering them. Hell, I would love to feel a little lonely."

When the dogs sense we are approaching them, they cease their hunt for the neighbor's squirrel and dash further away. I concede the futility of our pursuing them. "We better just go back home and wait for them to come back on their own as they always eventually do."

As we turn around and the yelping grows more remote, we can see our home, Gloria asks, "Is that a police car in front of our house?"

Chapter 12

I answer, "No, there are two police cars in front of our house."

In a minute, Gloria proclaims, "Ernie, better make that three police cars."

All of the bad memories of my previous run-ins with the police over our dogs, which I have suppressed since my last one, surge to my consciousness. I stop walking and let out a deep sigh. "The dogs must have really pissed off the neighbors for them to have three police cars called to our house."

She does not slow down and glances back towards me, motioning first to me and then towards where the two dogs seem to be far in the distance. "To hell with you and those damn dogs. You're on your own."

The police and I have come to an understanding about my dogs. Beagles let their noses rule their brains and, consequently, are never at the top of their obedience classes. Except for eating, which they do whenever the opportunity presents itself, tracking and hunting are paramount to their id. For them, what is hunting without baying? How am I to undo what centuries of inbreeding has perfected? The cops fully appreciate all of this. They know my beagles, boy do they know them, and agree that with my line of work I need good watchdogs at home. However, my neighbors shell out the taxes that pay their salaries. They, therefore, must satisfy the good citizens who live on my block and in the half-mile radius from my house that my dogs' howls travel and can be heard.

The county and I have confronted squarely and dealt decisively with my beagles' transgressions. In order to bring peace to the subdivision, when the cops come with their blue lights flashing to my house to arrest my dogs, they apologetically hand me the ticket and I gracefully accept it from them in a kind of businesslike transaction. Since it happens so frequently, Dumb and Dumber currently have their own public defender in doggy court, who arranges their bail. I no longer personally have to appear there to enter a plea; rather, the Clerk of the Court has my current credit card information on file allowing the county to receive a steady flow of income from me. The additional police presence from their visits to my house that is enjoyed by my neighbors and that I personally support through this arrangement offsets whatever inconvenience they must endure from the indiscretions of my beagles.

This morning's event may have indeed violated my pact with the cops. I can only imagine what the fine will be. Despite sauntering as slowly as physics will allow and taking the longest possible route home, I do finally arrive there with my spiel well rehearsed, *Officers, I can explain everything that happened. It wasn't the dog's fault. We just had an unusual occurrence. It couldn't be avoided.*

There must be six plainclothes and uniform officers standing in front of my driveway bathed in blue from the flashing light bars on top of their squad cars. Before hearing me out, the police captain pulls out his handcuffs and starts to play with them. "Ernie, I want you to meet Agent Johnson. He's with the FBI."

I am taken aback, to say the least. "Since when is barking a federal offense?"

In his navy blue windbreaker with embroidered "**FBI**" in yellow over his heart, both upper arms, and back, Agent Johnson is all business. Much taller and thinner than I am, he peers condescendingly down into my eyes as he sneers at me and ignores what I have just said. With one hand he takes off his dark blue cap with raised embroidered "**FBI**" in white on its front to comb his short blonde hair with the fingers of his other hand, before he asks, "Can you explain why a stolen vehicle was spotted at your house less than an hour ago?"

"Yeah, that's why the dogs got out. You see, the dogs heard the tow truck lower my son's van to the street and got all excited."

"Where's the van?"

"In my garage, I moved it there."

He puts his cap back on his head and gazes straight at me. "So, are you confessing to accepting a stolen vehicle?"

What can I say? "I guess if you put it that way, yeah. But the dogs got out when I went to search the van. I didn't realize that they would run away."

"Did you see the tow truck?"

"No. As I just told you, the dogs must've heard it and started making a racket in the house. I went down to find out what they were barking about. By the time I got there, only the van was in the street."

After pausing for a minute, he painstakingly inquires, "How did you tell there was a tow truck if you didn't see it personally?"

I train my fully extended left arm at the uniformed policemen. "Easy, as all of these officers will tell you, I have two beagles that are very good hunters and loud. They saw or heard the truck and started to bay."

One of the officers interjects, "It's true that they are loud, sir. I've heard them!"

Agent Johnson chooses to ignore him. "Did you notify the police that you were taking possession of a stolen vehicle?"

I called 9-1-1 and they brushed me off before I could tell them that! And, after all, it is my son's! "No, Why? Should I have?"

Directing his finger at me, Agent Johnson very seriously asks, "Sir, do you understand how much trouble you are in?"

I turn my head around and hear the far-off barking of my dogs. The sun is barely rising. "I think so. It's a pretty grievous situation."

"Do you mind if we inspect that van and your house?"

I have nothing to hide, but I feel obliged to inform him. "You're free to do so, but I can tell you that the dogs aren't in there."

"Good, they would only get in the way. I'm glad you are cooperating. I understand there were boxes in the back of the stolen van with valuable antiques in them. Do you have the bill of sale for them?"

I am confused. What do the things I bought at the auction have to do with my dogs scampering about the neighborhood awakening everyone? "Absolutely! But may I ask why you want to see them?"

His eyes show the contempt he feels for me. "I'm the one asking the questions, here."

"Do you want me to go get it?"

"Later when we examine the boxes. I want to corroborate that there hasn't been any changes made in their contents."

It finally dawns on me that perhaps he is not talking about my dogs. "I understand you're the one asking the questions, but does this have anything to do with my dogs getting loose and disturbing my neighbors this morning?"

Agent Johnson just stares at me. Finally, he says, "The Bureau could care less what your dogs did this morning, yesterday, or the day before that. I want to uncover what that stolen tow truck delivered here."

He has gotten it all wrong. How do I tell him? He is not the type to take correction well. "But, sir, it was my son's van that was stolen not the tow truck. We had the police investigate that last night. There hasn't been a single stolen government tow truck reported in the metro region."

He does not take my righting the facts well. "It was the tags on the truck that were stolen. I've been in three states searching for them. Last night someone reported them and this morning here they are at your doorstep. Why?"

"You're not listening! That's why I called the cops last night."

"Well, I don't buy that. You don't go to the White House and steal U.S. Government property for nothing, particularly, license plates. You have any clue to what you are able to do with them on your vehicle?"

I have not the foggiest idea what their significance is, but I am not about to ask him either. "Yes, sir."

His face is flush. "Don't yes sir me. Those tags belong to the Secret Service. And they want them back yesterday. Do you understand me?"

His anger only blossoms when I ask, "Why would someone rip-off Secret Service plates?"

"Good question! Unfortunately for me, I'm the one they ordered to find that out and get them back. Twenty years at the Bureau and I'm scouring the country for petty theft."

"Do you want to see the boxes now?"

He calms down and acquiesces. "I guess so."

We all descend upon my garage, which is down a little hill on the basement level of the house. Gloria has sneaked into the house via the back door and brewed some coffee. While they surround George's van talking amongst themselves, she opens the basement's door to the garage and asks, "Anyone want some coffee?"

162

The police captain speaks for the group. "Yes, ma'am. That's very kind of you. By the way, where are your dogs? Usually, when we come here they greet us."

As if on cue, Dumb and Dumber walk into the garage, thirsty. I tell Gloria, "The dogs would like some water, if you please."

She is not pleased and her tone of voice attests to that. "Do they want bottled spring water or will filtered tap do, dear?"

One of policemen asks her, "You give your dogs bottled water? You must really love them." She gives him the silent treatment and only glares back at him.

Agent Johnson starts giving orders to the policeman. "Someone dust this van thoroughly for fingerprints, same thing for these boxes. Wear white gloves when you open them. I want everything that can be fingerprinted to be fingerprinted. If I'm being removed from defending our country from terrorists to discover the punk, who lifted some license plates in DC, I'm damn well going to do so."

I feel this might be a good time to invite him into the house. "You're welcome to come in. I don't think there is anything in here that will be helpful to you."

"You're an antiques dealer aren't you?"

"Why, yes I am."

"Do you deal in Tiffany?"

"On occasion. Is there something you wish to buy?"

163

"Oh no. I couldn't afford anything as expensive as that. Did you hear that some idiot yesterday paid $600,000 for a tiny silver vase made by them? Can you believe that? He must have more money than brains. Or have clients that do."

How do you respond to that? After thinking it over, I mention, "I'm that idiot."

He is neither embarrassed nor apologetic. "No kidding. Then perhaps you can answer me this. Why is it worth so much?"

Sensing his interest is genuine and not flippant, I give him an honest reply. "It's a spectacular one of a kind object made for a World's Fair. Why do you ask?"

"Because there's a lot of interest in that vase at the Bureau. I think one of the old-time higher ups, who must have some dough, was considering bidding on it."

I am pleased to hear that. If Leonard's offer fails to materialize, I may have another customer for it. "Does he collect Tiffany?"

"No. Kennedy memorabilia, mainly stuff related to JFK's assassination."

"Then why would he be interested in that vase?"

"He didn't say. I thought you might have been told if it had been in the Kennedy family."

"That would be news to me. I bought it because it was one of the twelve Tiffany Columbian Exposition vases. It didn't come with any provenance."

He is no longer angry. In fact, he is most pleasant. "You wouldn't have it here so that I can see it?"

"Oh no, I don't keep anything that expensive at my home. I have it stored in a secure location."

"Good. From what I heard, a lot of people are interested in that vase. Supposedly, it vanished several decades ago. Everyone is curious about where it went."

I have found someone who may actually be able to tell me what all that discussion yesterday was about. "You wouldn't know why would you?"

Agent Johnson shakes his head. "That's a negative. I'm not into antiques. All I can disclose is just that when they heard it was up for auction, they emailed the auction picture to each other."

"Where did you learn it disappeared so long ago?"

"From what I overheard them say."

"What was that?"

With a grin on his face he says, "Look what finally showed up!"

Curious, I press him for more details. "How did they discover it was up for auction? John's auction house is hardly that famous. I mean, it's here, not in New York or London."

"We routinely surf the auction Internet sites for stolen items or material evidence in a criminal investigation. You'll be surprised what's available there if you only search for it. I've even picked up a terrorist who was stupid enough to buy a Top Secret Army manual on how to make bombs off of eBay."

"That's impressive. It must've taken you months to have done that."

"Nah. It wasn't that hard. Who do you think was selling the manual? Me, of course! The Army collaborated with the Bureau on this one. If he had actually gotten it, he would have had our entire database on explosives and the designs for weapons utilizing them. We showed just enough pages to convince him it was the real deal, but nothing that Al-Qaeda didn't already have.

"However, our meat and potatoes business with them is the used car sites. We find stolen vehicles, getaway cars used in bank robberies, and really fancy sports cars being sold by swindlers on Wall Street after the SEC indicts them."

I could understand the first two but not the last one. "Why the fancy sports cars?"

"Listen, those crooks hide their assets however they can. Those cars are registered in their deceased grandparents' names, their kids' name, and even their dog's name."

Recalling my two dogs, I found that hard to believe. "In their dogs' names?"

"Yeah, that's their favorite ploy. The dogs don't talk and don't divorce them. One of those chiseler's dogs owned both a Bugatti Veyron and a Lamborghini Reventon."

"Out of curiosity, how much were they worth?"

"A little more that $3,000,000. And it wasn't easy connecting the dots between the dog and that flimflammer. He used his wife's maiden name for the dog's surname."

"How did you eventually figure it out?"

Agent Johnson smiles. "No matter how smart they think they are, they always screw up on the details."

"And how did he screw up?"

"When you register a car, you need auto insurance. The cars' insurance was in his name, not his dog's. As you undoubtedly know, auto insurance companies do credit checks on their policyholders. The government doesn't yet issue social security numbers to dogs. However, the dog was credit worthy since he had at least two Swiss bank accounts and outright owned a Manhattan apartment on the Upper East Side without a mortgage."

I must admit that I am impressed. "You haven't answered my question about how the FBI discovered the vase was up for sale. It's not been reported stolen as best as John can tell, nor is it on the Interpol list."

He shakes his head. "I don't think it's anything that notorious. Best as I can tell, it's just part of an old urban legend that the old-timers in the Bureau believe in."

"Well then, what does the vase have to do with those stolen license plates?"

For the first time I sense that he is being disingenuous with me when he replies, "I never said it did. Why do you ask?"

He is the federal agent. Should he have not figured this out? "Obviously, Agent Johnson, whoever stole those tags was after the vase."

"I don't think you have the evidence to make that exact assumption. However, the Bureau is interested in who you bought the vase for."

He was privy to the answer to his question, "Do you deal in Tiffany?" before he had asked it. It is time for me to be circumspect about revealing my customers. "To be perfectly honest, I bought it with one client in mind, but he has yet to see it and commit to buying it. So, I guess I have to say it was a speculative buy."

"That's a shame. We were hoping that your customer might have a link to the theft in a counterintuitive way."

I am glad I did not name Leonard. "I don't quite follow you."

"The thief went straight from D.C. to here. Whoever he is does not want that vase to be sold by you."

"Is that what you believe?"

"I haven't been briefed enough about that vase to have any beliefs, but that's what the old-timers in the Bureau believe: someone immediately went to extraordinary lengths to deep-six that vase once it resurfaced."

Being in my robe all this while and not moving about, I am beginning to feel chilly. The policemen appear to be doing exactly what Agent Johnson wants. Anyhow, he is not issuing any further instructions to them and I can tell that he is not through with me. "Sure you don't want to come in?"

Chapter 13

Agent Johnson tells two policemen, "Get the boxes out of the van and bring them into the house." He turns to me. "Where should they take them?"

"The den will be best."

Indicating me with his hand, he instructs them, "Follow him and take them to the den."

The officers carefully place all of the boxes save one on the hand truck I have stored in the van. I lead the way. Agent Johnson shadows me and shepherds the officer with the trolley and the officer who is carrying the other box into the den. We follow the trail in my basement to the elevator to the two top floors. It is a path marked by junk, kitchen supplies that we do not have room for in the kitchen, and old furniture. I press the call car button. Agent Johnson asks, "Aren't you afraid a burglar could use the elevator to get into your house from the basement?"

"Not likely. Whenever we leave the house, we have the cab stationed in the kitchen and then turn off the power to the elevator."

When the cab arrives, I open the outer door and then the scissor door. He immediately detects the noticeable problem with its size. "Can we all fit in it?"

"Of course not. Just leave the boxes in it. I'll send it up to the first floor. We'll walk up the stairs to the kitchen. By the time we get there, it will be there."

After I press the button marked two and close both the scissor door and the outer door, I take them along the route to the stairs. One of the policemen jokes, "You need a guide just to maneuver in your basement."

I snap back. "Comes with being a pack-rat, which is an occupational hazard when you're an antiques dealer. We never throw anything away. Who knows what it will be worth?"

Once we are in the kitchen, Gloria hands each of us a cup of coffee. "This should wake you all up. I grind my own beans."

After each of them thanks her, they follow me to the den through the dining room. I good-naturedly warn them, "Don't touch anything. If you break it, it's yours and you'll have just bought it."

Agent Johnson scans the mahogany judges paneling that covers the walls of the large room as well as the display cases full of my own various collections before asking, "Anything in here not an antique?"

"Except for the TV and Gloria, no."

They place the boxes on the late nineteenth century Persian rug while I go retrieve my box cutter from the kitchen. When I return, he is on his knees fingering the tape on the boxes. "Where did you get this tape?"

"I didn't. The cheap plastic tape that John supplied me was removed. Whoever took the van replaced it with this stuff. It's definitely better than what I got."

"You can say that again. It's WAT."

171

"What's WAT?"

"Water-activated tape, it's the same type we use for forensics. Its hidden image technology provides a tamper evident seal. It's also tough as nails since it contains multiple layers with fiberglass reinforcement. Whoever took your van didn't go to a UPS store to have its boxes repacked."

"Why would they go to all that trouble?"

"It's strange; I'll agree to that. Unless, of course, they planned on keeping whatever is in these boxes and wanted to verify no one else got into them."

I shake my head. "You're making no sense. There is nothing in these boxes that would warrant such precautions. Most of these boxes are going to be shipped to my customers after they send me a down payment for them."

Agent Johnson stands up from kneeling on the carpet and goes down into the garage. He brings back the Captain. "What do you think, Captain?"

"It wouldn't be the first time someone tried to do it this way. I'll call for the dogs and get the DEA over here."

If Gloria's coffee has not fully awakened me yet, this does. My adrenalin is peaking. "What are you talking about and what dogs are you calling for? I've got enough trouble with the two I have here."

The Captain explains, "Drug dealers use that same tape to seal packages containing cocaine and heroin, among other drugs."

Again with drug dealers, once more I get that icy shudder bolting down my spine feeling. "Why?"

"They can tell in an instant if some law enforcement agent has opened a box. If they have, the drug dealers won't go near the parcel. They'll refuse delivery. That way we have no evidence on them."

This is all new to me. "Why would they do it this way? Don't they expect me to open the boxes before I would ship them to my customers?"

Agent Johnson intervenes. "You make the assumption they were planning on returning the cartons to you. Plainly, we were mistaken. They weren't after that vase after all. They wanted to use the antiques as a cover for the drugs. What I can't figure out is what convinced them to stop their scheme and bring them back to you."

"Well, I'm glad they did. I need the money to cover my checks to John."

He laughs. "You don't understand. All of the containers and their contents will be evidence. It's going to be years before you'll get these antiques back."

I groan before saying, "Oh, shit!"

"Yeah, oh, shit."

"Do we have to wait on the dogs? I really want to see what's inside them. After all, it's going to cost me a fortune if there's drugs in them."

Agent Johnson grabs the box cutter, sits back down on the rug, and starts to open one of the boxes. "No, we don't. I need the dogs for the van."

"Why the van?"

"It may be full of dope in its side paneling."

I plunk down onto a down stuffed Victorian wing chair while watching this nightmare unfold before my eyes. I rub my face with both of my hands. All I can think is *why me*. Agent Johnson gently opens the cardboard box. Shredded newspaper falls out of it. With his right hand, he pulls out a small clump of bubble wrap that is sealed with clear tape. He then puts both of his hands into the box and lifts out a much larger piece of bubble wrap also sealed with clear tape. More shredded newspaper flies onto the rug in a large circle. I can tell that it is heavy by how carefully he places it down on the rug. He then cuts away the tape and unfurls the bubble wrap. My eyes grow big while anticipating what I will and will not see. "Damn, it's that cut glass decanter. And there aren't any drugs in that box."

"Yeah, that's one down and how many to go?"

Mindful to preserve any evidence, he expertly proceeds to open each parcel. None of them contains anything other than what I had bought at the auction, and there is no drugs mixed in with them. I go to the desk in the corner of the den and get the sales receipt from John. I read off the list of items and Agent Johnson agrees that they are all there. He shows interest in only one of them: the mystery surprise box. "Why did you buy this?"

"I paid $2.00 for it. No matter what it is, you can

174

make money off of anything you buy at an auction for $2.00."

He opens the box and pulls out a rifle. "You have a license to sell this?"

"Of course, I do. Do you want to see it?" I reach for the top drawer of my desk.

"No, I trust you. What's the most one of these brings?"

"If in unused condition about $250.00 retail."

He holds up the rifle to inspect it. "Do you ever get an unused World War II Italian military rifle?"

"No, they're primarily on the Internet. I see its outside shows its age, but what do you think of this one otherwise?"

Before looking down the barrel, he grasps the bolt and pulls it back to establish that the chamber is empty. "I'm certainly no authority on them, but I an familiar enough with weapons. This one hasn't seen much action nor has it been oiled recently. You can tell that by its having some rust on the firing pin and spring. However, it's in such good shape that I wouldn't be surprised if its inners had been worked on years ago. If my memory serves me, Oswald used one of these same rifles to assassinate Kennedy."

I shrug my shoulders. "I wouldn't know anything about that. I'm going to put it out on my table at 'the show' and let one of the gun dealers there steal it from me on set up day."

"How much will you get for it?"

"Since the dealers won't have to clean up the firing mechanism other than removing that rust, perhaps a hundred dollars if it's inners are otherwise in as good an overall shape as you say they are."

"What will the gun dealer probably get for it?"

"It depends. As I said, $250 at most. Unlike machine guns and pistols, the majority of World War II rifles are worth more as scrap or parts than they are as rifles. That Italian rifle will probably be bought for target practice or perhaps rabbit hunting since whoever owned it before comes across as having intended to use it that way. Only an occasional buyer seriously collects them and then they want them to be in pristine condition. I don't really get into all of that. I just wholesale them to the gun dealers. I treat them right and they treat me right. Guns like this just help pay the booth rent for me."

He begins to gather up all of the shredded newspaper that covers the area in front of him on the rug. "Do you use this stuff routinely?"

I chuckle. "Hell no! John gives us cheap paper to pack up with. Whoever repacked my things went to a lot of expense to safeguard them."

"I've made quite a mess."

"It's all part of the business. As bad as that stuff is, those plastic peanuts are the worst. They stick to everything. It must be some static electricity thing. You can waste minutes trying to get them off of your hands or clothing. I hate using them. I'll get the vacuum."

176

Agent Johnson is perplexed. "Since there are no drugs in those parcels, you can keep your things. Hopefully, the van will also be clean. Do you have any idea why someone would steal Secret Service license plates, put them on a tow truck, then steal your son's van, take your boxes, empty them, then repackage them with the most expensive packing material and tape available, and return everything to you in the morning? It defies all logic, except if they were after that vase all along."

"You'll get no argument from me on that score. But have you considered that they were searching for something else and didn't find it. My friend, Mitch, agrees with your old-timers that they were after the Tiffany vase and returned everything when they discovered it wasn't in the van. But it could turn out to be a red herring."

"The vase wouldn't explain the license plates. They were stolen before the auction. Who warned them in advance to come after you or for that matter whoever else was going to get it? No, the vase, as you just suggested, has to be a red herring. Something else must've attracted them to you."

"For the life of me, I can't imagine that you are right. Should I feel honored that someone would go to all of this effort to steal my son's van to get to me? What else have I done?"

After we clean up the mess made by the packing material on my rug, Agent Johnson is about to leave for the garage and wait for the drug sniffing dogs when I go back again to my desk but this time to retrieve the opened envelope with the return address for the Allied Commercial Credit Company. After I hand it to him, he asks, "What's this?"

"It may help answer your question. The driver of the tow truck gave it to the valet parking attendant at The Blue And The Gay yesterday evening."

He takes the sheet of paper from inside and reads from it out loud, "Dear Sir: Your van has been repossessed for failure to pay last month's payment. Sincerely, The Allied Commercial Credit Company." He then inspects the photo of our van, its license plate, and a copy of the loan agreement. He asks, "How long after the auction did you get this letter?"

"At most 3 hours."

Holding on to them with his right hand, he waves the envelope and its contents in the air while shaking his head. "How would they have had the time to get all of this done if it was the vase they wanted? They had to target you beforehand!"

"I don't know unless somebody reported to whoever they are that I had won the vase immediately after I had done so."

"Even then it would have taken too long to have gotten the ACCC to approve this action. That would have had to have happened before the auction had started." He stops to rub his chin before completing his thought. "However, not if this is a forgery." Consequently, he holds the letter up to a light and pores over it intently. "Damn, it's the real McCoy."

"How can you say that?"

178

"The Agency has a special code placed as a watermark on all of the ACCC's paperwork. The watermark tells you who sent it. And this has it."

"Perhaps, it's stolen."

Agent Johnson scolds me with his eyes. "You don't steal anything from the Agency. If it's not them, someone from within it gave the envelope and paper to whoever took your son's van. But why?"

I blurt out, "Because an informant advised them that I was going to get the vase at the auction unless they did."

"Who would have been in a position to have done that?"

"Ira."

"Whose Ira?"

"Ira Wynn is the dean of the New York Tiffany dealers. He told me that one of my customers, Leonard, has been boasting to anyone who would listen to him that he was getting the Tiffany Wild-Rose Vase."

He is not impressed. "That doesn't mean a damn thing. Lots of people go into auctions claiming that they will be taking something home only to be disappointed."

Agent Johnson has been holding back on me. "You seem to know a thing or two about auctions."

"I haven't been chasing down terrorists my entire career. I've cracked a few auction scams in my day. You would be pleased to hear that I even was involved in a Tiffany theft early on."

"Which one?"

"Some mausoleum window from a cemetery in Brooklyn. It made all of the New York papers."

"You're not talking about the Alastair Duncan scandal, are you?"

"Yeah, him and a guy named Casamassina."

"Well, I didn't bid $600,000 for that vase without believing that Leonard would back me up."

"He's that well off?"

I smile. "If he wants something, he'll pay what it takes."

Agent Johnson leaves for the garage and I join Gloria in the kitchen. She asks, "Well, did he find anything?"

"No. Everything is as it should be. He's baffled. He can't explain what happened or why?"

"I'm going to be ecstatic when they leave. This past 24 hours has been just too stressful."

I check the clock on the wall. "Do you think it's too early to call Leonard?"

"He's on Central Time. You'll definitely need to call him on one of his cell phones."

I do just that but strangely get an error message on each of them stating that it is not in service.

Chapter 14

Leonard, more precisely Ignacio Vargas Leonarte, is an enigma to me. He is larger than life, both in his body size and his persona. He and a portion of his family came over from Cuba during the Mariel boatlift. Dirt poor as a child, he moved to Texas from Miami and made it big in the oil business, not here in the United States, but in South America and the Gulf of Mexico. How he earns a living is obscure. I guess the closest explanation he has given me to what I believe is the truth is that he is a facilitator. He makes deals happen, really big deals. The drilling for oil, its transportation, and its refinement are technicalities in the geopolitical world of energy. The big picture (who gets what contract, which government officials must be persuaded, and the terms of the final negotiations) is his forte. While never physically in the room when the haggling is occurring, his presence is always felt. Normally, he forges hookers, bribes, and the threat of blackmail into handshakes. His is not the type of man who usually has the sophistication needed to appreciate the nuances of Art Nouveau.

Regardless, Tiffany is his weakness, particularly exhibition pieces. Leonard pays only in cash, usually from a suitcase carried by his secretary. Flown in by his private jet, she can consummate a purchase even faster than a bank transfer. Since he is in oil, the ups and downs of its pricing directly affects his enthusiasm for Tiffany in an almost manic fashion. The higher the price of oil, the more choice an item must be to interest him. Finally, Leonard's word is his bond. Once he agrees to buy it, he never hesitates. He is the only customer I have who doesn't get buyer's remorse.

Even if Leonard had not told everyone that he is going to get it, I am still confident the Wild-Rose Vase will be an immediate sale with him. It meets all of his acquisition criteria: rarity, beauty, and, most of all, two other buyers at the auction wanted it as much as he did. There is an element of one-upmanship in antiques. Even if a collector does not like an object, the mere fact that others do and will pay a hefty premium to obtain it, especially at an auction, makes him want it all the more. Take Tiffany lava glass. I have never understood why it always brings more than the estimate. More intriguing is the fact that, when I do have an example of it, it is the first thing to sell at "the show" and for a whopping profit. For myself, I would not have it anywhere in my house.

Sitting at the kitchen table, I stay fixated on the digital clock hanging on the wall above the refrigerator, waiting for it to display 10 AM at which time Leonard should be at his desk in Dallas. Gloria jars me out of this haze. "A watched pot never boils."

"What's that?" I ask.

"Leonard's not going to get to his office any earlier because your eyes are glued to that clock. Go see what that agent is up to down in the garage."

"I'd rather stay here. He's waiting for some drug sniffing dogs and the DEA."

"In that case, go call the customers whose pieces we just got back. We need the money."

In all the excitement of the morning, I had forgotten that I was supposed to do just that. "You're right. Let me go get my address book." I move on to the desk in the

183

den and pull it out of the top drawer. Sitting in that Victorian wing chair, I start dialing my customers on my cell phone. Everyone is happy with what I got and the prices I paid for their lots. What started out as a very bad day is turning into a very good day. By tomorrow morning, except for the money for the vase, my obligations will be covered. Inspired by the prospect of a financial resurrection, I briskly move the stuff off of the den's rug onto the dining room table where I will pack them for shipping.

Gloria yells from the kitchen, "It's 10 AM. Go call Leonard."

Leonard's office number is on the speed dial directory of my cell phone. I stop what I am doing and settle down at the dining room table where, while sitting on an armchair, I enter it. His secretary answers, "Energy Solutions of Texas."

"Cynthia, this is Ernie. Is Leonard in? Neither of his cell phones is working!"

"I'm sorry, Ernie, but Leonard is unavailable."

I feel like my breath has been kicked out of me. He has never turned down one of my calls, no matter what he was doing. Once the shock from this is over, I take in a deep gulp of air and ask, "Cynthia, when should I call back?"

"Honestly, I don't know."

My heart starts racing. What am I to do? The $600,000 check will clear tomorrow! I decide to be bold. After all, I have nothing to lose. "What's up?"

"He's out of the country and can't be reached."

Leonard can always be reached. Both his personal and business cell phone numbers are also on my cell phone's speed dial directory. "I can't believe that."

"Well, Ernie, it's true. Yesterday, he got a call from Havana from his family that is still there that his mother suddenly turned ill and he needed to come to Cuba right away. He left the split second he got State Department clearance."

"Why can't I call him?"

"You can't, I can't. Nobody can get him. Because of the recent hurricane in Cuba, no phone carrier can call into there. He'll have to use a Cuban phone and call you. He's scheduled to call me later today to tell me what's up with his mother and when he should be back in Dallas. Yours will be one of many messages I will need to give him when he does."

"How sick is his mother, Cynthia? I just talked to him two days ago and he didn't mention her being ill."

"He's as surprised as you. She was doing well. Out of nowhere, she's in a hospital in Havana."

"Well, when Leonard calls, tell him how sorry I am about her becoming ill."

"I'll do that. He does have your cell phone number, doesn't he?"

I try to hide my extreme discomfort when I say, "Yeah, he does." When calamity happens in business, one thinks of every imaginable and unimaginable cause. Some seek revenge; I become paranoid. Years of experience have taught me that, when the unexpected bad happens, it usually is not a random event. I recall Ira Wynn's comment after the auction, "My friend, people back out of deals all the time for all sorts of reasons. I'm just suggesting that it would be prudent to take our offer in cash today rather than risk a freak collapse of what you think should be a sure-fire deal tomorrow." What did he know yesterday, and how could he have known it?

Gloria comes into the dining room to find out what Leonard said. "When did he say he'll deliver the money?"

"He didn't!"

Although standing right next to me, she shouts into my ear, "What do you mean he didn't. You said it was a done deal."

I wince before clearing my throat. "It is a done deal. I just can't get hold of him."

"What!"

The more upset she gets, the calmer I try to be. "His mother was hospitalized in Havana and he left yesterday for Cuba. No one can reach him there because of that recent hurricane."

Gloria sits down in one of the side chairs near me. "Oh shit! Was he expecting this?"

"No. Cynthia said it came out of the blue."

"Well, what are we going to do? That check will bounce tomorrow unless we shift our funds."

"I am painfully mindful of that. He's supposed to call Cynthia some time today. She's going to have him call me. Until then, we're going to have to just sit tight."

"That's cutting things too tight. Why don't we just shift the funds and then, if Leonard comes through, shift them back?"

I must admit that is a smarter plan. "OK, go ahead and do it."

Gloria gets up and leaves to call our bank from the kitchen. After I spend the next minute rubbing my eyes, I decide to call Mitch and Helen to ask them if they have any advice. "Mitch, Ernie."

"Ernie, what did the police say?"

"They came here before I called 9-1-1 back."

"How did that happen?"

"As I just found out, the license plates on the tow truck were stolen from the Secret Service at the White House. They came here after that tow truck delivered George's van. Moreover, they're still here."

"What are they saying?"

"The FBI agent isn't convinced that whoever took the van is after the vase."

I can tell Mitch is taken aback by that by the way he

asks, "The FBI is there?"

"Yeah, stealing federal property is a federal crime."

"What does he think they're after?"

"He hasn't a clue. He did say that, whoever they are, they have a contact within the CIA."

"He would! The Bureau is always trying to blame the CIA for anything illegal the government happens to do. What makes him say they're involved?"

"Mitch, you recall that letter from the ACCC. Well, it was written on paper that would have taken the help of a CIA operative to obtain it."

"Yeah, it could've been stolen or snuck out of the Agency. I'll grant him that. What's he doing now?"

"The police and he are waiting in my garage for drug sniffing dogs and the DEA to show up. They want to eliminate a drug dealer being involved in all of this."

He sounds dubious. "I thought we ruled that out last night?"

"We did. It's just that Agent Johnson hasn't. The boxes were wrapped with WAT and that's what drug dealers use."

When it comes to packing materials, Mitch is the expert. He has to be. When you routinely ship million dollar antiques cross country, you better have all of the tricks. I have stumped him with this abbreviation. "What's WAT?"

"I asked him the same thing. It's a special paper tape that conclusively shows that a package has been tampered with."

That satisfies him temporarily. "So, why did you call?"

"Mitch, something funny just happened."

Before I can finish my sentence, he interrupts, "And the rest of the stuff that happened to you today isn't funny?"

"Well, you're right, of course. But something really odd has happened and I need your and Helen's advice."

"What could that be?"

I again try to be calm. "Leonard got called out of the country on an emergency basis yesterday to visit his mother in Havana. He can't be reached. I'm screwed."

Mitch, who likes to joke about everything, asks, "What's the odd part of this: Leonard being called to go to Cuba or your being screwed?"

"Both, but it's Leonard's being called out that just doesn't seem right."

He promptly becomes serious and suggests, "Have you seen a psychiatrist yet? The stress of the past 24 hours has made you go nuts. I've never heard of anyone going to that length to kibosh a deal. Things happen to our parents, usually at the least opportune time."

"So, you don't think the New York dealers had

anything to do with it?"

Mitch is growing really concerned about my state of mind. "No! Rather than being paranoid, you need to figure out what you are going to do to cover that check and sell that vase straightaway."

I, though, have other issues I want resolved. "What about that message not to sell the vase?"

"You do need to see a shrink!"

No, I do not. I need an answer to what the hell is going on. "Why do you say that?"

"Because you need the money and who would be crazy enough to heed a wacky anonymous message like that?"

"After all that's happened to me recently, what should I believe?"

He decides to lay it on the line for me. "Take my advice. If Leonard doesn't come through today, start calling Ira. If he was willing to offer you $700,000 yesterday for that vase, he'll pay you $600,000 today, no matter how crazy his customer is. Boy, does that vase attract the nuts."

"But he said the offer was only good for yesterday, and he meant it."

Being a Tiffany lamp dealer, Mitch has dealt with Ira many times before. "That's just New York dealer BS. I get it all the time with my lamps. They figure that if they put the pressure on you, you'll cave in. The way they act, you would think that some of them got started in the boiler rooms on Wall Street."

I have my misgivings. "Why would that make that lady call me just after the auction?"

"Maybe she was there or maybe she saw that cable news clip about you. Your number is in the book."

"Assuming you're right, any idea what her motive may have been?"

"I guess she just wants to buy it from you."

Sometimes I say something really stupid. This is one of those times. "She could have done that at the auction by outbidding me."

"If she were dumb, that's exactly what she would've done. If she were smart, she would approach you after the auction, just like she's doing."

"And the reason why is?"

"You saw the way that bidding was going. Hell, she would have probably ended up having to pay over a million dollars for it since nothing was going to make you stop."

He is right, of course. "So, you think she decided to just buy it outright from me after the auction."

"If I were her, that's what I would've done. It's bound to be cheaper than entering that insane bidding war between you and that Hispanic dealer, who may have bid you up just for spite once he saw her come in."

191

"Speaking of him, do you think John would give me his name and contact information?"

Up until my asking that, Mitch had not considered me to be that desperate. "Why? You're going to sell it to him?"

"I may not have a choice in the matter. Gloria wants that vase sold ASAP."

As if on cue, Gloria comes back into the dining room. "Leonard's on the home phone. He says he's been trying to get you, but you've been on your cell phone all morning."

Chapter 15

The closest landline phone is in my den on the desk. I scurry back over to it to talk to Leonard, who is paying God only knows how much a minute to talk to me. I do not take the time to sit down and remain standing. "Leonard, I'm so sorry to hear about your mother. How's she doing?"

"Ernie, it's the damnedest thing. Her doctor called her up and told her to go to the hospital immediately. Some lab test had come back that showed that she was desperately ill, even though she felt fine. He had her admitted to what they call here an ICU, but even Parkland has better."

"Sounds like a lab error to me. Even here it happens!"

"You're a doctor and have to defend even the Cuban doctors, but she told me she hadn't had any lab tests in weeks. Nevertheless, he scared the shit out of my family and they called me and told me to get down here before she dies."

"How's she doing?"

"She's fine. She wants to go home, but they won't let her out."

"What do they say she has?"

"No one will talk to me, particularly, her doctor. I tell the nurses that I will be in the waiting room, but he doesn't come out to speak to me. I think he's scared of me. I do have a reputation down here in Havana."

Being all too familiar with what frequently happens when errors are made in hospitals, I note, "Perhaps he's ashamed of making a misdiagnosis and having you fly in from Dallas."

"I thought about that. But if that were the case, why hasn't he released her?"

"Doesn't make any sense to me either."

Fortunately, Leonard brings up the vase since I fear transitioning from his mother's hospitalization to it would be most indelicate for me to do. "Well, did you get the vase? I was about to call you to find out if you had won it, oh, I mean had your pilot customer come through, when I got that call. The timing couldn't have been worse. Funny thing about it was that it came from some Cuban official in Havana, who said he was calling on behalf of my family, who for some reason couldn't get hold of me, something about not enough civilian lines to Dallas from Havana after their hurricane."

Relieved by his question, I at last sit in the wing chair. "Yes, he did. But it wasn't cheap."

"How much did you pay?"

I try to be non-dramatic about the price when I say, "$600,000."

Leonard is surprised by it, to say the least. He raises his voice and speaks in a higher pitch when he declares, "I told you it wouldn't come cheap, but $600,000! That's

194

twice what the Daisy Vase went for."

"No kidding, but a strange bidding war developed over it. Some New York dealers and a Hispanic dealer kept bidding it up."

"Were they insane?"

"I thought so, but my friend Mitch talked to the Hispanic dealer after the bidding and he said I got a bargain."

That does not assuage his feeling that I had been ripped-off by the other dealers. "Why the hell did he say that, Ernie? It doesn't sound like a bargain to me."

"Mitch said he asked if I knew the history behind the vase, which of course I don't."

He then poses a question that stuns me. "He wouldn't have thought it came from Havana originally with a notorious past?"

"Why do you ask that? I say that because that Hispanic dealer and another one claimed that there is a duplicate of it in Havana at the Museo Nacional de Bellas Artes. That caused quite a stir at the preview."

After all these years of selling to him, I finally learn where Leonard found his passion for Tiffany. "At the turn of the last century there was a lot of Tiffany in Havana. Batista had some of the best pieces taken out of the country before the revolution's victory to 'insure their safety.' Eventually, they followed him to Portugal. Despite being a communist, Castro came from money and knew the artistic value of Tiffany, which, as it so happened, began having its current resurgence in popularity and price around the time he gained power. In the early days of his rule, after the US broke off diplomatic relations, he was forced to sell some of the liquid Cuban valuables that he had just expropriated. Antiques, including the Tiffany, raised much needed dollars since Eisenhower had also frozen all the Cuban assets in the United States. In point of fact, rumor in the Cuban community is that he was so short of dollars that one way he paid off his spies in the US was with Tiffany. Everyone in Miami is suspicious of anyone from Cuba, who owns a real Tiffany lamp or a rare piece of Tiffany glass and is not a recognized collector, like me."

Both out of curiosity and from being a dealer, I ask, "Well, if it did come from Havana does that increase its value as that Hispanic dealer implied?"

"As odd as it may seem, that's never come up. It's an interesting question. The Cubans who do own Tiffany that came from Havana, regardless of how they got it, don't sell it. It's willed to their children or grandchildren with a strict proviso to never sell it unless they are in desperate financial straits. And then only to another Cuban."

"Why's that?"

He pauses. I take it to indicate that he is being careful about what he is about to say. We both grasp that this call is being monitored. "You've got to understand Cubans. We all hope to come back. It would be a betrayal to our homeland to sell to Americans anything of value from here. It's all supposed to be reinstated when we come home to Cuba."

"So, would a Cuban pay another Cuban a premium for something that he truly knew had come from Havana in order to be able to return it to Cuba?"

He again hesitates, but this time to consider the question, itself. "I guess so. It certainly would make sense; but, as I said, I've never heard of it being done above all at an auction."

I become specific. "What about a duplicate to the one in that museum?"

"The issues, of course, are which was the real one from the Columbian Exposition and were there ever two of them in Cuba. And if it did come from Cuba via Castro, what did it pay for, and who owned it for fifty years and then sold it yesterday?"

The trace of suspicion about the authenticity of my vase that he just raised has me concerned. Does he really believe mine may not be the original? I am compelled to reassure him. "As for your second question, who owned it? Only John knows and he was requested not to reveal that. However, we debated your first question after the auction. My friend Paul thinks that Tiffany may have made a second one later on for the Presidential Palace. Having seen the bottom of the one I bought, I have no misgiving about its being the original."

His Cuban pride shows. "Don't be so cocky. Spanish silversmiths had been doing champlevé enamel long before LCT used it in that vase. Before the revolution, we had silversmiths capable of duplicating it here. So, it could have been copied here or in Spain."

One matter remains for him to explain. "How about

the markings, Leonard?"

"Yeah, you've got me there. I can't fathom why they would have cared to have put the exact same markings on the bottom unless, of course, whoever was exporting the real Tiffany didn't want it revealed that he was taking it out of the country and, therefore, had a duplicate made to hide the fact that the original was gone."

"That's entirely plausible. Even Castro must have had enough Cuban pride to have not wanted it trumpeted about Havana that he was using its historical treasures for currency."

"Ernie, you don't think his brother is trying to buy them back after all this time?"

"I'm not privy to who was backing that Hispanic dealer; but they had a deep pocket, fortunately not as deep as mine."

"You mean mine, don't you?"

I laugh nervously. "Of course, I do, Leonard."

"Obviously, he and his backer feel as secure as you do as to its being the real Columbian Exposition piece."

"There is a small mark that is only on those vases, which tells who the enameler was for each of those vases. Its presence is not published and is not common knowledge. It also doesn't show up in any of the photographs of the bottoms of those vases. Mine has it."

"You think he knew about the mark?"

"It's possible. However, it may be a moot point. He seemed to be more of an authority about that vase than anyone else at the auction, including John."

Leonard has yet to commit to buying the vase. I am beginning to get nervous and even more so when he says, "I'm going to go over to the Museo Nacional and inquire about their vase."

"How come?"

"For what that vase is going to cost me, I want it to be right and exactly what it is supposed to be."

That is not music to my ears. When he said, "Exactly what it is supposed to be," did he mean exactly as it is supposed to be? What do I say? My wallet is demanding an answer without hesitation. My brain deems it is better to be patient than to pressure Leonard, particularly with his mother being in the hospital. "When do you think you'll be able to get back to me?"

"This is Havana, not New York, things move slowly down here."

As I hang up the phone, Gloria approaches me. "So, did he buy it and when do we get the money?"

My face shows the frustration that I am feeling. "He didn't exactly buy it."

"Did he turn it down?"

"No, he didn't turn it down."

"Listen, since when does Leonard futz around when

it comes to buying Tiffany, especially a masterpiece like yours? What's bothering him?"

I sigh. "He wants to see the one in Havana."

His apparent sudden lack of confidence in me sparks her temper. She scornfully asks, "Why the hell does he want to do that?"

"He wants to authenticate that it's 'right and exactly what it is supposed to be.'"

"What are you talking about?"

I am as baffled about this as she is. "Despite the fact that the Hispanic dealer offered $500,000 plus the buyer's premium for it, he still wants to confirm whatever that Hispanic dealer apparently holds true about the vase's history."

"That's crazy. That dealer unequivocally felt it was right. What difference does its history make? What more could Leonard want to learn about it besides its being one of the twelve Tiffany Columbian vases?"

"You're preaching to the choir, Gloria. I think I've convinced him that mine is the true Columbian Exposition piece. It must be some sort of Cuban thing. He won't commit until he hits upon why there are two of them and why one of them is here in the US."

"Well, did he tell you when he would call back?"

Once again, I sigh. "Gloria, he said things move slowly in Havana."

"Great, I better verify the bank has our check covered."

As she leaves, I get up to go to the garage and keep an eye on Agent Johnson. The way today is shaping up; he will probably be towing George's van off to some police impounded vehicle lot. The dogs have arrived and are sniffing all around the van. The DEA agent is talking to Agent Johnson. "It sure sounds suspicious, but we've had no intelligence about something this bizarre going down last night."

"Neither has the Bureau. But just because you all at the DEA didn't hear about it and we at the FBI didn't hear about it, doesn't mean that it didn't happen. Someone went to a lot of expense and effort evidently to do nothing. And there's always the CIA!"

The puzzled DEA agent shakes his head. "I agree. That's what it sounds like, but why are you so persuaded it has to do with drugs or the Company?"

"Because any vehicle with those tags on it would go completely unchallenged anywhere in the US. They're from the Presidential entourage pool and have special secret holograms on them. With those plates, if a drug dealer had them switched onto this van, he could drive it into Langley and the security guard at the gate would salute the driver as he raised the bar without asking any questions. Who else would want to be able to do that and would be willing to take the risk if he were found out. It has to be a drug dealer working with a rogue agent."

"Agent Johnson, you're perhaps right. But it also could be part of some Agency payoff to someone in Pakistan or Afghanistan. And if there are no drugs found in that van, we don't have a case. Period!"

While walking towards them, I smile nervously. "Well, did you find anything?"

Their shoulders sag. In unison they answer, "No."

Hopefully, this part of the nightmare is over. "When does George get his van back?"

Agent Johnson is adamant. "Not until after we've inspected inside the paneling. If someone is using the Agency to transport drugs, I'm going to prove it."

Shocked by his innuendo, I simply stare at him before shortly asking, "You think the CIA is using George's van to traffic drugs?"

"You've got a better explanation of what has happened over the course of the past day."

The DEA agent adds, "They've done it before when they needed to cooperate with drug dealers to get information. More than 14% of the heroin in this country starts out from Afghanistan where Al Qaeda still controls most of its movement. Your guess is as good as mine when it comes to what the CIA may be up to."

"But why me?"

He then throws a curve ball out to me. "Are you familiar with a Mr. Ignacio Vargas Leonarte?"

Leonard! He is interested in Leonard. How come? After thinking about whether or not to answer him, I decide I have nothing to hide and say, "Why? Yes, I am. I was just talking to him."

"About what?"

"About buying something I got at the auction yesterday."

"Exactly what would that be?"

"A sterling silver Tiffany vase."

The DEA agent just says, "Huh!"

Chapter 16

I am standing in front of the DEA agent mesmerized by what he has just said. "What do you mean by that?"

"Oh, nothing much. I thought I recognized you as being the dealer who paid a fortune for that Tiffany vase at the auction house downtown. I saw your picture on the cable news last night. You're a big hit at the local DEA office."

"Yeah, so I heard. Why then did you ask if I knew Leonard?"

The DEA agent is being coy with me. "You mean Mr. Leonarte?"

"Yes, him."

"He's an interesting man who makes a lot of trips to Cuba in his own private jet and never goes through Customs."

I feel obligated to defend Leonard. "Well, he does have family down there, including his mother who just so happens to be currently in the ICU of one of the hospitals in Havana."

"Yeah, that's old news. Say something I haven't heard yet."

Either this guy is investigating Leonard, is a good friend of his, or is a very good liar. "Why are you so concerned about him?"

"Your crony is a person of interest to the DEA."

"In what way? I've never ever heard or seen anything to hint that he had been dealing in drugs."

He becomes defensive. "Oh, don't get me wrong. We don't think Mr. Leonarte is doing anything really criminal beyond the usual breaches of the law that international business in the Caribbean and South America dictates."

"What then are you saying?"

"He knows people who know people who we would like to know more about."

He has me completely confused. I finally ask him point blank, "What would that have to do with the vase and someone stealing my son's van?"

"Agent Johnson mentioned to me that Mr. Leonarte had been telling everyone in the Tiffany world that he was going to be getting the Wild-Rose Vase. There are people in Cuba and here in the United States who, let's say for want of a better word, would be pleased if Mr. Leonarte didn't take possession of that particular vase."

"Why would they care?"

"I'd rather not say."

Having had enough of his evasiveness, I get in his face and press him. "You better damn well tell me what's happening because I've had a really bad 24 hours."

"OK, OK, all I can say is that certain pieces of Tiffany are of greater importance to the Cuban community here and in Cuba than others. That one is categorically the most sought after piece to have come on the market in decades."

Turning to Agent Johnson, I ask him, "This wasn't what you were talking about earlier when you said there was some urban legend surrounding that vase?"

His expression tells it all. He is as ignorant about what the DEA agent is talking as I am. "I guess so, but I won't swear to it. That old-timer, I think, is from Cuba or his parents were. At least his last name sounds Hispanic."

The DEA agent volunteers one last bit of information that I find fascinating. "It should come as no surprise to you, because of all of the drugs coming out of South America and Mexico, we have a ton of Hispanic agents. Yesterday, the Cubans started a betting pool with the other Hispanics on whether or not Mr. Leonarte would get the vase."

I am blunt with him. "Why would they do that?"

"I have no idea. You would've thought they were betting on the World Soccer Cup by their intensity and the amount of money that will be had once it's settled who finally ends up with the vase."

I return to Agent Johnson. "Is the Bureau interested in Leonard?"

"Not that I'm aware of and, if they are, hardly to the extent that the DEA seemingly is."

The DEA agent adds, "The Bureau isn't involved in Latin America the way we are."

Leonard definitely is holding back on me. I wish I could be a fly on the wall when he goes to that museum in Havana to investigate their Wild-Rose Vase. I have one last thing to discuss with the two federal agents before I leave them to finish up with the van. "Would you two mind coming upstairs and listening to an anonymous voice mail message I received after the auction yesterday?"

"What's it about and why do you say it's anonymous?" asks the DEA agent.

"The caller blocked caller id and didn't leave her name. As to what it's about, she didn't want me to sell the vase! Mitch thinks she wants to buy it from me."

"In that case, by all means."

Although he and Agent Johnson follow me into the elevator, they ignore me and talk quietly to each other. Upon my closing the doors and pressing two on the control panel, the DEA agent asks, "Can the Bureau trace a voice message?"

"Perhaps if it's not too remote a call. Not likely if it's a cell phone call."

In a minute, I open the elevator's two doors and say, "It wasn't a very long message."

Agent Johnson notes, "Unlike in those old detective movies, we don't need 10 to 20 seconds to trace a call. It's all kept on computer logs in the switching stations at the phone company."

We walk to the den where I replay the message. "You have two saved messages. First saved message: message from unknown caller at 5:10 PM yesterday: 'Do not sell the vase. I repeat, do not sell the vase.' Click. To save this message press 9 to delete it press 7. To replay this message press 4." I press 9.

The DEA agent grimaces. "You can't say she wasn't succinct."

Shaking his head, Agent Johnson is suddenly perceptibly worried. "That sounds more like a threat or warning to me than someone trying to purchase that vase."

I am startled for I had not considered that. "A threat?"

"Yes, a threat, but what's it about? Did either of you detect any kind of an accent?"

Both of us say, "No."

"Neither did I. That's even stranger. Voice messages usually highlight accents. She was too perfect."

I take the bait. "Why do you say it was too perfect? It sounded fine to me."

"She had practiced it many times before. Even though it was brief, it was executed in a professional announcer's style, almost as if she were reading it from a script."

"You mean whoever sent that message had hired someone to give it?"

"Maybe or maybe she has an accent and worked on covering it up."

"Mitch said he thought he recognized the voice but couldn't place it."

Agent Johnson thinks about that. "That's possible. She may have hidden her accent but couldn't disguise her mannerism. Many times it's how we talk and not what we say that identifies us over the phone."

The DEA agent is more direct. "Regardless of how and what she said, do you think you can trace the call?" He promptly nods over to me. "So that we can find out who she is and why she is intimidating him."

"Since this can be considered a harassment call, I won't have a problem with the phone company having them try to trace it. You have some paper and a pen to write down your phone number?" After I do that, he leaves the room to call the phone company. When he is finished, he returns and tells us, "They'll call us back in a few minutes with the results."

While we are standing by my desk waiting for the return call from the phone company, I ask what to me is currently the question of the hour. "Why would anyone want to threaten me over that vase?"

The DEA agent reminds me, "I told you that there are Cubans out there that don't want Leonarte to get that vase."

"But how would they in particular have an inkling that I was offering it to him? Leonard may have been blabbing to everyone that he was going to get it, but I question whether he told them I was going to get it for him. Hell, she called me when the auction was barely over!"

Agent Johnson ponders that question. "Yeah, why would she presume that you would be calling him first unless he had somehow directly or indirectly told her?"

As we attempt to figure that out, the phone company calls back on my landline phone. I place it on speakerphone. "This is ATT. You placed a trace on a call from 5:10 PM yesterday to this number."

I answer back, "Yes, ma'am."

"Unfortunately, it was from out of state and done on a cell phone. That's all the information we have on it. I'm sorry."

"Thank you."

Agent Johnson nods. "That's what I thought they would say."

All of this intrigue has at last gotten to me. Fear makes you remember things that you have otherwise repressed. "I think I failed to mention something that Ira said to me after the auction had finished. He offered to pay $700,000 for the vase. When I turned it down and made him a counter offer to give his customer second right of refusal if Leonard passed on the vase, he said, 'If you buy the vase today, it will no longer be valid. Our client is funny about this. He insists that his name be on the auction records as the new owner, not yours.' My friends feel that Ira was somehow trying to protect me. What do you make of it?"

He smiles. "Perhaps if you had sold him the vase yesterday, I would be standing in his den this morning and not yours."

The DEA agent is less kind towards Ira. "He didn't represent any Cubans did he?"

I shake my head. "He didn't hint at who was his backer. The only one at the auction who would have been a blatant potential confederate of any Cubans would have been that Hispanic dealer, who didn't talk to me."

Agent Johnson laughs. "I just thought of an absolutely absurd explanation for Ira's offer."

What has he thought of that none of us had last night? "And that is?"

"What if Ira's customer just flat out didn't want Leonarte to even have a chance to get that damn vase?"

"You mean, you think he did all of this to spite Leonard! Why would he have wanted to do that?"

The DEA agent hesitates before observing, "There are those in the Cuban resistance who feel he is too close to Castro. To be blunt, they just don't trust him."

I have to ask him, "What the hell would that have to do with the vase? Since when is owning a Tiffany vase an international political issue?"

"The Cubans in my office were placing their bets on Castro getting the vase. They claimed that the word in Miami is that later on he so regretted ever having let that vase leave Cuba that he had a duplicate of it made and placed in a museum in Havana. Castro's getting old and wants it back!"

"Why then did he ever let it go?"

"They said something about his being worried about his health at the time. He told his inner circle that he bought a life insurance policy with it."

I have to confess that I like his idea best of all that I have heard. I never believed that Ira had my safety in mind when he made me that offer. If Agent Johnson had ever met Ira, he would laugh at the mere suggestion of Ira's being altruistic. By far, it is a more absurd proposal than Castro's having fallen in love with that vase.

Gloria joins us in the den. "When's the van going to be ready?"

The DEA agent eyes his watch. "Maybe now if the dogs didn't find anything."

"Good, let's all go down to the garage and get this mess settled."

Gloria leads the way. Rather than take the elevator, we walk down the stairs to the basement. When we pass through the door to enter the garage, one of the policemen who had been in the van shouts out, "Get a load of what we found!"

I stop dead in my tracks. It feels like all of my

blood is draining to my feet. I sense I am about to faint and lie down immediately on the cold concrete floor of the garage. Agent Johnson is behind me and helps me to the floor. He asks, "Are you OK?"

"I think so. I must've had a vasovagal reaction when I heard that officer say he had found something."

Gloria rushes over. "What a putz you are!"

Wavering about how to react to her callous response to my acute medical condition, Agent Johnson just stares at her. "You're not very sympathetic towards him."

"Vasovagal reaction, my ass. Hell, he hyperventilates and then faints all the time. When that happens, he has to breathe into a brown paper bag. Why do you think he never practiced medicine? The least bit of stress and he goes to ground. I never understood how he passed obstetrics. He had to have some other third year medical student do the circumcisions because he would hyperventilate and break out in a sweat just prepping the kid. Then his hands would start to cramp up and shake. He wasn't any better in surgery. That's why he went into forensic pathology. It's the one field of medicine that is stress free. You know all, do all, but too late."

Once I begin to feel back to normal, I get up and we all walk over to the van to view what the officer was talking about. Although he corners Agent Johnson and the DEA agent, he allows Gloria and me to eavesdrop on them. "We decided to completely inspect the insides of the van just in case the drugs were hidden in an unusual location. There was nothing in the side panels; however, when we explored the spare tire compartment under the

213

floor, bingo!"

My worse fear has materialized. The drug lords are after me. I begin to feel light headed again. I move over so that I can hold onto the van for support and see inside it better. "How much is there?"

"I didn't find any drugs, sir. I found this." In the palm of his hand, the policeman holds up a small rectangular object so covered with grease and grim that I can barely tell it is white.

Gloria asks, "What the hell is that?"

Agent Johnson turns to the officer while immediately responding to her, "It's a Spark Nano. Let me see that."

"As I just said, what the hell is that?"

"It's a transmitting GPS tracker."

"You mean, they left it in the van and forgot to take it out?"

The policeman hands it over to him before interjecting, "I don't think they forgot to take it out, ma'am. It was very securely held in place by a very strong magnet to the undercarriage of the van. Whoever put it there meant for it to stay put."

Agent Johnson wipes the tracker off with his handkerchief and then studies it with a jeweler's loupe he had in his pocket. Nodding smugly, he next gives it to the DEA agent. "It's not one of ours or yours. This came from the CIA!"

214

Gloria still does not understand what they are saying. "Why would they do that?"

The DEA agent explains, "That is the one thing about this case that's open and shut. When they didn't find what they were after, they decided to return the van and all of its contents to you. Since you wouldn't suspect anything nefarious had happened after all of your belongings were returned to you, they would use the tracker to eventually lead them to wherever you had stored whatever they were after. They planned to get it from you before you sold it to someone."

Just as I blurt out, "The vase," another policeman comes up to us and hands over to the DEA agent two more Spark Nanos identical to the one from the van. "I found these in their other two cars."

Chapter 17

The DEA agent is quick to say, "I think that wraps it up here. I'll file a report just stating that no drugs were found in your possession. The better part of discretion dictates that I not mention the CIA's participation in this." He then leaves and the policemen finish putting the van back together and cleaning up behind themselves.

Surprisingly, Agent Johnson is not as displeased as I expected. At the same time, he is not very encouraging. "Do you want me to arrange federal marshals to monitor your house and protect you?"

Since I am stunned by what has happened, I do not directly reply. Gloria, on the other hand, does. "Damn right I do. They obviously found out where we live and those bastards could ransack our house any day, even today, hunting for that vase."

"I'll get the paper work started. In the meantime, I'll have the local sheriff's office put out a squad car in front of your house. That should scare them off."

Things are getting out of hand. I do not like the idea that I may be under some sort of protective custody. I protest Gloria's and his plan. "Is all of this necessary?"

He is adamant. "Indisputably, there is a direct connection between the theft of both those license plates and your son's van and your vase. As long as the vase is in your possession, you are in danger. Whoever at the CIA are involved in all of this, they want it bad and they aren't playing by the rules!!"

I joke, "So, you don't think this has to do with a vendetta against Leonard any more?"

"No. By the way, do you have Ira Wynn's contact information?"

"I don't have his phone number, but that won't be a problem. He's in the New York phone directory under antiques dealers. He has a big ad in the yellow pages."

A short time later, Gloria and I are alone with all the doors and windows shut and locked, making us feel like prisoners in our own home. Gloria sits in the den doing her knitting. I pace. When is Leonard going to call back? The quicker I hand over that vase to his secretary; the better I will feel. The doorbell rings. I go over to see who it is and am thrilled to find two uniformed policewomen standing on the front stoop. "Gloria, Johnson really works fast. The police are already here."

I unlock the door and one of them says, "I'm Officer Cooper. We understand that you've had an incident here."

"That's correct. It happened early this morning."

With most of her brunette hair closely cropped and hidden by her cap, she has used just enough makeup to be attractive but not enough to appear too feminine. I cannot tell what her eyes look like since her dark glasses hide them. If intimidation is the first line of defense for the police, she has nothing to fear. Her upper body muscles, well developed by years of workouts in the gym, should even give the CIA second thoughts about coming back to my house. Straight-faced with a taut expression, she gets right down to business. "Can you tell us the details for

217

our report?" She takes a notepad and pen out of her shirt pocket.

I might as well come clean. "Well, first the dogs, we have two beagles."

I do not like the way she interrupts me. She is either rude or too familiar with my dogs. "We know all about the beagles."

"Yes, I figured you would. Anyway, the dogs started to bay at the front door and I came down to find out what had gotten them all riled up. When I did that, I saw that our son's van that had been stolen the night before was now at the curb in front of the house. Without thinking about the dogs, I opened the door to go examine the van. They then bolted out of the house. Gloria and I then searched for them."

"So, you admit that the dogs were loose without any restraints?"

This lady is a stickler for details. "Absolutely, and they were barking up a storm. They must've smelled something strange around the van."

"How long did they do that?"

Boy, is she thorough. I do not recall exactly how much time had elapsed before we gave up on them. It is not the type of thing you do before sunup when you are trying to round up Dumb and Dumber. "Quite awhile. They went on the hunt to find out who the strangers were and where they had gone to before finding a squirrel to chase. When my wife and I decided that pursuing them was going to be fruitless, we returned home. That's when the FBI agent arrived with a bunch of policemen."

For the first time, Officer Cooper stops writing in her notepad, lowers her sunglasses, and just eyeballs me. "Why was the FBI interested in your house?"

Good, we are finally getting to the heart of the matter. "He was investigating why a tow truck had come to deliver my son's van."

"Why would that be a concern of the FBI?"

"Because the tow truck had stolen Secret Service license tags on it."

"Did the agent do anything else?"

"Yeah, he called in the DEA to do a drug search on the van."

She perks up upon hearing that. "Did they find anything?"

"No, just something called a Spark Nano in the spare tire compartment."

She pushes her sunglasses back up and stops me. "I've heard enough. Your neighbors, all of your neighbors called in repeated complaints about your dogs waking them up this morning. We're going to have to ticket you. It's going to be a big fine. You really ticked them off."

"You mean you're not here to watch over the house?"

"No sir, I haven't heard anything about that."

She hands me the ticket and the two of them depart. I read the court date is in a month, but there is not a fine amount. Instead, she has written TBD. I call out to Gloria, "What does TBD mean?"

She does not come to see what I am talking about but rather cries out, "Why do you ask?"

"Because the police just gave us a citation for the dogs' running around the neighborhood this morning, and all it says under fine is TBD."

Gloria is undoubtedly not happy. "Shit, Ernie, that means 'to be determined.' It's going to be up to the doggy court judge to decide. And that's never good. Do I need to remind you how much I hate those two dogs?"

After all this, things can only get better today, or so I think. As the day progresses, they do not. Leonard does not call me back. The police by late afternoon have a cruiser stationed out in front of my house in plain view. When they do not leave, our nosy neighbors begin to call us wanting to pry out of us what is up. I have difficulty determining whether they are frankly concerned about us or are trying to time when both our dogs and we will be arrested and dragged away to the pound in handcuffs and whatever they use for dogs. I can only imagine that they do not want to miss out on lining up outside along our driveway and showering expletives on us as that occurs, especially when the police bend our heads down to avoid hitting the top of the rear door of the car as they push us in.

Meanwhile, I decide to put my mind at ease by

starting to prepare for "the show" at the end of the week. Usually, I try to have at least half of my booth be new stuff. Nothing turns customers off more than finding stale merchandise. Because Leonard has not bought the vase yet, I will not be able to buy on set up day, sort of like the original Loehmann's in Brooklyn. Customers who pay extra to get in then and dealers, who have either finished already or are waiting to start, congregate in front of the booths of dealers who have just unloaded their boxes and are unpacking them. A feeding frenzy then ensues. The smart dealers never have price tags on their things when they are unpacking. Judging from how many people are asking for a price on a particular item, they shout out one. If you pay close attention, many times later on in the day they will quote a lower price as they place their price tags on the items in the booth. I have never figured out why we put them on our merchandise. You would have to be an idiot to pay what they claim the cost to be. It is sort of like an auction in reverse. You start out at the highest price and work your way down.

For freshening up your booth in a hurry, nothing competes with set up day. It takes two people to be effective. One to man the booth to sell to other dealers and the especially obsessive-compulsive collectors, and the other to scout "the show." Gloria does most of our buying there. Her academic background in art nouveau has given her a museum curator's eye with regard to Tiffany, Steuben, Gallé, and Loetz. But her specialty is finding the sleepers in the crowd. I do not have the patience required to rummage through all the junk that is offered at "the show" to find the rare diamond in the rough. To her credit, she also does not get taken in by buying a fake.

Not everything a dealer brings is shown to the

public. Frequently, the best pieces will be hidden under the table and trotted out only when the target dealer or customer approaches the booth. Why is this done? I cannot fathom. If one mulls this over, it makes no economic sense, but it does have a tradition that will not permit it to go away. I laugh to myself when someone tells me that they *brought something this month just for me* because he is flat out lying. However, I also follow the rule never to haggle over the price of something *brought just for me*. That maybe the key to my continued success with the notorious hook, "I've got something special just for you under the table."

When money is tight and set up day is out, I resort to selling off the lesser pieces in the cabinets in my den. One of the better sales gimmicks is saying, "This came from my personal collection." It could be the garbage from dinner a year ago that I was too lazy to put out in the trash, but some schmuck will pay a premium for it, just because it came from my personal collection of garbage. Better yet is saying, "I've had this for 20 years." If it were worth buying, count on it that I would have sold it in the past 20 years. What I do have that is worth saving for 20 years, I have no intention of selling. My heirs will have that honor or, God forbid, the bankruptcy lawyers will, which, if Leonard reneges on this deal, may be sooner than later.

Best of all is bringing something that is a "one of a kind" to "the show" claiming all the while that you only brought it for bragging rights. "I will show it to you so that you can say you have actually seen one, but it's not for sale." Why the hell bring it if it is not for sale? As every dealer realizes, "the show" is not a museum exhibition. Despite it's being a transparent ploy, boy, does it work. I do not have to name a price. They will spontaneously make me an offer greater than I would have had the nerve to mention. Through the years, no one has ever suspected that I have at least one more at home as I begrudgingly acquiesce to part with that true rarity at a very handsome profit.

Set up day purchases are a different sale. Other dealers at "the show" not only have seen them but also have seen me pay for them. That is one advantage of buying something from under the table. Since only two people at "the show" are aware it is there, the dealer who sold it and me, how could whoever I am offering it to have an inkling what I was charged for it? I do not even tell Gloria how much they cost me. In a lapse of judgment, she might tell another dealer what a steal I got. And on the rare occasion that that does happen, as God is my witness, whoever buys it is immediately told by all the dealers, who have gossiped among themselves about what I shelled out for it, "You know, he robbed you. You do know what he gave for it?" If one plans to make a killing at "the show," it is best for him to keep it to himself. On the other hand, are the items that the other dealers passed on when they were offered them, but I bought and put up for sale as soon as I return to my booth. When the collector proudly shows the other dealers his triumph, they in an undertone mention, "You know, I saw that earlier, but passed on it." What the hell does that mean? They did not have enough money to buy it? They thought it was overpriced? They think something is wrong with it? Or, more than likely, they could not tell a real bargain if it were presented to them gift-wrapped on a sterling silver platter. Nevertheless, the piece is forever tainted for that collector.

However, the biggest issue with set up day purchases is whether to sell them at "the show" or keep them for a private sale or an auction. Gloria's selections regularly fall into this category. When you do stumble onto a true one of a kind object or a real museum quality piece, what is it worth? I do not have time on set up day to research it. There are collectors bustling around "the show" who memorize price lists and auction results for their specialty goods or have them on their portable computers. In this case they have the advantage.

I have no issue with my giving someone a bargain. Hell, that is why they come to "the show." However, if someone is going to get a real steal, that someone is going to be me.

I go to the basement and bring up into the foyer the boxes containing what remained from the last show. I do not need to see inside of them. They are each numbered and on my computer is a list of what they hold. They will do, but it will not be a good show. I start opening the cabinets and taking out stuff. I place all of it on the dining room table. This is one of those moments like the age-old question: "Which child is your favorite?" What am I willing to part with? Some things are no-brainers. Wine glasses always sell. If there is ever an antique that is a cash equivalent, it is the wine glass. People cannot get enough of them, and, since they do not take up much room, there is always space for one more. Although sets are no longer popular, pairs, examples, and one of each color are. Silver is next on the list. Even if it is junk, as long as it is sterling, someone will buy it for the right price. I cannot tell you how many times I have threatened never to sell another piece of sterling as I witness someone weigh a piece, buy it on the cheap, and then crush it by stomping on it on the floor with their feet. Why would someone do this overtly insane act? Because they got it well below an inflated scrap value, it will be melted down within the week and sold to some silver brokers at a slight discount to the spot market silver price quoted on the New York Mercantile Exchange that day. Oh, they crush it in order to maximize the number of pieces the shopping bag they bring to "the show" will hold. Some people would eat their own children.

Cameos and miniatures are excellent sellers. Their aficionados snap them up every time I offer some, which I try to do at each "show." Even so, I really hate to take them. While I love their enthusiasts, after all I make part of my living off of them, they are also my competition when I restock my inventory and can make it particularly difficult to find suitable replacements for my own collection. Finally, there is my cabinet full of Asian art: hot as a pistol these days, but tricky. Lots of really good fakes will be on the floor making my prices seem high. Worse, some items cannot be sold unless I have documentation of their age and origin. Ivory and animal tooth sculptures are the main problem. One cannot imagine how hard it is to sell a really old ivory chess set these days without the proper papers, even if it has been in a family since World War II, when a relative brought it back from China. They, of course, do not have the proper papers. It is so difficult that many dealers will try to sell the individual pieces as separate figurines.

Gloria puts down her knitting and comes into the dining room to find out what I have selected. She is not impressed. "Don't you have better to sell? I mean, this is good, but it isn't great."

"Of course, I do; but if Leonard comes through this week, I really don't want to try to sell our best pieces. With John's auction this close to 'the show,' there is going to be a lot of great stuff all about it. I'd rather wait until there is less competition. I think we'll do better then."

"But if Leonard doesn't come through, you're dead in the water when it comes to new inventory for probably the next two shows."

"You're right, of course, but my instincts tell me not to."

Gloria frowns. "You're just too tired to be thinking sensibly today. Go find some really good things and pack them up. If you find out that it will be a mistake to put them out, then don't unpack them. What's the downside, you carry a few more boxes than you need to?"

"I guess what's really bothering me is what to do about that vase?"

"In what way?"

I sigh very deeply before I say what she, most assuredly, will take as being stupid, "Should I take the Wild-Rose Vase to 'the show?'"

She is at a loss for words. After a while, she asks, "Where were you today? Why would you even consider doing such a thing?"

I grimace. "You won't believe this, but everyone there will be expecting to see it. It could get us our biggest crowd ever. Hell, someone there might even buy it."

"Or steal it."

"Yeah, that too."

She then smiles. "Let's call Agent Johnson and hear what he thinks?"

"Why would you want to do that?"

"If it were publicized that the vase would be at 'the show,' who can we assume would be there?"

I can imagine a lot of people. "Who?"

She taps my shoulder. "Whoever placed those damn GPS devices in the van and our cars, that's who, you idiot. He would be more than interested in buying it."

"Or stealing it." I get up and go to the desk in the den and pick up Agent Johnson's business card. I dial the number on it.

"FBI"

"I would like to speak to Agent Johnson."

The operator is curt. "He's not in, can I take a message?"

"Yeah, this is Ernie Kopp. He was at my house this morning regarding a Tiffany vase"

I am startled by what she says next. "You're in luck, he just walked in."

"Agent Johnson. Dr. Kopp, what's up?"

He is bound to be busy. I try to be brief. "Since

Leonard hasn't bought the vase yet, what do you think about my showing it at 'the show?'"

He acts the way I expected him to. "Why the hell would you want to do that?"

I am convinced that he thinks I am crazy, but I suspect I can turn him around. "Well, it will draw people to my booth in record numbers plus I just might sell it, perhaps to whoever placed those GPS devices."

He buys it. "I'll get back to you in a little while. You won't want to do this without our assistance. I am bound and determined to nab this rogue agent."

I hang up and move the chicken boxes out of the foyer to stack them in the den.

Chapter 18

Figuring we must be upset, Mitch and Helen early in the afternoon call to tell us that they will be coming over later with supper. They bring take-out Chinese, three bags full. Helen is holding one in each hand while Mitch has one in his left hand and presses the doorbell button with his right. If fine wines fuel high finance, the antiques world survives on take-out. It is not that we do not appreciate haute cuisine. Rather, we either do not have the time to leave to go to a fancy restaurant during "the show," since we have to man our booths, or are too tired to go out to eat after closing at 8 PM. There are plenty of fast food vendors and caterers there, some of whom are quite good and serve substantial meals. Nevertheless, we still prefer take-out pizza, Chinese, and barbecued chicken wings. I think it stems from the all-nighters during our college days.

Yes, most of us are college educated. Many dealers started out as art history majors whose first job was with an auction house as a specialist. Gloria was a Tiffany and Gallé specialist at one of the leading establishments in Manhattan. She became disheartened by her other duties there, such as the financial services and trusts and estates departments. The objects she had grown to love became mere commodities to be traded, hoarded, or protected from the IRS by individuals who did not appreciate what they had or were about to own beyond the appraised value she assigned to them. She particularly bristled at the accountants' concept of a well-balanced portfolio of art or antiques. These are masterpieces, not stocks and bonds.

Some of us come from pawnshop backgrounds. The non-degreed education provided to them there is by far more practical than anything they learned at the MBA programs they attended. Yes, that guy behind the counter at a pawnshop may have an MBA from Wharton. Pawnshops are at present big businesses, publicly traded even on the NYSE, and followed by Wall Street analysts. Believe it or not, there are also reality cable programs about them. Past experience tells the pawnbrokers that what will not sell at their stores will fly off the shelves at "the show": especially, fur coats, jewelry, collectables, and family heirlooms. In a counterintuitive way, they get a better feel for the economy sitting behind the counter of their pawnshops than they would at the bond-trading desk of a prestigious Wall Street firm. When things just begin to stink on CNBC, Fox Business, or Bloomberg, they have been rotting for a long time at a pawnshop. The lower the Dow, the higher pawnshop profits are. Others, like Mitch and myself, switched from being collectors to dealing when we burnt out on our day jobs or lost them in the last recession. We love what we sell and sell what we love.

Much to my surprise, Paul and Kelly are with Mitch and Helen when I open the front door. I had assumed that they had returned to Nashville. "Why aren't y'all back in Tennessee?"

Paul grins. "My conspiracy clients would never forgive me if I didn't hang around long enough to find out all of the details of your little adventure."

"Well, what do you want to know?"

"Mitch and Helen have pretty much filled us in on what's happened. I decided to stay here and see how this whole thing plays out. Is that police car a new addition to your permanent collection of lawn sculpture? I'll have to reflect about your moving into twenty first century modern manufactured art."

Gloria joins us in the foyer and finds nothing humorous in our predicament. "You haven't heard about the Spark Nano that the DEA discovered in George's van."

All of them are at a loss. Helen takes the lead for the group when she asks, "I think I've heard about them. It wouldn't be a transmitting GPS device, would it?"

"Yes, it is."

"How did it get there?"

"The FBI agent is tentative about that. But whoever put it there also put one in each of our other cars, too!"

Paul's eyes widen. "You've had both the FBI and DEA here today. My, my, this is getting even better than I imagined. I may need to start taking notes."

I interject, "And the tow truck that was at The Blue And The Gay had stolen Secret Service plates from the White House."

"Of course, it did. I told you it's all about Elvis. Somebody is trying to find him and is using that vase as bait. Elvis would never suspect someone who came in an official U.S. government car or, even better, a tow truck. Boy, is this ever going to make the big time in Nashville."

Mitch is not so sanguine about Paul's Elvis theory. "The DEA doesn't think drugs are involved in all of this?"

A broad smile crosses my face since I am very relieved to be finally able to state, "No, their agent signed off of the case."

"What then does the FBI feel is going on?"

"Agent Johnson is hesitant to say at this time, but the Spark Nanos came from the CIA. We've come up with a plan to trap whoever is involved in this."

Shaking his head, Mitch obviously does not like the sound of that. "Let's all move into the kitchen. I want to be sitting down when I listen to this plan, besides the food is going to get cold. Believe me, Ernie, when I say that when I was at Justice we were very careful about using civilians in police work, particularly when it involved the Agency. You're not the type suited for this kind of operation."

I protest. "Why not? I'm board certified in forensic pathology. I know a thing or two about the law."

He puts his right hand into his jacket's pocket and points his finger at me. "And you also will faint at the sight of a gun."

Once in the kitchen we gather around the breakfast table, open up the Styrofoam containers, and pass out plates. We all use the chopsticks provided by the restaurant. Mitch and Helen have brought more food than we can eat. We pile high on the steamed white rice in the center of our plates Szechwan-style prawns with dried

232

chilies, quick-fried lobster in hot bean sauce, tea smoked duck with scallions and ginger, and beef with snow peas. Midway through the meal Mitch asks, "So, tell me about this grand plan to catch the crooks."

I lay down my chopsticks and begin to outline our work in progress. "Actually, Gloria thought it up. She figured that whoever is after the vase will be at 'the show' if it is there because to quote Willie Sutton, 'that's where the money is.' We're going to announce that I'm bringing it to 'the show.'"

"How do you plan to do that? You don't have much time."

"With all the publicity I got after the auction, I figure a few phone calls to TV stations and the local paper will get us at least one article and a couple of spots on the evening news."

Mitch nods approvingly. "That part of this scheme makes sense. They'll probably even want to interview you and Gloria about it at 'the show.' How do you intend to protect it? Security at 'the show' is tight, but I don't think we've ever had anything comparable to this to test it."

I flinch a bit at his objection. I realize this will not be easy. "The FBI is figuring out how to do just that so that we can nab them if they try to buy it or steal it."

"Why would you want to do it that way? Sounds risky to me."

Gloria pounces on him. "I don't want that damn squad car in the front of my house any longer than it has to be there. If we spread the word that the vase will be at 'the show,' only a fool would try to break into our house. He can get it easier and legally there."

Mitch does not back down. "I can appreciate that. But what if someone else approaches you with the cash in hand to buy it? By the opening of 'the show,' a lot of Tiffany buyers will be aware of its being there and will come by to see it with the intention of buying it. How will you determine who is the one? I don't think the FBI wants to be charged with false arrest."

His having worked in the U.S. Attorney's office just after he finished law school gives Mitch insight into the fine details of a sting that I had not thoroughly thought through. "You have any recommendations?"

"First rule of a sting: whoever comes to buy that vase is probably a patsy, especially if he is working with the Company. If the FBI pinches him, he won't admit to anything worth divulging, especially who and where his ultimate boss is. You've got to figure out how to get the leader to make a presence at 'the show.' Second rule: they will have multiple patsies. They presume it is better than having just one guy try to pull this off alone since they plan on you trying to nab him. If one of them fails to pass the smell test and you grab him, there will be others who will follow him."

Helen interrupts. "If they've been trained by the CIA as their professionalism indicates, they'll be casing your booth. They even may send someone in just to test the water while others will try to figure out who the FBI agents are and where they are stationed. The bigger the crowd around you, the more comfortable they will feel. As they say, 'There's safety in numbers.' Besides, if they plan to steal it, they may use the crowd to create a diversion. However, the real buyer may not show up until Sunday just as 'the show' is closing, exactly when both the FBI and you are preparing to leave."

Mitch concludes, "Third and final rule of a sting: block their exit route. They don't want to be caught. Figure out how they plan to escape. That's not easy to do on set up day or after closing when all of those side doors are wide open to allow trucks and vans to drive onto and off the floor."

I am discouraged to say the least. "You're not very optimistic that we'll pull this off, are you?"

"I would be if I knew something about who you're really dealing with."

"Why do you say that?"

"Every covert group, be it CIA, FBI, the Mafia, drug dealers, or even a terrorist group, has its own way of doing business. It's almost like a fingerprint."

"What do you mean?"

After thinking about how to describe this, Mitch explains it by asking another question I had not considered. "How are they going to pay you for the vase, if they go the legal route: cash, cashier's check, credit card, or trade you something for it?"

I do not understand his question. "Who wouldn't use cash, a cashier's check, or bank transfer?"

"You're too used to dealing with legitimate

customers. You may be dealing with someone who doesn't have a bank account because he doesn't trust banks or can't access them?"

"Like whom?"

"Al-Qaeda for one avoids Western banks like the plague since their assets can be frozen. They pay in cash through the hawala banking system or phony Islamic charities. Heroin and cocaine may be traded in a strange bartering system. The Mafia doesn't like any paper trails attached to their true businesses. However, they've transitioned out of suitcases full of money into jewelry and real estate. Both are excellent ways to launder their money and to pay off associates. Drug dealers frequently launder their cash through friendly banks or bank equivalents and have the cash immediately turned into cashier's checks under $10,000 or wire transferred to other banks out of the country. Spies prefer cash or cash equivalents: money orders, bank transfers to Swiss accounts, or certified checks. You can tell a CIA operative because he passes out $100 bills with sequential serial numbers. No one uses American Express. So, how do you think you'll get paid for the vase?"

"Leonard always pays in cash in a leather suitcase that is brand new. Wire transfers are the more usual route for my other customers. But I hadn't thought about how a crook might do it."

Smiling Mitch advises, "Well, you better. It would be very awkward if you got a suitcase full of counterfeit one hundred dollar bills. The Mafia and drug dealers who are working with the Agency aren't above doing that to someone they think is a sucker. By the way, neither is North Korea. Have you thought about what you might

236

take in trade?"

I shake my head, no. "I hadn't considered it."

This is standard operating procedure for Paul who breaks in. "How do you think I got my new house? I swapped a Tiffany lamp I got from Mitch for it and I got $200,000 in cash to boot. If the real estate market hadn't collapsed, I would have had to take just the house."

Never one who regularly reads the Real Estate section of the paper, Helen adds, "I won't let Mitch do that. It's too much work moving and I like where we are living."

In the midst of air fiving her, Kelly concurs. "You can say that again, girl. I wasn't asked in advance." She grimaces towards Paul. "And it's something that won't happen again."

Always caught up in a deal, Paul chuckles nervously. "How about for a condo on South Beach or on the Upper East Side?"

Before she has an opportunity to answer him, I ask, "Won't the FBI determine all of these things?"

At the same time Mitch and Helen, both, say, "Hell, no."

"Why not?"

In view of the fact that she is overtly deferring to him, Mitch answers for them, "It's your project. They've only offered protection. It would take months for this to go through the usual channels to get approval as an FBI generated sting, particularly for what is so far only petty theft of license plates and maybe a CIA approved covert operation. Protection will be a lot easier to get approved by Washington."

Out of frustration with all of these obstacles, I beseech Mitch, "How would you go about doing this?"

"I adhere to the KISS principle. You know, keep it short and simple. Have them come to you. They can't find it and they want it bad."

Gloria does not like this at all and scowls at him accordingly. "How do we go about doing this in a reasonable amount of time? I don't like being a prisoner in my own home."

He waves at her. "Can the cops."

"What? Are you insane?"

"As long as you show them you don't trust them and have the police stationed outside of your house, you won't hear from them. If they really are crooks, even ones working for the Agency, they would have broken into John's auction house and stolen that vase."

"But it's a fortress!"

"Gloria, so is the White House, and they got Secret Service tags from there."

Recalling the ACCC note, I throw it out for general discussion. "Agent Johnson thinks it's someone in the CIA itself and not some contract person."

Helen is skeptical. "What makes him think that?"

"That note from the Allied Corporate Credit Corporation, which he claims was written on CIA stationary, and the Spark Nanos."

"As you know, I'm very familiar with their tactics. This doesn't sound like something they would be involved in."

"Why do you say that?"

"Ernie, the CIA wouldn't steal Secret Service tags or use the ACCC in that way. As for the tags, they could've just ordered them. The note from the ACCC is like handing you their business card. 'Dear Sir, you've just become a target of the CIA. Do not pass Go and do not collect $200. Go directly to jail.' They don't do that. Someone is trying really hard to make this for all the world appear to be the work of the CIA to people who've never dealt with it."

Gloria stares at her. "You mean someone is trying to frame the CIA at our expense?"

"It wouldn't be the first time one of their enemies did that. It's actually kind of easy to do. Ever since our attempts to make Castro disappear, Congress believes the Agency is capable of doing any kind of a screw up. From drug dealing and political assassination to anything having to do with terrorists including kidnapping and torturing them, some foreign operative has tried one or all of them to discredit the CIA. Getting bin Laden, though, really helped their image."

I again press Mitch, "How would you have them

come to me?"

"If you stop making this a federal case, they'll probably have someone like Ira approach you again about selling the vase to them. Insist on meeting the buyer."

Gloria scoffs at his idea. "If they're legit, then why the hell did they steal the van and search all of Ernie's boxes?"

Slowly moving his head from side to side, Paul asserts, "They in reality didn't steal anything, Gloria. It could be the Mafia coming after Elvis, as I said last night, or, from what I heard earlier today, it is even more likely that Elvis is trying to get back what is rightfully his. If he had found the vase, he would have left $600,000 plus a little extra for the inconvenience."

"What now makes you think it's Elvis and not the Mafia?"

"Only the King would be considerate enough to have returned your son's van right back to your house and taken such precautions that those valuable antiques in its cargo bay were left undamaged. He even used the same tape as the FBI does. Probably got it from them. You know the Mafia wouldn't have gone to so much trouble. Hell, they probably can't even safely pack an antique."

Unconvinced, she maintains, "I thought you said last night that he was covertly selling the vase."

"I did. But his Trust was the intended buyer and they were to return it to him. Yesterday Ernie screwed everything up for them! I bet you he even called to notify

240

you that he was bringing the van back today. He's just that kind of an upright guy."

Chapter 19

I never can tell how much of what Paul says is BS intended to stir things up and how much is just good guessing. Regardless of that, I ask him, "Do you want to hear the message?"

"You betcha. I'm curious as hell to catch the King's voice after all these years."

We all move into the den where the main telephone console is sitting on an Edwardian walnut end table next to the wing chair. I punch both the speakerphone button and the voice mail button. "Please enter your password or, if you have entered the wrong mail box number, press star." I key in my PIN. "ATT, you have two saved messages. To listen to your saved messages, press 1." I touch 1. "First saved message: message from unknown caller at 5:10 PM yesterday. To listen to your saved message, press 1. To re-save the message, press 9. To delete your message, press 7." I tap 9. "Message re-saved. Second saved message, message from unknown caller at 9:20 PM yesterday. To listen to your saved message, press 1. To re-save the message, press 9." Being a bit theatrical, I hold down 1 for a few seconds to build up the suspense. "Your car will be ready in the morning. Click. To save this message, press 9. To delete your message, press 7. To replay your message, press 1" Again, I hit 9.

Waving his arms in the air, Paul is ecstatic. "Sounds just like him, doesn't it?"

Everyone else, including Kelly, is gawking at him in amazement. Mitch eventually says what we all think,

"That doesn't sound a thing like Elvis. And you need to calm down!"

Paul pulls his arms down by his side but remains adamant. "Sure it does. Play it again, Ernie."

Once more I depress 1. "Your car will be ready in the morning. Click."

"Don't you hear that Mississippi/Memphis accent?"

The disdain in Mitch's eyes tells it all. "You're full of shit. There's nothing there except for perhaps a trace of a Southern accent."

Having had enough of all of this, I stare straight at Paul. "Did Mitch tell you that we had gotten a call last night about the van?"

He tries to cover up his smile but fails miserably. "Yeah, he did. I thought I would throw that in to get your goat."

"I figured as much." Seeking out each of them, I ask, "Have we come to any conclusion tonight?"

Mitch shrugs his shoulders. "I don't think so. In the morning, call that FBI agent and see what he has come up with. Plus, you need to find out if Leonard is going to take the vase before 'the show.' All of this will be moot if he comes through."

Once we clean up the kitchen, which is quick work since there is not much of a mess, after all it was take-out Chinese, they leave and Gloria and I decide to go walk the dogs and then water and feed them before we go to

243

bed. We do not want another early morning wake up call from them.

Saying we walk our beagles is a misnomer. They have been bred to be scent hounds. Slowly meandering down the streets and smelling their way through the neighborhood with their noses to the ground, they announce their discoveries of odors of interest by barking and howling. Upon establishing the trail to the source of the one fragrance that has intoxicated them, Dumb and Dumber raise their heads, begin to bay, and thrust forward towards it. Abruptly their leads snap straight and taut evoking sharp pains in our shoulders. The hunt is on with Gloria and I straining to control them. We only find relief either from their having lost the scent thus having to slow down to sniff the grass again to regain it or from our pulling back on their standard dog collars to where they repeatedly choke themselves from resisting us, which as well stops their howling, but only temporarily. It is no coincidence that the ads for dog harnesses never show one on a beagle. I personally feel that it is because the restraints would either have to fracture the dog's ribs or stop its breathing before the beagle would concede defeat and slacken up its pace. The instant the pressure is off their necks, Dumb and Dumber clear their throats and proceed to test yet again the strength of our hands and their leads, hoping that they can break loose. Their barking begins anew. It sounds like a goose honking and, when we walk them by the lake, even elicits friendly greetings from the geese that live there. To our uninitiated neighbors this all indicates that Dumb and Dumber are in pain from an injury or illness. Only those who have previously owned beagles or have accompanied us on one of these daily adventures understand that the dogs are enjoying themselves immensely.

Upon leaving our house, the dogs immediately run over to greet the two policemen at our curb and, after sniffing the patrol car's tires, raise a rear leg to spray each one to mark their claim on the car. Somewhat embarrassed by this, Gloria and I avoid eye contact with the cops and only silently wave at them before moving up the street. About 15 minutes into our ordeal, we see the headlights from a car that is behind us. Accordingly, we pull Dumb and Dumber off the street onto the sidewalk, which is not an easy feat to accomplish since this had been garbage collection day and they must thoroughly inspect each house's trash cans that remain by the curb. Much to my surprise, the lights slow down and a black stretch limousine pulls up beside us. We stop, and it stops. A very hefty man, with black hair combed straight back and held down with mousse so that not a single strand is out of place and wearing an expensive custom tailored dark suit, opens up the front door and walks up to us. He comes across like he had been a defensive lineman in college, if he had gone there. In a no nonsense manner with a heavy Hispanic accent, he states, "The Boss wants to talk to you." Nodding towards the car, he adds, "Inside! I'll take care of the dogs."

All I can think is *Oh my God, the drug Mafia is after me, after all*. However, I keep my cool. "I must warn you they are beagles. Do you feel you can handle them?"

"No problem. I have a way of getting people and animals to do exactly what I want them to do."

After giving him a quick going-over a second time, I say to myself, *I bet you do*.

Diplomacy is not one of Gloria's strongest suits.

She points her right hand towards her neck, holds its fingers barely touching each other just under her chin, and gently rocks it. "These dogs don't obey anyone, even wise guys, capisce? They got loose this morning and we had a time getting them back. Our neighbors and the police were all over our asses because of that. We've got to go to doggie court again because of it."

Sternly, he tries to reassure her. "Yes, ma'am. It's all about control and letting them know that you are the boss."

Already crotchety from being stressed out from Leonard not bailing us out and on top of that from having to go to doggy court once more, Gloria is showing her familial stubbornness and strong resistance to any form of intimidation. She has the Stoller gene. Family lore has it that Lenny Bruce was somehow in the Stoller kinship, enough said. "You really don't understand. They're beagles. Only their noses control them, that's all. Am I clear? I don't care who your boss is. Hell will be paid if they get loose again."

As far as he is concerned, Dumb and Dumber have finally met their match. He cracks a devious smile. "No one gets away from me."

I decide it's time to turn over the leads and get into the limo before he gets angry. "Gloria, just do what he says. He looks to me like he's handled a lot tougher assignments than Dumb and Dumber."

The side door of the limo opens as we hand him the leads. From inside, someone calls out, but with a Hispanic accent I think I recognize, "Please come in."

Gloria goes in first and then I follow her. I am shocked by whom I see sitting across from us. "Leonard, what are you doing here? I thought you were stuck in Havana."

"I said things move slowly down there. I didn't say I move slowly."

"What brings you here."

"To pick up that vase from Mitch's house."

Stunned, I pause. I have no idea how he found out that the Tiffany vase was there. Worse, if he knows that, who else does? Who might have been at Mitch's house when he and Helen returned home tonight? Is the vase even still there? "How did you get hold of our little secret?"

"Well, you went straight there after the auction yesterday. And the vase wasn't in your son's van. Where else did you have time to put it?"

A sudden thought crosses my mind. I cannot believe it, but have to ask the question anyway. "You didn't steal the van did you?"

"Of course not, why would you think I would've done that?"

"I didn't until you said that the vase wasn't in the van when we had gone to The Blue And The Gay."

He laughs at me. "Listen, Ernie, I knew it wasn't there before those idiots who stole your van did such an amateurish thing."

247

All I do is stare at him. "How?"

"How, what?"

"How are you so sanguine about that?"

"About whether they were idiots to steal the van or that you went to Mitch's house to store the vase?"

"That I went to Mitch's house."

"That's what Adolpho told me. And he's very reliable."

Gloria interrupts him when she asks, "Who's Adolpho?"

"You just met him." He gestures outside towards my dogs. "He's walking Dumb and Dumber."

I am at a loss for words. What do I say except to repeat myself. "How did he find that out? No one followed us to there."

"He didn't have to in person. He followed you after you left the auction on Google Earth Live."

"You can do that?"

"Yeah, you can do that if you plan in advance. It also helped that your son has a big ego."

"Why do you say that?"

"He has his business logo painted on the top of his van. It wasn't hard to tail you."

"Oh, then why did you feel the need to go to all of this trouble?"

"You still don't have a grasp on the history of that vase, do you?"

"Well, it's a fact that it was at the Columbian Exposition and that Tiffany made it."

He smiles. "That's all true. I verified it at the Museo Nacional de Bellas Artes. Yours is the original and theirs is a later copy."

I stare at him. Was that DEA agent right after all? "And you heard that from whom?"

"I was told that by the museum, itself."

One thing still bothers me about this, but I do not express myself well. "I don't believe you."

He takes offense at that. "Ernie, why would I lie to you?"

Quick to correct my error, I have to apologize. "I'm sorry. I didn't mean to say that you lied. I just find it hard to believe that a curator at a museum, even one in Havana, would admit that they did not have the original one but a reproduction."

"I never said the curator claimed to have a reproduction."

None of this is making sense to Gloria who usually is not baffled easily but is at present. "I don't follow you, Leonard."

In his mind it is settled that he now needs to unveil his surprise package and he, therefore, bends over to reach for a small mahogany stained wooden container, which in reality is a very large old cigar box. He places it on his lap and opens the latch. Inside, the box is lined, top and bottom, with a blue velvet cloth, which in a well surrounds a vase that he hands to me. "Once they showed me this one, I knew yours was the original."

My hands start to sweat. I reach for it and scrutinize it. From what I observe, it is exactly like the one I purchased at the auction. After flipping it over and going over the hallmarks, I must admit that to me they are identical. "I don't understand. It's the same. It's exactly the same!"

Leonard smiles again. "No it's not." He takes out a shiny chrome jeweler's loupe from his coat pocket and hands it to me. "Look again."

Holding it close to one eye to peer through it, I search the vase's base. "You're right. It's not the original."

Turning her head sequentially towards each of us, Gloria glares at both Leonard and me. "What makes you two say that?"

Answering her curtly, Leonard signals to me, "Ernie, tell her."

I cannot resist grinning. Very slowly and deliberately, I announce, "It doesn't have the enameler's mark."

This revelation has no effect on her. "So what?

Tiffany didn't have his craftsmen sign their works. That's a universally accepted fact."

"Gloria, while that's usually true, it's not for the 12 Columbian Exposition enameled vases. He was so concerned that they would get damaged in shipment that he had the enamelers sign the vases they worked on so that they could repair the very same vases they had created. He didn't trust his own paper records."

Leonard adds, "Only Ernie and I and a very few advanced collectors are privy to that. The curator in Havana isn't. He told me that his was the original one and that you had bought a fake."

We have not convinced her. With a finger stretched out towards it, she asks, "Leonard, how did you steal this vase and smuggle it out of Cuba?"

Unfazed by her directness, he defends himself. "I did neither of those things. They gave it to me."

"Why would they have done that?"

"The museum's director wants Ernie's vase and agreed to swap his for Ernie's."

"That's crazy Leonard. You expect me to believe that a museum would in good conscious exchange an original for a reproduction or, worse, a fake, as that museum's curator said it is."

"Yes, I do."

"Why? You are aware of the penalty for dealing in stolen merchandise?"

"Because the museum's director knows the true history of Ernie's vase and the curator doesn't. In Cuba information isn't readily passed on between colleagues."

Gloria has heard enough stories of Tiffany intrigue to be wary even of Leonard's claim. "If they are identical except for an enameler's mark, then why would the curator claim that ours is a fake and the director believe otherwise? Marks can be added and taken off by forgers."

Gently and carefully, he eases the vase from me. "Because the director's father made this one in Cuba."

"Did he tell you that?"

"Yes, and he proved it."

"How?"

Leonard slaps his hand on his knee. "It's too perfect. All of Tiffany was handmade and no two pieces were identical, even when meant to be a matching pair. He wanted it that way. He rejected the reproduction capabilities of the machines that were popping up all around him and being utilized by his competitors to make perfect copies of their sketches. Each piece of Tiffany was unique by his design."

Unyielding, Gloria asks, "In what way is it too perfect?"

"The work order number. They are the same. The director's father was a Cuban silversmith who earned his master's certificate in Spain both in silver and champlevé enamel work. In the 1960s he was ordered by Castro to make a duplicate of the Wild-Rose Vase in the old

President's Palace. Because he knew he was good enough to make a truly identical copy, which few of his contemporaries elsewhere could accomplish, but respected Tiffany's work too much to do so, he then conspired to leave two hints to future generations that his was the copy. First, he left off the enameler's mark, which others by mistake thought was a superfluous mark of no meaning since its significance was not in any of the Tiffany literature at the time."

I interrupt him. "And, I might add, still isn't."

Leonard nods. "You're right. The director's father knew better. Second, he made the work order number be the same. Since there had only been one Wild-Rose made by LCT, he felt confident that having two with the same order number should alert the savvy expert that something was wrong. The absence of the enameler's mark would tell which one was genuine and avoid the fraud from continuing."

"Did he say why Castro ordered the reproduction be done by his father?"

"Ernie, he was the dean of Havana's silversmiths and before the revolution had made most of the exceptional silverware in Cuba. Afterwards, he was ordered to make exact copies of the silver treasures of Cuba. The director said his father, without explicitly having been told this, figured out that Castro needed to do this to cover up his secretly selling off the originals to obtain U.S. dollars. In your vase's case, Castro demanded that his father take extra care when he fashioned the roses."

"Was Castro into roses?"

Shaking his head, he adds, "Castro never said anything beyond they carried some sort of particular significance and had to look real."

All of this is plausible to me, I interject, "He must want the original back home in Havana where it belongs and thinks I can pass off his father's as the original to pay for it."

Leonard nods in agreement. "Yes, and that's why we need to go to Mitch's house to compare the two to be convinced that all of this is really true. Even the museum's director isn't 100% certain about it. His father could have been innocently mistaken or, having been such a fervent opponent to Castro, he may have been capable of accusing Castro of doing anything nefarious. But if it is true, I'll buy yours for him."

"And if it's not?"

"Then we have a problem. Neither he nor I want the copy returned to the museum. If it does come back to Havana, it's only to be part of the director's family's collection of his father's work."

Before I agree to this deal, I have one last question for Leonard. "Why did you feel the need to trail me after the auction?"

"If yours is the real vase, as you and I believe it is, there are many who would go to any length to steal it. I wanted Adolpho around in case you ran into any trouble." He then motions to his driver to continue on to Mitch's house.

Chapter 20

I call Mitch to alert him that we are on our way to his house. Since he has sold Tiffany to Leonard before, he is not upset. Moreover, he thanks me for the heads up so that he can put out some of his best Tiffany pieces that are up for sale. On the way there, I finally get around to asking Leonard, "Why would I need Adolpho?"

"There are lots of rumors in the Cuban community about that vase."

"Like what?"

"They all center on why Castro felt the need to sell it. From the day the exchange happened, there have been questions raised about it by advanced collectors. You see, while his ploy to have a replacement switched for it initially worked outside the museum, within its walls people immediately suspected the swap. To this day no one, except possibly for members of his inner circle, was party to the events that were so critical that they forced him to sell one of Cuba's masterpieces of silver that had been the envy of the rest of the Latin American decorative arts world."

Thinking back to what happened in 2003, Gloria is not convinced that people would have perceived the substitution that promptly. "I bet you the director of the Sofia Imber Contemporary Art Museum in Caracas wouldn't be so confident that her staff there would be so observant. It had taken at least three years, maybe even six years, for her curators to discover that their Matisse's "Odalisque in Red Pants," which for twenty years had been one of the museum's prize possessions, had indeed been replaced by an elaborate forgery. Worse, only after she had been notified that the original was being offered for sale did she investigate the authenticity of the painting that was hanging on their wall. How did the Cubans uncover Castro's duplicity? It had to have been difficult, since it had to have been done clandestinely."

Leonard's being a silver collector makes it easy for him to explain why she is wrong. "As you know, old silver has a patina that new silver does not have. You can polish it out, but no one who respects old silver would do that, especially a museum. When the copy was placed in the very prominent case that the original had been in ever since Tiffany had given it to the President of Cuba in 1918, everyone who was into silver big time silently noted that the patina had changed. As I just said, it didn't take very long before all of Havana was speculating in private amongst themselves about what necessity had forced Castro to use that vase to finance it. When it was advertised that the vase was up for sale, all the old rumors resurfaced. Some people would like to make it go away along with the mystery surrounding it."

His last comment raises an issue with me. "What stopped the rumors in the first place?"

"Since that museum director's father held the two vases next to each other to settle in his mind that his copy was indistinguishable from the original except for the marks on their bases, no one has seen them together to substantiate that there had been such a severe deception made upon the Cuban people. That proved to be a very effective argument for the deniers within the government: 'OK, where's the other one?'"

This brings up another question. "What exactly are they denying?"

"Castro needed dollars to circuitously buy vital supplies from the U.S., such as medical supplies and replacement parts to cars, trucks and factory equipment originally made in the States. He also needed them to repair the eight planes in his Air Force that hadn't been destroyed in the Bay of Pigs Invasion until Russia came to his aid and resupplied his Air Force."

"That still doesn't sound like anything that would require denial by the Cubans."

He nods again. "It wouldn't. However, Castro had an extensive secret intelligence network in the U.S., particularly in south Florida and at the UN, whose primary assignment was to uncover and stop the CIA plots against him. Those agents required a continuous infusion of U.S. dollars to meet their forever increasing funding requirements."

Finding his "Spy vs. Spy" story to be funny, Gloria chuckles. "I don't think the fact that there was a ton of Cuban operatives in New York and Miami would've come as a surprise to many Americans or Cubans for that matter in the 1960s."

For Leonard this is all personal and he does not find any humor in it. Frowning his displeasure, he adds, "Yes, but what they ultimately did here would have! The Cold War may have ended in Eastern Europe decades ago, but it's still present in the Caribbean."

Hoping that perhaps with a little prodding he will reveal some of the dark secrets of the U.S./Cuban relationship that he has never disclosed before, I press on. "So, what the hell were they doing here that would still cause such a reaction by the Cubans?"

"At first Castro just wanted the facts about what the CIA was planning on doing to thwart him: everything from another invasion to the next assassination attempt against him. He followed Benjamin Franklin's dictum, 'an investment in knowledge pays the best interest.' We never got him because he always knew well in advance what we were up to. Then he discovered that the money he needed could be had for military intelligence of interest to the former Soviet Union and the current radical Arab countries. He also wasn't above selling information to Columbian drug lords."

While I welcome Leonard's opening up, it has not escaped me that my current situation may have a dark side, which demands that he not delay being frank with me. "That's all in the past. What would be so important to them today?"

He wags his finger in my face. "Do you think Castro would leave his spies out in the cold to fend for themselves against the FBI and CIA? Hell, some of them are double agents. He and his brother still need them."

Leonard is getting entirely too worked up about all of this. I try to cool him off. "Why? We're not about to invade Cuba or do any political assassinations there."

His face becomes flush, as he grows more irate. "You hope that or want that? If the truth about what they have done here in the U.S. were ever publicly divulged, it could be considered a legitimate provocation for all out war against Cuba."

258

I shake my head. "You Cuban expatriates are always seeking an excuse for the U.S. to attack Cuba."

"If just half of what has been said about that vase is true, even you, Ernie, would be clamoring for revenge."

About to reply, I spot that we have arrived at Mitch's house. Rather than pulling over at the curb, the driver continues on. I blurt out, "Hey, stop! That's Mitch's house!"

Annoyed by my outburst, Leonard both grimaces and glares at me. "He knows that, Ernie. We'll drive around the block to prove no one is tailing us before we stop."

After our brief tour of the neighborhood, we finally pause in Mitch's driveway with the engine still running. The driver gets out and surveys the street. Convinced we are safe, he walks around the car to our door. As he leans over to open it, I observe that he has a pistol in a shoulder holster. Rather than comment about it, I pretend to ignore it. Once both Gloria and I are standing on the walkway to the house, the driver hastily goes over to the street and again surveys it. He returns to the car and then opens Leonard's door. Because of his bulky physique, Leonard has trouble exiting the rear seat and uses the grab handle for assistance. With thick jet-black hair combed back without a part and an equally thick and black mustache, he has that very Latin look portrayed in the movies from the 50s. He turns around and bends over to retrieve his white linen suit jacket. He tells the driver, "You can turn the motor off."

"It's a bit warm to be wearing that," I observe.

Putting on his coat, he smiles at me and says, "Compared to Cuba, this is Alaska. You Americans keep your homes too cold for us Latinos."

Gloria points to his chest. "Where did you get that tie? Around here we don't see them with Cuban stamps."

"I picked it up in Havana. I thought the Cuban Red Macaw was particularly well done. As you can tell, I really like bright ties. They're good for business."

Noting that he is finally calming down, I kid him. "I guess you need them to close some of those infamous deals you are famous for."

"Whatever it takes, Ernie: power ties, fancy cars, Cuban cigars, whatever. Just so long as I don't go to jail." He then goes back into the rear of the limo to get the cigar box containing the copy of the Wild-Rose Vase and with it in hand joins us to walk to the house.

At Mitch's front door, I push the doorbell button. Mitch does not respond immediately and takes his time to open the door. In the interim, Leonard plucks an envelope out of his inner coat pocket. After thumbing through its contents, he lifts out a faded index card and hands it to me. "Read this and you'll know why the war continues. From the beginning it's been personal, not just politics."

There is typing on both sides. Flipping it over, I find the first sentence and read out loud a portion of what is written. "If Kennedy were not an illiterate and ignorant millionaire, he would understand that it is not possible to carry out a revolution supported by landowners against the peasant in the mountains, and that every time imperialism has tried to encourage counterrevolutionary

260

groups, the peasant militia has captured them in the course of a few days. But he seems to have read a novel, or seen a Hollywood film, about guerrillas, and he thinks it is possible to carry on guerrilla warfare in a country where the relations of the social forces are what they are in Cuba."

I turn it over and continue to read from it. "In any case, this is discouraging. Let no one think, however, that these opinions, as regards Kennedy's statements, indicate that we feel any sympathy towards the other one, Mister Nixon who has made similar statements. As far as we are concerned, both lack political brains." I stare at Leonard. "Where did this come from?"

"It's a portion of the transcript from Fidel Castro's 1960 Address to the U.N. General Assembly."

"OK, it's no secret that they hated each other. Kennedy even tried numerous times to assassinate him. But Castro wasn't declaring war then. So what war continues?"

I had barely finished when he pulls out another faded index card and gives it to me. "Read this. Castro wrote it to Celia Sánchez who served as his secretary when he was stuck in the mountains of the Sierra Maestra. It's about a farmer's house being attacked by rockets from Batista's air force, which was supplied by the U.S. The farmer had been a collaborator with the revolution."

After I return the other card to him, I study this one silently:
"Sierra Maestra
June 5 - 58

261

Celia: After seeing the rockets they shot at Mario's house, I've sworn that the Americans are going to pay dearly for what they are doing. When this war is over, a much wider and bigger war will begin for me, the war I am going to wage against them. I realize that that is going to be my true destiny.

Fidel"

"You consider this to be his declaration of war against the U.S.?"

Somberly, Leonard answers. "He did. It's not important what I think of it."

As I pass it back to him, I ask, "Why did you show me those two index cards?"

"Once we exchange vases, you become part of the resistance. You might as well be in on about why they are fighting."

Mitch finally opens the front door. He is very agitated. "Sorry to have taken so long, but someone just called me with a bizarre question."

Not liking the way this sounds, I ask, "What was it?"

"He said that he had been trying to get hold of you but was unable to. He asked how much you wanted for the Tiffany vase."

Gloria does not find that to be disturbing. "Mitch, lots of people at The Blue And The Gay know you and Ernie are friends. And your business phone number is not unlisted."

"You don't understand, Gloria. My home number *is* unlisted and that's the number he called."

She sighs before observing. "You're just paranoid. How many dealers have your home number? A bunch, I bet. Someone just gave it out to one of their good customers as a favor to Ernie."

"Then explain to me why he asked if Ernie had been here yet after I said I didn't have any idea what he wanted for it."

Leonard only raises one eyebrow before asking, "Did he say anything else?"

"Yeah, he insisted that he would counter any offer you made."

"Did he name me by my name?"

"Aren't you Ignacio Vargas Leonarte?"

"Yeah, I am."

Mitch smiles. "Well then, he named you by your name."

"Anything else?"

"He also asked if you had been here."

Leonard is taken aback by this question. He raises his other eyebrow, as well. "What did he mean by that?"

"To be precise, he asked, 'Has that son of a bitch shown up yet or are you still expecting him?' Of course, I denied being acquainted with you. I take it you are not close personal friends with this individual."

Leonard answers, "No," and then walks back to the limo and over to the driver who is standing between the car and the road and seems to be acting as some sort of a lookout. After a brief conversation, the driver re-enters the car and restarts it, and Leonard returns to Mitch's stoop. "He didn't happen to mention his name, did he?"

"No, nor did I ask for it. However, I should have his telephone number since I have caller ID on my home line."

"He couldn't be that stupid not to have blocked it?"

We all hurriedly move into Mitch's den where he punches in the numbers necessary to retrieve his last phone call. "It's 212-689-7215."

Startled upon hearing Mitch say that number, Leonard almost as a reflex and without hesitation declares, "That's the Cuban Mission!"

"How do you know that?"

"Trust me, I know that number."

"We'll call it and see." Mitch then dials the number on speakerphone.

In a broken, very thick Hispanic accent a man answers, "Permanent Mission of the Republic of Cuba to the United Nations, may I direct your call?"

He turns to Leonard and says, "You're right."

Leonard takes the phone and answers, "Miguel Garcia, please."

"I'm sorry but that is a restricted number."

"Tell him José Cuervo is calling."

After a brief moment of silence, I can overhear a female secretary say, "Mr. Garcia's office, may I say who's calling?"

Leonard answers, "Tell him Beckmann is calling and the ice is melting."

"I'll get him right away."

A minute later a man's voice comes across the speaker. "What can I do for you, José?"

"Tell me whose tailing me and why!"

"No one from here. By the way where are you? Aren't you in Havana visiting your mother?"

"Something came up and I had to return to the States. Someone is following me and left the Mission's phone number on caller ID."

"In that case, it's the CIA. They use our number whenever they are tailing our agents. Come on, we're not that stupid."

Chapter 21

I am flabbergasted. Who is Leonard? More importantly, what the hell have I gotten myself involved in? Antiques dealers are not political activists by tradition; rather we live in the shadows of the public celebrity where our clients are over exposed. When was the last time one of us was on the TV news besides the rare occurrence of somebody being carried away in handcuffs for defrauding his customers by selling fake or stolen merchandise? For that matter when was the last time one of us was on TV period except for appearing on the Antiques Roadshow or some lame reality show? Even Hollywood avoids us. Spies, villains, and heroes come from all walks of life in the movies but not from the antiques world. The most publicity for which we can hope is the fifteen minutes of fame that comes when one of us has set a world record price for an obscure item, like I just did at John's. Even that is an anomaly since it is felt best to do such a transaction as an anonymous telephone bidder. Everyone knows that those bidders, no ifs, ands, or buts about it, are calling from the room next to where the auction is being held in an effort to hide their identity from the other super rich bidders.

I genuinely love it when the really well-heeled collectors use an agent to bid for themselves. It is just another ploy. Who would pay millions of dollars for something they have not personally laid their eyes upon and let someone else have all the fun of successfully bidding for it? Besides, no one with that kind of wealth would completely trust an auction house. They are going to insure that they are not being ripped off. As for being anonymous, I can attest that is only true in their dreams.

They are merely hiding from the press and art thieves. By the next morning the gossip grapevine and blogs of us professionals has pinpointed who did it. After all, there are only a handful of people in this world who have the means and the desire to spend that kind of money on a painting, sculpture, or some piece of decorative arts. Plus, the true contenders are very well acquainted with each other.

Selling anything at auction is never done openly by us, even though we inevitably do so more frequently than we will ever admit to our clients. What kind of a salesman would reveal his need to use an auction house to turn over his inventory? No, we live a boring life that not a soul cares to explore in any depth. Today one and all, even pawnshop owners, cake bakers, and crab fisherman, has his own reality show on cable: everybody that is, but us. To add insult to injury, even our pickers can claim a TV show. Of course, there was that book and movie about a Savannah antiques dealer who killed his gay lover.

As for my suddenly being some sort of a freedom fighter, it is just plain outlandish. Hell, I do not even vote in elections. When asked for whom I am going to vote, I can honestly say none of the above. It is safer that way. Politics and religion are two topics that I like to avoid when talking to anyone other than a relative. They are excellent ways to lose a deal and a customer. The closest I ever come to meeting politicians is by owning their autographs on their photographs. But you are never really confident they are genuine. The sons of bitches cannot be trusted to give their supporters a real one despite their overly generous contributions. They have machines or their secretary do it for them. Yes, I am in completely uncharted waters.

Before I can confront Leonard, Helen who has been with us in the den the whole time asks him, "Are you some sort of a spy? Because that sure sounded like you were using passwords and codes to talk to that fella at the Cuban Mission."

"No, Helen, I'm just an opportunist. As I just told Ernie, I do whatever it takes to make the deal, as long as I stay out of jail."

"And I guess that would include avoiding a firing squad in Havana?"

"Especially that. Foremost in my thoughts is doing whatever it takes to restore Cuba to its rightful place in the world's economy. We have spent over a half of a century in economic purgatory."

"Why then are you so intimate with the Cuban Mission? Mitch and I always thought you hated Castro and were part of the resistance."

"Despite America attempting to make Cuba go away through its boycott, there are times both countries require each other. When events dictate it, someone needs to be the fixer. There has always been one since Castro took over. Today that someone is me. One day I may be on Cuba's payroll, the next day I may be on Washington's payroll."

"What exactly do you know about the vase, Leonard?"

"The proof of the existence of two identical Tiffany Wild-Rose Vases somehow is not in the best interest of either the United States or Cuba."

That observation is both something new to me and perplexing. "Why would the U.S. care about Castro's having had a duplicate made and selling the original one?"

Leonard falters for a second. "Beats me. But when I was at the museum, its director mentioned that the CIA had been there wanting to inspect the vase they had."

"They sent an agent to Havana?"

"I doubt they actually sent someone there since they have plenty of local collaborators who spy on the government for them. He was probably one of them. Anyway, when the upcoming auction of the real vase was announced, he showed up and wanted to examine theirs."

"Couldn't he have just evaluated it without alerting the museum."

"No! He wanted to study its base. He unquestionably knew what to find to determine which one was the original and which one was the fake."

"Why do you say that?"

"He came with a special camera that's not available in Cuba to photograph the vase."

"What was so special about it?"

"Per the director, it was a 1.4-gigapixel hand held digital camera. He said its images were so good you could see the tool marks on the vase."

Helen observes, "That would indicate that the CIA

had at least lent him the camera, because only our government has that level of resolution as prototypes. And they are being made for NASA to search space for dangerous objects that might be on their way to hit the Earth. But it doesn't prove he was working for them. He wouldn't have dared to be so conspicuous if he was actually in the employ of The Company."

"That's all true. But the Cuban Intelligence Service was there even earlier to do their photography. They positively identified themselves."

"Why would the CuIS want to do that? They couldn't have believed it's the genuine one."

"The director told me that they wanted to verify that an elaborate fraud was not about to take place. They openly feared that the fake could someway be switched for the real one at the auction and that they might end up buying back their own vase."

I laugh. "Isn't that what we are about to do tonight in some sense?"

Finding it to be kind of funny too, Leonard grins slightly before observing, "Yeah, but in the end the museum will get the real one back."

Still not satisfied, Helen insists, "No agent I've ever dealt with, would have been so transparent. He took incredible risks letting the director witness him having such a special camera."

"I would agree with you, Helen, except the director didn't seem to me to be a loyal Castro supporter. I wouldn't be surprised to find out that he has helped out the CIA in the past. Besides, I'm suspicious that the director himself took the pictures for them in the museum's photography room."

"What makes you say that?"

"From the quality of the photographs that he kept for himself on the museum's computer. Only a photographer, who was at ease with the CIA and they with him, would have openly shown the amount of pride in them that he did. More importantly, he was allowed by them to keep a set of copies."

"If that is so, then why would he have shown them to you?"

"Since it is no secret that I play both sides of the political fence when it comes to U.S./Cuban relations and never reveal my informants to the authorities, people in Havana are far looser with me than they would be with their own families. Even the CIA and CuIS hold my sources, when I'm involved, at arm's length."

Having come to a different conclusion, I add, "Perhaps he was just so proud of his father's work he wanted to have copies of the photographs and the CIA granted his wish. He has no guarantee that the copy his father made will ever return to Cuba."

"That last part is true. However, in this case his museum director's background overruled his family's pride. He wants the original, and he wants it bad. Which brings me to why I am here. Where's the original?"

Mitch walks over to the polished brass and glass cabinet and unlocks the door. We follow him. While

Leonard is placing the cigar box with the copy on a nearby large end table, Mitch bends over and hands Helen, one at a time, several pieces of Tiffany glass before revealing the vase. She carefully puts them on that same end table. He then lifts out the vase, passes it to Leonard, and asks, "You got it?" After Leonard acknowledges his securely holding it in his right hand by saying, "Got it," Mitch lets go of it and states, "This is the original." Then Helen cautiously delivers back to Mitch, again one at a time, the pieces of Tiffany glass that he very precisely returns to their original location in the cabinet.

Leonard turns to me and says, "Ernie, open that box on the end table and get out the copy." While I am doing so, he flips the original over and with his loupe surveys its base. "You're right, this is the original."

In the meantime, I take the copy vase out of its box and, holding it in both of my hands, scrutinize it. "This is magnificent. If I didn't know you had the original, I would swear this is it. In my humble opinion it's better done."

Leonard places the original on the end table while I set the copy next to it. All five of us encircle the vases and compare them. I go first. "I really can't tell the difference."

Mitch speaks next, "Neither can I."

Helen just shakes her head, no.

Although speechless initially, Gloria eventually opines, "If you hadn't told me otherwise, I would have never guessed they hadn't been made at the same time, in

272

the same shop, by the same silversmith, although I have to admit that I agree with Ernie that with them next to each other the copy seems to be slightly better."

Leonard finally says what I have been waiting to hear. "We have a deal. Let me go get the money." He then leaves the den and enters the foyer where he cries out, "Oh my God!"

All of us tear into the foyer. With his head tilted upwards, he just stares at the large Morgan size hanger. Mitch asks, "What's wrong Leonard?"

He answers, "Where did you get that!"

"From a house in San Francisco that was destroyed by the 1989 earthquake."

"Any clue where they got it?"

"Gloria thinks it originally came from the Presidential Palace."

"It did. Its mate is still hanging there. Were any of you told the *real* story behind it?"

Mitch seeks out Gloria. "I think Gloria should answer that. She's explored it more than I have."

Gloria recounts what she considers its history to be. "As best as I can tell, it is one of two later copies of the original hanger that LCT had made for J. P. Morgan, Jr. who wanted a bigger version of the Tiffany hanger he had seen in the newly constructed First United Methodist Church in L.A. The records from Tiffany Studios show that around 1923 the President of Cuba commissioned the duplicates for his new Presidential Palace after visiting Mr. Morgan's deceased father's library and falling in love with the one there. How it got to San Francisco is a mystery to me."

Leonard eyes his watch. "I don't have much time, but I will tell you all a secret. That shade came to be in San Francisco to pay for an assassination plot against then President Gerald Ford and then Governor Ronald Reagan at the Republican National Convention in Kansas City. The proceeds from its sale at auction went to the Emiliano Zapata Unit."

"Which was?" she asks.

"Gloria, they were a radical terrorist cell in the Bay Area that was responsible for several bombings. Castro sent it there to fund the hit they were to carry out in Kansas City."

Mitch is incredulous but delighted. If this were true, the value of the shade has just skyrocketed. Imagine owning the payoff vehicle for a Presidential assassination. "How did you learn all of this?"

"Unlike you Americans, we Cubans read everything written about the US/Cuban cold war. Google a Gregg Daniel Adornetto. He was big in 1976 when he turned on his old gang. He affirmed in his statements to the FBI that, while he was a member of the Weather Underground years earlier and had been in Cuba, he had met a Cuban Agent, Andres Gomez. From what he said, the Weather Underground sent its members to Cuba for terrorist training and to get support. He fingered Gomez, who he claimed was an agent for the Intelligence Directorate, as the 'Cuban link' to the assassination plot."

Each of us is curious about how this was all carried out. Mitch persuades Leonard to fill in the details. "How did they sell it?"

"It was consigned to a major auction house in San Francisco by a Cuban sympathizer who lived in Canada. He did a lot of this type of thing for Castro over the years. The import records in Toronto show that the shade was originally sent there from Havana. The Canadian drove it to San Francisco in the back of his VW van to avoid any questions from U.S. Customs officials. The border guards believed his story that it was a reproduction he had made and was delivering to a restaurant in the States. He immediately had the auction house appraise it and authenticate that it was genuine. They were delighted to handle its sale since they easily recognized it was a larger version of the one in a Methodist church in Oakland and expected the collectors in the Bay Area would too. The provenance of the one in Oakland was well documented: that church had received it as a gift from its original owner, the First United Methodist Church in LA. Plus, the Morgan hanger was an acknowledged exact copy of it. How could the auction house's customers not want the larger one? They even had its picture be the front cover of its spring catalogue for that year.

"From the beginning that guy from Canada had assumed the name of the leader of the Emiliano Zapata Unit and signed the documents as the consignee under that alias. The auction house's records confirm that he had shown them a passport and a driver license as proof of identity. Both turned out to have been forged with that pseudonym. To this day, his real name has not been disclosed. What's more, the bill of lading on its shipment to Toronto had his assumed name as the consignee."

"When it was sold, how did the Canadian transfer the money to that group?"

"That was simple, Ernie. The auctioneer per his routine made the check out to the consignee. Since it was in his alias, all he had to do was turn it over to the real leader of Emiliano Zapata, who deposited it into their checking account at a local bank. At that time the Federal Reserve and Treasury Department did not monitor such large deposits."

Recalling this case, Helen asks, "Wasn't it the IRS that found out about all of these financial dealings?"

Leonard nods, yes. "They investigated Emiliano Zapata for tax evasion since they were not registered as a non-profit organization. They traced each step of the sale up to the shade's arrival in Toronto."

There are so many tax scams in the business of antiques, mainly involving donations to museums, that my curiosity is aroused. "How did the IRS get wind of that particular deal?"

"When they conducted a routine audit of the auction house in 1977, they found the sale. $250,000 caught their attention. That was a lot of money back then. They were unable to document that the leader of Emiliano Zapata had ever paid income taxes in the U.S. and couldn't find his group in the listed non-profit organizations in California."

Mitch is elated with having discovered the provenance of his hanger. "So, some rich guy in San Francisco bought the shade at auction and hung it in the foyer of his mansion until the 1989 earthquake wrecked the place. Does the auction house have his name?"

"Somewhere in its archives it should. The IRS wasn't interested in that part of the plot since the actual sale was perfectly legal. However, unless it was some decorator or dealer who purchased it, you should be able to find that out, if not from the auction house then from the FBI records under the Freedom of Information Act. The Bureau thoroughly probes everything when they do an investigation. I wonder who there changed the records to indicate that it had come to San Francisco from New York instead of Cuba?" Leonard hastily leaves to go to the car, or so I think, to get the money he owes me.

While I wait for his return, I hear what sounds like a helicopter over the house. We don't get a lot of helicopters flying around our neighborhoods so we all go out to see what it is up to. There in the middle of the street the helicopter is attempting to land. Leonard's driver is diverting cars away from it. Once it lands, Leonard ducks under its still rotating propeller and takes out a suitcase from the passenger's seat. He next trots over to me and hands me the suitcase and the key to its lock. "This should more than adequately cover your expenses and your commission." Before I can open it, he scurries into the house to get the vase.

With what feels like gale force winds blowing about and making me fumble with the key, I try to unlock the suitcase. Meanwhile, Leonard is walking back to the helicopter with my original vase in its presentation cigar box from Cuba securely nestled in both of his hands. When I finally unfasten the suitcase, I discover it is full of money--lots of money!! As Leonard climbs aboard the helicopter, I holler to overcome its motor's whine, "How much is in here?"

"Two million, six hundred thousand dollars in $100 bills."

I am overwhelmed. "That's way too much!"

"No it's not. You will need every penny of it, trust me."

"What do you mean by that?"

"I don't have time to explain. I have to return this vase to the museum in Havana before it opens in the morning and someone discovers it's missing. Besides the CIA will be here momentarily. My driver will take you back home. Good luck!"

Chapter 22

Leonard's chopper takes off, preventing us from asking him any further questions. Gloria in particular does not understand his aside. "Ernie, what did he mean you *will* need every penny of it?"

"You got me there. All he said is that he wants me to sell the copy to pay for the original. Who's going to pay $2,600,000 for it?" Mitch laughs. I do not sense anything that is amusing in my predicament. "What do you find to be so damn funny in all of this?"

"Remember that caller from earlier today. He said he would top anything Leonard offered you. Perhaps you can sell him the copy as the original and make out like a bandit."

Helen pokes him in his ribs. "You idiot! Weren't you listening? That guy is from the Agency and is probably on his way here if Leonard is correct. You don't want to screw around with them."

I have to agree with Helen. "It definitely would be reckless for me to misrepresent the copy vase. I'll admit that I will take advantage of an unsuspecting and naïve widow on occasion, but selling a reproduction for over $2,600,000 is something I could go to jail for or worse. Like Leonard, I try to avoid doing potentially life-threatening things like that."

Mitch is a dealer and has the dealer's ethos. "So, how *are* you going to sell it? It was consigned to you to be sold."

Shaking her head, Gloria disagrees. "Not exactly. It was Ernie who advanced that the museum director's intent was to pass off his father's copy as the original in order to pay for it. Leonard agreed but never said we had to do that or where the money actually came from, only that this vase would pay for the original."

"Are you playing word games with us, Gloria?"

"Yes, and so is Leonard."

"In what way?"

"Mitch, how many consignments do you handle in a year?"

"Hundreds, you think I personally owned all of those expensive lamps?"

"Well, how many times have you done it without anything in writing and a minimum price being established for the sale."

He rapidly concedes. "I can't think of one."

"Of course, not. No one does it the way Ernie has described. All Leonard said was that passing off the copy would help pay for the original, isn't that right, Ernie?"

"Come to think of it, if I remember what I said correctly, you are right."

Helen has found one issue that no one has considered. "Is there a specific person who is supposed to receive the copy as the original?"

I stare at her. "What do you mean by that?"

"Just as I said, does the museum director have someone in mind to pass the vase on to? Maybe getting the copy to the right person will be enough payment for him."

Gloria again shakes her head. "If that were the case, Ernie would have been told to do that and the individual would have already been named."

Suddenly, I recall one of the messages that had been left on my home phone. "Someone did do that."

Having forgotten about what I am talking, Gloria asks disparagingly, "What do you mean?"

"Remember that message some woman left on the phone, 'Do not sell the vase?' Perhaps she's the one who is supposed to get it."

"How the hell does she expect you to figure that out, much less, find her? She even had her telephone number on caller ID blocked."

"Good point. I guess the only way of doing this is to have it at 'the show' and wait for her to come to me."

Helen becomes very excited. "I just had an epiphany."

Mitch rolls his eyes. "What is it?"

"What if the copy is the original?"

"You are crazy! No one the least bit familiar with

Tiffany would consider a reproduction, no matter how good it is, to be an original."

"Yes they would!"

"Helen, it's late and you need to go to bed. You are obviously overtired and not thinking straight."

"No, I'm not. Now hear me out!"

Mitch backs off. He realizes he has pushed her too far. I ask her gently, "Please explain what you mean. At first glance it doesn't seem plausible."

"Everyone knows that Tiffany made a Wild-Rose Vase for the Columbian Exposition. Only a handful of people know that a silversmith made an exact copy of it for Castro. Perhaps it is the copy that everyone is seeking."

"OK, I can understand all of that. But why would they care that much for a reproduction? That violates the rules. All other times, everyone wants the original and ignores the copy, no matter how good it is."

"Did Leonard have an explanation why Castro had the museum director's father make the replica?"

"Not exactly. He said the director thought it was to cover up Castro's selling the original one to obtain dollars to pay for some necessity."

"Precisely! Without the copy, there is no proof that Castro did that."

Where is Helen going with all of this? "So what?"

282

"So, it could be evidence of some misdeed he had done and Cuba wants forgotten, just like our hanger is."

Mitch is chagrined. "I have to apologize to you Helen. What you just said is conceivable. In a court of law the copy would be the original piece of evidence of a conspiracy to defraud the Cuban people."

Breaking her silence, Gloria remains unconvinced. "I've been thinking about what Helen has proposed. While it's possible, why didn't Castro just sell the reproduction as an original? From what you all have been saying, very few back then would have had the insight to look for that enameler's mark. And isn't it easy to overlook? Practically everyone would have missed that it was a counterfeit."

Helen's response is quick in coming. "That's self-evident."

Unfortunately, it is not to me. "It is? I think Gloria has made a good observation. Perhaps we have it totally wrong."

Helen is adamant. "I don't think so."

"Well, you haven't thought it through then. Forbes accuses Castro of having siphoned off hundreds of millions of dollars. I think it was $900 million dollars last time I saw their listing. He might have wanted that vase for himself."

"What are you saying, Ernie? He made a copy so that he could own the original."

"Exactly. It wouldn't be the first time a country's

283

leader stole from his citizens."

Dissatisfied with the direction the conversation has taken, Mitch sighs. "That's ridiculous, Ernie."

"Why do you say that?"

"Because it never would have left Cuba if he owned it. And John would not have auctioned it off. And you wouldn't own it."

Helen bursts in. "That's BS. Both his daughter and his sister left Cuba as exiles. Either one of them could've taken it and later sold it. Hell, he may even be a softy deep down inside and gave it to one of them as a memento. Besides, if it were a payoff, he had to have sent the original since the agent contracted to obtain or do whatever he wanted done would have had to have it authenticated in order to sell it, despite Gloria's feeling otherwise. Forgeries have been made for eons. It would have been too important a piece even in the Sixties not to be vetted. He couldn't risk having the putz find out it was a fake and being stuck with it! What would the sap have done or said: nothing, I bet, that would have pleased Castro, who knew better than to screw one of his operatives."

Once more, Mitch agrees with her and nods his approval. "You're right again. In the Sixties Tiffany had the archivists and records to validate their earlier work. They would've hunted for the enameler's mark. It would've been too great of a gamble for Castro to take if it were made for a payoff, especially for something nefarious like espionage or worse, a hit. So, the question is was the copy in Ernie's possession made for a payoff or for a sovereign theft?"

Frustrated by all of this futile speculation and with an impending need to know what Leonard meant, I call for a halt to it. "Let's be smart. The CIA and the Cubans aren't worked up about these vases because some relative of Castro took one without permission or was given it in the past and then sold it. Leonard didn't pay $2,600,000 for one of Castro's toys. No, there is more to this than that. It must be what Helen first said it was: some sort of evidence of a misdeed. So, who are the good guys and who are the bad guys?"

Before we have a chance to settle the issue, Leonard's driver approaches Gloria and me. "We need to go, Sir."

"How come?"

"The CIA will be here presently and it would be best if you weren't here when they arrive!"

"If I'm not here, they'll just go to my house. What difference does it make?"

"They won't come to your house."

"How come? That makes no sense."

"Adolpho's there."

"So?"

Impassively, the driver confidently declares, "They won't mess with him."

"You are talking about the United States Central Intelligence Agency?"

"Yeah, the guys from Langley."

Helen's past interaction with them forces her to ask, "And why won't the CIA mess with Adolpho?"

"He's from JM/WAVE."

"That's ridiculous. They closed JM/WAVE in the late 60's."

"Yes, ma'am. They closed JM/WAVE in 1968 to be precise, after RFK was assassinated."

"Why then do you say he's from JM/WAVE?"

The driver remains stone-faced. "Because he is."

"You mean they officially closed JM/WAVE, but they didn't really close JM/WAVE."

He reluctantly allows a smile to creep up. "Yes, ma'am. I can tell you have some experience with The Company."

"Where is JM/WAVE currently?"

"I've not at that level, ma'am. You'll need to ask Adolpho or Mr. Leonarte."

Enough of this, I finally have to intervene. "What the hell are you two talking about? Who or what the hell is JM/WAVE?"

The usually circumspect Helen matter-of-factly explains, "It was the CIA's station in Miami that oversaw our anti-Cuban activities during the Kennedy and

286

Johnson administrations. Because of LBJ's change in foreign policy emphasis from Cuba to Viet Nam it was officially considered obsolete in 1968 and closed. Its leadership team was transferred to Laos. A smaller operation took its place in Miami."

"Why would this man claim it's still around, if that were true?"

"JM/WAVE took on a life of its own. The real reason it was eventually closed after a slow death was that Langley could no longer control it, particularly after RFK was gone. They had planned another invasion of Cuba for 1965 to coincide with the successful assassination of Castro. It literally had become an intelligence agency separate from but still within the CIA. Some within the Agency described it as an independent country nestled within south Florida. Worse for Washington, some of its alumni never accepted its closing. The Agency must've had to reactivate JM/WAVE just to figure out what its now-disjointed 15,000 plus member army was up to and to block some of their more harebrained plots."

"Who were these men?"

"Castro's worst nightmare. They were fanatics who could not and would not accept his still being in power. And they were powerful. They spun a web that incorporated the Mafia and the extreme anti-communist far-right movements in the U.S. In the 1970s the banks of Miami were once described as the Wall Street for drug dealers and the city itself the main cog in international fascism."

I turn to the driver. "What's Adolpho's involvement

in all of this?"

"He tells me he is the designated driver among a bunch of drunks."

"What does that mean?"

"How about the only adult among a bunch of overly tired children?"

"I still don't understand what you mean?"

"I'm sorry but that's how he describes his job. He claims that there is a feud among the Cuban people and neither side is willing to compromise. He comes in and tries to bring some sort of sanity to this dysfunctional family. Left to their own means they would kill each other off one bomb at a time."

"Why then does the Agency leave him alone?"

This question the driver likes, grins broadly, and smugly states, "He's above them."

My limited familiarity with the intelligence agencies of the United States prevents me from believing that statement. "How is someone above the CIA?"

"He works under Mr. Leonarte, who enjoys the good graces of the White House and the President of Cuba. Each of our countries has decided that he's the one who can keep insane acts by extremists on either side from precipitating a nuclear war."

My grimace belies my attempt to hide my reservations. "They're still worried about that? I thought the missile crisis ended that."

"Do you have a premonition about what Russia would do if we invaded Cuba?"

"No."

"Well, neither do the Russians." He then opens the passenger door for us.

Chapter 23

Three blocks from our house, we hear dogs yelping uncontrollably. Even from this distance we can tell that they are Dumb and Dumber. Gloria and I stare at each other. Both of us hope otherwise but understand that something is wrong. I can only imagine what the police stationed in front of our house will have waiting for us. Is there a limit to how much a doggie court can fine someone for infractions incurred within a 24-hour period? This routine issue has brought us back to reality. Gloria is more upset about it than I am. "So much for that macho Hispanic BS about, 'I have a way of getting animals to do exactly what I want them to do.' I wonder who he is going to say is presently in control, him or Dumb and Dumber.

I do have one positive observation to make once we can see our front lawn. "At least they're not loose. He did say, 'no one gets away from him.'"

As we slow to a stop, Gloria gestures towards our house and shouts out, "You can say that again!"

The police car parked in front of our house has both of its front doors wide opened. A nearly full moon and the streetlight illuminate the two officers who were in it when we left. They are now head down in the grass with Dumb and Dumber licking whatever exposed parts of their faces our dogs' long tongues can reach. On either side of them are Adolpho and Leonard. Both have pistols drawn and aimed. I ask the driver who, like me, is also taking in this scene, "What the Hell is going on?"

He shrugs his shoulders. "I don't have the faintest idea. I thought Leonard was on his way to Havana."

No longer her usually confident self and definitely showing a lot of agitation, Gloria asks haltingly. "Should we get out?"

The driver pauses to consider the situation. "No, I'll go and see what's up and see if it's safe for you two."

He opens his door. Leonard hollers, "Stay inside. I'll call you when it is OK to come out." The door slams shut.

We all watch Adolpho use the officers' handcuffs to shackle their arms behind their backs. With his pistol he nudges them onto their feet. Dumb and Dumber, upset about no longer being able to slobber all over them, start barking anew before moving on to sniffing their shoes. Gloria begins to laugh. I ask her, "What do you find so funny in all of this?"

"Watch the dogs. You do see what they are about to do to those policemen's feet?"

Hearing me giggle too, the driver turns around to find out what we find to be so funny. "Am I missing something?"

Gloria answers, "Just keep your eyes on the dogs! Dumb and Dumber are about to pee on those two guys shoes. I know their routine."

When they do just that, we all snicker. Leonard waves to the driver, who lowers the front passenger side window to hear what he has to say. "You can come out now."

The driver opens his door again and walks over to where all of them are gathered. I can tell that he is not happy with whatever Leonard and Adolpho are proposing. He walks back to the limo and opens our doors. "Leonard wants to speak to both of you."

I am curious to hear what their argument was all about. "It appears that you disagree with Leonard about something."

"Yeah, he wants me to put those two in my limo wearing *those* shoes!"

Gloria and I open our doors and cautiously approach Leonard and Adolpho. She asks, "What are you two doing to these police officers?"

Adolpho speedily replies, "They aren't police officers."

One of them interrupts and says, "Yes, we are ma'am. These two lunatics are in big trouble. They attacked us and now they're trying to kidnap us."

Signaling him to keep quiet, Leonard aims his pistol at the officer.

I have never encountered Leonard acting this way before. What am I to do? Finally, I decide to confront him. "What are you up to? And where the hell did you get that gun? You always claimed to be a pacifist."

"It's a gift from these two gentleman who are the CIA agents who stole your son's van and after returning

292

it have been patiently waiting for you to return with the vase."

"I thought they knew better than to mess with Adolpho, at least that's what your driver said?"

"We did too. But they're stupid."

"In what way?"

"They never learn and are too stupid to shut up."

After giving them the once-over, I admit, "I don't understand."

He jabs his pistol into the ribs of the closest one. "When Adolpho recognized them and said that Task Force W was the stupidest police unit he had ever seen or heard of, these two clowns started to argue with him."

"Why would that cause you to arrest them or do whatever you two are doing to them?"

"Ever heard of Task Force W?"

"No. Should've I?"

"Probably not and neither should a regular cop." Leonard pushes his pistol even harder and deeper into the officer's ribs, making him wince.

Gloria butts in. "What was Task Force W?"

"Back in the Sixties it was the CIA's unit that ran "Operation Mongoose. Wasn't it fellas?"

She is not satisfied. "What the hell was Operation Mongoose?"

Leonard asks the two officers, "Does one of you want to tell her or do I have to?"
Neither of them speaks. "So, all of a sudden, you've decided to keep quiet. I guess you two, have learned your lesson after all. Operation Mongoose was Kennedy's effort to overthrow Castro. It was ended over 40 years ago." Leonard pulls his pistol away from the officer's ribs only to place the tip of its barrel on his nose. "Wasn't it?"

Sweat begins to bead up on his forehead as he answers Leonard, "Yeah, it was."

"But some of you guys in the Agency think the Special Group still exists or should, don't you?"

Having lifted his head to free himself from the gun, the officer insolently responds, "Damn straight we do! This country has done nothing but go down hill ever since we surrendered to that communist pig. And you're nothing but a traitor, Leonarte, to both of your countries."

His tirade only heightens Leonard's fury. He throws that officer to the ground before confronting the other officer, grabbing his collar and twisting it tightly around his neck. "Am I a traitor?"

Suddenly breaking Leonard's grip, the officer straightens his back and lunges at Leonard. Adolpho quickly moves to restrain him, but not before he says, "Absolutely! The worst kind."

Leonard's contempt for them is striking when he smiles while caressing his gun. "You two idiots will get us all killed. I keep telling the Agency to lock you both up."

That officer wiggles free of Adolpho and is face to face with Leonard. "You're as much of a coward as that asshole President of ours was. If he hadn't chickened out we wouldn't be the second class country we've become in the eyes of the rest of the world."

With his left hand again squeezing the officer's neck, Leonard puts his gun to the temple of the officer's skull. "I take it back. You don't learn, do you?"

Alarmed by Leonard's apparent loss of control, Adolpho comes over and seizes him by the arm. "That's enough. If you kill them, then you'll only be doing what they want you to do. No one will come to your defense if they end up dead."

Promptly, Leonard seems to calm down. "You're right. Some goody two-shoes from Justice will just indict me. Those retards would love to throw the entire CIA in jail as war criminals."

Once he has helped the officer get up off of our lawn, Aldopho pulls both of them back away from Leonard and then asks, "What do we do with them for now?"

"I'll drop them off at Guantanamo on the way back to Havana. Go put them in the limo, Adolpho."

I cannot help from mentioning, "Agent Johnson would like to arrest them."

Leonard wrinkles his forehead. "Who the hell is

he?"

"An FBI agent who's after these two for stealing Secret Service license plates."

"Fine, I'll let him interrogate them before leaving for Cuba."

Gloria who is really annoyed by Leonard's judgment of his prisoners butts in. "But they're U.S. citizens!"

"You see any citizenship papers on them? I don't. And you won't either. Their kind never has real IDs on them. Terrorists don't deserve the rights of real Americans. They're enemy combatants as far as I'm concerned. How about you, Adolpho?"

Before he has a chance to answer, she insists, "They haven't done anything that would be considered terrorism. Stealing yes, but not that."

"That's only because once again I've caught them in time. If they had gotten that vase, they would have caused plenty of havoc for the U.S. to clean up."

One of the officers spits on Leonard's face as Adolpho begins to lead them to the limo. "I spit on you. I spit on your mother in Cuba."

Leonard takes his handkerchief out of his suit jacket's breast pocket and wipes the spit off. He is about to strike that officer with the butt of his pistol; however, he abruptly stops and grabs from the officer's belt a second pair of handcuffs. He wraps them around the back of the officer's neck to pull him closer to himself.

"You're not worth the piss those dogs sprayed on your shoes." He then drags the handcuffs around to the front of the officer's neck and pushes up, choking him.

Adolpho hands off the officer, who did not confront Leonard, to the driver who then puts him in the limo. He swiftly goes back to retrieve the other officer from Leonard's hold and pushes him to the car. Still coughing from the chokehold, this officer remains defiant and struggles to get loose. Adolpho warns him, "How many times have I told you, 'Don't fuck with him, you idiot!' There are things worse than death!"

Once the two officers are in the limo, Leonard orders the driver, "Take them to the airstrip. I'll be there in a bit. By the way, find a FBI agent named Johnson, who's in town. Tell him to meet me there. He wants to talk to those two." He then takes out his cell phone and calls someone. All I hear him say is, "Come here!"

Meanwhile, Gloria goes over to the limo and gets both the suitcase full of money and the vase out of it. Next, she walks over to the police car and puts them down on the curb next to it. She pushes its doors closed. Patting the police car while still standing beside it, she snidely asks, "What do you want us to do with this, Leonard? Someone will be missing it."

"I forgot all about it. I'll get Adolpho to have it towed."

"Won't someone from the Police Department be suspicious that the cops they had protecting our house are gone and so is their car?"

"They've never been cops guarding your house. It's

been the CIA the whole time."

I just do not follow Leonard's statements. "Whose side are you working for?"

He straightens out his tie before answering me. "We don't worry about that. In my line of work that is a philosophical concept sort of like which religion is the true religion. Right and wrong eventually just don't exist. That's why so many spies become turncoats and take the money."

"Then what do you believe in?"

"I've always told you I'm a fixer. I make things work. In this case, I'm trying to keep Cuba and the U.S. from going to war. Didn't you say I claim to be a pacifist?"

Gloria shakes her head. "Isn't that being a bit bombastic? After all we're not even discussing the possibility of war with Cuba in this country."

"Maybe you haven't. Maybe the Congress hasn't, at least, not recently. But within the intelligence agencies of both countries it continues to be a constant topic for debate."

"Why?"

Leonard points his finger at her. "I know you won't believe me." He then points at himself. "But despite all that I'm privy to, even I don't have the answer to why, but a peaceful resolution has not been a viable option. For decades, ever since the Cuban Missile Crisis, regardless of what has happened and who has been killed, it has just not been enough. There has been this hunger in the belly of our relations demanding a final military solution; winner takes all. Call it a grudge match, if you want. I've been told that the reasons behind all of this have been buried for a long time. Somehow that vase is a critical piece of the puzzle."

He is right. I just cannot accept that. "There must be someone in our government who does."

"If there is, he or she isn't talking to me about it. For over 50 years there has been a fixer for Cuba, someone who both sides have decided to trust and who is responsible for keeping both of us from doing something really asinine." He motions towards the limo. "Like what those two would have us do. They don't let me see the papers of my predecessors. Hell, I'm kept in the dark about who they are, except for the first one, who in DC is held in disgrace as *persona non grata* and an example of what not to become. Once you retire from this job, officially you never had it."

"Sort of like the *Men in Black*!"

"Yeah, but they're not real."

Gloria joins us. "What really happened in the early Sixties? Is that why the first fixer is held in such contempt? After all, we had the Bay of Pigs and the Cuban Missile Crisis. It doesn't seem that he did a very good job."

"Those records have been expunged."

"What do you mean by that?"

"I have searched for them everywhere, including the CIA. They're just gone."

"What about all those tapes and first hand accounts that have been made public?"

"They're there. They're real. But the story we have is like Swiss cheese, full of holes."

I have read all of those accounts of what went on during the Cuban Missile Crisis and do not recall anything being left out. "What kind of holes are you talking about?"

Leonard sternly says, "What really went on in Havana."

"What do you mean?"

"Despite later claims to the contrary, it is no secret that it didn't take much persuasion for Castro to accept those Russian missiles being sent over to Cuba 'in the interests of strengthening the socialist camp.' You see, Castro initially feared retaliation from the U.S., but Khrushchev reassured Che Guevara sometime in July 1962. He said something to the effect, 'You don't have to worry; there will be no big reaction from the U.S.'

"Khrushchev's confidence stemmed from the Vienna Summit in June 1961 where he was neither charmed nor threatened by JFK who he felt was 'too intelligent and too weak.' Kennedy gave an even harsher judgment of his own performance there describing the meeting as the 'roughest thing in my life. He just beat the hell out of me.' If you remember, shortly in less than three months Khrushchev built the Berlin Wall.

However, he would later regret giving such encouraging counsel to the Cubans.

"Right in the middle of the missile crisis, as it worsened, an emboldened Castro went on to send a letter to Khrushchev on October 26, 1962. His letter was coldly received in Moscow, since they believed it advocated a preemptive strike on the U.S. They feared Castro was trying to instigate a war when he had earlier ordered his anti-aircraft weapons to shoot down any U.S. plane that came close to Cuba. In fact, Castro was a man of his word and did just that the day after that letter had been sent when his defense force hit a U2 with a Russian missile. This, of course, could have provoked what Castro was desiring: some sort of an American retaliatory attack.

"World War III would have been precipitated, since Khrushchev initially had left it solely up to the Russian field commanders in Cuba to decide when to launch their tactical nuclear weapons. How naïve he was! Those Russians weren't required to have a direct order from Moscow to start a nuclear war in the event the U.S. had been foolish enough to strike back militarily!! Kennedy wisely did not fall for Havana's bait, that U2 incident, and Khrushchev immediately upon hearing about it insured that he was in complete command of the nuclear weapons in Cuba."

I still do not understand him. "So, what went on then that today we aren't aware of?"

He puts his hand into his inner coat pocket and pulls out that envelope full of faded index cards. After shuffling through them, he finds the two he is after and reads from one of them, "You have to appreciate the mind-set that had taken over Havana. Che Guevara

301

precisely articulated Cuba's position at the crisis's peak, 'Direct aggression against Cuba would mean nuclear war. The Americans speak about such aggression as if they did not know or did not want to accept this fact. I have no doubt they would lose such a war.'"

After placing the second card in front of the first, he continues, "Two days after it was all over, Castro in a letter to Khrushchev reiterated Che's sentiment, 'No, Comrade Khrushchev. Few times in history, and it could even be said that never before, because no people had ever faced such a tremendous danger, was a people so willing to fight and die with such a universal sense of duty. We knew, and do not presume that we ignored it, that we would have been annihilated, as you insinuate in your letter, in the event of nuclear war.'"

His eyes shift from that card straight into mine when he says, "You know, he really meant it then, because years later he is quoted as saying that if attacked, 'We would have used nuclear weapons and we would have been destroyed.' 'Irrational,' was all that Khrushchev would say about Castro shortly after the crisis was over. Incidentally, Castro had operational missile sites at San Cristobal and at Sagua la Grande that he was ready, willing, and able to employ through out the crisis."

Gloria reiterates my question. "Leonard, while you have indubitably shown that Castro had become delusional during the Cuban Missile Crisis, you still haven't answered Ernie's question: why do you hold that first fixer in such esteem?"

"Someone made Castro stand down and it wasn't Khrushchev. A little more than two weeks later

Khrushchev warned his people in Havana that Cuba still, 'wants practically to drag us behind it with a leash, and wants to pull us into a war with America by its actions.' Castro at the same time called him a 'son of a bitch, a bastard, an asshole.' Nowhere in the records that are still secret or that have been made public is there mention of that someone who personally sat down with Castro and told him that his promise of June 5, 1958 was not going to be fulfilled."

He returns the two cards into their stack in the envelope before thumbing again through them to select a third one, which he hands to me. "You remember when I showed you this one. I've committed to memory what on that day he swore to do, 'The Americans are going to pay dearly for what they are doing. When this war is over, a much wider and bigger war will begin for me, the war I am going to wage against them. I realize that that is going to be my true destiny.'" He puts the card back into the envelope, which he then replaces into his coat pocket. "Zealots like Castro don't make oaths like that lightly and certainly don't forget them. More important, they are not easily dissuaded from carrying out what they sense to be their fate. And don't you discount what the fixer in those days in October 1962 did, even if none of us can fully appreciate what that was."

I turn towards the limo. "Well, who the hell are those two guys?"

"Castro and his brother have never abandoned his perceived true self-destiny. The descendants of those who died at the Bay of Pigs haven't forgotten their forebearer's providence either. Somehow, I guess out of loyalty to their fallen heroes, the Agency doesn't get rid of them. Every once in awhile the progeny of those who

303

fought at the Bay of Pigs emerge out of Little Havana ready to provoke the all out war that their families feel they were denied. Those two brothers, given the opportunity, would go to Cuba and try to assassinate Castro even today. If those two didn't know enough to really blackmail the Agency, they would've been let go years ago."

Chapter 24

The helicopter, which had picked up Leonard before, is back. The dogs do not like the noise and wind and are especially vocal as it lands. Before he gets in the helicopter, Leonard shouts over the roar, "Adolpho will stay with you to keep thieves from coming back. If you run out of cash, he can arrange for you to get whatever you may need. Remember that things may not be what they appear to be at 'the show.'"

As the helicopter rises to take Leonard to the airport, Adolpho walks up to reassure me. "Hopefully, I will not need to call him back again."

Gloria asks him, "Where do you want to sleep? We have a guest room on the first floor and then there's George's old room."

"I think the guest room would be best. If someone thinks about breaking in, I want to hear them."

It is incontrovertible. He has never stayed at our house. Both Gloria and I laugh before she explains, "You don't have to worry about that. Dumb and Dumber will be more than happy to alert you and the neighbors."

We go back to the police car bathed in the light from the lamppost next to it. I get the suitcase and Gloria picks up the vase in its wooden crate. She begins to return to the house with the dogs to set up the guest bedroom. I stay with Adolpho while he inspects the car with a flashlight, starting under the hood, "Who exactly are those two guys that you and Leonard apprehended?"

"Some of Jose Miro Cardona's followers. Although he died in 1974, they carry the torch in his memory."

"Who was he?"

"If the Bay of Pigs invasion had been successful, he would've become President of Cuba. To this day, a copy of the speech he gave at the dawn of the invasion is still carried in the wallets of the members of the Cuban resistance. Here, I think I still have my copy." He gets out his billfold and fumbles through several sheets of paper. "Yes, this is it." He hands one to me.

I hold it up and angle it towards the streetlamp to get enough light to read the paragraph highlighted in yellow. "It is our duty to our revered liberators to expel the tyrant from our soil. To arms, Cubans! We must conquer or we shall die choked by slavery. In the name of God we assure you all that after the victory we will have peace, human solidarity, general well-being and absolute respect for the dignity of all Cubans without exception." I hand it back to him and ask, "They still believe that?"

Once he has returned the sheet of paper to his wallet and put it in the back pocket of his pants, he closes the hood and starts to scan under the front seats before searching the glove compartment. "The true believers, like those two young men, do."

Which brings me to ask, "Why does Leonard dislike them so much?"

"He doesn't really hate them. He's trying to keep them alive in spite of themselves. If they die, they become martyrs. The last thing he needs is for them to actually get close enough to Castro to kill him. Their

306

deaths, while accomplishing that, would revive passions that we have been trying to moderate for decades. Castro's death at their hands would cause a war."

Are we talking about Fidel? "But Fidel Castro has retired!"

He shakes his head. "You think the Jews would have given Hitler a pass if he had retired to The Berghof?"

Only one matter remains unresolved. "Why does the CIA still have them in its employ?"

Lying on his back while spotlighting what's under the dashboard and the steering wheel with his flashlight, he smiles. "It's a form of hush money. No one in the Agency wants the truth about our past relations with Cuba fully disclosed, especially what happened in the Sixties. If we don't hire some of them, their families threaten to leak inflammatory information. They want to learn what we are up to as much as we want to learn what they are up to." He laughs. "Besides, we follow the old saying, keep your friends close and your enemies even closer. In this case, despite their working for us, until the issue with the vase is settled, we need to keep them really close."

"Leonard said something about their being enemy combatants. How did he come up with that?"

Finished with the inside of the car, he walks over to the back and explains, "The faithful exiles in the resistance have never renounced their Cuban citizenship, since they believe they will return any day. He'll use that as a technicality."

"Isn't it illegal?"

He raises a finger for emphasis. "My friend, by the time the courts get around to rendering a final opinion, this uproar about the vase will have blown over. That's all that matters. Why those two are so interested in obtaining it overrides any Constitutional issues." He opens the trunk.

I chuckle. "You think the Supreme Court will agree with that glib assessment?"

Stone-faced, he speaks slowly for emphasis. "Listen, I don't know all the details. But from everything I have heard, that will be this country's least concern about all of this." He closes the trunk of the car after a prolonged search inside of it, including lifting up its carpet. "Well, I'm finished here. It's a mystery how they obtained it, but it undoubtedly is a regular squad car. There isn't any evidence it's been booby-trapped and I don't find any special equipment in it. I'll have it picked up tomorrow morning after I do a search to find out which police precinct is claiming it. After all, I do need an address to deliver it."

Before long, we are in the foyer. Gloria is holding the box containing the vase in both of her hands. "Where do I put this?"

Adolpho slowly reaches for it. "This stays with me. But first I want to see what is causing all of this trouble."

We move into the den. I carefully take it from him and set it on the end table. After opening the box, I lift out the vase and with both hands position it underneath the table lamp by the telephone. When I turn on the light,

Adolpho gasps. "I've seen that vase before, but I don't remember exactly where."

I state what is obvious, "Perhaps you saw it in Havana. It's been sitting prominently in the Museo Nacional de Bellas Artes for almost five decades."

"No, it wasn't there. You see, I've never been to Havana."

"You mean you saw it here in the U.S.?"

"Must have."

"But you don't recall where?"

He gradually shakes his head. "Not really, at the time it wasn't mentioned as being anything of importance."

"Can you think of what they did say about it?"

Rubbing his face with his right hand, he hesitates. "Something on the order of part of a retirement plan or, maybe, a life insurance policy."

For what Leonard paid for it, that was not a bad appraisal of its worth. "That's all! Was its owner a Tiffany collector?"

"Well, I wasn't told who owned it. The collection was nothing like Leonard's. There were several nice pieces of Tiffany that Leonard commented on as being worthy of any collection."

Wow! Leonard had seen the original before and

must have been aware of the copy since he goes to Havana frequently. "He never said anything more about it or the other pieces of Tiffany?"

"No. But if my memory of that day is correct, I do recall who showed us the Tiffany. Leonard was always very careful when he was around that man. God only knows why. If you saw his house, you would have thought he was destitute. It wasn't very big. As I recall, it had wood siding with white paint peeling off and a tin roof. The steps to the gray painted porch had holes in them. I remember almost stepping into one of those holes. When you drive around the Old South you see lots of these houses in the rural areas. You also see their red brick chimneys standing alone in the middle of what must have been the yard. They are real fire traps."

"What then was so strange about it?"

His recollection of the place begins to return to him. "First, it wasn't close to anything. Second, you had to drive up this dirt road to it. A thick forest of briars surrounded that path. At least, that's what we seemed to be going through."

I am surprised that he can't tell me more. "All this detail and you still draw a blank about where all of this happened?"

"Well, we were in the back of a limo with very dark windows. I wasn't paying attention to where the driver was taking us. I don't believe Leonard even wanted me to ascertain where I was going. I only went there once and found out where we were going only when we landed. We flew into some small landing strip that was basically unmarked except for the fluttering red windsock. A limo, which drove right up to the plane, picked us up. When you travel with him you don't ask many questions. You just listen."

This I believe to be true. "Did it take long to get to the house?"

"Surprisingly, no. I haven't the foggiest idea why there was an airport, if you can call it that, which could handle a small jet in the middle of nowhere."

"What did Leonard do when he went there?"

"I wasn't party to that. As I said, all Leonard told me was he wanted me to come with him on a day trip. When we landed, he said he wanted me to be there to meet this man and above all his daughter and another girl. I kinda baby-sat the two women while they and another man wandered about the property, which was a small farm, as best as I can tell. That other man gave me a tour of the house. Except for the Tiffany there wasn't much to be seen there. For what it's worth, Leonard usually had the first man fly into Dallas. They would talk in private. I was never privy to one of their conversations. I just knew he was coming because I suddenly would have an out of town assignment."

"Why do you say it was a farm? Most of the farms I've seen had pastures or fields with rows full of crops in front, not briar forests."

"There were a lot of farm animals all over the place: cows, pigs, goats, even geese. The first man's daughter loved the geese. She had one as a pet that she dressed up as Mother Goose. If there was ever an attack goose, that one was it. Someone must've trained it to be her bodyguard."

"Come again?"

"That goose would peck at you and even bite you if you got too close to her."

"Where was the Tiffany kept? It doesn't sound like this was a very extravagant house."

"There was a room that was paneled with old heart of pine where all of these mementos and the Tiffany were kept. You would have expected them to be locked up in cabinets. But there were none. Everything was out on top of furniture so that you could touch it if you so desired. I thought better than to do that.

"Someone also must have been an avid hunter. He kept one rifle hung up on his wall. It wasn't very fancy, sort of the type of gun you would use to hunt rabbits when you were a kid. From the prominence he gave it, I gathered it was his first hunting rifle. He had some other rifles that were locked up in a gun cabinet in his living room. They appeared to be much more valuable."

"What makes you say that?"

"Well, they were newer and had been better maintained. As best as I could tell, that hung-up one hadn't been touched in decades except for dusting while those other ones had wood with a fresh high gloss polish on it and their metal was nice and shiny. Plus, they all had fancy telescopic sights. I remember them well because I thought when I saw them that if I were a paid assassin those would be the weapons I would have at home."

"Perhaps he used them to hunt deer?"

"That's what I assumed they were for. Which ever one of those two men owned those rifles struck me as the sort of guy who would be self-sufficient and have a freezer on his back porch full of deer meat and other game he had killed." He laughed. "I don't think Mother Goose's mistress would let him shoot ducks and geese."

Beginning to yawn and stretch her arms, Gloria asks me, "It's way past my bedtime. It's been a long day. Ernie, are you coming to bed?"

"Yeah, you're right. I'm beginning to get sleepy. And tomorrow I have to get ready for 'the show.' That's always an ordeal."

We show Adolpho to his room. He places the vase on his nightstand. I do not realize how tired I really am until I finally lie down on our bed. While waiting for Gloria to finish up in the bathroom, I fall asleep without getting fully undressed.

Well before I am ready to get up, Dumb and Dumber discover that Adolpho is in the house. You would have thought he was a rabbit from the intensity of their howling. After I decide to go downstairs and take them out to relieve themselves in the hope that that will calm them down, I put on my robe. They suddenly turn quiet. Either he has killed them, a thought that had crossed my mind this morning, or he has taken them out himself. When I go into the kitchen, I see he is playing with them in the backyard. I join him. "Boy, you're up early this morning."

On his knees, rubbing one of the dogs' stomachs, he

313

states, "I get up early every morning. It's my routine."

He really does seem to be in command of our usually unruly beagles. I ask him, "Where did you learn to handle dogs so well?"

"My first job in the FBI was as a dog trainer."

"How did you get that job?" I jokingly say, "I thought all FBI agents were lawyers or accountants who try to catch tax evaders like Al Capone."

He laughs. "While they do that, they do a lot more. My family has a long history of being circus animal trainers in Cuba. For a while I trained all of the drug and bomb-sniffing dogs in the Bureau. We had a lot of beagles trained to smell for contraband and explosives."

"How did you go from dog trainer to assistant to Leonard?"

"Family connections."

"What do you mean?"

He stops rubbing the dog. "The Cuban Mafia, and I'm not talking about The Corporation. The Cubans who hate Castro have this informal organization. Leonard's and my family are part of it. He heard about my being in the FBI and contacted me to see if I wanted to work with him."

I raise my eyebrows. "That makes no sense. He works with the Cubans as much as with us."

"Yeah, funny isn't it. There is a split within the

Cuban Mafia. Some, like those two yesterday, want retribution: an all out war, a battle to the death with Castro vanquished. Others follow Nixon's approach to China and Reagan's towards Russia. They want to crush the communist through capitalism. They feel once the Cubans start to have a better lifestyle they will abandon Castro's socialism, as the Russians have with Lenin's and as the Chinese are in the process of doing with Mao's."

"So, they want to completely end the embargo and travel ban."

He starts petting the dog between its long ears. "Exactly, it hasn't worked in 50 years and, if it isn't lifted, our families will grow permanently apart. Time is our enemy. Many of the original exiles will die soon without having seen their families in Cuba since the revolution, just like what is happening in the Koreas. Within the Mafia a sense of urgency is developing. We don't want to have Cuba's civil war continue on indefinitely as is undeniably happening in the Koreas. Some of our elders are arguing that we are in a new crisis. For them it's now or never. Many are too infirm to go to Cuba. They are seeking any legitimate excuse to invade Cuba and liberate their relatives so that they can come to the U.S. Leonard, on the other hand, is hopeful he can work with Raúl better than he could with Fidel and bring about a peaceful reconciliation."

"How come?"

Back to rubbing the dog's stomach, he observes, "Raul's not as much of a zealot as his brother."

"In what way?"

315

"First and foremost, we didn't try to assassinate him God knows how many times. Fidel has never forgotten that and has never forgiven the U.S. for it. He further remembers all who were killed directly or indirectly by the Eisenhower and Kennedy administrations and still recites many of their names from memory on Cuban Liberation Day. In his eyes, they were not only friends but are also martyrs whose deaths live on in infamy. He equates the Bay of Pigs to Pearl Harbor, but in this regard he was the victor. He has always felt it is his destiny to avenge those deaths. I've been told he feels the Cuban Missile Crisis was a bittersweet victory. Yes, he successfully stood up to the U.S., which has not tried to invade Cuba since then. However, because of Khrushchev, Guantanamo Bay remains in the hands of the U.S. He was denied his full vengeance. Second, if Fidel was the rigid visionary, Raúl is the pragmatist who maybe willing to bend and make some deals. At least, he has shown some signs of it. Third, Fidel's almost eighty. There is no announced succession plan for the Cuban government once the Castro brothers die off. This dictatorship will have to begin to delegate power to the younger generation at some time or face what happened to Russia. Leonard wants to be in the good graces of Raúl in order to influence him in a positive fashion when he comes to that realization."

Chapter 25

Gloria calls out. "Guys, breakfast."

The morning of the day before "the show" calls for a big breakfast. Gloria and I will be working all day quite intently. The three pieces of equipment needed today are a hand truck, adult diapers, and chicken boxes, lots of diapers and chicken boxes. What's a chicken box? They are the staple of the antiques show. Waxed, rectangular cardboard boxes that are incredibly strong with hand holes on opposing sides and separate tops. They are designed to ship whole chickens or their parts in ice to restaurants and stores. Occasionally, one will see them used to transport fish. For our purposes they are just the right size and can be stacked on each other. Did I mention that they are also inexpensive? As for the diapers, the flat, rectangular ones without any elastic are the perfect packing material. One just rolls the object in the diaper and with a little practice, voilà, it is protected in less space than with bubble wrap. With diapers I can safely stuff twice as much merchandise in a chicken box than I can with anything else. It is easy to tell when "the show" is near. The stores run out of the diapers.

After breakfast, we begin the routine. Gloria has made it clear to me that we should take our usual full load this weekend. All the boxes from the last show that contain things that did not sell are stacked in the den. We use the hand truck and the elevator to spare our backs while bringing up the remaining boxes in the basement that are my inventory. Searching through them takes the most time. I will never admit it to Gloria, but I forget what I have in them even though they are numbered and I have a computer list of what is supposed to be in each of them. I must unwrap everything and decide whether it is their time to be sold. This is not a trivial decision. If done too early after an auction or show, too many people will remember what I paid for it. My customers will only begrudgingly give me half of what it is worth if they find out that I got it on the cheap. They will even quote to me the auction price that I gave for it, as if I did not know it! It also has to be timed according to the market. If a collector decides now is the time to unload his entire collection at auction, for the next few months the rarest of the rare in that genre can be found everywhere.

I can remember when an estate sold off at auction over one hundred museum quality punch bowls. Every booth at "the show," even mine, had one, and none of them sold. Customers would not believe us when we told them that they were incredibly scarce and should sell at a premium. They would say, "Just look around you. All of you have them. You're just hyping your stuff and pricing it beyond reason." It took us, all, three years to get rid of them. Since then, you will not find one at the show. Not that we will not carry them; we just cannot find high quality punch bowls.

Although not always feasible, I try to have a prospective buyer for each major item I pack for the show. Insight into your customers and their financial health is crucial to a good show. If a correction in the stock market occurs the week before the show, I might as well not go. Nothing is more boring than an antiques show in the middle of a bear market. Of course, there is always someone with disposable income who will show up. They just want me to give away my things. Vultures can learn a few things from collectors in economic downturns.

Finally, I must have a showpiece. What is that? Something I can call all of my customers about and tell them that they must come down and see, even if they cannot afford it today. If I do not have a showpiece, some people will not come to "the show." This week that is not a problem. I have the Tiffany Wild-Rose Vase. No one needs to be called. They have already left voice messages alerting me not to sell it before they have a chance to see it and, of the highest priority to them, hold it in their own hands.

Only after all of this is done, do I reconsider my personal collection that is not already on the dining room table. If my booth is not strong enough, I will need to part with one of my own little precious gems. The pitch to sell them is an art unto itself. "It's from my personal collection. I had to debate with myself to see if I could part with it. Gloria didn't want me to bring it. Where will I find another? You know, I may never hear about another for years to come, if then. But I need to upgrade the booth. My loss is your gain." Sounds convincing, does it not? But to be honest, I should say, "Please take it. I have no more room in my house. If I don't sell it here, I'll be forced to place it on eBay, God forbid." You see, dealers are always being offered the treasures of the Nile for their own collections. Unfortunately, most of the time we either do not have the funds to buy them or the space to display them at home. They go hand in hand. If we do not sell enough, our curios are full but, unfortunately, our wallets are light as well.

By late afternoon, the foyer is close to impassable with the chicken boxes piled up five high. I do not feel the need to fill the booth entirely with stuff from the house and am ready to call it quits. With the cash that Leonard gave me the day before, I can buy from the floor on set up day what I need to complete the booth. Besides, the Tiffany vase will command so much attention that it will outshine most of what I will bring. I call George to tell him we are ready for his van. He is not busy and, therefore, promptly delivers it and helps me load up the chicken boxes. I park it locked inside my bolted garage. After supper, Gloria and I go to bed early since we will need to be at "the show" by 5 AM to take our place in line.

The morning of "the show" is basically hurry up and wait until I actually get my van into the building. However, although given a specific time to enter the building based upon their booth's location, everyone tries to be there when the gates of the parking lot open so that they can either set up or walk the floor while dealers with the earlier start times are setting up. My best finds at "the show" were purchased while a dealer had just pulled the treasure out of his box and was unwrapping it. Allowing others to praise an object, or worse actually inform the dealer what he has before you get to it, only makes the price go up.

There is a lot to do before I wander about. Folding tables need to be arranged and covered with black cloth. Glass display cabinets must be wiped cleaned, shined, and placed in the very back of the booth. Both of these we rent at "the show." There is just so much that we want to schlep back and forth. Only after all of this is done, do I begin to unload the chicken boxes that are still heaped up inside the van parked in front of the booth. Once all lined up on the front tables, we empty the boxes of their contents, which are temporarily placed on other tables and in the glass display cases. Their diapers are carefully laid back in the now unfilled boxes so that after "the show" ends I can conveniently pull them out to wrap up what has not sold. Gloria helps me do all of this, but leaves the final placement of the merchandise to me. The "WOW factor" is paramount in this decision. The booth must not only appear pretty, but also make a customer want to stop and inspect what is in it. I have never sold anything at "the show" to someone who just window-shops without asking, "What's the price?"

Today, though, is different. I have the FBI supervising security. By some miracle, they on such short notice arranged the booths directly behind mine and on both sides of it to have been rented to them. No one has told me this, but I suspect these "dealers" are frequently at "the show" and other shows across the country. They are very efficient at setting up and have the types of merchandise desired by those people who are specifically not interested in discovering their provenance, wink wink, nudge nudge. Behind me are old masters paintings, to my right are Gallé and other art glass from Daum Nancy, and to my left are Tiffany lamps and windows. They are all "priced to sell." "The show" must give them good leads on dealers in stolen property and fakes.

In the middle of my set up, Adolpho comes over holding the box with the vase inside. After placing it on one of the tables, he pulls me aside. "Ernie, what do you want me to do with this?"

"Good question. Do you think it is safe just to put it out in a locked cabinet?"

"Well, we don't want anyone to be suspicious of our motives by doing what you wouldn't ordinarily do."

He is right. I decide to do exactly that. "Let's just put it on the top shelf of the center glass display case.

Either Gloria, you, or I will be in front of it and the FBI is directly behind it."

This unmistakably does not please him. "Shit, they're here!"

"Why are you upset?"

Adolpho lowers his voice so as not to be overheard. "Let me just put it this way, over the years, Leonard and I have done a few things that have kept us off of their Christmas card mailing list."

It would be better if I didn't ask this, but I cannot resist, "Such as?"

"We deal with individuals, some of whom are in 'The Corporation.' On occasion we've had to protect our sources from the FBI. Needless to say, this upsets them."

"What exactly does 'The Corporation' do?"

He scans around us before speaking. "The usual organized crime syndicate types of things. Without going into the details, let's just say, they are not boy scouts."

"Why does Leonard feel the need to protect them if they are criminals?"

"The heads of 'The Corporation' go all the way back to the Bay of Pigs invasion. You can't do what we do without their assistance."

I remember one of the things Leonard had mentioned about his line of work. "Is that what he meant when he said, 'Right and wrong eventually just don't exist?"

"Among the other compromises we make, yeah."

"Well, let me introduce you to Agent Johnson. He's in charge here."

Adolpho and I go to the booth to the right of mine where Agent Johnson in civilian clothing is helping set it up. "Agent Johnson, this is Adolpho, I'm sorry, he's never told me his last name. He works with Leonard."

Agent Johnson turns around to eye Adolpho. "We've met before."

Adolpho, though, does not recognize him. "Where?"

"A few years back, you screwed up a big sting operation we had going on in Miami by identifying a terrorist suspect who had infiltrated 'The Corporation.' He was going to blow up a jetliner and blame it on Castro."

Adolpho pauses for an instant. "As I recall that incident, we called you and told you to arrest him before he got the bomb aboard the plane."

"Something like that. He had been one of 'The Corporation's' hitmen and had worked his way up from just plugging a guy to using explosives to take care of the Mexican gangs that were moving into south Florida. He was going to use the skills they taught him to advance his own political agenda. You never did tell us why 'The Corporation' turned him in."

"While they liked the idea of blaming it on Castro, as worthy as that would have been, they didn't agree with killing innocent Americans. That isn't something 'The Corporation' does or endorses. They also thought it would be bad for them both as Cuban businessmen and members of the resistance if it somehow were traced back to them. That possibility made them suspicious he was a double agent for Castro. They envisioned the headline, 'Cuban Exiles Linked To Commercial Airliner Bombing.' You can imagine the backlash they foresaw coming their way."

"One thing I could never figure out. Why didn't they just knock him off? He could have given us lots of incriminating information about them."

"Deep down inside, those wise guys are very loyal to this country and don't want anything bad to happen to it or its citizens. Besides, they can in no time locate where his family is in both Miami and in Cuba. He knows better than to rat on them."

I must ask, "How did this screw up a sting operation?"

Agent Johnson turns to me. "You arrest one of them, even if one of the higher-ups snitches on him to you, the rest of them get paranoid real bad and have a witch hunt. We had to get our man out of there real fast before they figured out who he was."

Adolpho has had enough of this. Both excited and upset, he says, "You rather have had us keep quiet and let him kill all of those innocent people? It wouldn't have taken long before everyone would have said it was Castro's revenge for exiles' placing bombs on Cubana flight 455 in 1976. Of course, eventually that idiot would have been found out, since either he would've never kept quiet or Castro's people in Miami would've figured out who really did it. Then, thanks to them, the Miami Herald would have had banner headlines for weeks."

"No, it just ruined several years effort." He smiles somewhat. "However, Leonard's turning in those two Cubans makes up for it."

Needing to return to my work, I start walking towards my booth. I glance back at them and say, "Hopefully, this weekend will be less exciting."

Adolpho follows me. Once he has caught up with me, he quips in an undertone, "Asshole. We hand them crucial data that the Department of Homeland Security, the FBI, and the CIA don't have and he bitches about not being able to get some petty crooks."

"How do you know that?"

"It was part of the deal. We force the FBI off of 'The Corporation's' back for a while and they help us save a 747."

I cannot believe I am about to say this, "That seems like a fair deal, I guess."

"Hell, if they weren't so goddamn arrogant, we could've told those Keystone Kops where to find the damn drugs, saving them all that effort. But they would've blown our cover and 'The Corporation' would've never spoken to us again."

"In what way?"

The muscles in his face tense up. "The FBI goes strictly by the book. Everyone at the CIA feels that the FBI is incompetent. Leonard was emphatic that the FBI would've somehow named us in the damn search warrant."

I try to calm him down. "How was Leonard going to do it?"

"He wanted to just tell the Mexican drug lords where 'The Corporation's' warehouse was. He figured they would go after it and the FBI could be conveniently there to arrest the Mexicans."

"He didn't think that would piss off 'The Corporation?'"

"Any day the Mexicans get arrested and jailed or deported is a great day for 'The Corporation.' Leonard felt they eventually would congratulate him despite initially losing all of that money. You see, they would make it up very soon afterwards from the absence of the Mexican competition. In the long run, they would've seen it was worth it to them and forgiven Leonard."

"Did he approach the FBI with his idea?"

"No. If they don't initiate it, they aren't interested in it. Besides, they don't trust the CIA or Leonard. He's Cuban and they believe we all stick together in the end. I'm surprised Johnson showed any gratitude for Leonard handing over those two Cubans. They must've been up to some really bad no-good."

Back in my booth, I resume unpacking the boxes for the front table. These are never particularly valuable.

Usually, I try to have the stuff the other dealers and pickers would want placed there early in the morning. I can finish up setting up the booth and sell them at the same time. It further affords me an opportunity to see if the pickers might have anything I would want. They troll the countryside, as well as garage sales and classified ads, in quest of anything on which they can turn a profit. I am always amazed by what they bring to "the show." Of course, I have to recognize what it really is since they almost never do. You do not have to worry about them selling fakes since their offerings genuinely show their age. They do not bother to hunt for hallmarks on silver since that would mean they would have to clean off decades of tarnish. I have even had them sell me sterling silver as plate because they did not polish it. Unfortunately, when they recognize that they have a find, they always demand too much for it. Not that you overpay, just that there is not as much room for profit in it. Pickers view "the show" on set up day as a supermarket for bottom fishers. What do we need to unload for which their dealer customers will pay handsomely? I put out the rifle that I bought for $2 at the auction. It should sell before the afternoon is over.

Adolpho takes an interest in it. "Where did you get that?"

"It was a mystery surprise box at the auction. I paid a whopping $2 for it. Gloria thinks I should've held off for $1. Why? Are you interested in buying it? For you, I can give better than dealer cost."

"No. I don't collect guns. It just looks familiar."

"Hell, you find these World War II rifles everywhere. This one's Italian."

He picks it up and examines it. "By god, I've seen this rifle before."

"Of course, you have, probably hundreds of times. Oswald used the exact same model to kill Kennedy."

"No, not that. I mean I've seen this very same rifle before."

"Adolpho, I assure you that you've never seen this weapon before. John's mystery surprise boxes hardly ever contain anything of true value or rarity."

"Ernie, I have this feeling that I have. I just can't place it."

He then walks over to the box containing the Tiffany vase and takes it out. "We better put this up before you put out too much stuff on this table. Someone might walk off with it." Prior to my unlocking the center display case, I place the vase next to the gun. I hear him say, "Oh my God!"

"What's the matter?"

Adolpho cries out, "Now I remember. It was in that guy's house hanging on the wall over the vase!"

Chapter 26

I have to be blunt with Adolpho. "That's impossible. The crap that John puts into those mystery boxes would never, I repeat, never be owned by someone who could afford that vase. You just saw one of the thousands of these rifles that have made it to the U.S."

He is adamant. "I know you think I'm crazy, but I'll say it again, that vase and that very rifle lived together in that man's house."

"Even if what you say were true, it still isn't worth much."

About an hour later, my gun dealer customer meanders by the booth. "Word at 'the show' is, Ernie, that yours is the booth not to miss."

"Yep. I got this very rare Tiffany vase. You want to see it?"

"I'll take a gander at it, but remember I won't fully appreciate what I'm looking at."

I lead him over to the back glass display case. "There it is. A one of a kind Tiffany vase made for the Columbian Exposition."

"That's right nice. Too bad Tiffany never got into guns or rifles."

"Why do you say that?"

"Because that's about the best metal work I've ever seen. I betcha he would have made a rifle that would have been too pretty to shoot. Well, Ernie, what do you have for me this month?"

We return to the front table. "How about an Italian World War II rifle in great condition that I can sell real reasonably?"

He grabs it and peers into its chamber. He then holds it up towards the overhead lights to examine its barrel from its inside and its outside. "It's in great condition compared to most of the Model 91/38 Carcano short rifles brought into 'the show.' It certainly hasn't seen much action. I know it before you say it. Oswald used this same model to assassinate Kennedy. Doesn't mean squat as far as value is concerned."

"Well, then, what will you give me for it?"

He pulls out a small magnifying glass from his front pocket. "Let me see its serial number on its barrel before I answer that: T 3164. Huh!" He then takes out his smartphone. After a minute of searching a file, he says, "I can't make you an offer on this rifle."

I am shocked, to say the least. My prices are so low that he has never before turned down a gun or rifle from me. "Why not?"

"The serial number isn't right."

"In what way?"

"It must've been changed some time in the past. They never made one with a T in the serial number in

1940 when this one was made."

"So, why can't you buy it?"

"The Feds would be all over my ass if I owned, much less tried to sell, a rifle with a fake serial number. They would claim it had been used in some sort of a crime and altered to conceal that fact or the previous owner's identity. I'm surprised you even have it."

"To be perfectly frank, I got it at John's last auction. It was one of his mystery surprise boxes."

"That would fit. Whoever consigned it to John wasn't interested in anyone researching it before they bought it. They probably knew that the serial number isn't right."

"In that case, what should I do with it?"

"If one of these FBI agents who seem to have surrounded your booth won't take it, find a wall in your house to hang it on."

"What makes you say that there are FBI agents here?"

"Ernie, I sell weapons. I can spot a police officer, DEA, FBI, or ATF agent a mile away. Hell, most of them are on my email list. They must suspect something is going to go down here at 'the show' for them to have this much of a presence."

I decide not to comment. "Well, I guess I'll see you next month."

Adolpho has stayed close enough to be within hearing range and approaches me as the gun dealer leaves. "If he could tell they are FBI, maybe whoever is after the vase will too and be scared away by their being here."

"From your mouth to God's ear."

"Really, Ernie, just having them here may help."

"In that case, I'm going to explore the floor. Want to come along? Gloria can watch the booth."

"No, I think I better hang around here to guarantee that nothing happens."

"No guts, no glory."

I need a break from setting up. Strolling through the aisles and viewing what other dealers have brought is refreshing for me. I learn a lot from just asking what something is. A late middle-aged bearded dealer from New Orleans has the booth directly across from mine, which normally goes to Jim Cook, who for some unexplained reason has dropped out of sight. I do not recognize him. He is just like any other dealer, except for wearing a necklace with an ornament that is an odd, dime store purple cloth coin purse. It hangs by a heavy gold chain from around his neck and covers his heart. I think to myself how out of place it is at "the show" to have a patently valuable chain holding such a cheap pendant. Once I have had my fill of gawking at it, I superficially scout around his booth without introducing myself.

Since his stall is filled with stuff from Louisiana that I never sell, I pay little attention to anything in particular in it until I end up at the front table. I had saved it for last since frequently that is where the most interesting items are kept to draw a crowd. Prominent in its middle is a closed wooden box, almost perfectly square with an enormous carved cross on its top and a lesser cross incised on each of its four sides. Nothing is near it. I can easily tell that the box is a real antique from its worn and weathered patina. There is no varnish left on it, just stained wood with a brown background and occasional red streaks. It has the hinge for a pad lock but there is not one on it. It does not resemble anything like the decorative Victorian English and French boxes that are common at "the show." I stand directly in front of the small chest, pointing at it, when I ask, "What is it?"

Gazing up from the paper he is reading, he takes a moment to see what I am referring to. "Oh that, something you've never beheld before, I'll bet." He gets up from the metal folding chair he has been sitting in and walks over to it from behind the front table. As he pulls open the top, I barely hear him whisper, "A vampire slaying kit from New Orleans. I date it from the mid to late Nineteenth Century."

"Can I take a peek inside of it?"

He again speaks up. "Be my guest, but it is heavy so be careful if you move it."

He is right. It weighs about 20 pounds. I pick it up so that I can view it close up. "What kind of wood is this?"

"Linden tree with maroon velvet inside. It was assembled in Transylvania by a Romanian monk, who brought it with him when he came to New Orleans in

1892."

Inside, within the center of the top is a wooden hammer about 6.5 inches long with four 6 inch wooden crosses with each of their bottoms fashioned into a sharp point with a silver tip. These stakes form a semicircle underneath the hammer. They and the hammer are individually affixed to the velvet of the top panel by a single thin strip of grayish cracking leather. Each stake has a small silvery metal holy cross embedded on one side of where its two pieces of wood join to form a much larger cross. The hammer has two of the metal crosses one on both sides of its head. "The stakes were fashioned from aspen since it drives off evil spirits and makes them one of the few weapons suitable to kill a vampire," he volunteers.

At the top of the box is a deep multi-divided tray with a large compartment that holds two mirrors, one beneath a clearly very old leather bound prayer book with a large crucifix embossed onto its front cover and the other under a Bible with the same appearance as the prayer book. I thumb through several pages of the prayer book to read from it only to discover that it is printed in some ancient language I cannot identify. "What language is this written in?"

"Chirilica."

"What's that?"

He bends forward to answer me in a very serious, almost eerily solemn, tone of voice. "An old holy Romanian language from the Tenth Century. We date this book from before 1860. Since then only true vampire slayers can recite and understand what is written in it.

They and only they have the power to subdue the dark forces of evil. They and only they are empowered to kill demons, vampires, and the other demonic creatures of the night." He then watches me with an odd almost longing expression while awaiting my reply.

"How do you know that?"

I am confused by his sudden, conspicuous disappointment in my response that his face shows. He straightens back up. "Because that's when Alexandru loan Cuza, the first Domnitor of the United Principalities of Wallachia and Moldavia, ended the use of Chirilica in their religious writing and turned to Latin as the language for what would become the Romanian Church."

Above the prayer book and Bible is a long but narrow compartment with an unusual 13-inch knife. When I pick it up to study it in detail, I see that it has a very heavy handle that has a U-shaped front bolster, which holds two blades! The handle is also intricately encrusted in a gothic motif with prominent fangs. To the right of the prayer book, is a compartment that holds two small candles and a muzzleloading pistol with its ramrod, powder flask, and a crescent shaped brown cracked leather pouch, which I open. It is filled with spherical lead ball bullets coated with tarnished silver that I count to myself to be a total of 10 rounds. In addition, scads of small brass cylinders with green tops surround the shots "What are these things among the bullets?"

"Percussion caps. The slayer couldn't shoot the bullets to kill the vampire without them."

After I close the pouch and return it next to the powder flask, I spy a 5.5-inch pliers like tool, upon which

I briefly place my left index finger. "What's this?"

He unbuckles the leather straps holding it in place and takes it out. With an almost wicked smile, he grasps its handles in his right hand, thrusts it very close to my mouth, and twists it before jerking it back away from me. Afterwards while stroking it sensuously, he slowly asks, "Surely, you've seen a Dentol before. Haven't you?"

I shake my head. He continues. "The slayer would use it to extract the fangs from the vampire's mouth after killing it." He then fastens it back into the box.

To the left of the prayer book is a compartment that holds a silver chain with a large, well crafted silver crucifix, a rosary, and a metal box with a crucifix welded on its lid. I lift off the top of the box and see inside of it are an antique metal syringe and several long needles. After his little demonstration with the Dentol, I feel it is the better part of discretion not to ask him for what they were used and place the cover back on the box before quickly moving on. There are two outer compartments, one to the left of the chain with a crucifix and the box with the syringe and one to the right of the prayer book. Each holds five identical very dark amethyst, almost black, bottles with clear glass stoppers and brown crumbling oval paper labels and one bigger jar. After inspecting them individually, I suspect eight may still have some sort of fluid content in them. "What are the liquids in these bottles?"

I do not think he could get any creepier but he does. As if revealing ancient forbidden ritual secrets, he raises each bottle as he deliberately reads from its label and precisely specifies what's in it: "Pamant (holy soil from the site where Christ was crucified in Jerusalem. It would

336

be placed on the grave or body of the vampire.); Agheazma (holy water from the Vatican, which the Pope himself has blessed. The slayer would sprinkle it on himself for protection and onto the vampire where it would burn whatever flesh it touched.); Mir (an anointing oil from a clay vessel placed inside Christ's tomb by Mary. The slayer would rub it both on himself and the skin of the vampire.); Tamaie (resins from exotic shrubs and small trees planted by the pharaohs in ancient Egypt that have been used as holy incense ever since. Their smell would ward off the evil spirits within the creature's body.); Usturoi (liquid garlic); red serum; blue serum; and a secret potion whose ingredients only the monk knew and took to his grave. The serums and the secret potion were repellents to the unholy. The monk would use that syringe with those needles you just saw to inject the liquid garlic and the secret potion into the heart of the creature after impaling a stake into its heart with the hammer. Only then would he guarantee that it would be dead for evermore." He next unstops the smaller jar that contains a dusty material. Its label says Usturoi. "This is a powder made from dried garlic. The slayer would throw it into the bloodsucker's eyes to blind and disorient it." He returns the stopper to the jar. Finally, he uncorks the other larger jar, whose sticker also reads Usturoi. He pulls out dried out whole garlic cloves strung together to form a chain. "The slayer would wear these to protect himself from as well as to ward off the undead."

While he slowly lowers the garlic necklace back into its jar, I motion to the pistol. "Why the silver bullets?"

"Because of its unique pure qualities, silver is very toxic to all the creatures of the night. Bullets casted from it and blessed by a priest will temporarily 'kill' not only

337

vampires but also werewolves when fired into their hearts." He then lifts the tray out of the box and brings out a large wooden handled cleaver with a thin silverplated blade. "Once the creature is stunned, the slayer would use this to cut off its head to terminate its undead existence and forever preclude its supernatural vitality from causing it to arise, reborn anew to live again in the same form as it had before it had been attacked, like the phoenix. "

I bite my lower lip to keep from laughing. "Does the kit work?"

"The monk had a great and legendary following all the way from New Orleans to Natchez. His powers were felt to almost rival those of Queen Marie Laveau by the many who believed in the root work along the Mississippi. His services were called upon almost every Friday night, when the vampires are at their weakest."

Over my years in the medical examiner's office, I had occasionally run across voodoo and subsequently taught myself lots about it, although not to an expert level. However, I am having too good a time and, therefore, play dumb to string him along. "What's root work?"

"Hoodoo, or as you call it voodoo."

Nodding to indicate my grasping its meaning, I finally ask dealers' favorite question. "How did you stumble upon this relic?"

"The monk was a great, great uncle of mine. It has been passed from one generation of my family to the next. I have just recently inherited it. Unfortunately, I am illiterate in Chirilica. As a result of that, tradition dictates that I must sell it but only to one who can read from the prayer book. I go from antique show to antique show seeking the one, as you do. So far, only you have shown any interest in it here."

He is very good. What a spiel! For the right price he would sell it to anyone! He almost has even convinced me to buy it. It is without question something I do not have and would expect to sell at "the show" before Halloween. And if it did not sell, I would not be upset since I would assuredly take it to The Blue And The Gay's All-Hallows-Eve party where it would be the hit of the night. Adolpho taps me on my shoulder. "You need to return to the booth. Someone wants to see you about the vase."

I salute the dealer from New Orleans. "Excuse me, I need to go back to my booth."

He uses the oldest of the lines that dealers have in their repertoire for arm-twisting. "I don't want to pressure you, but I'll be showing it to a very promising prospect this evening."

As I turn around to speak to Adolpho, I ask him, "Who's there?"

"These two Cuban dealers who claim Leonard sent them to buy the vase, but I don't believe them. He never mentioned them to me."

Glancing up, I recognize one of them from the auction. I mutter into Adolpho's ear, "The one to the left bid against me at the auction for it. Mitch stated he was pissed that I got it and said that I didn't know its history."

339

Adolpho waves his hand to signal the FBI agents in the booths on either side of mine. They stop what they were doing and start paying attention to the two Cubans. We move swiftly to greet them. I ask, "What can I do for you gentlemen?"

The taller and darker of the two speaks for them. The other silently holds onto an attaché case. "We're interested in the vase."

I address him reservedly. "Weren't you at the auction?"

"Why, yes, I was. You outbid me that day. I was not prepared as well as I should've been. That is not the situation today."

"Well, I have had a very steep offer for it."

Not giving me a chance to finish, he interjects, "Yes, Leonard's offered you $2,600,000 in cash for it. We can do better. But first I need to see its base."

"Of course, you do. Are you interested in anything in particular?"

"I want to see if it has the enameler's mark still on it."

I restrain myself in an effort to hide any signs of emotion after he said that. "Oh, go ahead. It's unquestionably genuine. Everything about it screams that it's real. And where would I get another?"

"We'll see if it's right."

I unlock the cabinet doors and carefully hand him the vase, which he turns over. He then takes out his 14 karat gold jeweler's loupe and scrutinizes the base. "How much will you take for it?"

To be honest, I had not considered what price to ask for it. "What will you give for it? You without a doubt know its true value."

"I am authorized to offer you $2,900,000 cash for this one." Nodding to me, his partner raises the attaché case just a bit allowing me to observe that it is handcuffed to his left hand, meanwhile he taps it with his right hand.

Of what about its history are they aware? "Well, I must say, you do know its true worth. I'll have to confer with Leonard to see if he can top that most generous offer."

"We'll be back tomorrow to pick it up. I doubt that even the great Leonard will give more for this one."

He must realize that there was a switch after the auction. Why else would he have said, "For this one?" And if he does, why is he being so generous? After they have left, I ask Adolpho, "Who exactly are they?"

"For sure, they are from Cuba, but I've never been given their names."

I sarcastically say, "I could have told you that they are Cuban."

He is a little bit upset with me. He raises his voice and slowly states, "No, I mean they are from the Cuban mission in New York."

"Oh! Why would the Cuban mission want to pay $2,900,000 for the replica that they just allowed out of Havana? Besides, Leonard has just brought the original back there? And he must've seen it was the copy since he specifically sought out the enameler's mark."

"It doesn't have an explanation, but I'm going to find out."

Agent Johnson comes over. "What did they want?"

I crisply reply, "They want to buy the vase for $2,900,000."

"Why would two DGI agents want to do that?"

"You know them?"

Nodding, Agent Johnson immediately names them. "Yeah, Miguel Garcia and Jesus Sanchez. The Bureau can't figure out what they are currently doing in the US."

"What do you mean by that?"

"They're in charge of the anti-resistance department in Havana and, when in the States, usually stay in Miami where they operate a front selling phony antique art work made in Cuba and South America to the exiles who aren't very sophisticated in such things."

I have heard about those fake Gallé and Tiffany pieces from South America, but despite many attempts never discovered who was importing them. "Why do they do that?"

"At that store they and their agents hear all of the

gossip. No one suspects antiques dealers to be spies. They are always donating something to the raffles and silent auctions at the dinners held to benefit the anti-Castro forces. Plus, Castro has for decades sold such good reproductions that even unsuspecting museums buy them. He started doing it in Miami to raise dollars in the Sixties. The elders in the Miami Mafia remember seeing the objects in Havana during their childhood. They would die if they found out that they have been supporting him all these years."

"Why don't you guys blow their cover and just shut them down?"

A big smirk crosses Agent Johnson's face. "And lose our best pathway to deliver false intelligence to the DGI? Are you crazy?"

"Not as crazy as those two."

"Why do you say that?"

I at last smile. "At what they've just offered me, they'll never be able to resell that vase for a profit."

As we finish unpacking, I make a mental note to show Gloria the vampire slaying kit on the way out. It is so weird that she just might let me buy it.

Chapter 27

Friday morning of "the show" is never exciting. It too is a financial waste of time. Since both the dealers who are not part of "the show" and the collectors have for the most part bought what they are going to buy on Thursday at set up, few of them venture back on Friday morning. Consequently, only an occasional dealer from "the show," typically one who arrived there late on Thursday after having had transportation problems, or a deranged true collector, who is usually an amateur dealer in reality and comes to "the show" everyday in order to avoid missing out on something that had not been put up for sale previously, buys antiques before noon on the Friday of "the show." Regular retail customers will only start to roll in after lunch. They have a life. Over the years, I have made my grand entrance to "the show" later and later on Friday mornings. When Gloria and I finally do arrive, we can tell that this Friday morning is different than all of the others we have experienced. At the entrance to "the show" there is an ambulance and scads of police cars with their blue lights flashing. All of the dealers are standing outside huddled together. Gloria is amazed. "What the hell is going on? We took that damn vase home with us last night."

"I can't imagine what has happened. By the looks of it, someone must have been shot dead in there."

"Why do you say that?"

"Well, they don't usually send an ambulance to a robbery scene. And only a single fire truck accompanies the ambulance to a heart attack, not a whole precinct of cops."

Gloria nods in agreement. "That's true. And there isn't a fire engine in sight."

We park George's van as close to the crowd of dealers as we can and walk to them to find out what has happened. Just to be safe, I carry the vase, which I had brought back home last night. Before I have a chance to ask anyone what's up, the manager of the show approaches me. He is short and fat with his horseshoe shaped mound of poorly dyed red hair all tousled. Always an impeccable dresser on the days "the show" is open, he must have selected and put his clothes on in a hurry this morning. He takes his cigar out of his mouth and states in a very serious tone of voice, "The police want to talk to you."

From my experience as the medical examiner for the county, I am shocked that they would think I had any material evidence to share with them. "What about?"

"They've asked me not to discuss this with you."

"Can Gloria come?"

"I can't see why not."

The three of us work our way through the crowd to the entrance to "the show." A police officer opens the glass door and leads us to the large manager's office. Silently sitting in it are Agent Johnson, a uniformed police sergeant, a plainclothes detective, and Leonard. The detective, blond, clean-shaven and average in height but so thin that he barely fills his gray suit, stands up and does all of the talking after Gloria and I take the two remaining empty chairs. "Dr. Kopp, I'm Detective Nuntz." He nods to the uniformed sergeant. "That's Sergeant O'Brien. I take it you've met Agent Johnson and Leonard before."

"That's correct."

"Did you talk to the dealer whose booth is directly across from yours yesterday?"

"Yes, I did."

"What about?"

The detective begins taking notes on a small pad he holds in his left hand while I speak. "He had this antique vampire slaying kit that his great, great uncle had left him. He showed it to me and told me all about it?"

"Did he mention to you how much he wanted for it?"

"No. In fact, he said he would only sell it to one who could read the prayer book and Bible in it."

The detective's eyes go from his writing straight to mine. "Did you find that to be strange?"

"Well, to be honest, I thought it was part of his hyping it up. You know, all of us will sell whatever we bring to 'the show' for the right price. The more reluctant we seem to be about selling something, the more eager the buyers become, and the higher the price they will pay."

"What did he tell you about the prayer book and

Bible?"

It was such a bizarre spiel that I remember it almost verbatim. "Well, he dated them to before 1860 since that was the year that some ruler of Romania, whose name escapes me, changed the Church language to Latin. They were written in something that he said sounded like Churlicca. I couldn't make heads or tails of what was in them."

"Did he mention why he would only sell the vampire slaying kit to such a person."

Why would the police care that he was so eccentric? "Yeah, now this was weird. He said something to the effect that they and only they could fight the dark forces of evil and kill demons, vampires, and other fiendish things."

The detective's eyes return to his notebook. "Did he say, 'They and only they have the power to subdue the dark forces of evil. They and only they are empowered to kill demons, vampires, and the other demonic creatures of the night?' And did he mention he was seeking the one?"

"Why yes. As I recall, those were his exact words. For some strange reason, he seemed to be disappointed with my response to that."

Leonard explodes, "Shit! I knew it!"

Fed up with these bizarre questions, Gloria finally asks, "What's all of this about? Is Ernie in some new kind of trouble?"

Getting up from the stool that he had been sitting

on, Leonard stands next to her to explain, "Early this morning, when the manager unlocked the door to 'the show' after his head of security called to tell him that none of his officers were checking in with their hourly reports on their cell phones as required, that dealer was found slumped over the front table of his booth, stabbed in his heart with one of the silver tipped stakes from that box."

"Oh, my God! That must've been a bloody mess."

"You would've thought so, but all of his blood had been drained out of his body ostensibly before he was placed there. We can't find any trace of it."

This is definitely not your usual murder. Someone had to have spotted something. I interrupt. "What about the guards and the surveillance cameras? Didn't they see anything?"

The detective continues, "The guards were locked up in one of the storage rooms. The surveillance system had been turned off before that. Although we've searched everywhere, the guards' cell phones and keys are nowhere to be found. All that we have determined is that some very expert hitmen overpowered the guards, who routinely work nights here, and left no trail themselves."

"Was anything stolen?"

"Just the prayer book and the Bible, very peculiar!"

He is right, very peculiar. They have no value except possibly to some vampire freaks, but they do not come to "the show," except just before Halloween when they hunt for really bizarre stuff for their parties. "Why would anyone take them? They were in some dead Romanian holy language."

Having moved over from Gloria, Leonard stands in front of me. "The Cubans sometimes use Chirilica to send secret messages. They get these old texts and apply something like the Bible Code to conceal the hidden messages."

"What's the Bible Code?"

"It's a complex code technique using equidistant letter sequencing, for instance, every 15th letter followed by every 8th letter and so on. If you haven't been given the sequence that tells you how many extraneous letters separate the true letters in the message, it takes a computer to decipher it."

"What exactly are you saying, Leonard?"

"He was trying to hook up with a contact at this show and it was no coincidence that he was situated directly across from you."

"The show" manager butts in. "The same time the FBI instructed me to rearrange the booths surrounding yours with their booths, another government agency ordered that he be placed directly in front of your booth. They somehow had conveniently made Jim Cook disappear. When we tried to contact him to find out if he objected to being assigned another booth, all we could find out was that he was not in town. Even more bizarre, his cell phone had been disconnected. You know, he lived and died by his cell phone."

If a guy selling a vampire slayer kit was who the

government so desperately wanted to be my neighbor at "the show" that they kidnapped Jim, who in it cares about the occult? I am straightforward. "Which agency would that be?"

"That's still up in the air. I thought it was the CIA, but neither Leonard nor Agent Johnson can figure out who had come by to arrange that I rented the booth to the deceased. He left his CIA business card with me but they aren't convinced it's real."

Agent Johnson interjects, "The CIA will neither confirm nor deny his existence. If he is for real, he would have to have been out of their New Orleans station. They have issues down there."

Between Katrina, that oil spill, and just dodging the bullet with Hurricane Isaac, New Orleans has had a plethora of problems. How the CIA had added another one escapes me. "What kind of issues?"

Before he can respond, Leonard answers for him. "Like JM/WAVE in Miami, the New Orleans station has had a certain amount of independence from Langley when it comes to Cuba. Even I am not privy to what some of their operatives are up to."

While I can buy that, it does not explain what they had done to Jim. "So, why was the deceased here?"

"As I said earlier, it would have been too coincidental for that agent to have suddenly shown up here the day after you had bought the vase and arranged a booth in front of yours for the deceased. What made him assume that this would be the first show where you were going to bring that very same vase to be sold?"

"But, Leonard, that dealer showed no interest in that vase."

"I don't think he cared about the vase per se as much as he wanted to see or, more likely, contact whoever was interested in buying it."

"Why would've he wanted to do that?"

His frustration with me shows plainly in his grimace, his loud protracted sigh, his muttering something in an undertone in Spanish, and his then commenting, "You antiques dealers would make lousy agents. He wanted to give 'the One' the prayer book and the Bible. They must have some secret message encoded in them that explains the importance of the vase."

That does not ring true. I pause for a minute to recollect what happened just after talking with him. "I don't think it was the DGI agents that he was seeking."

"What DGI agents are you talking about?"

Agent Johnson speaks up, "He's referring to Garcia and Sanchez. They were here yesterday."

After spinning around to face him, I keep on about the Cubans. "Yeah, those two. Adolpho pulled me away from his booth to come back to mine since they were inquiring about the vase." Since Leonard does not appear to be surprised to hear this, I figure Adolpho has already filled him in on this.

Agent Johnson continues. "What did they do?"

"They specifically asked to view the base of the

351

vase."

"Who spoke to you?"

"The taller and darker one. They didn't introduce themselves."

"That would be Sanchez. He actually is somewhat of an expert in antiques. Garcia could care less about them. He's strictly in the information gathering and disinformation dispensing business. What did Sanchez say specifically?"

I am so shaken up by the events of the day that I am uncharacteristically vague on exactly what he did say. "I remarked that I recognized him from the auction and he mentioned that he had been there. He then said something about not being prepared enough for it. He next said he knew Leonard had offered me $2,600,000 for the vase and was prepared to better that offer if the base of the vase was OK."

Leonard asks, "Did he mention the enameler's mark?"

I turn back to him. "Yes, he said that exactly. He wanted to see if it was there?"

"Did he say 'was there' or 'was still there'?"

While I cannot recollect, Gloria emphatically states, "He said, 'still there.' I remember that because when he said it, I thought we were in trouble."

Leonard raises an eyebrow. "Is there anything about that vase that they haven't been informed about?"

Having had that same thought, I comment, "I actually mentioned that to him after he offered me $2,900,000 for it. I think I said something to the effect that he must know its true value."

Gloria disagrees. "No, you said true worth. I thought that was an odd way of saying that."

After pausing to consider what we have said, Leonard asks, "So despite his having proven that this was the copy, he still offered you $2,900,000 for it?"

I nod. "That's right."

"At the auction, do you remember at what price he dropped out of the bidding?"

Despite what Leonard has already given me for the vase, Gloria is still upset about what I paid for it. "The son of a bitch raised the bid on his own to $500,000."

"So, in less than a week he is willing to pay almost 6 times as much for the copy as he was for the real deal, interesting. I assume he claimed that this was all that he is authorized to offer you."

I nod again. "Yes, why did you ask that? I figured that was all his line of credit would permit."

"He gets his money straight from the Banco Central de Cuba in Havana, which usually gives him basically a blank check for these sorts of things. For some reason, the folks there weren't willing to do that for the original but are willing to do so to have the copy returned to Havana."

The detective asks, "Interested enough to kill for it?"

Leonard shakes his head. "That's not Garcia's and Sanchez's style. They don't do any heavy lifting. They're strictly in the information side of things."

"Maybe they had someone else do it?"

"No, if they really want to get the vase, they will pay whatever it takes. They have to maintain their image of being legitimate Cuban exile businessmen. Trust me on this, when the DGI orders a hit, those two are completely oblivious to it, on purpose. Besides, the prayer book and Bible were stolen, not the vase. Ernie, did they show any interest in the vampire slaying kit?"

Now shaking my head, I assert, "None, and I don't think they were aware it was here. They didn't enter that guy's booth when I was there and left immediately after giving me their offer. Plus, they said they would be back today to pick up the vase."

Once he hears that, the detective dramatically perks up. "You mean to say that they will be back here today."

"Yes, that's what they said and what I just said."

"Well, that may take them off the list of suspects."

"Why?"

"Dr. Kopp, professional hitmen never return to the scene of the crime. Whoever did this will be in another state or country by noon. They plan their exit strategy in minute detail. Only an amateur or patsy would still be in town today."

"Who then do you think did it?"

Having already decided that those two Cubans were not involved based upon what I had just mentioned, the detective states, "Well, they're probably from New Orleans."

"What makes you say that?"

"They went to a lot of trouble making this for all the world seem to be a vampire murder: using that stake and draining out his blood. They even left two puncture marks on his neck. And they must've had extensive experience doing this sort of thing. For whoever they are were damn efficient and tidy. Draining all that blood should have made a helluva mess. So far, the only trace of his blood that we can find is what's on his clothes. Those Cajuns still practice voodoo. The way this hit was done was meant to send a message to someone who believes in voodoo. And whoever did it is very familiar with its jinxes."

Although what he has just said is reasonable, I am not convinced. "The Haitians in south Florida also practice voodoo. Why couldn't it have been someone from Miami?"

"We found a doll with red pins stuck in it by his body. That's part of New Orleans Voodoo, not Haitian Vodou. No, the hitmen are from Louisiana not Florida."

"Why couldn't it be Cuban Voodoo?"

"This was an old expertly made New Orleans style

doll just like a guy in the French Quarter used to sell decades ago, not the cheap rope dolls found in Cuba today."

His concern is palpable when Leonard puts his hand on my shoulder. "Regardless of who the real target is, you're leaving 'the show' today. These guys are too good. I don't think Adolpho, even with the help of the FBI, can assure your safety here."

"What about my selling the vase?"

"Well, whoever that someone is that your dearly departed colleague was seeking to find is going to have to contact you some other way."

It is unheard-of for Leonard to lack Latin bravado. Gloria is nervous. "Are we safe in our house?"

Chapter 28

Leonard is always one step ahead of the crowd. "Adolpho is working on finding you a safe house."

Crossing her arms in protest, Gloria's grim determination is further evident when she insists, "We're going to stay in our home. You all will have to figure out a way to keep those creeps away."

I am more surprised by her tone of voice than by her wanting to stay at home. "Why are you so opposed to his plan?"

"Thinking this over, I don't think they are after us. I don't even think they are after the vase."

"Who do you think they are after?"

"That woman who called and told you not to sell it. She, I'll bet you, is the contact person."

Although this is the first time Leonard has heard about that phone message, he does not act exactly clueless regarding to whom Gloria is referring. "Did she have any kind of accent?"

I abruptly answer him. "No, she sounded American."

"Are you definite that she didn't have even a trace of a Cuban accent?"

"If she does, she's really good at hiding it."

"Did she say anything else?"

"No, and she blocked her number on caller ID."

That surprises Leonard. "How did she expect you to get back in touch with her?"

"We assumed that she planned to come to 'the show' and meet me here."

"Gloria, why don't you think they are after the vase, itself?"

"Leonard, I am shocked that you haven't figured this out yet! Where did the vase come from?"

"That museum in Havana, of course."

"Exactly, if Castro's people wanted that damn vase, you damn well know they never would have let you take it out of the country. And you want proof? Is the museum's director in prison or behind his desk at work this morning?"

"You're right. I should have seen this. He was back at the museum when I delivered it."

"So, why would they go to all this trouble and murder someone or us, for argument sake, to get back what they just allowed to leave the country."

"I can't imagine."

Ready for the kill, Gloria smiles. "Because only the copy was what she would want and would come to the show for. The original for whatever reason wasn't of enough interest to her for her even to come to the auction."

Although all of this is making sense to me, there is one thing that Gloria has not addressed. "Then why are those two DGI agents willing to pay so much for the vase. Castro must've expected that I was going to sell it to the highest bidder to pay back what that museum director gave for the original. Wasn't that part of the deal, Leonard?"

He nods in agreement. "Yes, the director insisted, 'Get the most you can for my father's work.'"

With her confidence swelling, Gloria is not stymied. "Maybe they figured that she couldn't afford to pay cash for it. Ernie, you don't have a reputation for extending credit or giving away one-of-a-kind Tiffany silver as overly generous charity donations. Unless she has something else to trade for it, they had to presume you aren't going to just give it to her. I mean, this is turning out to be the deal of your life." She hesitates before going on. "Come to think of it, this all may have been a trick to lure her out and make her dig up something from the past that's she's had hidden and they desperately want."

She has swayed Leonard who continues nodding his head. "If you're right, she may have owned the original or was calling for whoever did, and one of them consigned it to John's auction house in order to raise the money to buy the copy. Besides, who would've ever figured that that museum director would have paid $2,600,000 dollars for the original? I still can't fathom why he did that. If he honestly envisaged getting his money back, he set the bar awfully high."

359

"Unless, of course, it was his intention the whole time to keep it away from the DGI, and he figured that she would be able and willing to buy it with what he paid Ernie for hers. We all had assumed that their $500,000 bid for the original was the top price they could afford. He may have foreseen a better offer."

I do not quite follow Leonard and sense that he may be holding back some information. "You do know who she is and what this is all about, don't you?"

"Maybe. But if she is who I suspect she might be, I don't understand why whoever is after her is all of a sudden trying to flush her out as Gloria has proposed? She's never personally been involved with Cuba."

Pleased by her apparent victory, Gloria goes for his concession. "So, I'm right after all. She intends to trade something for the vase."

Leonard finally admits, "I believe so. And that something must be something that museum director wants awfully bad."

From his expression, the detective undeniably has no idea what any of us are talking about. "Please, explain to me why that dealer was executed New Orleans style."

Having finally connected the dots, Leonard enlightens him. "Not all Cubans went to Miami from Havana. Some went to New Orleans where there have been centuries of commerce between the two cities. If she is the daughter of whom I'm thinking, then her father was from New Orleans. Someone in the Cuban community, either here or from Cuba, does not want her to complete her father's mission."

"And the dealer from New Orleans was going to help her do that?"

"I can't say that definitely. But I'm fairly certain that something in the missing prayer book and/or the Bible would've been of tremendous interest to her."

A glimmer of hope that this weekend will not be a bust has arrived. "If Gloria and I are not the target of these people, why do we have to leave the show? You know, I have paid booth rent for this month.'"

Realizing that I may have a legitimate point, Leonard lingers to consider my request. "What if she comes and they are here?"

"I think you're right. I'll start packing."

Sergeant O'Brien, who is Irish, talks with an Irish accent, and, except for the lack of the appropriate beard, could play Santa Claus at Christmas, accompanies us to our booth. "I hope it won't bother either of you, but we haven't had time to remove the body. We're still obtaining evidence and taking photos."

With my forensic pathologist's morbid curiosity being fully intact, I have no problem with that. "Mind if I have a glimpse?"

"Come again, sir?"

"Before I became an antiques dealer, I was a medical examiner (ME). I'm kind of fascinated by what really has happened here and, besides, I might be of some help to the guys from the ME's office."

The Sergeant mulls over my request. "I can't see how it could hurt. And I know you know this but remember don't touch anything without permission."

Gloria winces at my wish. "Sergeant, count me out. If you could put up some sheets so I don't have to see what's over there, I would appreciate it."

When we arrive at our booth, I return the box with the vase in it to the back glass display cabinet, which I lock. "It will only take me a moment, Gloria."

"My mother warned me not to marry a medical student, and she was right when she said you all are gross."

Choosing not to defend myself, I ignore her, step over to the crime scene tape barrier, which I lift up, and bend down under it to enter the deceased dealer's booth. Fortunately, one of the assistant medical examiners recognizes me from my days in that office. In her white laboratory coat and wearing red horned-rimmed glasses that match the color of her hair that just curls out at her shoulders, she is the picture of the feminine professional. "Dr. Ernie, I haven't seen you in ages. Can you help identify this guy?"

"No, I only momentarily met him yesterday. He was a strange bird."

"You can say that again. Put on some gloves, let me show you some stuff you won't believe."

I put on the gloves as requested and pull back the sheet covering the victim. "They weren't kidding when they said that the murderers had drained out all of his

362

blood. He is white as the sheet covering him."

"What we can't figure out is how they did it without making a bloody mess?"

"What do you mean by that?"

"We can't find the puncture site they used to place a line to drain the blood."

After a cursory inspection, I ask, "How about the heart?"

"But the stake is still in it."

"The stake could have been placed later at the entrance wound for the trocar they used to drain the blood."

The assistant medical examiner looks askance at me. "That would mean that he was killed somewhere else and brought back here."

Taken aback by her being surprised, I ask her, "You thought it was done here?"

She stares at me again. "Of course."

Perhaps I can be of help, after all. "Look, yesterday evening when they closed this building down, all of the dealers, including him, left. Then the guards searched the site to confirm no one was hiding inside. They use German Shepherds to do that. Then they locked the doors from the inside. No one is allowed in until the show manager arrives the next morning."

"So, you're saying they attacked him elsewhere, had the blood drained out there, and then placed the stake in his heart."

"Unless you believe he was a vampire that's how it had to happen. Take a gander around here. There are no signs of a struggle and no blood. Trust me, they would have had to clean all night to have returned this booth to its previous bloodless state. And they didn't have the time to do that."

"Any idea what the murder weapon was?"

I go to the vampire slaying kit, lift up its lid, grasp the leather pouch, open it, and start to count out loud, "1,2,3,4,5,6,7,8,9."

She cannot figure out what I am doing. "What are you counting?"

Pointing to the revolver, I say, "Silver bullets. There were exactly ten rounds in this pouch yesterday. I know because I counted them then. There are only nine in it today."

"What do you think happened to the other bullet?"

"If I were a betting man, I would put all of my money on that it's in his chest, probably his heart." I reach for the pistol in the box and smell the barrel. "And this gun placed it there."

Mortified, the assistant asks meekly, "Anything else I missed?"

"Yeah, this box was not here when he left the

building. He took it with him."

"How did you deduce that?"

"Oh, it's nothing that involved. Gloria and I left after he did. I was going to show her the vampire slaying kit to see if she would let me buy it. I thought it would be a hit at Halloween either here or at the big shindig at The Blue And The Gay. But it wasn't here. He had already taken it to show it to someone in town who he had said was a hot prospect for purchasing it. Since it's here now and he's dead, I have to presume that he indeed took it to the supposed 'vampire slayer,' who shot him with the pistol from it, returned the pistol to the box, and brought the box and its contents back with the corpse." I turn around and glimpse at the deceased again. "And yesterday he was wearing a gold necklace with a purple cloth purse like bag, which seemed to be shielding his heart. It's not here!"

I am on a roll and she wants to be a part of it. She pursues my theory. "OK, what was the motive?"

"Like most homicides, theft. The police say the prayer book and Bible in the box are missing. Whoever killed him wanted to explicitly make him an example to someone, so they broke in here to do just that." Since he had told me that no one besides me had shown any interest in the box yesterday, one thing causes me to hesitate before continuing with my scenario for the crime. "How did you all determine that the books are missing?"

"That was simple. He had an inventory of what was in the vampire slaying kit stuffed inside a hidden drawer in the box."

"Anything else missing from the booth?"

"Not that I can tell. He had an eclectic collection of memorabilia from the Mississippi Delta and a nice collection of old, used books. He must have been a fan of JFK."

"Why do you say that?"

"He had a helluva lot of material on the Kennedy assassination from Jim Garrison's estate. It's a bunch of the documentation that Garrison used in his prosecution of Clay Shaw. There are tons of photos of JFK along with a copy of the complete Warren Commission Report signed by Earl Warren and Garrison's copy of the screenplay for the movie JFK. He even had copies of JFK's, Jack Ruby's and Lee Harvey Oswald's death certificates."

"How about voodoo? He seemed to care a whole lot about it when I talked to him."

She shows me a postcard pinned to a pole in the booth. It has a recipe for a cure-all printed on its front. "In a glass add enough jimson weed to make you happy, but not enough to turn you red as a beet, dry as a bone, blind as a bat, and mad as a hatter. Add a little sulphur and enough honey to make it sweet as tea on a hot summer's day. Find a black as tar black mama cat without any white and rub the filled glass against her fur. Sip from the glass real slow. Good for the cascade and runs, the asme and the shakes, and the bad blood, the high blood, and the low blood, and all disorders of the bladder." Next, she grabs a book from under a pile of voodoo dolls and opens it up. "It's full of voodoo spells."

366

"Anything else this son of the Cajuns had that's unusual?"

She does not speak. Instead, she turns around, goes over to the table in the front of the booth, and snatches something from on top of it. Returning to me, she holds up a modestly and flimsily made medium-sized jewelry bag attached to a leather cord, "Yeah, he had this necklace hanging from around his neck. We removed it to take photos of the entry wound. He must have exchanged it for the purple one you saw yesterday"

Momentarily she hands it to me. I inspect it but do not recognize it. Of interest is the absence of bloodstains despite its having been in such close proximity to the entry wound. "What's this? Is it some sort of a pouch with a drawstring?" I feel the fabric once more. It is a non-dyed, hand-stitched, natural fiber cloth, a fact that jogs my memory. "This can't be made out of the stuff undertakers use for burial shrouds?"

"Well, we haven't yet analyzed what it is or what it was made out of. However, we suspect it has some voodoo significance since it held some mighty strange things."

"Like what?"

"How about a bat's wing, the liver from what we think was some sort of a bird, a dried lizard, two cat's eyes, a dried up frog with one eye, the heart from a bird, possibly it came from the same bird as the liver. Oh, and, there was the little finger from some black person."

Did she say strange? This is outrageous! "May I see them?"

367

"Sorry, they've already been taken to the crime lab. The detectives really wanted to see if they could ID whose finger it is and were in a rush to get it to the DNA lab ASAP."

"I hate to ask this, but is there anything else that's out of the ordinary?"

"Yeah, in the back of his booth hidden in an old blanket chest we found a ton of skins from a bunch of snakes."

"Show me." She leads me to a herpetologist's treasure trove. I am very impressed. "Wow, someone must've spent a helluva lot of time in the Louisiana swamps to get this many different venomous snakes."

"Yeah, but who would buy one?"

"Snakes are central to voodoo. Its believers worship with them and use their pulverized dried skin to cast spells. Unfortunately for them, the New Orleans police don't take kindly to their citizens dancing with live lethal snakes, most of all ones housed in their homes." I take one of the rather long snakes, the one with the biggest fangs, and approximate them next to the two puncture marks on the deceased's neck. "The vampire was a leather serpent."

My young colleague has one final question. "If you are right that he was brought back here, do you have any idea why they did that?"

"Leonard feels that they did that to warn someone off from doing something. By the way, has anyone established his name?"

368

"We have found his wallet. It was full of fresh one hundred dollar bills, but no IDs. The manager here has his booth rental papers that have a name on it and his signature. Agent Johnson is running it along with his fingerprints to see if that was his real name or an alias."

"Any idea when you'll get his body to the morgue. This kind of thing spooks my wife."

"Once Officer O'Brien is satisfied, we should be ready to put him on the gurney. Thanks for your input. I'll call you if we find that silver bullet in his heart when we do the autopsy."

After I take off my gloves, I return to my booth to help Gloria with the packing. "Well, Ernie, did you solve the case?"

I nod. "Yep, the hitman abducted him after he had left here last night. Subsequently, he shot that guy in the heart with the pistol and a silver bullet from the vampire slaying kit. Then in some inexplicable voodoo-style ritual, the culprit used the bullet entry wound to place an undertaker's trocar to drain his blood from his heart, replaced the trocar with a vampire stake, and finally brought him back here where they found him this morning. And the motive was theft by taking. They stole the prayer book and Bible."

"Who does that sort of thing?"

What I have just seen is so unfathomable that I am forced to shake my head. "Not the Mafia. They either leave the bodies where they shot them or dump them where no one is supposed to ever find them. Spies don't go to this much trouble. They would have plugged him in

369

his truck and taken the entire box with them."

"Well, when do you see such a bizarre murder?"

"Grudges. Whoever did this knew him, probably had been his associate or even friend. Somewhere along the course of time they had a parting of ways. Then he either did something that his former acquaintance could not tolerate or maybe he was just about to do it."

"Pretty gruesome way of saying you ticked me off."

"In my experience, gangs do such grotesque executions most frequently. It's one of their definitive punishments to reinforce bonding and prevent betrayal, sort of like cutting off an offender's head and hanging it in public. Of course, there are those reports of vampire cults doing similar rituals when they need blood for their ceremonies to 'cure' the sick. Or as Leonard said, this may have been a voodoo warning to someone!"

Chapter 29

While we are loading up the van, Leonard ambles over to speak to me as I roll diapers around some art glass pieces before positioning them in a half filled chicken box. I use this as an excuse to break away from my task at hand. "Ernie, I want to take you somewhere tomorrow morning. My limo driver will pick you up."

"Where are we going?"

He answers haltingly, "To the home of that woman who called you."

At last! I slap my hand on the table in front of me. "So you do know her! I thought so!"

From his tightening the muscles in his face, it strikes me that he feels he has already said more than he should have, and he falters. "Yeah, I called her and she confirmed that she was the one who called you. She wants to see the vase, and you need to bring that suitcase full of money that I gave you."

"I can understand her desire to inspect the vase, but why do I need to bring the suitcase?"

"She may have something of interest to show you. If it's what I hope it is, you're going to have to pay dearly for it."

Suspecting that to mean that she does indeed have to what Leonard had been referring when he said I would need every penny of the $2,600,000, I glance over to the crime scene where they are finally removing the body. "Her invitation for me to see her wouldn't have anything to do with that, would it?"

"Possibly, that Cajun may have been pursuing her in order to reach her father. Unfortunately, both of them are now dead."

Being a bit punch drunk from the event of the day, I am stunned by this apparent coincidence. "Her father was just killed, too!"

Leonard shakes his head. "Oh, no. He died of natural causes years ago. However, it wasn't well publicized." He bites his lower lip. "To be perfectly honest, quite a ruse was undertaken to hide that fact. He became sort of a zombie within the government's inner circle. It was advantageous for some of the higher-ups there to have him live on well after his funeral."

"What makes you say that our recent dearly departed was searching for her and, even more so, for her father?"

"I can't speak for her, but he would have had no difficulty reading the missing prayer book and Bible or deciphering them, for that matter."

He is definitely still holding back some facts. "Any other reason?"

Leonard sighs before elaborating. "Ernie, I guess I need to be candid with you about all of this. When he told you. 'They and only they have the power to subdue the dark forces of evil. They and only they are empowered to kill demons, vampires, and the other demonic creatures of the night,' he was seeking a coded response." He points to across the aisle from us. "Since we have proof that his being at that booth was no accident, he must've been briefed about your having that vase and was somehow testing your knowledge about it. Otherwise, he would have never said it to you."

That explains the fleeting bout of frustration he had shown but still does not make sense to me. "That's ridiculous. He, by your own admission, was probably hunting for that woman's father. I couldn't have helped him. Hell, I don't even know who you are talking about and that includes her."

"Of course, you're right about that. But then again, perhaps he was trying to get to me through you. His handlers probably figured that I would intervene on their behalf."

"That would presume that you are prepared to give the proper response."

Leonard places his right hand opened flat just below his chin with his thumb fully extended vertically. His other four fingers without any space between them are stretched perpendicular to his thumb and with it outline his jaw. The whites of his eyes are fully exposed. He then lowers his voice. Why he does that is not intuitively obvious, since except for Gloria we are all alone. "They and only they know the truth contained within the Chirilican teachings."

I feel a cold chill crawl down my spine. "You're good, you're really good. Ever thought about going into the movies?"

"As a fixer, there are many coded messages I have committed to memory. This is a very old one referring to the slayers."

"Are you talking about the same vampire slayers as that dealer from New Orleans was?"

"There are several types of vampires, each needing its own unique slayer. Those demons who willingly suck the life blood from others for their own personal benefit are a plague upon nations."

I am beginning to realize that we may no longer be talking about Dracula and his ilk. "You wouldn't be referring to Castro, would you?"

"Many in the Cuban community would consider him to be an unholy."

"In his booth he had a lot of documents from Jim Garrison's estate regarding the Kennedy assassination. There wouldn't be any connection between that slayer's kit and JFK, in particular?"

"There were many in the Cuban community, both here and in Cuba, who would have also considered JFK to be an unholy. Some even believe that next to Castro he was the most hated man in Miami in 1963."

My eyes light up. Finally, I may have stumbled onto the rationale for the Cajun's murder. "So, there is something in those two holy books that might be material to the Kennedy assassination!"

"I didn't say that and I sure as hell won't speculate if they contain anything relevant to it. However, having said that, someone felt it was imperative to kill to get their hands on those books and keep them from being passed on."

"Am I to take it that her father was a slayer?"

Leonard laughs long and hard at my accusation. "Oh, no, far from it. However, he would have been in a position to be acquainted with the slayers and able to contact them."

"Have you ever met a slayer?"

"Except for one, no, her father never revealed any of the others to me. The identity of slayers is a very closely held secret, which one takes to his grave."

Feeling that statement to be ironic, I observe in jest, "Finding slayers is a tricky business. Seemingly, only the dead know who they are."

My joke falls flat on Leonard, who is unusually somber. "The whereabouts of slayers is passed onto only those who are worthy of the knowledge and only given out when they have a need to know it. After thinking about all of this, I could make the argument that he may have even been trying to get in touch with a slayer or a slayer's daughter."

I restart rolling the diapers around the glass. "Leonard, you're becoming entirely too creepy for me. I just want to get rid of that vase. It seems to have some sort of a curse upon it: first the van, then those Cubans, and now the Cajun."

"Well, I'll see you in the morning, say 10

O'clock?"

"That will be fine."

Gloria comes up to me. "What will be fine?"

"Leonard wants to take me to see that woman who called me."

"Good! Maybe she'll take that damned vase, and things will get back to normal."

Friday night I walk Dumb and Dumber around the neighborhood while Gloria gets ready for bed and watches the news on television. My neighbors strangely fail to venture out of their homes to exercise their dogs during the customary prime time to do so. Since I am exhausted, this does have the welcomed timesaving benefit of preventing mine from having their usual raucous conversation with each fellow canine they meet. In fact, except for my dogs, I am completely alone and do not encounter any of our neighbors despite the particularly inviting weather we are experiencing.

My worst fear does not materialize when I return home. I do not find a police car waiting at the curb in front of our house. For the first time since the auction, I begin to feel that things are reverting back to normal.

After showering, shaving, and getting dressed Saturday morning, I dart down the stairs to the kitchen table, eager to read the newspaper account of the vampire murder while eating breakfast. I have never been able to figure out who in the medical examiner's office leaks the crime scene photos to the press. Those reporters must pay a lot for them since they got their copies before I got mine when I worked there. Gloria has beaten me to the paper and holds the front page up to me. "Ernie, there's no mention of it!"

"Of course, there is. A murder at 'the show,' especially one that bizarre, is too hot for them to ignore. You've just missed it."

She is miffed by my not believing her and just glares at me before stating, "No, I've scoured each page of the paper and even went to its website. Nothing! And the only thing about 'the show' on the television news last night and this morning were its own ads." She shoves the first section over to me. "Here, look for yourself."

After a cursory search of it and the rest of the paper, I capitulate. "Leonard is the best. I can't believe he did it, but he suppressed that murder. I wonder what he told the news media to convince them not to broadcast it. They live and die by hyping that sort of thing all evening before their late night news programs. You know they wouldn't have willingly passed on a vampire story just before midnight, and there was a harvest moon out last night."

"The paper isn't any better. It would've put pictures of that cross in his heart on the front page with the headline, 'What's a Real Dracula Worth?' After all, its editors think you all are nothing but a bunch of mercenaries."

"Yeah, just what you want to see when you are devouring your bacon and eggs. Plus, I can only imagine the accompanying story, 'Antiques dealers were heatedly debating amongst themselves how much the fresh corpse of a son of Dracula would go for at 'the show' Friday.

The question was raised whether the absence of his original coffin would affect the price their customers would pay for an otherwise absolutely pristine vampire without any sign of the decomposition that turns off all but the most advanced collectors. The rarity of such an offering, unencumbered by the usual costly restoration required for the more commonly encountered specimens from Russia, Germany, and the western Slavic regions, seemed though to outweigh this omission. It was generally conceded amongst them that there would be little difficulty in unearthing a suitable substitute. In order to resolve how much of a deduction in price could be expected, some searched for past auctions on the Internet to find the latest winning bids for Egyptian mummies with and without their caskets for comparison.'"

"I think that's a bit over the top, even for you, Ernie. Besides, you'd better quit playing comedian and eat up. Adolpho will be back here any minute. It shouldn't take him long to move his car to make room for the limo."

Gloria is right. I barely finish my breakfast before Adolpho is ringing our doorbell.

I go into the den and grab the box with the vase and the suitcase full of money, $2,000,000 to be precise, both of which are on the floor near the door. When I get to the front door I feel a bit foolish since I have no free hand to open it. I holler for Gloria who rushes over, unlocks it, and opens it for me. Adolpho immediately sees my predicament and says, "Give me the vase."

As I hand it over to him, I poke fun at its checkered past, "Hopefully, this will be the last time it's in my house. With all the bad luck it has brought, you would've thought it had come from King Tut's tomb."

"What are you talking about?"

"The vampire murder at 'the show!'" He just stares at me. I find his acute amnesia to be both strange and somewhat disturbing and so keep on. "You know, that Cajun who was killed because of it: stake in his heart and all of his blood drained out."

Outwardly genuinely concerned about my story, Adolpho finally declares, "No one was killed at 'the show' yesterday! You were misinformed. Some guy from Louisiana died of a heart attack, that's all."

His statement shocks Gloria. "We were there, you weren't! I had to deal with his sheet-covered body with that stake sticking out the whole time I packed up yesterday. What are you talking about?"

He remains adamant. "No, no, nothing like that happened. If it had it would have been all over the papers and on the TV news. Did you see it there?"

I now understand. "How did Leonard get that story out?"

He smiles. "Well, the body was taken to the FBI's crime lab in Bethesda instead of the ME's office for the autopsy. Leonard instructed the ME to put the cause of death down as heart attack. When reporters inquired as to what had happened at 'the show,' everyone played along. 'The show' was more than happy for us to do anything that would avoid any bad publicity from scaring away its customers this weekend. The police routinely defer comment about the cause of death to the ME's office, which is busy enough that they were happy to unload the case onto the FBI and make it a federal crime."

"Didn't anyone there object to falsifying the death certificate?"

Adolpho chuckles. "If you think about it, Ernie, it was technically an attack on his heart."

"How did he get the FBI to cooperate?"

"That was easy. The guy who had placed him here had a CIA business card. Agent Johnson was more than willing to assist us in investigating the murder of a fellow federal agent, particularly one who was undeniably working deep undercover and whose murder may be material to the theft of those license plates."

"I was led to believe the Agency didn't use antiques dealers as agents. Leonard claims we all make lousy spies."

"You all do. He got killed, didn't he? Good agents don't make amateurish mistakes like not recognizing Cuban hitmen."

"I thought whoever did it was from New Orleans, at least that's what the detective said the voodoo doll implied."

"Listen, Ernie, Cuban hitmen are in New Orleans, as well as Miami. Anywhere the Cuban exiles are active so are they. Besides, some of those hitmen may not be Cuban by birth. Castro is not above tricking others to do his handiwork. He especially likes using drug dealers."

"Leonard told me that his post mortem appearance was designed to be some sort of a warning or threat."

Adolpho does not let me finish. "Yeah, they are after someone from New Orleans, who they want to keep as far away from you as possible."

"I gather it's Leonard's plan to introduce me to that person."

He starts to leave and prompts me to do the same. "And the sooner the better. He's very upset about how brazen they are and is taking their threat very seriously. The last thing he wants is for them to discover her whereabouts."

I begin to walk to where the limo should be parked. It is not there; rather the limo driver is piloting a small helicopter, which landed on the cul-de-sac several doors down from us. "I take it we're not going somewhere that is on the GPS maps."

He scrunches his face. "Some people value their privacy. We're going to meet Leonard at the airport and fly to her farm. Besides, this way whoever is after her won't be able to tail us."

Peering down from the helicopter as it ascends, I realize that Leonard had taken extreme precautions that I was not disturbed last night. I wave at all of the police cars that have effectively barricaded my neighborhood. "You don't think that's a bit excessive?"

Adolpho shakes his head. "Sergeant O'Brien felt it was best. He, like Leonard, was impressed by the professionalism of those Cuban hitmen. If they could enter 'the show' undetected, they easily could get to you. Besides, it kept your nosy neighbors at bay. You didn't see anyone checking out the helicopter, did you? They may not leave their homes for weeks after what the cops told them was the reason for the road blocks."

Not currently being on the homeowners' association's most favored list, I am afraid to ask but do so anyway, "What exactly did the cops say?"

"Something about your name and address being found on a target list on an international terrorist group's website. After that, they didn't object to cops searching their cars."

"Y'all couldn't have shown some restraint in all of this?"

"Hey, we didn't do house to house manhunts with bomb sniffing dogs as the SWAT team wanted."

In a few minutes we arrive at an airport that is not on any map. "How private is this place? I've never heard of it."

"It's not private at all. It's owned by the public."

"As in government owned?"

The limo driver, turned helicopter pilot, rotates his head to congratulate me. "You're finally catching on. You have to have the highest security clearance to use it."

"If this is owned by the CIA, why do I see all of those MPs down there."

Adolpho answers, "I told you, Leonard was really shaken up by that hit. He's taking no chances."

When we land, Leonard bends down to meet me under the rotating propeller. He needs to shout at me to be heard over the whine of the motor and the wind still coming off the propeller as it slows down. "Glad you could make it. And in the nick of time, I might add. Are you familiar with root work?"

"Come again!"

"Root work, you know, unhexing someone."

Chapter 30

The flight to wherever Leonard is taking me does not last more than 45 minutes. From the very rural nature of the landscape on the approach to the airstrip, I expect that we will be touching down in any minute on a cleared out cow pasture and wonder to myself how the pilot can land this small corporate jet safely. Much to my surprise, out in the middle of nowhere is a commercial grade runway with a limo parked on its apron. After I put the box with the vase and the suitcase in its trunk, Adolpho, Leonard, and I get settled in the car while the pilot returns to being a limo driver and starts the engine. Leonard reaches into his coat pocket to take out a folded sheet of paper and then sits up to tap the driver on the shoulder. He turns around to face Leonard who hands him the map with directions. "Follow this route exactly."

Despite examining it thoroughly, the driver is still confused. "But there are no names for the streets."

"That's because they're all dirt roads. I don't expect much traffic to slow you down. By the way, unless some farmer is hunting for a cow that has gone astray, there won't be anyone to give you directions. And don't bother with the GPS; it won't work either. So, don't get lost."

The driver laughs. "I'm already lost and we haven't even started."

In a while, we arrive at a driveway with a locked gate and a tall brick fence with barbed wire on top that extends for at least a mile in either direction. Leonard shouts out, "Stop here," and then gets out of the limo. He searches his pocket and pulls out a small random number generator that he holds in his left hand. A surveillance camera follows his every movement. Reading from the device's screen, he punches a six number code onto the keypad on the gate, which slowly opens after he has finished. He gets back into the car.

As we drive down the long single lane dirt path, I observe. "Whoever lives here must be plenty paranoid. That's one expensive fence for a house that no one could find even if they wanted to."

Leonard is not amused. "Dudley Nichols said it best, 'Fear is the highest fence.' She has her reasons."

The wide-open cow pastures suddenly end and we enter a pitch-black tunnel formed by prickly vines thick enough to keep all remnants of the sun out. Is this what Adolpho was talking about? "The neighborhood kids must love coming to her house for Trick or Treat."

Still in no mood for levity, Leonard curtly asserts, "She doesn't get a lot of visitors."

Just as my eyes adjust to the darkness, the sun bursts out and I squint. A small well-kept front yard leads to a freshly painted century old white washed farmhouse. There are geese everywhere. I have forgotten her name, but finally conclude that this must be the home of that woman Mitch and the other dealers were talking about at The Blue And The Gay. "Leonard, I've heard about this lady from the other dealers. Her father worked at the White House in the Sixties. She wants to sell his papers for some God-awful sum of money, which none of the dealers in town will pay, even Mitch, who told me you referred her to him."

"You're partly right. Denise's father did work in the White House as the first fixer for Cuba; however, his papers are probably worth every penny she is asking for them. Mitch should've taken her offer. He has the bankroll needed to close the deal."

"Why does she want to see the vase?"

"I can't rightly say. She asked me to bring both you and the vase. Denise doesn't do that unless she has a good reason."

After surveying the yard, I am compelled to ask, "Maybe you can tell me why she has all of these geese?"

His hand makes a wide sweeping motion by the window. "You mean these Chinese geese. They are her watchdogs. Unlike real dogs, they get alarmed about anything. Nothing happens outside of her house without them alerting her. Besides, goose eggs make wonderful omelets and baked goods. She claims they are her secret weapon at the County Fair. Her cakes haven't failed to win a blue ribbon in decades."

When the limo stops, the geese surround it, stretch their necks forward taking aim at us with their beaks, and start to hiss in unison. They are indeed intimidating. "Is it safe to get out?"

Leonard smiles. "Show no fear, and you'll do fine. I haven't heard of them pecking anyone to death recently."

A late middle-aged woman, with her long blonde hair tied back in a bun and a red polka dot apron partially hiding her yellow blouse and blue jeans, opens the front door of the house. She immediately starts to shoo away the geese with a very odd looking broomstick and makes a path to the limo. Her swiftness at reaching us indicates how much she is in firm command. Standing by the rear door of the limo closest to the house, she announces, "It's safe to come out now, Leonard."

We all together get out and surround her in the area free of the geese. Leonard introduces me, "Denise Reid, this is Ernie. He's the dealer who bought the vase and the rifle and he's a doctor."

As I shake her hand, I detect a vast uneasiness about her. She ignores what I had considered to be my real reason for being here and to my great surprise only asks, "Are you learned in the root?"

What's with root work: first Leonard, now her? I stare at her. "It's been a long time since I've had to treat someone who's had the root put on them."

The apprehension so evident in her expression softens somewhat. "But you have! Good, come on in and see what you can do."

We walk past the grey stained wood plank porch, which was repaired since Adolpho was last here, into the living room. Except for the nests with geese sitting on their eggs, it is not all that different from many I have visited in my quest for hidden treasure. Immediately, we make a right turn into the hall leading to a bedroom. In the middle of the floor in front of the door to the bedroom is a large mound of what resembles coffee grounds but smells more like some exotic spice. Nestled right in its scooped out center are the contents of three unfertilized goose eggs, cracked open with such considerable skill that no yolk was broken while placing them there. From the number of flies clinging onto them, I take that they have been there for a while. A fat line of sparkling glitter goes from the coffee grounds straight into the bedroom. Its only sources of light are the many candles burning on a makeshift altar in one of its corners and a single window with white curtains drawn tightly closed allowing only a sliver of sunlight to enter the room. Each candle has a scrap of paper crudely torn from a brown paper bag and then tied around its middle with a thin metal wire. When I cross the threshold, my shoes kick up a fine white powder, which lightly dusts them. Its trail rings the room. Denise does not wait for me to ask the question. "That's Demon Stay Away Powder. And watch out for the three sticks in the center of the floor. Don't disturb them."

The further I enter the room the more I perceive the strong odor of peppers coming from the ceiling. The sunlight from the east outlines an object between the quarter-opened window and the curtain. I push the curtain aside and see a large tree just beyond the window. Attached by a string to one of its branches is a crude doll stuffed with white cotton and covered with sewn together torn pieces of a black cloth dress. It is sitting on the windowsill, with its head supported by the window's rail. I grasp the "doll" and notice cayenne pepper stains the small cut out strips of paper that are pinned to it. By all appearances these are from the same grocery sack, which was ripped apart for the candles. Each has someone's name printed on it in pencil.

A larger note is also pinned to it. I hold it up so that the light from the window lets me read it. "To whom it may concern is holding her. Hang. Cut her a-loose. Or have all kind of trouble, worries yourself to death until you turn her loose." I try as best as I can to return the

388

"doll" to the window exactly as I had found it.

Before long, curious to see what the notes attached to the candles say, I move over to the altar and read them. One commands, "All demons attacking me leave me now." Another proclaims, "I declare victory over the dark spirits." A third has an even more intriguing message: "Death to those who harm a slayer or a slayer's child."

Finally, I approach the only bed in the room. It is directly across from the altar and is also encircled by Demon Stay Away Powder. In its center, fully dressed in hand-stitched white cotton, a Hispanic appearing woman lies flaccid in a stuporous state. I can see where incense had been burning at each of the four corners of the bed. I pick up a cardboard tube that had fallen onto the floor and still holds a small amount of unused powdered incense, which is all that is left. It is labeled "Witchcraft Killer." I ask Denise, who is standing attentively by the bed, "How long has she been like this?"

"Since yesterday. She came here all in a dither after seeing photos of that Cajun dealer, who was killed by a stake piercing his heart at 'the show.' Once she had performed each and every one of the voodoo anti-demon rituals that she knew from memory, all the while declaring that someone had put a death root on her, she crept into this bed. Then she slowly lapsed into this catatonic state."

Leonard becomes very disturbed upon hearing this. "How did she see them? I thought I had buried that story so deeply that she would never hear about it."

"One of her protectors in the CIA felt he knew better. He told her she was in danger and to get the hell

389

out of town. When she asked what did he mean, he showed her the photos. So, she came here. Where else would she go?"

"Shit! She's not even their target, you are. When will the Agency learn to do a thorough run down before reacting?"

"It's funny that you think I'm their target since she's the one who called me to tell me that her father's prayer book had finally surfaced and would be at 'the show.' I told her that I would go there to get it to complete my father's work. You probably don't know that it's the last link in the chain of evidence. She, though, insisted on going without me after saying that I wouldn't be able to tell if it was the right one. You see, she didn't think it would be a good idea for the both of us to be there at the same time. I had to agree with her about that. But now, without her, none of this is any good." Stern-faced, she then eyes me and forcefully clamors, "Ernie, you've got to do something."

Like what? I cannot conceive how to help them out here where even cell phones do not work. Nonetheless, I cannot back off. "Leonard, you've always said you're the fixer. Get me a 1000 cc bag of normal saline, two 200 mg tablets of Pyridium, a 20 mg vial of IV Lasix, an IV set up, a pole to hang the saline, and some smelling salts, preferably ammonia capsules. And, if you can, bring some Wahoo bark."

Without flinching at my requests, he asks, "Is that all you need, Ernie? That's not asking very much."

"If you can find me a voodoo doctor costume, it may help."

It is unclear to me if he realizes I am kidding about the costume when he quickly leaves and goes to the limo. A few minutes later, he returns. "It will all be here in a half an hour. I also asked for a nurse. I don't trust your ability to put in an IV. You haven't touched a live patient in how many decades?"

"How did you do that?"

"The limo's equipped with a satellite telephone. You don't think I would go anywhere where I couldn't be reached."

"Speaking of that limo, it's awfully familiar."

"Of course, it is. You've seen it hundreds of times on TV. It used to be the President's until he got a more fuel-efficient model. It's here for Denise's needs. The Secret Service maintains it."

I glance towards her. "Who exactly are you?"

Coldly, she answers, "I am my father's daughter and that makes me a problem for our government."

"In what way?"

"Same as Ángela. We embody a truth that both Washington and Havana would prefer be remained buried along with those responsible for it. For almost five decades, both governments have successfully hidden what they had done. Now in a few years, those same governments have promised to reveal what they claim is the 'truth.' Both of us stand in the way of that."

It is such an odd thing to say that I am taken aback

by her stating that. "Why would you want to do that?"

"The documents that are to be released by Cuba and our country do not contain the full truth. It is here on my farm! My father ordered me to insure that his story is finally told when our government starts to spread its distortions. I have granted you the right to review his papers and, after you pay me for them, do with them what you think is best. Leonard tells me that you will do just that. My father in his will set out the terms of their purchase: $1,000,000 to read them, $1,000,000 to take possession, and $1,000,000 in October 2017 upon their sale."

"That's a lot of money for records of what happened a half century ago. How can I realistically expect to recoup my investment? No one may still be interested in them despite your father's feelings to the contrary."

Staring straight into my eyes, she unnerves me by frankly asserting, "You don't."

Leonard hastily interjects, "But you will!"

After acknowledging his endorsement simply with a nod, Denise continues. "My father felt that the best way to get the real truth out was to have his papers sold at auction. The stir that will be generated after their re-emergence should thwart any attempt to denigrate them. He felt it would be best if I did not directly participate in any consignment."

Up until that I follow her father's logic; however, I do not understand his objection to her being the consignee. "How come? You appear competent enough not to be ripped off by those sharks."

"He wasn't afraid of that. Rather, he was certain that there were people who would try to block the sale from ever occurring if I were to do it. Someone, whose reputation for honesty is irrefutable and well established among auctioneers, in his mind would have a greater chance of success. For my father, proving that I did not somehow selectively edit the information to exonerate him in DC was paramount. At the same time, it could both be difficult for me to do as well as potentially embarrassing to my family and me. You see, he feared a smear campaign once I started to shop his papers."

Since how well I comprehend the intrigue in the Executive Branch is open to question to Leonard, he explains, "When things go down badly in the government, someone in the inner circle needs to commit seppuku figuratively to save face for the President and to preserve his reputation and historical standing. Denise's father was such a designated fall guy. A huge disinformation campaign was created to obfuscate the truth about what had happened. Those documents to be released in 2017 will prove beyond any reasonable suspicion that her father was a traitor to his country and had committed high treason."

All I can think about at this juncture is how do I gracefully get out of this transaction. No one will pay $3,000,000 for another Benedict Arnold's papers. I breathe deeply before asking, "Was he?"

"No, just the opposite. Those at the highest levels knew he was innocent, but, nevertheless, concocted the scheme you will see. He agreed to be 'banished' to this farm that does not officially exist in any governmental

393

records and where his every need would be met. Sort of like a witness protection program, but with royal treatment. He fell on his sword to prevent World War III and the nuclear annihilation of the civilized world. He accepted the blame for failing to prevent Castro's assassination of JFK and consented to others implicating him as the instigator of it all to deflect serious inquires into Castro's role in it. He thus prevented the predictable reflex repeat of the Cuban Missile Crisis, but this time without a happy ending. All those conspiracy rumors of CIA involvement, an FBI role, even a Mob hit were allowed to worm their way to him. Eventually, Ángela and her father came to live here."

As always, follow the money trail, and this deal definitely has one. I turn to Denise. "Why did he want $3,000,000 for the truth if all of your family financial needs were being met forever?"

Unfazed by my bringing up that large sum of money, she states, "In 2017, when all the official records are to be disclosed, the contract with my father will end. The original agreement between President Johnson and my father was that the documents, including my father's personal papers, would be kept secret and sealed until December 2013, fifty years after the assassination. They felt that everyone involved would be dead by then, even Castro. Johnson's intent for the release of everything was to eventually set the historical record straight. Anticipating how essential my father's account would be to do that, both of them felt secure that my family and I could use the proceeds from the sale of my father's documents to support ourselves. $3,000,000 dollars was a lot of money at the time my father made out his will. Bush modified the deal when he signed the JFK Assassination Records Collection Act in 1992.

Everything was moved back four years to October 2017."

It could be that Leonard is right. But I am not yet satisfied. "Do you have any independent corroboration of what you just said?"

"In October 1968, just before he left the White House, Johnson felt it would be prudent to tell one trustworthy reporter of his plan in a circuitous way. Howard K. Smith quoted him as saying, "I'll tell you something that will rock you. Kennedy was trying to get to Castro, but Castro got to him first. . . . . It will all come out one day."

That is not actually the proof I need. "But you claim the official records are tainted."

For the first time, Denise becomes animated. "Exactly, those who wanted to maintain the Camelot image of the Kennedy years resolved that specific things would need to be continually suppressed for 'security reasons.' Even as late as December 2009 Obama unwittingly continued this cover-up. He created the National Declassification Center with the motto: "Releasing All We Can, Protecting What We Must." Strangely, his executive order included the Kennedy assassination papers, which was unnecessary since they were already covered by the JFK records act, except it gave a way to circumvent that act." The excitement in her voice picks up. "What about those papers must still be protected? Why does the CIA insist on continuing to withhold 1100 assassination records after the 2017 release date? It has already prepared its appeal to whoever is President then to postpone their release. What does the Agency claim that's in them will cause an identifiable harm to the military defense, intelligence operations, law enforcement, and conduct of foreign relations of this country of such gravity that it outweighs the public interest in the disclosure? Again, fifty years later, after the fall of the Soviet Union and the deaths of the major players of the day except Castro, is it possible that there is anything that could outweigh the public interest in knowing why JFK was assassinated? Hell, they've even finally released the rest of the 'Pentagon Papers' that Daniel Ellsberg didn't give to the New York Times." She slams her hand on a nearby bedside table. "But they won't release all of the JFK papers!"

I have to concede that point and move on. "OK! Now answer me this: what's with all of the secrecy and James Bond type things that I have encountered since I bought the vase?"

She does not calm down. Once more she hits that table. "There are those within the Cuban DGI who wish to keep Castro's false claim of innocence perpetuated to avoid retribution. And there are those within the CIA who wish the same as the DGI, as well as others within the CIA who want to prevent the truth about the JM/WAVE connection to the JFK assassination from ever surfacing. At least three covert forces have coalesced to keep my father's story from ever being told and believed. Fortunately, some within the Cuban resistance want Castro's guilt unveiled and are fighting to achieve this." Denise shakes her head in disgust. "Regrettably, their motive is to force a military overthrow of the current Cuban regime, rather than prove my father's innocence."

Pointing at the bed, I ask, "OK, then who's Ángela?"

Without delay she exclaims, "The sole living

relative of the slayer of Kennedy, his daughter."

This is getting even weirder. I think back to the now deceased dealer from New Orleans and my discussion with Leonard about vampire slayers. "Why is she here?"

Leonard straightaway takes over. "To keep the ploy intact, Johnson had Denise's father protect the slayer and his daughter by having them live here. No one in the government could figure out a way to try the slayer, even in a military court, without the details somehow finding their way to the press. I'm certain you're asking yourself why, but they couldn't just execute him. This is the compromise they conceived. With all of the principals now dead except for some in Cuba who aren't talking, Ángela is the only substantiating witness, so to speak, of the cover up. Their existence is such a secret that I only met them once and was told to just deny they were alive if ever asked about them. Adolpho also only met Ángela once but was never told who she is. The CIA has, up to the present, prevented the DGI from getting to her and eliminating her."

Not entirely satisfied by this explanation and wrongly disturbed by my poker face, Denise is worried that I suspect all of what has just been said and adds apologetically, "Unfortunately, only she is privy to what's in the prayer book and the significance of the copy of the vase, details that her father took to his grave. She is literally the key to the truth."

Chapter 31

For a second time I feel Leonard is probably spot-on. Those documents do appear to have real historical importance, a true attribute, which makes dealers begin to hear the ca-ching of cash registers. In our lingo that sound translates to mean big profit. While waiting for the medical stuff, I figure I ought to take this opportunity to find out what is in the boxes. "I guess there is no time like the present to see what you all are talking about. Let's take a peek at what the CIA wants deep-sixed."

The change in Denise's face shows that she is pleased. "I was hoping you would say that." She then leads us to her kitchen.

There is barely any empty space left in it due to all of the white storage boxes stacked high upon each other. Moreover, it is so crowded I cannot figure out how anyone can cook in it. As the guys at The Blue And The Gay had claimed, the boxes were numbered and sealed with official-looking government tape with the White House logo imprinted on it. My quick count suggests there are over fifty of them. "How many are there?"

"Fifty seven."

"Your father was thorough in his record keeping, I see."

Her entire countenance transforms as we begin discussing her father's papers. The tension is gone. "He had to be. He knew that if anything went wrong, he would be the fall guy. I have an index of what's in each box that may help you decide if you want to pay to find out what indeed is in all of them."

She abruptly leaves the kitchen and then returns in a few minutes. In her right hand is a yellow manila envelope with brown spots on both sides, signs of its age. She presents it to me in a surprisingly formal manner. "I just want you to understand that my father spent an inordinate amount of time cataloguing everything in those boxes and preparing the proper chronology. It really became an obsession with him that historians should eventually get the story right. He always felt that the Viet Nam War overshadowed the true significance of all the things that had been done invisibly during the Cold War with their long-delayed and long-lasting consequences. Once he was officially elected President, it didn't take Johnson very long to begin to wind down JM/WAVE and send its people to Laos."

After I undo the metal clasp, I pull out ten single-spaced typed sheets of paper. While I originally thought the Bay of Pigs would be the hot topic at an auction preview, my attention is immediately drawn to the documents in box 32 listed under the broad headline, "Assassination Attempts." These are the cloak and dagger secrets that can make the bidding at the auction itself go through the roof.

Under the caption, Jack Esterline, he has "Spring 1960 LSD aerosol spraying of radio station from which Castro is broadcasting his speeches" and under Dr. Edward Gunn, "Fall 1960 botulinus toxin contaminated cigars."

Next, he has a new heading, "The Beard: Trip Outside of Cuba" with two subtitles: "1) Thallium powder in boots and shoes" and "2) Animal testing for best dose to cause depilation of beard but not paralysis."

The list of documents jumps in size with a series of articles under the unexpected category, "Gambling Syndicate Phase-1. August 1960-May 1961," The name Cornelius Roosevelt is recorded over a group of odd sounding subjects: "Pin to deliver highly toxic shellfish poison," Bacterial infested liquid," "Bacterial treatment of cigars or cigarettes," and "Handkerchief laced with bacteria." Following that is what turns out to be a major topic called "Poison Pill: Santos Trafficante, Juan Orta, and Varona." I ask Denise, "Do you know who any of these people are?"

"Like who?"

"Santos Trafficante, sounds Italian to me, not Cuban."

"That was Joe, the courier. He was the chieftain of the Cosa Nostra in Cuba. He ran their gambling casinos."

"Oh, how about Juan Orta? He sounds Cuban."

"The Mob's man inside of Havana. Officially, he was Office Chief and Director General of the Office of the Prime Minister, basically, Castro's chief of staff. Orta supplemented his government salary with kickbacks from the various casinos in Cuba. He began to have financial problems when in 1959 Castro initially closed them to native Cubans. Things only continued to degenerate for him until the fall of 1961 when they were shut down entirely. Then, in January 1961, Castro ousted him from the Prime Minister's Office. After Trafficante vouched for him, Orta was designated to be the man to put the

CIA's poison pill in Castro's tea or bouillon. Although Orta begged off the assignment, he did help recruit another insider who made repeated unsuccessful attempts."

"Who was Varona?'"

"Dr. Manuel Antonio de Varona y Loredo was a former Prime Minister of Cuba and the head of the Democratic Revolutionary Front, which despite its communist sounding name was a leading force behind the Bay of Pigs invasion. It was purported that the Mafia financially supported his operation in order to regain their gambling interests in a post-Castro Cuba. He claimed to have a contact in one of Castro's favorite restaurants, who agreed to put one of those poison pills in Castro's meal. Unfortunately for the Mob and the CIA, after they had paid Varona off and given him the pills but before he could implement the plan, Castro found out about the plot and quit going there."

Next came: "Gambling Syndicate-Phase 2. Late 1961-June 1963." It is full of code names, such as, Operation Mongoose, ZRRIFFLE and QJWIN but does not have a very long log of papers. I am intrigued by the shortest entry so far, "1963 Desmond FitzGerald, Caribbean Mollusca." "Your father had a special interest in seashells?"

"No, but FitzGerald, who ran the Cuban operation for the Kennedys, thought that they could rig up a 'spectacular sea shell' with explosives. Ian Fleming may well have first proposed the idea to JFK at a White House meeting at which he further submitted attacking Castro's manliness by making his beard fall out. That's what the thallium was supposed to do. It turns out that Castro liked

401

to skin-dive and the idea of a booby-trapped seashell that would attract his attention and then blow up when he lifted it up was enticing enough that it was explored. They even thought of having the attorney for the Bay of Pigs conspirators, while he negotiated for their release, give Castro a goodwill gesture: a skin-diving suit impregnated with a fungus that would infect him with a chronic, disabling skin affliction. The accompanying breathing apparatus was to be designed to deliver tuberculosis. Unfortunately for the Agency, that same lawyer decided that presenting Castro with a fancy skin-diving suit, sans the biological weaponry, would advance his cause. He did so on his own without first consulting FitzGerald."

A rather lengthy listing is "Project AMLASH-Rolando Cubela." "Who was Rolando Cubela? Your father had a lot of information about him."

"As well he should have. You know the expression, 'Keep your friends close, but your enemies even closer.' It applies to him. Rolando Cubela Secades, code name Amlash, was both a physician and a major in the Cuban army. He had been second in command of the Directorio Revolucionario 13 de Marso and personally assassinated Batista's chief military intelligence officer, Blanco Rico. His group and Castro's group were allied in the revolution against Batista, but weren't exactly friendly afterwards. He, to say the least, did not like the communist direction the now Prime Minister Castro was heading Cuba towards. From early on he talked about killing Castro.

"In 1961 he became a CIA undercover agent. Such things as blowing up an oil refinery, the execution of Carlos Rodriquez, one of Castro's subordinates, along

402

with the Soviet Ambassador were schemes he dreamed up. In 1963 Cubela approached FitzGerald, who had told Cubela that he was a personal representative of then Attorney General Robert F. Kennedy. Cubela wanted an assassination weapon that he could use to kill Castro from a long distance, preferably a high-powered rifle with telescopic sights."

Scanning further below AMLASH'S heading, I come across a titillating entry. "What's a Black Leaf 40 poison pen?"

"Later in 1963, Dr. Gunn of the lethal cigar and poison pill plots developed the Black Leaf 40 poison pen device. A Paper-Mate pen was converted into a hypodermic syringe. Black Leaf 40 is an insecticide primarily 40% nicotine, which would kill Castro if injected into him. Cubela was given the pen by his CIA case officer in Paris on November 22, 1963 but refused to use Black Leaf 40, stating that there were better agents to use. He also requested 20 hand grenades, two high-powered rifles with telescopic sights, about 20 pounds of C-4 explosive, and a few other items to stage a real coup against Castro. Just as the meeting broke up, those at it were informed of JFK's assassination that ironically had occurred while they were plotting to do the same to Castro."

I quip, "That should have ended his espionage career."

"Unfortunately, it didn't. In the spring of 1964, two FAL 7.62 automatic rifles made in Belgium were obtained for Cubela along with 10 magazines of ammunition. However, he wanted silencers, which eventually were fabricated for him by the CIA. In July

1964, the rifles with their silencers were put down on the north coast of Pinar del Rio. For the next year, Cubela continued to plan the overthrow of Castro. To get the needed manpower, he recruited Manuel Artime, who was introduced to him by the CIA and ran a 300-member army in Central America, which was paid for by the Agency. In 1965 during Castro's annual July 26 address at the beach resort, Varadero, Cubela was to kill him. At the same time Artime was to lead an attack from the sea on to the nearby northern coast of Cuba with the collusion of dissident Cuban military officers stationed there. It never happened. Nevertheless, in March of 1966, Cubela and some others were captured in Havana. They were convicted of treason and jailed but, without explanation, not executed."

Denise is anything but the weirdo that my colleagues had described. "How do you remember all of this minutiae?"

She smiles. "Some of my friends' fathers told them World War II stories when they were growing up. Such as, tell me what you did in the Great War, Daddy. Mine told me the history of the Cold War as it pertained to Cuba. I probably have committed to memory pretty much everything of any importance in those boxes. I told you he felt that the historians had gotten it wrong due to Washington's slight-of-hand and smoke-and-mirrors tricks and the 800-pound gorilla in the room, Viet Nam. If those records were somehow destroyed, my father made me their human backup."

"I understand the geese are here to protect you, but why do you let them live in your house?"

Pointing to the west, she explains, "I don't live

here. I live in a very comfortable underground bunker over there. My father always felt that some day, someone would come after us. He didn't trust anyone, particularly anyone connected with the intelligence agencies of the governments of Cuba and the U.S. If they did attack us, they would only take geese as prisoners. By the way, don't try to pet the geese that are in here. They are wirelessly connected to a defense system that will blow up this place if they are approached in a threatening manner. That was a 'retirement present' from some of his true friends in the Agency, who feared for his safety."

I am at this instant convinced that this may indeed be the deal of the century and am about to hand over the suitcase full of money, when Adolpho sprints into the kitchen. "They just arrived with your medical equipment."

Denise immediately leaves to attend to the geese that have surrounded Leonard's medical team.

Fearful that Denise will be disappointed in what I am about to do, when she returns, I warn her. "Now, don't ask any questions. Just trust that I know what I'm doing. If you interrupt me or challenge what I'm about to do, you may ruin it."

Misinterpreting this, she is a bit concerned. "You aren't going to do anything dangerous, are you?"

"Of course not, just the opposite. I don't want you to be surprised by how simple unhexing is." I glimpse at Adolpho, "Did they really bring a witch doctor's costume?"

He is visibly displeased. "Yeah, they did. It reminds

me of something from a Halloween costume store. I don't think you should put it on. You'll look ridiculous. Everything else is already in the bedroom except the Wahoo root. The nurse couldn't figure out what you were planning to do with it."

I meet up with the nurse in the living room. She hands me the witch doctor's outfit. "Sorry, but it's all we could find on such short notice. I know, it's the circa 1930s Tarzan movie crap they sell at Party City."

Holding up the costume to inspect it, I immediately decide that she and Adolpho are right and forgo the idea of dressing up. I am not troubled since it strictly was a joke. As I lead her into the kitchen, I ask, "Have you ever unhexed someone?"

"No. Is it anything like the exorcism in *The Exorcist*?"

I shake my head. "Hardly. It's really very basic. Just don't laugh at me. You're going to have to pretend to be very serious and concerned. Adolpho says you have the Wahoo bark?"

"Yeah, it wasn't as hard to locate as we all thought. A local herbal medicine shop had it."

"Good, hand it to me."

She takes out a plastic packet from a small white paper bag she is holding and passes it to me. I silently read the label. "Yep, that's the stuff. Let's go brew a strong tea from it." We step into the kitchen and find a small pot in the cabinet over the cooktop. After filling it with water from the tap next to the oven, I place the pot on a burner and turn the heat up to high. I wait until the water boils, pour the entire packet of Wahoo root bark into the pot, and stir intermittently with a spoon. Ten minutes later, I turn off the burner. From the freezer over the refrigerator, I grab some ice cubes, which I dump into the now steaming water. I note, "That ought to cool it off enough." I carry the pot out of the kitchen.

When we enter the bedroom, I intone, "This is a very serious case of root work. We will need to use the big guns if anything will save her life."

The nurse is pretty sharp and has figured out what I am about and, in addition, must have done some acting previously. Her improvisation is perfect. "Do you think the red death will work?"

"It will have to. It's all that's proven to kill the demons associated with this type of death root." I then place the pot of Wahoo tea on the left bedside table.

Denise, Leonard, and Adolpho are already standing by Ángela's bed. All three of them are holding 7-branched menorahs with 6 lit small solid black candles and one lit 9-inch long jumbo double action and reversing candle. Its top half is pure white and its bottom half is jet black. The black and white candle is in the large center branch cup with three of the small black candles on each of its sides in the smaller branches cups. Seeing me stare at them, Leonard speaks up, "You're not the only one who's been in contact with voodoo."

I position the nurse by the right side of the head of the bed and I go over to the left side. I order her to, "Crush one of the ammonia capsules and place it under her nose."

Almost as soon as she does that, Ángela wakes up coughing and slaps the nurse's hand away with her own right hand. Before I gently rub the tepid Wahoo bark tea onto Ángela's brow with my thumb, I move her arms against her chest to cross herself. While I bathe her forehead, I loudly exclaim, "Wahoo, Wahoo, Wahoo, Wahoo, Wahoo, Wahoo, Wahoo." Each of the seven times I say "Wahoo," I press a X-cross on her forehead with my thumb and then dip it back into the pot of tea. Immediately after saying "Wahoo" and making the pass over her head for the seventh time, I grab her by her wrists and uncross her arms and throw them as far apart as I can. Finally, I pick up the pot of Wahoo tea and take it to the window where I open the curtains and raise its lower sash. After I cast the tea to the east onto the trunk of that large tree standing just beyond it, I go back to the bed and say ominously, "Ángela, the nurse is going to put a needle into your vein so that we can give you a most powerful medicine that will kill the evil red spirits that have entered your body and flush them out of you. You will see that they are gone when your urine turns red. Is that all right with you?"

With her eyes closed, Ángela barely nods her head. The nurse rolls over the IV pole and places the bag of saline water on one of its arms. She inserts the IV tubing into the bag and, upon removing the plastic cap at its other end, flushes out the air in the line, spilling a few drops of the solution onto the bed. She then replaces the plastic cap onto the end of the tubing. She next ties a tourniquet around Ángela's arm and tightens it. While rubbing alcohol on the increasingly distended veins on top of Ángela's hand, the nurse selects a vein for the IV needle and proceeds to insert it. Ángela's arm flinches a bit. The nurse grabs it and warns her, "Now, don't you move or I won't be able to get it in."

I can see blood flow backwards into the plastic tubing attached to the cannula. The nurse says, "See, that didn't hurt so much." She attaches the male part of the IV tubing to the female adapter on the plastic tube of the IV catheter and with clear plastic tape finally secures the needle onto Ángela's hand and the tubing onto her forearm.

Noticing that everything is ready, I solemnly decree, "Let the evil spirits be driven out and banished forevermore. Let the hex be nullified for now and eternity."

Understanding me, the nurse turns the blue plastic ball of the clamp of the regulator that controls the flow rate of fluid going into the IV until a steady stream of saline solution pours down into the collecting drip chamber. I mandate, "Now flush out those demons and hand me their poison."

The nurse plays along, gives 20 mgs of Lasix IV, and tosses the Pyridium over to me." Once I have the pills, I eye Ángela and implore her to take one. "I want you to swallow this uncrossing and cleansing medication. It won't hurt you, but it will dispatch all that is devilish."

In my hand I have a round maroon 200 mg Pyridium tablet, which, after I open its blister pack, she takes into her hand that does not have the IV in it. I carefully monitor her to verify that she does indeed swallow the pill after she puts it in her mouth. "Good girl. Presently, without delay, the medicine will slay all of the fiends that have invaded your body. Once they are no more, you will expel them out. Your urine will turn red, but don't panic, that will be the sign of their having been obliterated and cast out."

409

Outwardly she is calm and accepting of everything we are doing, although without speaking. Her eyes remain closed the entire time. I cannot tell if this is part of the curse or she is still too scared to talk or observe what is happening to her. Silently, the five of us are keeping vigil over her. Suddenly, Ángela begins to shake as if she is having a seizure and starts to smack her lips. Just as abruptly, she sits bolt upright in the bed with her eyes wide open and screams with the remnant of an accent that is half Cuban and half New Orleans Yat dialect, "Help me up to the bathroom. I've got to pee something awful!"

Denise puts her menorah on the bedside table. With the nurse grasping under her arms and Denise helping her stand straight up and not fall, Ángela makes her way to the toilet. Shortly, I hear Ángela say, "Thank God! They're gone!"

Chapter 32

When they arrive back at the bed, Ángela's persona is completely different. Sitting against the bed's headboard, she is smiling and very talkative. Based upon what little I know about her, I do not expect her to be articulate, but she is. Plainly, despite having been raised in isolation, both she and Denise had been well tutored by the government. Fingering the other Pyridium pill, I say to myself, *I guess I won't need this.* I ask her, "Why do you want to see the Tiffany vase?"

"The vase you bought at the auction is the copy made in Cuba. The vase you got from the museum in Havana is the original made by Tiffany. It belongs to me. I inherited it from my father."

I am at a loss for words. I know she is wrong. "No, you got it backwards. The vase I have now is the fake. It doesn't have the enameler's mark on it."

She is courteous but firm. "No, you are the one who is mistaken. None of the Columbian Exposition enameled vases had an enameler's mark on them originally."

"But the one at the Metropolitan . . ."

"So, you've seen the bottom of the Magnolia Vase at the Met. Beautiful isn't it and such a great work by Tiffany." She smiles curtly. "It's also a fake."

"But its provenance is impeccable. The woman who donated it bought it for the Met from Tiffany, himself, a few years after the exposition."

"That's all true. Nevertheless, almost from the beginning Castro has been selling fake Tiffany, Gallé, whatever as the real deal to make money or use in lieu of cash. A supporter of his worked in the Met's conservation department in the early Sixties. One day, when that vase was taken off display to be polished, he swapped it with the one made in Cuba by the Havana museum director's silversmith father. He showed the enameler's mark several years later in the early Seventies to a new curator and to a new conservator, who each had just arrived at the decorative arts department. He took advantage of a rare opportunity when a large number of retirees left the museum over a short period of time. On that day the myth of the mark was born."

I can believe that; however, it does not answer one question. "Why did you have the fake vase to begin with?"

"Castro's deal with my father was complicated. In exchange for assassinating Kennedy before Kennedy got him, Fidel promised my father the Wild-Rose Vase. However, both of them had a problem with the execution of the transaction. If my father was caught with the vase then it could be used as evidence of Castro's ordering the hit. Something neither of them wanted to happen since it would provoke a war with the U.S. You see, after the Cuban Missile Crisis Castro no longer sincerely felt he could count on Khrushchev to back him up with nuclear weapons."

Finally, I get it. "The replica was sent as some sort of a marker!"

"But not just any IOU. Very carefully detailed in my father's prayer book were various intentional inconspicuous differences that only the silversmith in Havana knew about and no one else would notice unless they were held side by side with the prayer book as a guide. Those variances would serve as the proof, if necessary, that the vase was a fake and hardly something a slayer would have received for payment."

"Within the Cuban community in Miami there seems to be an urban legend about your vase. How did that come about?"

Ángela winces. "Unlike what happened at the Met, the switch in Havana did not go completely unnoticed. To make the stunt work, Castro felt he had to have the reproduction temporarily exhibited at the museum in Havana in place of the original."

"Why did he think he needed to do that? The original wasn't going anywhere."

"He became very paranoid that after the assassination, someone would be able to link him with it. He didn't know when my father might want the real one. Therefore, he did the exchange ahead of time to see what the reaction would be in Havana."

"Market research?"

"You could say that. As I said, it didn't go over well. Everyone in Cuba who knew silver at that time silently felt that the true Tiffany vase had been sent out of the country when, all the while, it was sitting in Castro's safe in his Havana residence. He returned the original back ten months before Kennedy's assassination. That really confused everyone. Whenever my father or his heirs needed the money, Castro promised to exchange the original for the reproduction, which he has just done."

All of a sudden, the significance of the prayer book is strikingly evident to me. "Without that book, I can't prove that the vase Leonard gave me is right and the one I bought at John's isn't right and therefore not of any value beyond the silver used to make it."

"Not you, not anyone!"

This brings up a very pertinent question in my mind. "Why did any of this have to happen at that auction?"

She stares at me as if I am an imbecile. "With the way things still are between Cuba and the U.S. diplomatically, how else do you think we could arrange the transfer? I can't leave the U.S. safely, and the government won't let Castro's agents come to visit me here even if it could be done safely. And the vase is not exactly something you would FedEx. Above and beyond that, doing it in private would not allow me to eventually sell it since the question of provenance would always overhang such a sale."

"So a public auction overcame all of the obstacles you all envisioned."

"All of them except for you. You got in the way! No one figured that you had the wherewithal to outbid us. The Cuban dealers had been monitoring your recent top bids. Your wallet appeared to be thin to them since you seemed to become short of cash fairly early in the auctions they attended. As an extra measure in the previous auction, they had forced you to bid way too much for the lots you won. Who would've thought you still had the reserves to outbid them at the next auction?"

Jim Cook's sudden disappearance comes roaring to my mind, as does what happened to that Cajun dealer. "You all didn't kill Jim Cook, did yah?"

She laughs for the first time. "Of course, not! We knew that he, unlike you, had more than enough cash to outbid us. We just had him detained in a friendly sort of way. He's having a VIP, all expenses paid vacation at Fidel's suite at the Paradisus Rio de Oro Resort & Spa in Holguin, Cuba. It's the best!"

"How much of a pain in the ass was I?"

"A major one. You see, the New York dealers were to bid among themselves to establish a preset auction price for the vase that I could subsequently use as a minimum appraised value when I wanted to sell it. After all, they and their cartel are the ones who usually determine the retail market price for Tiffany. But with last minute bids at the auction, the Cuban dealers were supposed to ultimately buy the vase and the rifle you bought and return them to Cuba. Castro's man in Toronto was to come back to the auction house with the real vase demanding his money back, claiming quite rightly that John had sold his agents, the Cuban dealers, a counterfeit one at the auction."

"And you were going to arrange that, how?"

"We had set up the FBI to leak a story to the New York Times immediately after the auction to verify just that conclusively. What's more, the Cuban dealers started a rumor questioning its authenticity two weeks before then in order to scare away other bidders, like you. In

Miami it really reawakened all of the decades old suspicions about the vase in Havana."

I think to myself *it didn't do so poorly at the DEA in Washington, either.* "And you would without a doubt gracefully return your proceeds from the sale of the fake vase and take possession of the real vase."

"Absolutely, unfortunately for John, he would be forced to reluctantly return his commission and the buyer's premium. If it had come off as planned, I would have the original vase and the Cuban dealers would have been reimbursed by the Toronto agent, all without it costing anyone a penny."

"Except for John."

"Yes, except for John."

While I can understand their using the auction house for the hoax, one thing she mentioned still makes no sense to me. "Why would those dealers want that $2 rifle?"

"Their Latin tempers got the better of them when you outbid them. They stormed out of the auction house. They left the weapon my father used to assassinate Kennedy to be won by you unchallenged."

I think I had heard her right but do not believe her. "Can you prove that?"

"I can if I had my father's prayer book."

"Do you have any idea why someone killed the Cajun dealer for it?"

Unexpectedly, Ángela becomes angry and raises her voice. "Of course, Fidel was an honorable man when it came to his loyal followers. Raúl, on the other hand, has found it expedient to take advantage of many who had helped his brother out in the early days of the Revolution. He has done this to solidify the new reforms and image he wants to create for Cuba."

"I gather my having the evidence that Fidel ordered the assassination of JFK does not fit in Raúl's plan."

"No question about it. He wants the world to forget all about it. Without the book my vase is worth a fraction of its true value, Denise's papers aren't worth $3,000,000, and your rifle is just another Italian World War II weapon. More important to Raul, Cuba is off the hook for the assassination of one of America's most popular and glamorous presidents."

"Why his change of heart?"

"Not wanting to offend Fidel, Raúl allowed Fidel's original contract with my father to be initially executed. Now that you screwed that up, Raúl has found it necessary to do a double-cross behind Fidel's back before the promise can be completely fulfilled. By winning the vase, you have created the possibility of its secret being divulged without the benefit of Denise's father's papers tempering it."

I am flabbergasted by her accusation. "How did I do that?"

"Since you own the vase, how were we to get it back? That vase and Denise's papers have to be sold together for the truth to come out. Fidel was furious at his

417

dealers for not getting the vase at the auction, and they knew it without his having to say it. I can attest that they were afraid for their lives when you outbid them! He wants public vindication for what he had done before he dies, and you are standing in his way. Don't underestimate him. Fidel is used to getting his way!"

"Is that where the $2,600,000 came from?"

She nods. "Precisely, he made you an offer you couldn't refuse. On top of that, he gave you the money needed to buy Denise's father's papers. Once he found out about Leonard's involvement in your bid, he felt comfortable that he could trust you to do the right thing."

"May I safely presume that Raúl, on the other hand, wants both vases back in Cuba under his lock and key, as well as your father's prayer book?"

She nods again. "He knows that without them Denise's father's papers will only make for interesting reading."

Are the Castro brothers at war with each other? I ask, "So, Raúl is secretly thwarting his brother's attempt at exoneration for Kennedy's assassination?"

"Not exactly, he's trying to prevent it from being the justification for an American invasion of Cuba."

"Why then does Raúl want you dead?"

For Ángela this should be obvious to me and is patently irritated at my having to ask her that. "Look, if they are successful in eliminating me, no one else in the U.S. will be able to read my father's prayer book. As I

418

said, without that book the hidden meaning in those records will remain indecipherable to any one in the U.S. Plus, that vase and rifle will not be enough to overturn the lies and deceptions that the government is about to put out in 2017."

"So, they will be just some more merely interesting conspiracy junk from the Sixties corroborating nothing?"

"Worse, without that book there won't be any directions to unearth the truth about the assassination."

I accept that but remain puzzled by one thing. "You still haven't explained why they killed that Cajun for having the prayer book!"

She raises herself up from the bed. "That dealer wasn't bumped off because he had my father's prayer book. He was ritually executed because he didn't! If he had had the book, they would have taken it and that would have been the end of the story. They would have let him live to tell me that they had it. Because he didn't have it, I became their target!"

Recalling how determined he had been to find someone who could read it, I interrupt her. "I gather without you the prayer book is mute in the U. S., regardless of where it is or who has it."

"Have no doubts about it, Raúl's people are afraid that with the vase's resurfacing they don't have the time to find the book on their own. Removing me ends their need for any further searching. The way they murdered that dealer from New Orleans was a voodoo message intended to tell me that I'm next if I keep hunting for it! They graphically telegraphed to me that the manner of his death will be mine, if I already have the book or get it."

Leonard interjects, "In that case, we'll need to act quickly."

"The sooner the better. Cubans in New Orleans, myself included, take the root most seriously. I recognized the Marie Laveau death gris-gris bag over his heart in the photos of him. It was placed there after he was dead and was meant for me. They aren't likely to fail on their next try!"

Chapter 33

Denise, who had been remarkably silent throughout the unhexing, interrupts Ángela. "My father may have an answer to our problem."

Ángela, however, remains profoundly distraught, especially about the prospect of another voodoo death root jinx, and does not welcome Denise's proposition, which she feels is naïve. "He's dead! How's he going to help? Since I put that vase up for auction, Raúl thinks I must have my father's prayer book or am about to get it and am ready to reveal its truths."

Years of indoctrination from her father have so hardened Denise that she remains unwavering about his having even foreseen this threat. "There's a sealed envelope that he entrusted to me with the instruction to give it only to whoever pays for his documents. He told me that it would lead to the truth, whatever that meant."

Silently reminiscing about the conversations he had had with her father, Leonard too remembers him saying something similar about them. "Denise, your father always said that his documents were only the foundation for the truth. I never could figure out what he felt was still missing."

Past experience tells me I have heard enough. All of my instincts are compelling me to believe that her father had not relied on Ángela's being part of the deal. Men of stature and men, who have held positions of power, do not do that. He had gone to far too much trouble to correct what he had to have felt was a grievous injustice and to prove his legitimate position in history to let someone else interfere. He made the ultimate gamble that in the end all of his documentation would lead to his being declared a patriot.

Amid all of this suspense and friction, I am able to slip out of the bedroom without being missed, go to the limo, in which the geese fortunately had by now lost interest, and bring back the suitcase. As I hand it over to Denise, I explain, "It's time to call your father's bet. Here's the $2,000,000, give me that envelope. I want to see if he was bluffing!"

My directness stuns Denise who had expected me to have a sudden change of heart after hearing what Ángela had just said. "Thank you. But are you positive you want to do this? I certainly can understand your wanting to back out of this deal and hope you realize that I can't promise you that what's in the envelope will make you any money."

Ángela is equally surprised by my quick action that she is confident is ill-advised. She points at me while reiterating Denise's concern. "I too hope you know what you are doing." Next, she gestures fervidly towards the kitchen. "That's a lot of money for a bunch of old government documents that are worthless if we can't find the prayer book."

Strangely, I smile. I have never before felt so self-assured. With everything I have learned from my past risky deals telling me that I am right, I state my case, "If that rifle I paid $2 for is the weapon your father used to assassinate JFK, it will be worth a lot more money than that. The man who sat across the desk from Castro and convinced him that it was time to fold, swallow his Latin pride, and face the humiliation from his being snubbed during the resolution of the Cuban Missile Crisis was too good a poker player for me to bet against him. I think it's worth $2,000,000 to see what ace he had up his sleeve. And almost assuredly, so does Fidel, who is seeking absolution based upon what is in those papers and that prayer book."

Impressed with my gambling analogy, Leonard in his own fashion congratulates me. "So, you really do understand what he did back then."

"Yes, and hopefully he didn't take all of his secrets with him to his grave."

Finally reassured that I want to do this, Denise has one last concern. "I don't have it here." However, suddenly, even before I have a chance to reply, she explains, "The envelope is in a safe in the bunker. It will only take me a few minutes to get it." She then leaves.

Once more Leonard pulls that stained envelope from his inner coat pocket. He shuffles through the several index cards before offering me one. "Denise's father entrusted me with these cards. He intended for them to be his ultimate defense against the rewriting of history he knew would be forthcoming. They are his collection of the definitive quotes regarding Cuba from the kingpins of the Sixties. Read this. He told me that it's Castro's only direct public admission of ordering Ángela's father to do the hit." After I initially glance at the card, I spot the White House return address on the yellowing envelope that Leonard is currently holding in full view.

Coming back to the card, I silently read its two

sentences, typed in bold letters for emphasis and enclosed in quotation marks, **"United States leaders should think that if they are aiding terrorist plans to eliminate Cuban leaders, they themselves will not be safe. Let Kennedy and his brother Robert take care of themselves since they can be victims of an attempt which will cause their death."** Once I am finished and as I hand it back to him, I ask, "When did Castro say that?"

He knows these cards well and answers without hesitation or tentativeness. "September 7, 1963 at the Brazilian embassy in Havana, just ten weeks before he blew away Kennedy. He told that to Associated Press reporter Daniel Harker in a three-hour supposedly impromptu and extemporaneous interview. It was not just a bit of friendly advice he was trying to give JFK through that reporter; it was a well thought-out, non-coded message that was an integral part of his good cop/bad cop plan to end the Kennedys' obsession with killing him. This had been brought to a head after the U.S. had sponsored another lethal air attack on Cuban soil at Santa Clara the previous day. To boot, Castro's spies had just informed him about Cubela's meeting that very day in a safe house in Sao Paulo, Brazil with the CIA to discuss rubbing him out. He chose to speak to Harker because he had recently been transferred from Colombia and had covered the guerrilla war there. In the sentence just before that one, in words no one could misinterpret, he had threatened, 'We are prepared to fight them and answer in kind.' He publicly repeated his transparent warning to the Kennedys when one month later on October 7th he declared, "They are our enemies, and we know how to be their enemies."

This is a pretty bleak picture of Castro, one which

sounds like something from the Cuban Missile Crisis days or what the anti-Castro Cubans would make up. "Was Castro unwilling to negotiate a truce with the Kennedys?"

"No, Ernie, just the opposite, at the same time he was being the bad cop promising to fight to the death, he was trying to jump-start détente discussions with the U.S. They were languishing despite his initiating them in January 1963 through the lawyer who had been hand selected by the Kennedys to seek the return of the Bay of Pigs prisoners. Two months later in March, he attempted a resolution to their differences in earnest with a letter to U. N. Secretary General U Thant. In April he granted a filmed interview with Lisa Howard, an ABC reporter, and in private conveyed to her his interest in improving affairs of state with the U.S. The CIA deputy directory, Richard Helms, even sent a memo to JFK outlining the thrust of her discussions with Castro after he had debriefed her." Leonard fishes out another index card from the envelope and reads from it. "'Lisa Howard definitely wants to impress the U.S. Government with two facts: Castro is ready to discuss rapprochement and she herself is ready to discuss it with him if asked to do so by the U.S. Government.'

"Then, with the help of Denise's father, over the course of the next three months, Castro arranged meetings between the CIA and European businessmen upon their return to their homelands after visiting Cuba. Those businessmen communicated on more than six occasions his interest in reconciliation with the U.S. He was still sincerely playing his good cop role when he found out that the CIA and the Pentagon had just hatched their most adventuresome plot since the Bay of Pigs, which, if carried out, had a very good chance of assassinating him and installing a new government friendly to the U.S."

Shaking my head, I have to laugh at the black comedy that Leonard is describing. "I guess that must have really pissed him off!"

"You could say that. On November 2, 1963, Ángela's father and another Cuban were scheduled to get Kennedy on his visit to the Army-Air Force football game in Chicago. But the trip was canceled after the Secret Service warned the White House of an imminent threat. That was a gross understatement of the facts since they thought they had uncovered two separate plots. One week before November 22, 1963, Castro had thirteen 'Cuban CIA spies' executed, sending a fairly overt message to Washington that he no longer believed the U.S. was sincere in seeking a peaceful resolution to their differences. As well, there was the November 18th mess in Tampa and Miami, which I seriously doubt you've ever heard of."

The best and the brightest were in the inner sanctum of the White House back then. They could not have been clueless about what was happening. "You mean to tell me that with all that Kennedy didn't see that things were getting out of hand?"

"Getting out of hand; that's putting it mildly. Death threats were rampant in both Tampa and Miami. Kennedy was scheduled to visit Miami on November 18, 1963. A typewritten post card, dated and postmarked Miami Beach, Florida, November 16, 1963, addressed to the Chief of Police, Miami, Florida, was received by that department and subsequently surrendered to the Intelligence Unit of the Metropolitan Police Department for investigation." He puts back into the envelope the index card he was still holding and hands me another. "What's on this card is what was typed on the post card."

In silence I read: "The Cuban Commandoes have the BOMBS ready for killing JFK and Mayor KING HIGH either at the AIRPORT or at the Convention Hall. A Catholic PADRE is going to give instructions at the Cuban Womens Broadcast at 8:45 tonight by "RELOJ RADIO" and then all are invited to dance at Bayfront Park Auditorium and take along a BOTTLE of wine, Wiskey, ETC., to decide who will throw the bombs. At King High because he did sign the Ord. About taxi drivers being only American Citizens and sending refugees away, ETC. Mary."

Once finished, I hand it back to him and say, "The Secret Service must have been very busy in Miami."

"Worse, they had déjà vu about what had happened thirty years before to FDR when he was down there. And it wasn't just from Miami that the threats were coming to them. Earlier that day JFK was to arrive in Tampa where Chief of Police J. P. Mullins and the Secret Service since October had been following at least one of three suspects, who purportedly had threatened JFK's life. One of them was arrested and kept in jail under heavy bond for five days or more. The other two were believed to have moved on to Dallas."

"So, what did Kennedy do to try to defuse the situation?"

He reaches again into the envelope that he has yet to return to his coat pocket and after exchanging index cards brings out one more. Expressionless, he replies,

427

"Castro was not swayed by JFK's coded attempt at signaling his interest in settlement given that night in Miami during a speech to the Inter-American Press Association. By the way, things in Miami were too hot for the Secret Service, so JFK arrived at the Americana Hotel via helicopter. He did not ride in a motorcade in Miami like he had in Tampa. To that Miami group he said," Leonard now reads from that card, "'Cuba had become a weapon in an effort dictated by external powers to subvert the other American republics. This and this alone divides us. As long as this is true, nothing is possible. Without it, everything is possible.'"

Knowing what happened next, I utter what is now unambiguous, "So Castro didn't believe Kennedy and proceeded with his bad cop scenario!"

While Leonard stows the index cards into the envelope and deposits it back into his coat pocket, he nods his head. "Speaking of November 22, that was truly a day of infamy in U.S./Cuban relations. On that very day, the CIA in Paris was arming Cubela to kill Castro and overthrow his regime. JFK, while still skeptical about the sincerity of Cuba's desire for reaching an accord, had Jean Daniel, editor of the left-of-center weekly newsmagazine *France Observateur,* interview Castro in Havana in order to assess his true interest in the normalization of relations. In Washington, at the behest of Robert Kennedy, the CIA was holding a top-level meeting with members of the nucleus of an impending Cuban coup, possibly to be carried out as early as nine days later. Castro was undertaking his final solution to the Kennedys in Dallas. Incredibly, he had the head of one of his counter-intelligence units fly into Dallas that morning and leave that evening so that he could have his own observer to the events that were to unfold there. If it

428

weren't true, you would have thought it had come straight out of the movie *The Godfather.* As they say, fact is sometimes stranger than fiction."

For Leonard, who normally keeps everything close to his vest, this is more than he ever will discuss about anything or any subject. He is so unreservedly passionate about what happened half a century ago that I become a bit unnerved. Does he protest too much? Could even he have been taken in? I press him further to find out all that he knows before Denise returns and the deal is consummated. "So, you are certain that it was Castro who had JFK assassinated. This couldn't be some grand con by the CIA, FBI, and/or even Hoover and his good friend and former neighbor, LBJ, to hide their involvement?"

I do not have to wait. He repeatedly points his finger straight at me and even raises his voice, another thing he rarely does. "No qualms about it. In 1968, an agent of the CIA who had been its section chief in Mexico City during the time of the assassination told an LBJ confidant that Castro had sent that man, I just mentioned, to Dallas to be his observer. Forty-two years later, that very man, who was then head of Castro's personal security detail, refused to confirm or deny whether Oswald had shot Kennedy. The most 'Castro's man in Dallas' is quoted as saying directly about Oswald is, 'One day we will know whether or not the Americans really did land on the moon and if Oswald shot Kennedy or not.'

"It was Denise's father's undoing. He knew Castro well. He heeded Castro's warning from the week before the September 12, 1963 meeting of the Cuban Coordinating Committee in the Department of State. There he tried to stress upon those in attendance the folly of their actions. His very words are even quoted in the minutes of that meeting, 'There is a strong likelihood that Castro will retaliate in some way against the rash of covert activity in Cuba.' Despite everyone there agreeing with him, Cuban exile attacks continued. First, they blew up a sawmill on September 30. Next, they struck two oil-storage tanks along with two patrol boats on October 22. Once Denise's father let it be realized that he held such strong feelings against what was happening, Bobby Kennedy never again completely trusted him. Therefore, he kept her father out of the loop when on October 4th the Joint Chiefs released their next version of OPLAN 380-63. Then just three days later, Castro declared that he knew how to be the Kennedys' enemy,"

Not recalling seeing anything about OPLAN 380-63 on the list provided to me by Denise, I do not know about what he is talking. "And that was?"

He pounds the bed table with his right hand. With his voice rising to a crescendo, he shouts, "Something those idiots who called themselves the Joint Chiefs of Staff drew up. Getting Castro had become the top priority within Camelot. It called for our sending in Cuban exiles in January 1964 to infiltrate Cuba. Seven months later on July 15, we would place US conventional forces in there. Then on August 3, a D Day style air strike was to start. If Castro had still not been 'removed' by October 1, a full-scale invasion was planned. What were they thinking? Did they think Khrushchev would sit idly by and allow the U.S. to renege on its recent public agreement never to invade Cuba. Did they want World War III? Didn't they suppose that Fidel would find out and be furious? Those Cuban exiles in Miami were telling anyone who would listen that an attack was imminent. Some were even giving out the first of December as the day. After his brother's assassination, Bobby Kennedy was so furious that Castro had won and that he had failed to consummate his promise to his brother of having a friendly regime in Havana before the November election that he called for someone else to fall on his sword. That someone was Denise's father.

"Yes, Castro had JFK killed. The only question is how he did it. I just told you Daniel was interviewing him when word got to him that JFK had been shot. After feigning shock and surprise, Castro is quoted by Daniel as saying, 'This is an end to your mission of peace. Everything is changed.' and then asking, 'What authority does Johnson exercise over the CIA?' Strange question for a supposedly dismayed, innocent man to be posing at that time. Makes you wonder if he knew that LBJ did not share the same fixation as did the Kennedys about making him disappear or as LBJ later put it, 'Operating a damned Murder, Inc, in the Caribbean.'"

One thing remains vague. I wonder to myself, why would someone, whom no one outside of the inner circle of the administration knew, be the scapegoat? "Leonard, what exactly did Denise's father do and why would Robert Kennedy distrust him if he was working in the White House?"

Leonard's face is flushed, as he becomes even more impassioned, if that were possible. "Not everyone in the Kennedy Administration was as focused on Cuba as Bobby. I think he took their defeat at the Bay of Pigs personally. Dean Rusk, for one, was more concerned about Berlin. He felt that all the attention towards Castro could backfire by complicating our Cold War struggle with Khrushchev. Our actions in Cuba might compel him to be tougher in Berlin, which would force us to commit more troops to Europe. McGeorge Bundy, on the other hand, wanted an all-or-nothing approach. He advocated either an invasion with overwhelming force and victory or rapprochement with the goal of normalization of our relations by 'enticing Castro to our side.' Denise's father was the invisible, non-policy making man at the White House, who had to mediate the opposing policies and, even more importantly, egos. As Bundy said later, 'We didn't have a department of peaceful tricks.' He could have gone on to say but we had Denise's father who kept a lid on explosive situations."

So far, I couldn't see what her father had done that had been very helpful. He may have cooled off Castro during the Cuban Missile Crisis, but that had patently not been long lasting. "Did her father have any successes?"

"It was no accident that Lisa Howard nabbed all of those high profile interviews that led to her interviewing Castro. When it became evident that both JFK and Fidel were exploring a way out of a collision course, he made it possible for the right people to become available to talk to both sides and pass on what one side wanted the other side to hear. During the Cuban Missile Crisis, he had Anatoly Dobrynin personally convey and Edward Murrow broadcast over the Voice of America what Kennedy wanted Khrushchev to know. Meanwhile he was stuck in Havana calming down Castro, who felt he was being ignored and betrayed by being excluded from the talks between the U.S. and the Soviet Union. Castro was particularly miffed that Guantanamo Bay was not even discussed and in the end remained in the hands of the U.S. This may well have led to Castro, on his own, feeling out our interest in stabilizing matters between us a few months later while discussing the release of the Bay of Pigs prisoners, another thing her father helped arrange."

He had yet to explain Robert Kennedy's beef with Denise's father but another issue became evident to me. "Why was Castro so friendly with him, after all he was one of Kennedy's men?"

My question seems to relax him somewhat and even brings on a smile. "Castro comes from a wealthy family and is a lawyer by training. He is no fool and comprehends the importance of back-channel negotiations and understands that frequently there is a need for a go-between, such as Lisa Howard. Denise's father was one of Fidel's classmates at the University of Havana. Although they strongly differed on Cuban politics, they remained strong personal friends. Throughout his life, Fidel would call upon Denise's father to help him out of tight spots."

Adolpho remembers one incident that unquestionably would qualify as a tight spot. "Like when Castro was released from prison in 1955 after being imprisoned there since the failed 1953 coup attempt?"

Leonard's grin broadens, and he nods to Adolpho. "Precisely. Who do you think saved him and Raúl from being summarily executed when they were captured after their disastrous attack on the Moncada Barracks? Two years later Denise's father as well successfully pleaded for the general amnesty from Batista. Ironically, both of those triumphs may not have been as difficult to obtain, as they would appear to have been. Despite being a bitter political enemy, Batista had a personal relationship with Fidel and had actually given a $1000 wedding present to Fidel upon his first marriage."

There is no need for him to say it. I can see what happened. "Robert Kennedy must have grasped all of that and afterwards never trusted him to be enough of a true believer to have Castro actually be eliminated."

Suddenly, he throws up his arms in anger. "Worse! He accused Denise's father of somehow discovering the details of the OPLAN 380-63 plan and passing them on to Havana causing Castro to order the hit on his brother. It got really nasty in Washington the months following the assassination. Kennedy's people felt that they should still be in power and tried to undermine LBJ in anyway they could. Robert and the CIA, possibly on its own, were successful in blocking access to the tape recordings and documents that would explain what had led up to the assassination and started plausible rumors to divert attention away from their own covert anti-Castro activities. Indeed, they were so successful that in 1975, at the Church committee, there were sworn statements by all the surviving major members of the Kennedy administration against the veracity of Drew Pearson's and Jack Anderson's 1967 report of the Kennedy administration ordering an attempt on Castro's life by the CIA. Things just degenerated to such frenzy that the CIA, the FBI, and even the Secret Service, Israel, and LBJ were accused of being complaisant with or cooperating in some sort of conspiracy in the plethora of canards being passed around."

I ask, "How do you feel so secure Robert Kennedy was embroiled in all of that?"

"Because why else did he refuse to call for reopening the Warren Commission or having another definitive investigation into his brother's assassination? He could have put an end to all of the scuttlebutt that was so prevalent at that time on the Washington grapevine. But he didn't. Why? Because he knew the truth would have also detonated that political H-bomb Pearson and Anderson claimed LBJ was sitting on. Instead, RFK sought public revenge only on the Mafia leadership. They may indeed have had a role since some of the same Mob figures, who the CIA recruited to whack Fidel, were also fingered in the JFK assassination plot. And you know Bobby would have gone after LBJ with a vengeance if he had been implicated in any way.

"As for others who have been rumored to be collaborators, Bobby would have done the same thing to any guilty members of the Council on Foreign Relations or the mysterious 'Power Control Group,' which supposedly included J. Edgar Hoover. The believers of Hoover's involvement neglect to mention that he was on a first-name basis with Joseph Kennedy. If truth be told, they were so tight that the elder Kennedy urged Hoover to run for President on either party's ticket in the 1956 election and promised to give him his biggest campaign contribution and work tirelessly for his election.

"Immediately after the assassination, the Kennedys were so popular that they became the closest thing America has had to royalty. Any one, who threatened them or harmed any of them, particularly the children, once ferreted out, would probably have been tried and executed on the spot, like in the old Wild West."

I make an off-the-cuff remark. "Like what happened to Oswald in Texas?"

He then laughs. "I hadn't thought about it like that, but you're right. I never have figured out how Sirhan Sirhan has survived as long as he has. Getting back to the

435

matter at hand, there is no valid explanation for Bobby's silence on this issue unless he already knew who it was and there was no way he could go after him."

"You mean Castro."

"Absolutely, immediately after his brother's murder only Castro or Khrushchev would have been untouchable as far as he was concerned and then only because of the threat or more likely the real possibility of a nuclear war."

Chapter 34

Having gone back to lying in the bed while listening intently to Leonard's rendition of the events leading up to her father killing JFK, Ángela now sits up to correct him. "My father could not have pulled it off alone. He devised a brilliant scheme where the very people who had most adamantly tried to get Castro ended up helping him get Kennedy, all the while thinking they were going after Fidel."

Leonard's jaw drops. This is conspicuously the first time he has heard of this twist to the conspiracy theories. He thinks about what she has just said before asking, "How could he have done that? Only an insane zealot would kill the President of the United States in order to kill Castro."

She nods. "And there were plenty who were just that. In order to find them, my father networked with the anti-Castro forces in Miami. He used false documents and photos to establish that he had worked in Cuba with Huber Matos, who as you know had been a major ally of Fidel's in the Revolution. Like Cubela, afterwards he turned to denouncing the communist direction, which Raúl and Che were pushing Fidel towards."

He adds, "Matos was so effective that he spent his full twenty year sentence for 'treason and sedition' in one of Castro's maximum-security prisons on an island south of Havana."

"That's right. That's why my father used his name. He found that contrived relationship to be very useful to hook up with another disgruntled former ally of Fidel's, who he found to be quite rational and well connected in Miami. Matos was in no position to deny my father's claims if anyone in Miami had tried to contact him. From that link my father gained entry into the anti-Castro community of Miami where he rounded up the genuinely crazed exiles."

"I take it that whatever he needed to complete his mission that he found difficult to obtain those fanatics arranged for him to get from the Mafiosos who were in cahoots with the CIA in their assassination plots against Castro."

"No doubt about it. Some times he even had to restrain himself to temper their enthusiasm."

Leonard just shakes his head since he is still dubious. "What kind of a mission did they think he was on?"

"Kennedy was losing face fast among those who had been involved in the Bay of Pigs. All of that rapprochement talk in the beginning of 1963 had them worried that Fidel would be successful in normalizing relations before OPLAN 380-63 could be implemented. You see, OPLAN 380-63 had one flaw in their eyes: it needed an excuse to be activated."

He points to her. "Yeah, I can see how JFK's initial change in attitude after the removal of the Russian missiles at the end of the Cuban Missile Crisis caused them consternation. He suddenly was opposed to an overt war against Cuba. However, he softened his position after Castro vetoed UN on-site-inspection of their withdrawal."

"That was the opening anti-Castro forces were hoping for, and, boy, did my father exploit it. In earnest they sought something to swing the President and the public to favor invasion of Cuba. My father planted the seed into their discussions that the assassination of a major American political figure, say the U.S. President, would without a doubt so sway public opinion for immediate retaliation that Johnson could not oppose openly and militarily eliminating Fidel."

"Sounds like a twist off of the Northwoods operation, which was as insane as this."

"And those fanatics went bonkers over my father's idea: another Pearl Harbor, Remember the Maine."

This is beginning to sound like our country had been taken over by lunatics. What are they talking about? I ask, "The Northwoods operation?"

A pained expression overtakes Leonard. "If you want to learn about some of the crazy plots Denise's father was up against, the Northwoods operation of the spring of 1962, well before the Cuban Missile Crisis, will teach you. The Joint Chiefs of Staff actually proposed to JFK that he approve a series of provocative actions to justify an invasion of Cuba. Among the more ludicrous schemes were: a terror campaign within the US including sinking a boatload of Cubans en route to Florida, conducting attempts on the lives of Cuban refugees in the U.S. that would inflict actual wounds in acts intended to make headlines across the country, exploding plastic bombs in designated strategic sites, hijacking civilian air and surface crafts, and simulating a Cuban aircraft shooting down a chartered civilian airliner carrying college students. All of these operations were to be blamed on Castro, which as I mentioned would cause a ground swell of public support for an invasion of Cuba."

"Were there others?"

"Oh, yes, Ernie, some even more outrageous! In Operation Bingo they even planned to sink Naval ships while attacking Guantanamo Bay and attribute it to Castro. But the most bizarre 'dirty trick' to receive serious consideration by the Joint Chiefs of Staff of the United States was the appropriately named Operation Dirty Trick contained in Operation Mongoose. It proposed, should John Glenn's rocket explode on take off, to make up evidence that would be irrevocable proof that communists caused it to happen by having Cuba provide electronic interference during the launch. After nixing these plans, it didn't take Kennedy long to change Chairmanship of the Joint Chiefs of Staff. Frankly, the more realistic JFK became about dealing with Fidel, the more fanciful or desperate the others became in their plots."

Ángela smiles. "As my father told me, the problem was not selling the concept, it was getting the opportunity to do it. The one instruction he was personally given by Fidel was not to leave any trace of a Havana connection to the assassination."

Leonard notes, "Robert Kennedy did not have any problem finding leads to people in the CIA, FBI, the Mafia, or Secret Service."

"By design. You see, my father left multiple unmistakable trails to each of them. The Mafia got involved not so much to get Castro and return to operating casinos in Cuba as to get rid of Robert

440

Kennedy. Once JFK was gone, they believed RFK would no longer be Attorney General since there was so much ill will between him and Johnson."

With everyone lining up to murder JFK, I have to ask, "What role did Oswald have?"

"It was mandatory that the hit had to be done from a long distance to allow my father a realistic exit strategy; and he needed a patsy, someone nuts enough to be a diversion and take the blame for him without knowing anything about him. At my father's urging, the Mafia convinced Oswald, while he was in New Orleans, that killing Kennedy was the only way of stopping the United States' interference in Castro's Cuban Revolution."

To me this was risky. "How did your father do that without violating Castro's primary directive?"

"He had the Mafia place a plant, CIA or Mob, my father never said which, in the Fair Play for Cuba Committee to persuade him to do it and then egg him on. That November 18th speech, which was supposed to have a veiled message offering an olive branch to Fidel, was presented to Oswald to be just the opposite. He was convinced that it was a signal to Cubans to rise up and overthrow Castro and then everything would be righted. That proved to be the kick in the pants that Oswald needed."

Overwhelmed by what I am hearing, I cannot believe that her father avoided being on the Secret Service's radar before November 22 and on the FBI's most wanted list after then. "He did all of this and got away with it?"

Pounding her fist on the bed, Ángela raises her voice answering me. "Now this is key, neither my father nor anyone else directly told Oswald to do it or even hinted that he do it. There was no traceable order or order giver. It was almost like they had brainwashed or hypnotized him into seeing how good it would be for Castro if Kennedy were eliminated without having to say do it. He really felt he had come up with the idea on his own. My father, on the other hand, left nothing to chance."

"Did he ever meet Oswald?"

"Never! Oswald was an enigma to my father when he was alive and throughout the rest of my father's life after Ruby shot him."

"Why did he feel that way?

"Oswald never made any sense. He was crazy at times. Would you have the Fair Play for Cuba office in New Orleans be right next to Guy Banister's office?"

"Who was he?"

Leonard answers, "A retired career FBI man. Big time anti-communist and anti-Castro Cuban supporter. Still buried in those unreleased documents is the truth, but there has always been a notion that he was in cahoots with the CIA. He and David Ferrie, another of the New Orleans anti-Castro players, were suspected by Jim Garrison to have put Oswald up to the assassination."

I have trouble believing her father would want such a flake on his side. "What did your father think about all of this? Wouldn't he have been concerned about

442

which side of the fence Oswald's loyalties lay?"

"No, and surprisingly he didn't care. He needed a patsy and if the Mafia vouched for Oswald, that was good enough for him. In point of fact, he once told me that Oswald's being so fucked-up made him the perfect patsy. No one would believe anything he said!"

"Could your father trust the Mafia?"

Ángela is put off by my question. "Absolutely! He had the Mafia arrange for some of their friends in the anti-Castro movement who had everything from vague to strong CIA connections to the Bay of Pigs to befriend Oswald. They too told Oswald how Kennedy's peace settlement talk was only a ploy to entice Castro away from the Soviet Union. The Mafia were as compulsive as my father was about leaving nothing to chance."

Leonard nods. "Despite their best efforts, it was difficult for them to tell exactly which side the Cuban expatriates were on. Even Cubela could have been a double agent."

She agrees. "By June of 1963 the boss in New Orleans had his misgivings about Oswald. One night while my father was still in his costume in full makeup from a booking and had just finished loading up his van to go home, he paid close attention to a black Cadillac limousine pull up to the curb ahead of him. An Italian hooligan in a dark suit got out of the car and signaled him to come over. He tensed up and started to finger the white gris-gris bag in his pocket until he recognized the ruffian as a frequent guest at the Mafia sponsored parties where he regularly performed. As my father told me the story, he asked, 'What's a rough 'em 'up like you doing slumming in this part of town?'

"The thug did not smile but rather pointed to inside the car before saying, 'Mr. M. has a business deal to discuss with you.'

"Believing full well that, voodoo or no voodoo, even Marie Laveau could not stop Mr. M. from having your body pulled out of Lake Pontchartrain in a couple of days if you pissed him off, he did not bother to pursue the issue any further. After hastily locking up his van, he just climbed into the limo. Mr. M. signaled for the driver to move on. For the first few minutes no one spoke. Each of them just gawked out of the window. Finally, seeing that protocol dictated that my father was expected to start the conversation, he faced Mr. M. and asked, 'What can I do for you that you've gone to all this trouble to find me?'

"Mr. M. rested my father's hands between his own and then went on to say, 'Something all of the gris-gris bags you've made for me over the years put together can't do. I need to insure that a particular man does this job a valued associate of mine had me offer him. He seems to be getting nervous about doing it despite me personally using my legendary and, I might add, well-proven persuasive skills on him. It's an important job that many in the family would be greatly displeased with me as their confidant if this man does not come through. The humiliation I would be exposed to would be insufferable. Because of the nature of the job, I have a problem. You see, I can't use all of my usual inducements to convince him to not let me down. I want you to use your considerable powers to make my anxiety disappear.' He then let go of my father's hands.

"My father understood him but could not figure

out how he was going to accomplish this. He plainly put it to him, 'Where will I meet this man?'

"Mr. M. paused to think this over. After mulling it over for a minute or so, he declared in an official tone of voice, 'No. It would be best if you didn't.'

"This complicated things for him. Mr. M.'s request wasn't what he had originally thought it was going to be, which was to act the part of a witch doctor to scare the hell out of this man so that he would do his assignment. Instead, he wanted my father to place a spell on him from a distance. My father played along and made his demand. 'Then I will need some certain items that belonged to him or came from his person.'

"Stooping down to pick up a hand towel that was on the car's floor and then passing it over to him, Mr. M. replied, 'Will these do?'

"My father opened up the towel on his lap. There were some military dog tags and a comb with hair on it. Upon reading Oswald, Lee on the dog tags, he became panicked. His plan all along was never to be linked in any way with the man. He had to think on his feet since Mr. M. did not know he had two separate secret personas and it was imperative that that situation be preserved. The only way he figured he could get out of this tight spot intact was to convince Mr. M. that he had come to the wrong man and that there was someone else far better to guarantee that he would have no more problems. You see, with men like Mr. M., you don't refuse to help them. Acting as humbly as he could, he answered back, 'To be perfectly honest with you, this requires powers far greater than mine. You need the best voodoo priest in Norleans to cast a spell over this Lee Oswald.'

445

"Where do I find him?' asked Mr. M., who from years of friendship sincerely felt my father's turning him down was both heartfelt and genuine.

"My father's response was deliberately slow in coming, for he didn't want to appear too eager to pass on helping out Mr. M., 'Go to Lugat's, I'm sure you know the place.'

"Mr. M. nodded out of familiarity with the place. His goombahs frequented it to collect the mounting gambling debts owed by Lugat, its owner, who eight years later ended up being fished face up out of Chaplain's Lake over in Natchitoches.

"Because my father wasn't aware how well-informed he was about the bar, he unnecessarily gave explicit instructions on what to do there. 'Ask Sam, the bartender who's always there, for Lugat. Tell him you need to meet Pappa S., a man who like you commands both trepidation and reverence in his community. Lugat will have no difficulty setting that up since Pappa S. uses his bar to hold court.'

"My father went on to further assure Mr. M. that if anyone could and should do it, it would be Pappa S. There was no skepticism in anyone's mind that the mob boss would persuade Pappa S. to cooperate. Scared the hell out of that poor black man being picked up at 9 PM the next day in front of Lugat's and riding around down Grand Street to Canal Street with Mr. M., who he felt for sure had never before had a black man in his limo who lived to tell about it. My father had made certain that everybody had left their fingerprints indirectly on Lee Harvey Oswald, everyone that is except him. Everyone was only somewhat guilty; therefore, no one was really guilty, except, of course, the patsy, Oswald. You see, so many people admitted later on that they were involved that no one from the government who was investigating the assassination believed any of them. Finding it to be too absurd, they created excuses to ignore the blatant huge web of involvement that my father had spun."

If he was going to all this trouble to do it in Dallas, how did he have time to plan an attempt in Chicago? I ask, "What about Chicago?"

Ángela swells with pride. "My father had a similar strategy in many cities. In Chicago there was a right-wing nutcase and Kennedy hater, who was planning on doing it anyway and who his connections there found to be a willing patsy. It was far easier and took less time for him to set up the Chicago hit than the Dallas one."

"You don't hear much about Chicago. How come?"

"Because both that lone wolf and my father's assistant got sloppy, Kennedy never came. The patsy was caught with a M1 carbine, a handgun, and 3000 rounds of ammunition the morning of the visit. My father was not much better in Chicago. He slipped up on that same day and left automatic rifles with telescopic sights and a map of the planned Kennedy route lying on the bed of his motel room. His Cuban intern made a real amateur's mistake by leaving the door unlatched to go for cigarettes. This allowed a maid to discover their weapons when she came to clean the room while my father was in the shower. She rushed to bring it to the motel manager's attention. Enough time lapsed before they returned to my father's room to allow him and his intern to slip out undetected. The Secret Service was in a panic. They thought they had uncovered two separate plots."

"It sounds like Chicago failed miserably."

"Yes, it did. But it proved the effectiveness of the patsy ploy, which he also had in place in Tampa, Miami, Houston, and Dallas. He was more circumspect from then on since his overarching problem became not letting the Secret Service find out in time to cancel the trip. 'Loose lips' were what botched the plans of the Tampa November 18th plot when someone snitched to the police days or even weeks before Kennedy's visit there. His Houston trip on November 21 had been targeted too but was spoiled by someone talking. On the next day Bush 41 reported to the FBI that he had overheard someone claiming that he would kill Kennedy if he could get close enough to him."

Did I hear her right? "You mean, he had five assassinations lined up?"

Seemingly indifferent to and unrepentant for what her father had done, Ángela is still showing her veneration for him. "Actually more. The true genius in each of his plans was that he did them without leaving a money trail. It also helped that Castro gave him a very long time to set up a series of assassination attempts in major U.S. cities."

Leonard notes, "Her father was a master at organizing assassinations. Probably the best vampire slayer there has ever been."

Taking this as a compliment, Ángela acknowledges it with a smile. "Thank you. You see, Castro first directed him to begin organizing them just after the Bay of Pigs. However, it wasn't until the very end of 1962 that Castro realized that he would either have to make peace with the

Kennedys or eliminate John. That's when he told my father to arrange them in earnest. In particular, my father started working on Oswald in early 1963."

Curiosity gets the better of me. "Why Oswald?"

"Oswald's having lived in Russia in the past, marrying a woman from there, and being so openly pro-Cuba had caught my father's attention. He was truly convincing."

Leonard adds, "Even Nixon in 1964 called Castro 'a hero in the warped mind' of Oswald."

"Since so many Cuban CIA operatives were unwittingly involved in the conspiracy, the possibility that Oswald was a double agent didn't bother my father, so long as he would play along and keep his mouth shut. The Mafia was to cover that. Such long advanced planning really paid off in Dallas."

Knowing how close presidential visits are revealed relative to their actual date, I find that difficult to believe. "How much time did he have?"

"My father had less than 2 months to implement a final course of action for the hit there once Kennedy's visit was publicly announced on September 26. He had to really hustle to orchestrate Oswald's moving back to Dallas and getting that job at the Book Depository in the middle of October. Oswald's communist, pro-Castro past had to be kept well hidden, particularly from Secret Service agents. My father expected that days in advance of Kennedy's trip they would be snooping around the buildings along the planned route for the presidential motorcade."

449

"Why the Texas Book Depository?"

"He had scoped out Dallas well ahead of then and correctly decided that Dealey Plaza would make the best spot to do the shooting since it was the only logical way to get to Stemmons Freeway from Love Field by the most commonly used parade route in Dallas: down Main Street."

"How did he stop the loose lips in Dallas?"

"Although claims have been made of at least two unheeded warnings before Dallas, they didn't come from anyone who was directly involved primarily because most of the planning had been done in New Orleans. There was no Mafioso or any one physically involved in the happening in Dallas who was in it for the money. Rather they helped kill the President of the United States as a matter of principle. Per their well-deserved reputation, the Mafia has been and is exceptionally adept at enforcing a secret, far better than any government agency. That's why no one directly involved talked before November 22 and some took it to their graves."

Chapter 35

Denise conveniently enters the room just as Ángela is finishing describing what her father had told her about the dealings surrounding November 22, 1963. She walks over to the window across the room from Leonard to be close to me and is tightly holding onto a small envelope with her right hand. I am dismayed since I had expected something on the order of a manila envelope full of papers. When she hands it to me she jokes, "Kind of a let down, isn't it. $2,000,000 doesn't buy what it used to."

I rip it open and unfold the single sheet of paper contained in it. Is this some sort of a diagram? The longer I examine the hand written directions and line drawing, the more certain I am that it is indeed a treasure map. I hand it back to Denise. "Do you recognize where these directions are leading?"

After a cursory glance, she laughs loudly and boisterously. "Yeah, that big X marks my father's headstone."

Glancing over to Leonard, I can see he is as shocked as I am and, therefore, only shrugs his shoulders. Since he is of no help, I return to her and ask, "Why would a map to your father's grave lead to the truth? That's what you said he told you, isn't it, Denise?"

"Yeah, that's what he kept telling me, 'Denise, you tell whoever buys my papers to use whatever is in this envelope to unearth the truth.'"

Leonard is standing strangely quiet with his brow

furrowed, contemplating what she had just said. I turn towards him again and wait for him to speak. Finally, in a muted tone of voice, he requests, "Please, hand me that paper, Denise."

Obligingly, she passes it to me, and I walk over and bow before formally delivering it to him. "Here it is Long John Silver."

After he scrutinizes every word on it, as well as, the map itself, he comments, "Denise, do you have any shovels here?"

That is not what she had expected him to say and chuckles. "Hell, Leonard, this is a real farm. We have shovels, tractors, even a backhoe. Why do you ask? In the trunk of that car, you have some dead Cuban spy you want to lay to rest like Jimmy Hoffa where no one will find him?"

"Just the opposite. We're going to have to exhume your father's coffin, which according to this map is somewhere on this farm."

"Yeah, in the old Walker Cemetery. Several generations of that family who used to own this property are buried there. What's more, this was their farmhouse. But why do you want to bring him up now? We're talking about Ángela's father."

Both aggravated and surprisingly troubled by this unexpected complication, he is not pleased with her levity and immediately scowls at her. "Very funny. It would appear that your father literally took his and Ángela's father's secrets to his grave. He must have had their most confidential documents buried along with him so that only whoever paid for them could get them."

One of the reasons I changed professions was a medical examiner's unpleasant duty to do autopsies on exhumed corpses. I am a little disgusted at the thought of digging up this coffin. On the other hand, since I have anted up $2,000,000 for this honor, grave robbing will remain probably the only thing I have not been accused of doing in the course of either of my careers as an antiques dealer seeking buried treasures or a forensic pathologist paid to uncover buried clues. "So that's what he meant when he said unearth the truth!"

Leonard nods. "Precisely. He even tells you where to dig and how deep to dig, four feet east of the head stone and five feet deep. Denise, who was at his funeral here?"

Trying to remember back to that sad event, she sighs. "Our immediate family, both of LBJ's daughters, and a few Agency people who knew the truth. As I recall, you were stuck in Cuba and couldn't come."

"That's right. Raúl had just taken over power after Fidel's surgery. With regard to the funeral, I'm sorry but I obviously wasn't clear. I meant to ask who actually buried him, dug the hole and filled the dirt back in?"

Even with all my training and experience in forensic pathology, I cannot imagine to what Leonard is alluding. I do not recall a prosecutor ever asking that question to me in court, nor an undertaker being subpoenaed as an expert witness on how the grave was dug. "Why the hell do you care about that? Are you screening funeral homes to use in the near future? Maybe you have some sort of pre-need issue? Or are you comparing prices?"

He is not appreciating either of our jokes today and scowls at me. "NO!! I just want proof it's not booby-trapped."

We are not talking about entering a newly discovered Egyptian pyramid and looting the bounty from a pharaoh's tomb, are we? However, with all of the recent voodoo events, I cannot resist quipping, "Why would he have done that? Was he a vampire and didn't want anyone disturbing his sleep?"

This just further irritates him; so he snaps back at me, "NO!! But he had his reasons. There are many in our government who would like to have whatever he took to his grave categorically buried forever."

Denise finally decides to end my fun at her father's expense. "He had it in his will which funeral home to call and several of his former buddies hung around to supervise its filling in the grave. I thought it was odd at the time, but, to be honest, after living with him all my life, I don't think I really know what being really normal is like."

This is exactly what Leonard fears. He does not hesitate before saying, "In that case, I'll get Adolpho to have an explosives sniffing dog team brought in before we do the dig." He then walks out over to the living room where Adolpho has been waiting, all the while being careful not to alarm the geese.

I am somewhat skeptical about his level of paranoia and quiz Denise, "Do you think your father would really have had his grave booby-trapped? We're hardly in

Hollywood."

"Oh, but are you mistaken! That's entirely within the realm of the world he lived in. However, the map doesn't take you to his grave."

Is she being honest with us? Stuck in the back of my mind are the warnings of the dealers at The Blue And The Gay. Is that not what she had just told Leonard? "What are you talking about?"

"The X is where his grave marker is, that's for sure; however, the written directions take you to the grave next to his."

Is this more CIA double talk? "What do you mean?"

"On the face of it, they interred next to his grave over another's casket whatever he wanted hidden. His instructions are to dig four feet east of his headstone. He never liked the sunrise, but he loved the sunset. He left strict instructions to be buried so that the head of his coffin and his feet faced west not east."

"So, who's buried east of the headstone?"

"He always had a sense of humor. He claimed that's what got him through the day when he worked in the lunatic filled world of the Kennedy White House. You had to be able to laugh at some of the screwball ideas that crossed his desk, such as 'Elimination by Illumination' or Operation Good Times."

"Sound like folk remedies."

455

"Well, they weren't medicines, but they were intended to cure the Fidel cancer. An Air Force brigadier general came up with the idea that if we could prove that Castro was Satan and was, therefore, preventing the imminent Second Coming of Christ, the Cuban people would rise up and overthrow him. I know, you don't have to say it: Cuba is a Catholic country and was not full of a bunch of born again Christians back then. That didn't stop the good General Edward Lansdale from seriously wanting the Navy to launch from a submarine phosphorescent shells that would create huge bright, white starbursts all over Cuba as a harbinger of the approaching Second Coming. The CIA, if nothing else, was good at eponyms. They gave it the code name, 'Elimination by Illumination.'"

I have to snicker at that. "I assume it was at least planned for the 4th of July."

"No, he offered All Soul's Day in order 'to gain extra impact from Cuban superstitions' and create panic in the streets with a subsequent uprising. Needless to say, it never got any further than Operation Good Times another bright idea from one of the good general's military planners, Brigadier General William Craig. He thought it 'should put even a Commie Dictator in the proper perspective with the underprivileged masses.' They were going to doctor up a photo of Castro to make him look obese. In a lavishly furnished room he would be consuming delicacies not available to the average Cuban citizen. On top of that, Castro was to be caught 'with two beauties in any situation desired.' As you can tell, General Craig was most clever and thus, not unexpectedly, had a title for this photo, 'My Ration is Different.' Then the Air Force, remember Lansdale was an Air Force general, would bombard the island with them. My father loved telling folks about that. His punch line was that they wanted the taxpayers of the U.S. to pay for porn for the Cuban men that would have been illegal to have been shown to American troops at Guantánamo! And the Cuban men were to risk their lives because of that photo! To give the devil his due, General Craig did have one idea that Jimmy Carter could have used during the Mariel boatlift when he was President: Operation Free Ride. Those same planes were to airdrop onto Cuba valid one-way airline tickets on Pan Am or KLM to Mexico City, Caracas, anywhere but to the U.S. You'll love this. He even realized that the 'validity of the tickets would have to be restricted to a time period.' He thought of everything."

"So, tell me who's buried east of the headstone."

"His favorite watchdog, a pit bull! Who better to guard his papers?"

Without any warning, Ángela slithers out of bed, drops to her knees beside it, and with clasped hands raised upwards begins to chant a prayer:
"Give ear to my prayer, O God; And hide not thyself from my supplication.
Attend unto me, and answer me: I am restless in my complaint, and moan,
Because of the voice of the enemy, Because of the oppression of the wicked; For they cast iniquity upon me, And in anger they persecute me.
My heart is sore pained within me: And the terrors of death are fallen upon me.
Fearfulness and trembling are come upon me, and horror hath overwhelmed me.
And I said, Oh that I had wings like a dove! Then would I fly away, and be at rest.

457

Lo, then would I wander far off, I would lodge in the wilderness.
I would haste me to a shelter from the stormy wind and tempest.
Destroy, O Lord, and divide their tongue, for I have seen violence and strife in the city.
Day and night they go about it upon the walls thereof: Iniquity also and mischief are in the midst of it.
Wickedness is in the midst thereof: Oppression and guile depart not from its streets.
For it was not an enemy that reproached me; Then I could have borne it: Neither was it he that hated me that did magnify himself against me; Then I would have hid myself from him:"

I am curious why she is praying. I whisper in Denise's ear, "What's she doing?"

She says in an undertone, "Ángela claims it's a banishment and equalizer enchantment in which she's beseeching God to shelter her and chastise whoever placed the root on her. When she first came to my house and started to recite it, she told me that she would have to say it each day for nine straight days."

"It sounds familiar."

"It should. It's Psalm 55."

When Leonard comes back into the room, he announces, "They'll be here within an hour."

Ángela finally rises from reciting the entire 55th Psalm from memory and straightens her dress before lying back in bed. Having another hour to kill, I decide to ask the one question she has not answered and may not

458

want to answer. "Did your father ever tell you why he did it?"

She answers immediately without any forethought. "He did it because he had to."

Chapter 36

I don't understand. "We all have free will. He could've refused."

Ángela is unyielding. "Sometimes you just can't. World events can spiral downward and out of control to an abyss where there is no good solution or alternative. For my father, he didn't see a way out."

Not believing what I just heard, I look askance at her. "We are talking murder here, like the Sixth Commandment. And don't forget he was the President of United States."

Surprisingly, she does not seem to take offense at my criticism. "I don't want to sound like the Mafia, but it wasn't personal for him. Now, for Castro it was. John Kennedy had basically allowed the CIA and Pentagon to become sub-governments when it came to Cuba. His brother, Robert, was personally managing and overseeing plots to assassinate Castro. He was fighting the 'losing' Cuba image the Republicans were pinning on his brother, the President, after the Bay of Pigs fiasco. Don't forget Truman was heavily criticized for losing both China and Korea."

I concur. "That fear of being blamed for allowing a country to go communist ultimately led to our getting stuck in Viet Nam, the domino theory, you know."

"Precisely, the Kennedys fell into that trap with regard to Cuba. They foresaw all of Latin America going red. Getting back to Robert, he wanted 'plausible deniability,' which meant he didn't get involved in the particulars. When you team up with the devil, you better watch your backside. Robert didn't do that. He allowed the unholy marriage of the CIA and the Mafia. A professional Agency Black Operator and a Mafia boss were given the authority to manage the operation to annihilate Castro without the direct daily supervision of the Attorney General."

"Why was he so seemingly careless in the chain of command?"

"That miserable failure, the Bay of Pigs invasion, cut deep into the Kennedys. Afterwards, Robert promised, 'We will take action against Castro. It might be tomorrow, it might be in five days or ten days or not for months. But it will come.' And he later made their mission 'the top priority of the U.S. government - - all else is secondary - - no time, money, effort, or manpower is to be spared.' My father had me memorize those statements. He used them whenever someone said he should have waited and seen what negotiation would have brought."

"That still doesn't explain sloppy control. He wasn't dealing with the type of individual who you sort of leave alone after saying surprise me."

Leonard intervenes. "Robert kept an arm's length distance from the every day details to maintain the 'plausible deniability' that Ángela mentioned. When asked by one of his agents to define the scope of the operation for guidance, the then CIA director said, 'Use your imagination.' He did not want to incur the wrath of the Kennedys. He is quoted as describing the pressure he was feeling from his superiors by saying, 'You haven't lived until you've had Bobby Kennedy rampant on your back.'"

"So, this fervor begat a Hatfield-McCoy type blood feud between Castro and the Kennedys, which led to the Cuban Missile Crisis?"

She winces. "Worse, despite having brought the world to the brink of nuclear war, the Kennedys did not really back off. The secret and, palpable to Castro, unregulated scheming persisted. But it wasn't so secret. The Cuban exiles were not tightlipped. They made life easy for Fidel's spies, some of whom may have been double agents, to alert him very promptly. The visceral, vendetta-like distrust persisted even when reconciliation was seriously being considered."

Leonard adds, "This led to the well-grounded Cuban perception that unless the Kennedys were stopped, nuclear war was inevitable. Khrushchev had informed Castro that in 1961 JFK considered and briefly had the Pentagon work on a nuclear first strike option. He had declared while running for President that if the situation in Berlin deteriorated and threatened the West's being driven from there than that 'is worth a nuclear war.' He reinforced his position at the Vienna Summit in June of 1961."

Ángela smiles. "My father always claimed that Kennedy was the real war monger. There he was at a summit and all he did was threaten war. JFK opposed the Soviet Union's signing a peace treaty with East Germany that restricted access to West Berlin. Khrushchev warned, 'Force will be met by force. If the US wants war, that's its problem.' In his reaction to the Soviet leader, JFK reaffirmed his campaign promise. 'Then, Mr. Chairman, there will be a war. It will be a cold, long winter.' My father prevented World War III. Wouldn't you?"

"He could've gotten Castro." I innocently add.

"He thought of that. However, Fidel was smarter than the Kennedys when it came to self-preservation. He's still alive. They aren't. As Castro has said repeatedly, 'If surviving assassination were an Olympic event, I would win the gold medal,' He claims to have thwarted at least 637 attempts on his life. No, whacking Fidel was not feasible. Rather, the option was which Kennedy to target. Eliminating John in Castro's view ended the immediate peril for all practical purposes. But, in the end, he had to get both of them. Once Robert Kennedy became a viable replacement for LBJ, all Castro could see was the nightmare returning."

Upon hearing that, I raise my eyebrows and stare at her. "Your father killed both of them?"

Ángela shakes her head. "No, he was in protective custody here when that happened. That assistant he was training in Chicago did that hit. A close-up Mob style headshot wasn't my father's forte. Interestingly, the Mob refused to use that approach on Castro. They wanted long-range rifles with telescopic sights and silencers. They claimed they didn't have a hitman who was that suicidal. Anyway, my father always preferred something where there was no chance of being caught. But, otherwise, they ran the RFK hit pretty much the same way as my father had done his brother's. Sirhan Sirhan was a willing patsy."

"How come?"

"Months of pumping him full of anti-Zionist propaganda about the Six-Day War and RFK's staunch support of Israel was enough to do the trick of converting him from a Robert Kennedy supporter to a resolute, pathologic hater of Robert Kennedy. Watching him wave the Israeli flag at a May 14th Israeli Independence Day celebration was Sirhan's watershed moment. But his final commitment to doing the assassination was made when he heard and read Kennedy declare his unflinching commitment to Israel's survival and his plans to sell bombers to Israel. It didn't take much to have him believe that the idea was all his since he was pretty fanatical about Palestine to begin with."

Did she just say what I think she said? "You mean to tell me that they made him their chief hitman?"

Ángela again shakes her head and pounds the bed with her fist. She is perturbed, perhaps even insulted, by my question. "Hell, no! I just said he was the patsy! Castro's agents aren't that stupid. Others were in place along the planned primary exit route. I mean, would you have an untrained assassin, who later claimed to have been drinking just before doing it, be your key hitman. That's why he was stationed by that ice machine where RFK wasn't supposed to go. He was the accidental assassin."

"That would explain why he was such a sloppy assassin. He had no exit strategy. There were hundreds of witnesses."

"Boy, was he ever sloppy! He was so careless that, when he visited the hotel two days before to see where exactly the ice machine was, he left a trail for the prosecution to follow, which they used at his trial to prove that he had cased the hotel then. But did he ever make a great patsy. Castro mustn't have believed his eyes when he read that Sirhan Sirhan had declared, 'I can explain it. I did it for my country.'"

Leonard notes, "A leading expert in hypnotism who examined Sirhan's behavior after the fact claimed he may have been hypnotically programmed, which had been the impression of many who saw him just after he was accosted. All of this helped fuel the theory he was a decoy for the real assassin."

She says, "Well, they almost had it right. Once more, no money trail to Havana. Best of all, even to this day there are only disputed claims of Mafioso or former CIA agents from the Bay of Pigs being at the actual scene. They can't pin it on anyone else. It hasn't been until 9/11 that Americans have realized that rational people actually do suicidal attacks in the name of a cause or religion. Before then, they had always believed that these people had to be insane."

Dumbfounded by the extent of her in depth understanding of this, I beseech, "How are you aware of all of this?"

She calms down and nonchalantly states, "The Secret Service used my father as an expert to determine what had happened in L.A."

Speaking of not believing one's ears, I am doing just that. "That's incredible. You can't really mean that."

Denise nods her head. "Ernie, it's all true. Ángela's father in exchange for a deal actually turned himself in. I know, you're curious why he would've done that. Castro didn't want him to return to Cuba. Too risky if someone stumbled onto the truth from questioning the Cuban exiles, mobsters, or former CIA agents who had had contact with him before the hit. Or can you imagine the blackmail potential, if after the fact, one of those accomplices figured out what he had been really up to. The press getting hold of that would have meant invasion, exactly what Castro wanted to avoid after learning the lessons of the Cuban Missile Crisis. Ever since then, he never trusted Khrushchev to protect him, which in his mind meant going all the way to a nuclear World War III. To prevent any proof of Cuban or Russian involvement with Oswald emerging, both the Cuban and the Soviet embassies in Mexico City earlier turned down his request for a visa that fall. He was not pleased to say the least."

Talk about ingratitude. I interrupt her. "I can only imagine. Here he was going to help get Kennedy and they ignored him."

"By the way, LBJ didn't want invasion or war with Russia, either."

Leonard points out, "While Castro may have had his misgivings about Russia's stomach for all out war with the West, Johnson sure as hell didn't. He felt he had to convince the country to the extent that it was completely 'satisfied' that if Oswald had gone to trial the evidence would've persuaded a jury without any reasonable doubt that he was the sole assassin and acted alone. The Warren Commission was a sham. From its inception Johnson had only one purpose for it and that was not to discover the truth about the assassination. Nixon thought that LBJ and that commission carried out 'the greatest hoax that has ever been perpetuated.' And that was Nixon, who knew a thing or two about dirty tricks!"

Upon hearing this, I am at a loss about what to say. Everything I had thought was true about the Kennedy assassination was being proven to be either untrue or a cover-up. "Then, Leonard, what the hell did LBJ charge Earl Warren, the Chief Justice of the United States Supreme Court, to do?"

"He was explicit in his instructions to both Warren and Senator Richard Russell that they were to disprove any connection between Oswald and Cuba and/or the Soviet Union. Fear was pervasive in DC that such a link would be used as a reason for 'kicking us into a war that can kill forty million Americans in an hour,' since such an insinuation of their involvement in the assassination might lead to a nuclear World War III. McNamara had given LBJ an estimate 'that at first strike we would lose sixty million people.'

"Alexander Haig, when he heard about Ángela's father and the deal he had with LBJ, asked Johnson why he had agreed to it. He quoted LBJ as explaining it away by saying, 'We simply must not allow the American people to believe that Fidel Castro could have killed our President.' He felt Johnson's intentions were also politically motivated due to his foreseeing a subsequent right-wing uprising that would lift the Republican Party to dominance for the next two generations if the public was informed about the truth. Haig claimed that LBJ felt so strongly about this that, despite his being convinced of Castro's guilt in the Kennedy assassination, he never publicly proclaimed it and 'took it to his grave.' Haig was correct except for that one incident with Howard K. Smith."

The irony in what Leonard has just said makes Denise laugh. "If it weren't true, it would be funny. Both LBJ and Castro tried to do the same thing: make Oswald the patsy to hide the Cuban connection."

"So, how did LBJ get out of the quagmire that Ángela's father had created for him?" I ask.

"My father was brought out of 'retirement' to make the arrangements. We would place Ángela's father under arrest and imprison him under twenty-four hour home confinement in exchange for similar treatment for our assassins who had been caught in Cuba, Cubela, for instance. It came as no surprise to the White House that Castro in 1966 intervened in Cubela's trial for planning his assassination and prevented the compulsory execution."

"What did Castro do?"

Denise smirks. "He sent a letter to the prosecutor. In it he wrote: 'I suggest that the court not ask the death sentence for any of the accused.' You know, Cubela and his six co-conspirators got off with incredibly light sentences compared to what they were originally going to face: the firing squad for four of them and thirty years confinement for the other three. Hell, two of them didn't even go to prison. Castro reportedly sent Cubela books to read while incarcerated and after thirteen years even allowed him to emigrate to Spain. Contrast that to the treatment he gave Huber Matos, who he tortured on several occasions. My father suspected that, if Cubela were a double agent, then this may have been a set up to get Ángela's father favored treatment by the US. You take care of our man, and we'll take care of yours. However, spending thirteen years in a Cuban prison would've been a helluva assignment and hardly would've been considered favored treatment. Of course, he just may not have wanted to turn any of them into a martyr by taking them to the wall."

Completely unfamiliar with that last term, I ask, "What does 'to the wall' mean?"

"'*Paredón*' (to the wall) is what the crowds cried out at the political rallies in Havana when Castro asked for a show of hands in favor of the execution of arrested counterrevolutionaries. In an odd turn of events, Ángela's father moved in here with his family for his own safety and to protect our operatives in Cuban jails. No one in the federal penal system could guarantee his safety. If he had been killed in one of our prisons, God only knows what would have happened to our people locked up in Cuba. Most likely, many would have gone to the wall."

Leonard mentions, "Incidentally, once his true identity was divulged, no foreign government wanted Ángela's father, even when told that he was just a minor part of the assassination. Oswald was still held up as the lone gunman. At that time, harboring an associate of the murderer of JFK wasn't very popular even with the Soviet Union. He in essence had become an international *persona non grata*."

I am dumbfounded. "Speaking of that. Didn't anyone object to his basically getting away with assassinating JFK?"

Amazed at my naivety regarding Washington, Leonard shakes his head at me before crying out, "Who? Bobby! He was too busy covering up his and his brother's past activities along with protecting their collaborators in Havana. It didn't take very long for the tape recordings of past conversations in the Oval Office to be sequestered. Can you imagine the uproar if it had become publicly disclosed that the Attorney General of the United States had been designated by the President to actively organize the assassination plots against a foreign leader. Or worse, I would hate to think what the headlines would have been like after they were found to have been in cahoots and literally in bed with the Mob. In a New York minute, the Press would have turned on their recently sainted President of the United States upon learning he had been sharing a mistress with a notorious Mob boss, who he had recruited to assassinate Castro. Congress would've been in pandemonium trying to figure out what to do about their planned all out invasion of Cuba on a phony, contrived pretext without Congressional advance enlightenment much less advice and consent. Last time I read the Constitution it said that Congress is supposed to approve our going to war."

"You mean to say that Robert Kennedy screwed up the entire Cuban faceoff?"

Leonard smiles. "No! He did one downright smart thing with regards to the Castro assassination plots. And that was to surround himself with people who would never make credible witnesses! No one believed them even when for once in their lives they told the truth."

"How about afterwards? There were tons of investigations into the assassination."

"Bobby's cover up lived well past his own assassination. Why do you think all of the assassination inquiries up until the Assassination Records Review Board was created in 1992 were denied access to the

470

relevant documents about what had been going on between the Kennedys and Castro? Why didn't any of the many investigations into what happened on November 22, 1963 answer one simple but glaringly obvious question: who ordered JFK's body be stolen from Parkland with weapons drawn?"

I am unfamiliar with what Leonard is talking. "I thought it was the Secret Service. Mrs. Kennedy wouldn't leave Dallas without his body!"

"The agents there didn't have the authority to have acted alone in this regard. Someone in DC had to have called in an explicit order to move the body to Bethesda."

"Couldn't have LBJ done it? He was at Parkland."

"No, he didn't have the authority either. He hadn't yet taken the oath of office. Technically, he only had the powers of the Vice President. Only the Secretary of the Treasury or the U.S. Attorney General could've given the Secret Service orders then."

I second-guess him before he completes his thought. "So, you think Bobby did it."

Leonard nods. "The Treasury Secretary wasn't in any position to have done it. He was on a plane over the Pacific heading to Tokyo. Ironically, the plane didn't have the proper codebook on board. In all honesty, Bobby wasn't legally empowered to do what he in truth did. You see, assassination of the President wasn't a federal crime back then. Only the State of Texas and the City and County of Dallas had jurisdiction over JFK's body. More important, the County Medical Examiner refused to release the body."

"If that were the case, why didn't the State of Texas prosecute the responsible Secret Service agents?" I ask.

Both shaking his head and shrugging, Leonard is at a loss. He answers slowly and deliberately, "Good question! I'm clueless! However, the DA of Dallas County and the Attorney General of Texas had a helluva case against the Secret Service."

"So, that botched autopsy legally should've never happened?"

Leonard suddenly acts surprised. "What makes you think it was botched, rather than orchestrated? Bobby spent a good portion of the afternoon of November 22 talking to the head of the CIA and later to a trusted Bay of Pigs veteran. Besides blaming one or more unidentified CIA anti-Castro operatives, what else did he discuss with them?"

This time I am puzzled. "Why would've he wanted to do that?"

Denise lowers her voice as if she were telling me a dark secret. "In an odd twist of fate, Bobby and Lyndon, though bitter enemies, both conspired to have the autopsy of JFK, which was revealed to a grieving American people, done not at Bethesda but in the Oval Office. The Kennedys and those who had served under them in 'Camelot' were more interested in getting it back than getting immediate justice. My father always thought Bobby might even have felt that he couldn't get the just revenge that he so hungered for until he was occupying the Oval Office."

Adolpho knocks on the doorframe of the bedroom

to get our attention. "The bomb squad is here."

Chapter 37

Denise helps Ángela put her shoes on and assists her getting out of the bed. Although still wobbly, Ángela says, "Thanks, Denise. Root or no root, I can't miss this." She grabs a black crocheted shawl from inside the drawer of a nearby nightstand and wraps it around her shoulders. "Now hand me one of those candelabras sitting on the table. I may need it." She takes the menorah from the obliging Denise with her right hand and with her left hand snatches a plastic bottle from the same nightstand. "Demon Stay Away Powder, I may still need it to keep them from interfering with my getting in touch with the spirits who reside at the cemetery. If I am to find the one you seek, I must learn all about those spirits of the dead. Once I establish contact with *that* spirit, I will have to pay it for its services. Doing that will not be easy nor quick. No, no, no, there is much that I will need to find out before I can negotiate with it: what's its name, how it died, and how close its grave actually is situated to the gates of the cemetery. Once paid, then and only then will it reveal to me what is most essential to you, where it wants you to dig: at its head, its heart, or its feet. Denise, do you have an unopened bottle of whiskey in the house?"

"I think so. But why do you ask?"

"Spirit may want it as compensation for what's been hidden in its grave. If we steal it rather than give what the spirit demands for it, that will make the spirit grow mad." With her expression suddenly becoming quite foreboding, Ángela waves her finger in front of her face as she slowly shakes her head from side to side. She speaks deliberately as she warns, "Trust me, you don't want to do that."

Maybe she did not hear for whose spirit we will be searching? Denise tries to explain, "Ángela, it's a pit bull. It probably would prefer a box of Milk-Bones."

She is not troubled by that and nods approvingly. Gesturing at Denise with that same finger, she says, "If you have an unopened one, bring it, too."

It takes her a few minutes to find the Milk-Bones and the bottle of whiskey. Once the offerings are at hand, we start to walk out of the house over to where the bomb squad is waiting. The dogs present a problem. Although they are well trained and do not pay attention to the geese, the geese do not reciprocate and are all in a dither, hissing and flapping their wings. Denise goes into the broom closet and brings out what comes across as a very well made, indeed custom-made broom. Its handle is a bright shiny gold plated color and the bristles are neither straw nor plastic, but something else. I ask, "Where did you get that broom. It looks like the Rolls Royce of brooms."

Matter-of-factly, she says, "The CIA."

I blurt out, "The CIA!"

"Yeah, it came with the geese. It somehow transmits radio waves that deactivate their wireless transmitter temporarily. I'll need it to shoo them away as we head out to the barn. Otherwise, the house may blow."

With Denise in the lead, brushing the geese out of our way, we all walk over to the red barn. She goes to a latch where its two doors abut, rolls a finger over a sensor, and then pulls a lever on the lock that allows her to push them aside. Although they are only parted just enough for all of us to see what is inside, Leonard is impressed by what she has in it. "You really are well equipped. Do you actually use every vehicle in here?"

"Absolutely! I told you this is a functional farm, not some CIA mock-up. After realizing what was really happening out here, my father decided that we ought to listen to Thoreau. He renamed it Walden Farm. For all intents and purposes we're fundamentally self-sufficient. Periodically, the Agency will send out some of their burnt out agents with their families to live here while they regain their sanity. It uses the excuse that I need someone to protect me to do that. The agents fill me in on what they are allowed to talk about and I reciprocate by teaching them the history of the Cold War that's not in the textbooks or their manuals. You know, things have changed a lot. I don't think what happened in the Sixties would be tolerated currently."

"Well, maybe not here in the US, but in Russia or the Middle East," Leonard pauses for a moment and shakes his head, "I'm not so sure. Hopefully, today we will get the last bit of evidence of what really went on back then."

Denise enters the barn and then mounts the driver's seat of a backhoe and starts its engine. She next signals to Leonard to climb aboard a tractor that has an attached trailer half-filled with hay and yells at him over the roar of the motor, "Can you drive one of these?" She then turns to us and orders, "Ángela and the rest of you get into that trailer. It's a piece to the cemetery."

476

Once Leonard is in the tractor's cab, he salutes Denise and calls out to Adolpho, "Open those doors wide open and then grab some shovels and jump on board."

The cemetery is in a remote corner of the farm, about a twenty-minute ride from the barn. I can see why Denise's father called it Walden Farm. There is a large wooded lake in that area. The cemetery itself is typical of the small family farm cemeteries that used to be a feature of the South. A wrought iron fence with an understated, simple gate outlines its perimeter. The vines of honeysuckle and wisteria cover most of its railings. Well into the past, one of the Walkers planted a southern magnolia tree on both sides of the front of the entrance. They have grown to an impressive size and have left a fresh blanket of their very large waxy green leaves and cone-like fruit covered with red seeds over the adjacent older graves. In each corner is a solitary concrete bench. The Victorian ornateness of the older tombstones distinguishes them from the newer plain ones further in the back. It dawns on me that Denise's father had not been hasty in choosing his plot, which faces west overlooking the lake. Despite the sun's still being overhead, I can sense how absolutely gorgeous the sky becomes here minutes before twilight. Once we have all assembled at the entry gate, I ask Denise, "How big is this farm. It seems to be huge."

"To be perfectly honest, it's classified and they haven't told me. After the Cuban Missile Crisis, the government bought it originally to be the FBI and CIA headquarters in case of an imminent nuclear attack. Whoever came up with that plan was goddamn naïve!"

"Why do you say that?"

477

"Ernie, they couldn't stand each other before the damn crisis, and they still don't!"

"What exactly were they going to do here?"

Denise holds back from laughing. "They wanted to build enough bunkers to house several hundred families for the duration. If the Russian missiles didn't get them, their damn bickering and in-fighting would've. Hell, I wouldn't put it past either one of them to poison the lake if they thought they could get away with it without killing their own kind." She becomes more serious. "Getting back to your question, I'm confident I've not been informed where all of the bunkers are. We were given one to live in with the understanding that we would maintain the property as a working farm as a cover for its intended purpose. There are even areas on it that I'm not permitted to enter." She finally chuckles. "As far as I know, Elvis could be living here, or Hoffa could possibly be buried here."

"How about visitors? Your gate is not very inviting, and your path of briars is something out of *Sleeping Beauty*."

"With the geese and my eccentric ways, few of the neighbors venture out here. Most of them think I'm crazy anyway. Rumor has it that I must be a Russian spy, or worse, an alien."

Leonard raises his eyebrows. "Where did they get that idea?"

"We have a bunch of sophisticated satellite receivers and transmitters on the property for the intelligence agencies to use in case of a national

478

emergency. They figure I use them to communicate with Moscow or the flying saucers that periodically land out here."

"Flying saucers?"

"Yeah, Leonard, that was my father's idea. He had the Agency build some experimental drones that he would test out here. Some really did resemble Martian flying saucers."

"Why the hell did he do that?"

"You are privy to how paranoid he got. He would send them up to survey those dirt roads to confirm no spies were coming to attack us. Although at this point we just Google it up on the computer from some spy satellite, the military still tests the experimental ones out here. The production ones are being used over in Afghanistan and Pakistan. My father would've been proud to learn what his paranoia nurtured. You see, he was certain that someone would try and get Ángela's father, not so much for what he knew about the Kennedy assassination but rather to force him into planning others. Within the world of assassins, he was the King, as Leonard said. No one has come along who understands the fine art of discovering and training really good patsies to believe that it was all their idea and that they did it alone as well as he did. To this day, not one of them has varied from the story line he wrote for each of them. If you think about all of the books written about the assassinations that he helped arrange, all of them fail to uncover what actually went on. I've never told anyone this before, but Nixon after the Munich games had the Mossad use him to instruct their agents on how to do assassinations without leaving a trace back to Jerusalem."

479

Leonard spies Ángela, who is preoccupied with spreading the Demon Stay Away Powder, moving the menorah around to find just the right spot for the candles, and establishing a rapport with all of the spirits of the cemetery. "Denise, what's with her?"

"I'm not aware if you were ever told this, but her father was a voodoo priest. That was his cover. Everyone in New Orleans thought he was mentally deficient, so to speak. Even the Secret Service didn't take seriously the multiple warnings about him that they received. He claimed to be a direct descendant of some monk who was a legend in the Mississippi Delta for his root work. There were many other practitioners of the root, white and black, who found it financially beneficial to claim to be one of the monk's direct descendants."

An international hitman tramping around as a voodoo priest, what a helluva cover! Since I cannot imagine how he pulled this stunt off, I ask, "Where did he operate out of?"

"From a dump of a store in the French Quarter, where tourists would buy his crap, particularly his dolls, the best in the city I am told, listen to him sing voodoo songs, and recite both spells and cures for hexes. At midnight, all made up just like Baron Samedi, he gathered them there to lead them on graveyard tours of the Lafayette, Saint Roch, and St. Louis Cemeteries where he would evoke the spirits of the cemeteries. My father told me that he was quite convincing and had to turn down an offer to be on Johnny Carson's The Tonight Show for fear that it might blow his cover."

Leonard is not yet thoroughly persuaded. "How was he able to carry out his hits, if he was doing all of that

BS?'"

Denise is disappointed by his remark. "What made the charade so good and work so well was that after a while people started to pay him to be their entertainment at parties, you know, like a magician or psychic reader. He would bring an altar upon which he would make voodoo dolls or gris-gris bags while telling people's fortunes interspersed between ghost stories. Occasionally, he would do a snake dance. But what he was most popular for were his gris-gris bags, which were accepted throughout The Big Easy to in fact convey good luck and fortune. That's how he ingratiated himself into the high society of New Orleans and got introduced to the FBI and CIA agents working the anti-Castro plots with the mobsters. All of them had him come to their birthday parties to place a good luck spell on them and make them a gris-gris bag for protection for the next year."

Finding that to be credible, Leonard nods and strokes his chin. "How about the Mafia?'

"The Mafia *LOVED* him. Nothing like having a little black magic and the Mojo on your side before a hit. Furthermore, that's how a target for a whack was marked. A voodoo doll from his shop would have the victim's name pinned on it and handed in secret to the assassin. Gave real credence to the legend about the powerful forces they call Loa down there."

Ángela's father was one weird dude. I remark, "He must've had a sense of humor to have accomplished all of that."

Denise giggles. "Yeah, her father had a sense of humor, a twisted one at that, which he frequently displayed before a hit. 'In the spirit of voodoo' he even made a doll up as LBJ and gave it to a member of Bobby Kennedy's Hickory Hill gang, who, as expected, presented it to Bobby as a gag gift at a party there in October 1963. They had a great time passing it around and sticking red pins in it."

Leonard is finally a convert. "So, exactly how did his operation work?"

"As you can see, in a remarkably short period of time, Ángela's father had established a network where he could locate or arrange whatever he needed, be it weapons, patsies, or being in the right place at the right time. Since everyone felt he was a little off base, they felt comfortable talking in front of him about matters that they would otherwise have kept secret. If Castro wanted to find out what was happening in the Cuban community along the Delta, all he had to do was have an agent visit her father's store. When Castro had an assignment for him, he would have an agent go to the French Quarter, cryptically tell her father what he wanted done, and hand over a list of the people who were trusted to help him out. Her father would take it from there. Many of those on the list he already knew. Since he didn't even have a bank account, social security number, or telephone number, he was invisible to the authorities except for his rundown store among a bunch of other rundown stores that laced the French Quarter at the time."

She had yet to explain one important thing. Leonard asks, "Well then, Denise, how did Castro pay him off?"

"In his alternate life, he was a 'picker' for some of the high-end antique shops along Royal Street. The same people, who saw him the night before dressed up as a Loa at a voodoo event party, didn't recognize him the next morning when he would walk into their stores clean shaven in a suit from Maison Blanche on Canal Street. Little would they have guessed that he was carrying in his hands a box with a piece of sterling silver or Tiffany glass from the old Presidential Palace in Havana."

I butt in. "So, is Ángela sincere or just carrying on the family act?"

Denise flinches. "I can't tell. That murder at 'the show' was too close to home. Besides the fact that the voodoo doll they found next to that dealer had come from her father's store, she knew him personally. He was an old friend of her father back in New Orleans."

Leonard observes, "When we first got here, you said that Ángela's the one he was expecting to meet at 'the show.'"

"Yeah, he was afraid to do the deal in New Orleans since the place is full of Castro's agents. How they found out he was going to 'the show' is still a mystery to her. He had avoided being in Louisiana for three months by doing other out-of-state antique shows to throw them off of his tracks. No doubt about it, whatever you did made her feel safe. You won't believe this, Leonard, but she claims that she didn't exactly know who you were, but had been told to rely only on you and Aldolpho." Denise turns to me. "After I called Leonard when she first came here, I told her that he would bring you, Ernie. She said that you could be trusted because she had been told to trust only whoever Leonard sent."

I remark to him, "Good thing you were able to get what I needed so quickly. It had to have helped convince her that both of us could be trusted."

Denise says, "Perhaps. The one thing you need to be conscious about Ángela is that she is wise to more than she lets on. Every once in awhile she slips up and discloses something that she is supposed to be ignorant about."

"Like what."

"Like the connection between that prayer book and my father's papers. He never told me it."

Chapter 38

Ángela comes up to us. "The spirit of Butch has instructed me where the spot to dig is and accepts our offering as payment in full for whatever we find there."

Together we, including the bomb squad and their dogs, with Ángela in the lead follow the path designated by his spirit. She has her father's gift for theatrics. Along the way, at each of the many graves we encounter, she stops, covers her head with the crocheted black shawl from her shoulders, and touches the headstone with her hand. Slowly she descends into a trance to commune with the spirit below. Upon awakening and removing her fingers from the gravestone and the shawl from her face, she tells us its history and in vivid detail how it departed this life.

We are all awestricken by the number of inexplicably grotesque and fantastically macabre homicides that have been committed out here in the sticks. Has no one in these parts died of natural causes? Even I, an experienced medical examiner, am shocked by the previously unheard of techniques for inflicting extreme physical pain or disfiguration by hideous mutilation. All done per Ángela either in the course of dispensing punishment for the likes of adultery, blasphemy, and even petty theft or offering human sacrifice that it sounds as if was routinely carried out for capital crimes, such as witchery, heresy and, of course, murder. Who invented these devices that would have been the envy of medieval torturers during the Middle Ages? How many impalements, spike penetrations, crushes, whippings, or burns does it take to kill someone?

Vilest of all, justice was felt to be served by a trial where eating half of a divided ordeal bean from Africa determined guilt or innocence? In this variation of Russian roulette, the wronged live, and the culpable die an insanely excruciating death preceded by seizures and rigid paralysis culminating in asphyxiation. I abruptly conclude that the Walker Family was perhaps the inspiration for *The Addams Family*. If not, they still would have had the number one rated reality program in their day, had there been cable back then.

Ultimately, we arrive at the tombstone marked "Butch." Demon Stay Away Powder encircles the area. The menorah with all seven candles ablaze sits on the flat top of the basic rectangular headstone and from behind it emanates the smell of burning incense. Where she got them, I can't imagine. In a loud voice while raising her arms, Ángela announces to our crowd that has surrounded the grave, "Butch accepts the Jack Daniel's and the Milk-Bones as payment in full for all that has been entrusted into his gravesite for so many a year." She then aims a stick she found somewhere in the cemetery to an unremarkable location on the grave. "Dig, here."

The bomb squad leader hovers his metal detector all around the area. "How did you decide to go here?"

"His spirit told me that this would be safe."

"Well, it is the only place that isn't suspicious for explosives."

With the metal detector and the two dogs sniffing away, guiding each shovel before it strikes to remove a blade full of dirt, Leonard, Adolpho, and I take turns burrowing in the site designated by Ángela. It is not easy digging five feet straight down, but that is what the bomb team insists we do. It is very slow going. Out of desperation, we search for a post hole digger, which we find tied to the rear of the backhoe. Thankfully, the dirt is not packed hard and does not have any stones.

At about five feet, Adolpho hits something hard with the post hole digger. Getting it up the hole turns out not to be trivial. Fortunately, the post hole digger is able to grab the object and lift it up out of the hole. Once it is on the ground and after everyone moves hastily away, one of the dogs is sent back in to investigate the situation. Subsequently, the dog gives it a thorough smell test, does not show any concern, and walks away from the hole. The bomb squad leader then creeps forward. He uses a metal detector to see whether it is safe to proceed. Whatever Adolpho hit; one thing is definite; it is not metal. He pokes about it with a shovel and finds out that it is also not very big. Painstakingly, he brushes off the dirt, revealing a wooden box, and next carefully lifts it up to inspect it. Finally, we hear him say, "It's clean."

We glimpse at each other. No one speaks, but we are well aware of what each other is silently thinking. "How do we determine who lifts up its top?"

Leonard breaks the quiet. "This is ridiculous. Give me the damn box."

He takes it in his hands and finds it opens without much effort. Inside is another box. This one is smaller but made entirely of plastic. It has a little clasp on it, which Leonard easily undoes. He turns it upside down and a plastic bag for storing leftovers in the refrigerator falls on the ground. It is opaque so I cannot tell what is inside of it. He bends over to pick it up. Upon retrieving it, he unseals the bag and sticks his hand in it to pull out its contents. I wish he would say what he is feeling in there, but Leonard is concentrating too intently on what he is doing to discuss anything with us. All of a sudden he takes the hand holding what he has found and reaches to the sky with it. "It's a book!"

My heart sinks. There is no mistaking it; this is not Denise's father's most secret documents. From a distance the best it could be is a diary. Diaries are tough sells unless there is sex or scandal in them. Trust me on this fact. Never, I repeat never, invest in a diary unless it contains intimate details about a celebrity and the very ones the celebrity is publicly trying to suppress. Of course, if it explains why one of them committed suicide, such as Marilyn Monroe's purportedly missing diary allegedly does, I would buy it in less time than the government takes to spend a million dollars. You see, if the celebrity is still alive, they always claim the damn thing is stolen unless you have it proven without question, not even a reasonable doubt, by that I mean no doubt about the fact that they sold it to you in good faith and not while on alcohol or drugs. Another thing, believe me, about such a purchase: get a blood alcohol level and drug screen on the celebrity at the time of the purchase. Private collectors are one's best bet for a really hot diary. Unfortunately, most historical figures' diaries draw a lot of interest from the wrong customers, such as museums and libraries, all of which are always claiming poverty, and, worse, always want me to donate whatever they find appealing.

Motioning with very melodramatic gestures, Leonard brings his hand down to inspect the book. But before he does that just to add some suspense, he stares at Ángela. "Do you recognize this book?"

She moves over, takes it, and opens it. She glances at the front cover of the book and smiles. "It's an old prayer book."

Great! If diaries do not sell well, old prayer books are direct, immediate Goodwill donation material. No one buys them. I never suspected Denise's father to have been so religious that he had a prayer book buried on top of his pit bull and think to myself that I have just lost $2,000,000. Terribly disheartened, I begin to amble over to one of the concrete benches in the corners of the cemetery. My lips and fingertips start to tingle.

Without further comment, Ángela examines the back cover and swiftly leafs through the pages before stopping at one page, which she reads to herself. Once finished, she adds, "It's the one I thought that dealer from New Orleans had." I turn around and wait for her next statement. "And it has everything in it!"

Although he already feels it, Leonard asks nonetheless, "Are you certain?"

"Absolutely, I inscribed my name on the back cover. My father had me do that to hide its ownership and, at the same time, attest to its authenticity. You see, he always had me write my name on the front cover of all of his books, except this one. He said it was special and needed to be signed differently. And the list is still here."

Next, as if to add to the spectacle, Leonard acts confused. "What list are you talking about?"

"Whenever he had an assignment for my father, Castro would have the prayer book rebound with pages inserted into it that told in code what it was, who his contacts were, what equipment to use, and where to obtain it. It's all here." She reads from the book, "Sam Giancana, John Rosselli, Santos Trafficante, Carlos Marcello, Clay Shaw, E. Howard Hunt. And then there is the rifle identification number, T 3164, and the Zip Code where to get it, 11182."

Those numbers sound familiar to me. "Can you go over those numbers again, Ángela?"

"T 3164 and 11182."

Much to my surprise, Denise perks up upon hearing them repeated. "Aren't those the numbers on the Tiffany vase?"

Ángela is taken aback by her asking that. "Of course they are. That's why that vase was used. The model number corresponds to the Zip code prefix for the main post office of Long Island City, New York. It told my father to go there and ask for a package for delivery to box 82, which he had been given the key for when he received the vase at his store, hand delivered with the prayer book by Castro's Toronto connection. The package was a 1940 Model 91/38 Carcano short rifle with a new serial number that matched the order number of the vase."

Something about the bit concerning the Toronto agent passing along the vase abruptly confuses me. "I know you said this before that the vase was payment for the hit and you just mentioned it again, but I just remembered that John handed me a copy of the receipt your father got when he supposedly purchased the vase. If Castro gave him the vase, why did he need a receipt? And if my memory serves me correctly, it didn't come from Canada or Cuba, but from Tiffany Tom."

She does not miss a beat answering me. "Shortly before my father died, he came to realize that he needed something to prove ownership of the vase and some sort of provenance in order for me to ever sell it as the real Wild-Rose Vase. He had Denise's father have the FBI obtain a phony receipt of purchase from Tiffany Tom along with an appraisal of its worth for estate tax purposes and a letter of certification of authenticity."

"Is that why he refused to let John use his old letter of certification of authenticity for its auction?"

"I would guess so. Tiffany Tom had to be suspicious about why the FBI wanted him to do all of that. Plus, they swore him to secrecy about it. If you ever ask him, he will never admit to it."

While I am preoccupied with the issue of the receipt, Leonard is trying to figure out another thing. "Why would the vase have the rifle's serial number on it?"

"It's kinda complicated and has to do with my father's plan to hide any connection to Castro. According to his plan, the Mob, still thinking they were part of some sort of a Castro assassination plot, had a crate containing 10 Carcano short rifles belonging to a firearms company in Manhattan removed from its bonded warehouse in Jersey City and transported back to Italy. There they used their connections to have the rifles' old rusty barreled action, which bore the old serial number, replaced with new ones. Ernie's was stamped T 3164, which is the order number on the vase. On top of that, they retrofitted a firing mechanism so finely tooled that each example was exactly the same as the other examples fabricated. The nine other rifles were treated the same way, except that each retained its old unique serial number and a silencer that didn't leave marks was made only for T 3164. The Mob adored the silencer. Get Castro and he wouldn't even hear it coming."

"And the reason they went to all of that trouble was?" Leonard asks.

"As I've said, my father left nothing to chance. He didn't want there to be any evidence of the refurbishing of the rifles. That discovery might lead the FBI to seek who had done it and where it had been done. Since there was no American source for spare parts, he and Castro weren't interested in their having concerns about that. His being sort of an antiques dealer taught him well how to fake age. To confuse the FBI, if they ever examined the rifles, he had the Italian workmen allow some rust to grow on their firing pins and their springs. They also put identical signs of wear on the nose of the firing pins. That's what took so long to get them back to the States. Finally, they had all of those overhauled rifles rebored multiple times. The very workers, who had made the parts for the rifles originally, were specifically selected to do all of this with the same equipment in the same factories in Italy where the parts for the rifles had been made in 1940. They were careful not to alter the outside appearance of the rifles. Later, no one could tell that they had been restored beyond what an Italian factory prior to their being originally shipped to the US had done."

Leonard has not questioned Ángela about this, but I do. "The firing mechanism and rebored barrel, why did they work on them?"

492

"For their intended purpose, these rifles had to be accurate. They even fooled the FBI firearms specialist who after examining Oswald's rifle stated, 'It is a very accurate weapon.' He never pursued why. Castro was smart; don't let anyone convince you otherwise. To avoid raising any red flags regarding the Mob's intention, he had these rifles and many more, including M1s, done by the Mob under the guise that they were being upgraded for the impending invasion of Cuba. No one, even in retrospect, suspected some other motivation, probably because they anticipated that the other ones would indeed end up being used for that invasion. You see, John Rosselli failed to inform the anti-Castro Cubans that the CIA's offer of $150,000 for Castro's assassination had been withdrawn in mid-February 1963. This meant that Castro also had not heard anything about its cancellation."

That all seems plausible to me, except how did the rifles ever end up in the right conspirators' hands? "I can buy that the Mafia was capable of heisting weapons from a warehouse in Jersey. That was probably a routine job for them. But once they had been restored, how did Oswald and your father actually get them?"

"Following orders from their anti-Castro Cuban connection, who was in reality a double agent working for Castro through my father, the Mob had the ten upgraded rifles shipped from Italy to that agent in Toronto, who after inspecting them, arranged for their return to the warehouse in Jersey City. No one ever reported them to be missing from there. The New York firearms dealer couldn't explain later why his records showed Oswald's weapon was sold to Klein's Sporting Goods in Chicago in mid June 1962 but not received by them until late February 1963. You see, it wasn't until two days before Klein's received them that an unwary worker at the Jersey City warehouse per Mob orders included the crate with the 10 refurbished rifles in a 100-rifle shipment intended to partially complete a month old order for 200 rifles from Klein's.

"After their arrival," she adds, "they sat there again per Mob instructions. Later Klein's advertised a sale on Carcano short range rifles among others because they had arrived too late for hunting season. Upon receipt of A. Hidell's money order and coupon, and once more at the request of the Mob, another worker, this one at Klein's, had two specific rifles mailed parcel post on March 20, 1963: C 2766 to post office box 2915 in Dallas for Alek J. Hidell and T 3164 to post office box 82 in Long Island City for my father. All three of those workers believed they were carrying out just another routine Mob job and never gave it a second thought."

I think to myself *that was way too complicated and risked a slip-up. There must have been a reason for it.* "OK, How did the convoluted delivery of the two rifles hide any connection to Castro?"

"Unless the two rifles were examined at the same time, a bullet fired from either of them would be a close enough match to be felt to have been fired by the other rifle even when the silencer was used. By routine FBI ballistics testing, the FBI would be obligated to say they came from the same rifle. You see, the Canadian contact had demonstrated that Oswald's weapon was the best match to my father's prior to having them transported back to Jersey City. As I said, it was my father's way to insure that they would trace the bullets to Oswald rather than to him and, accordingly, to Castro."

She smiles broadly. "And it worked! About a week after the assassination Hoover told LBJ, 'Two of the shots fired at the President were splintered but they had characteristics on them so that our ballistics expert was able to prove that they were fired by' Oswald's C2766 Carcano."

"You mean to say that Oswald really did kill Kennedy and not your father?"

"Hell no! Are you kidding? My father didn't trust Oswald's marksmanship. My God, everyone who knew Oswald knew he couldn't even hit the window at General Walker's house. Because of that, my father had the Mafia, without their knowing it came from him, make it perfectly clear to Oswald not to take the obvious clean shot when Kennedy would be within a short distance of him moving very slowly towards him, going north on Houston Street. The almost certain miss would prevent my father from being able to take his shots later on."

"So, what was he told to do?"

"The plan was for Oswald to start shooting when the limo was near the midpoint on Elm Street heading west to the freeway. From his research on the usual presidential security, my father had expected that two secret service men would be riding on the bumper of the presidential limousine. Therefore, Oswald would had to have picked off the one on the right first in order to have a clean shot at Kennedy. Once he did that and fired his next round, my father would get his shots off creating a crossfire when everyone, including Kennedy, would be either staring up in the direction of the sixth floor of the book depository or at the fallen agent if Oswald had been lucky enough to have gotten him. All along he had counted on Kennedy from natural curiosity turning around to see what had happened, which would've allowed Kennedy to appear for all the world to have been hit from the rear and by only one rifle."

History tells a different story. I blurt out, "But that's not what happened!"

Ángela begrudgingly smiles and nods. "You're telling me! My father couldn't believe his bad luck when those two agents were ordered away from the limo. Instead of everything seeming to have come from behind, there were two wounds in Kennedy's neck: one almost midline in his throat below his Adam's apple and the other at the very base of his neck in the back. Fortunately for him, the Warren Commission wasn't interested in the truth but only in proving that Oswald had acted alone. The agents' absence, Oswald's missing Kennedy and instead hitting Governor Connally, and the matched rifles made the single gunman theory credible. As you know, Arlen Specter created that tortuous argument that the wound in Kennedy's throat noted three times by the surgeon at Parkland on November 22 to be an entry wound was actually the exit wound for the bullet that went on to strike Connally in his back."

"Didn't anyone later on become suspicious about the special treatment the rifles received?"

"Except for the Toronto agent, every man jack involved in the production and delivery of the rifles, who asked, was told they were part of a plot to kill Castro. Why else make the silencer? And don't forget, the Mafia was involved. Each and every one of them knew better than to go beyond that, no matter how bizarre the request was. Also, remember there was a greater than eight months delay between anyone handling the rifles and the actual hit. No one ever connected the two rifles to what happened in Dallas. Thanks to the Warren Commission, everything would steer to Lee Harvey Oswald having fired the fatal shot from his Carcano short-range rifle, and only him. By the way, the Chicago, Tampa, and Houston plots had similar arrangements for their weapons."

I can buy what Ángela is saying; however, how did her father do this without being detected? "So, where was he when he did the hit?"

"Remember that there was a picket fence and trees on top of the grassy knoll. No one wanted to be behind that fence or near the trees since they would obstruct the view of the President. He was somewhere near the top of the embankment behind that fence where there was a cluster of trees, not far from the pergola. He and his assistant were dressed as secret service agents and even had real badges that the Mafia had obtained for him. They were convincing enough that they even shooed away the few stragglers standing near their spot without raising any suspicion. At the time of the hit he was concealed from anyone's view by the picket fence in front of him; the trees behind him and to his sides along with their shadows, particularly the shadow from a tree in front of the fence; and his assistant standing to his left and hunched over towards the fence. Plus, the silencer on his rifle caused enough confusion about his shots being recognized as such that to this day there is controversy over them."

I think I have finally pieced it all together. "So, the vase was both a marker for payment whenever your father may have later wanted the original and had the code numbers for the delivery of the rifle to be used."

"Precisely, in addition, it was his cue to proceed with the Dallas hit. With the delivery to his store of the silencer, the book and the vase, he had the required duplication of what to use to kill JFK and where to get it. Once he confirmed by peering through his telescopic scope that he had delivered to JFK that fatal shot, which blew out the back right side of his head, my father and his assistant drove away from the grassy knoll completely overlooked."

"What about Oswald?"

Ángela rubs her face while sighing. "Oswald! Oswald! Wow, Oswald created that really messy diversion. Except for exiting the Book Depository on schedule and thereby making himself the prime suspect, which was his second job, he screwed up everything else. His first job was to get everyone to look up towards the Book Depository with those three loud rifle blasts and, if by some miracle he could pull it off, hit both the Secret Service agent and Kennedy in the back. Well, the agent never materialized and he missed Kennedy. But he did shoot Connally, who was never an intended target, and it was in his back. And, let's not forget, one of his rounds hit a curb, and a fragment from it nicked a bystander's cheek."

"Was killing that cop part of the plan?"

Her voice grows with revulsion at Oswald. "Killing that cop was insane and never was part of the plan. After all, his 'friends' in the pro-Castro movement had expressed to him that they would protect him, no matter what. He was specifically told not to resist if he got into 'trouble.' By the way, they never defined 'trouble' for him. However, they told him to call a Mr. Abt if he ever did get into 'trouble.' Oswald really believed that he was going to get away with it. He honestly thought that he was a patsy when he said it. He should've anticipated killing that cop would've made his trump card, the promised transfer to Mexico City and prisoner exchange, impossible. Hell, that's why he tried to get the visas. On his own, he assumed he would need them for the exchange that his 'friends' assured him would occur if he ever got into really big 'trouble.' Since he was unaware of where exactly he was going to go, he went to both the Russian and Cuban embassies for them. He panicked, what can I say? In the long run it didn't matter for him. He was toast even if Ruby hadn't gotten to him first."

I have to ask her one last question. "Did your father ever say who Jack Ruby really was?"

"No. And in all likelihood no one ever mentioned him. My father's responsibility and his need to know ended once he left the grassy knoll. He couldn't even tell me for sure that Oswald had done the shooting from the book depository. All Mr. M.'s men notified him of was that the patsy was there. Actually, the code was, 'The pawn is about to checkmate the King.' Hell, Oswald could've been eating lunch on the second floor when all this happened as far as my father was aware or cared! Whether or not he was the one at the sixth floor window didn't matter. Oswald's scheduled entrance in Act II was when my father exited the stage."

Ángela shakes her head. "He never could figure out why Ruby, five days after shooting Oswald, asked for a specific ranking Dallas mobster to visit him in jail. But the next day, Campisi and his wife did, in reality, visit him. My father always thought the last thing the Mob would have wanted to do is associate itself with Ruby,

499

especially in prison and that close to the score, if he indeed was their hitman. After all, why go to the trouble of having Ruby kill Oswald to keep him from squealing and then make it transparent to the police that you are one 'of (Ruby's) best friends, closet friends?' Why incriminate yourself by going to the Dallas County Jail to tell Ruby not to spill the beans. None of that ever made sense to my father."

As we are leaving the cemetery, Leonard approaches Ángela and puts his arm around her. "Tonight I'll be in Havana. Raúl and I will have a late dinner."

Epilogue

Six months later, after I had had enough time to read all of Denise's father's papers, I return to John's office in his auction house and sit in the chair across his desk from him. My left hand holds the rifle, which is leaning against my chair. My right hand cradles the vase on my lap. All of the cartons of those documents are in George's van parked behind the auction house. Two cars full of Leonard's agents, one in the rear of the van and one in its front, back up Adolpho, who is in the driver's seat of the van guarding them. Recalling all of the trouble he had had trying to sell the vase originally, John is visibly upset at seeing it again with the rifle. He nervously starts drumming his fingers on the top of his desk as he stammers, "Why have you brought them back, Ernie?"

I smile. "Let me tell you a story. Do I have a deal for you!"

Made in the USA
Lexington, KY
26 July 2015